Liane Gentry Skye

Hannah Murray

Nicole North

Leigh Court

Volume 27

Secrets

Satisfy your desire for more.

SECRETS Volume 27
This is an original publication of Red Sage Publishing and each individual story herein has never before appeared in print. These stories are a collection of fiction and any similarity to actual persons or events is purely coincidental.

Red Sage Publishing, Inc.
P.O. Box 4844
Seminole, FL 33775
727-391-3847
www.redsagepub.com

SECRETS Volume 27
A Red Sage Publishing book
All Rights Reserved/July 2009
Copyright © 2009 by Red Sage Publishing, Inc.

ISBN: 1-60310-007-5 / ISBN 13: 978-1-60310-007-6

Published by arrangement with the authors and copyright holders of the individual works as follows:

HEART STORM
Copyright © 2009 by Liane Gentry Skye

THE BOY NEXT DOOR
Copyright © 2009 by Hannah Murray

DEVIL IN A KILT
Copyright © 2009 by Nicole North

THE BET
Copyright © 2009 by Leigh Court

Photographs:
Cover © 2009 by Tara Kearney; www.tarakearney.com
Cover Models: Kayleigh Stanley and Scott Klein
Setback cover © 2000 by Greg P. Willis; GgnYbr@aol.com

Printed in the U.S.A.

Book typesetting by:

Quill & Mouse Studios, Inc.
www.quillandmouse.com

Volume 27

Satisfy your desire for more.

Heart Storm by Liane Gentry Skye

Sirenia's the last fertile mermaid of her brood. Racing against a hurricane, she must search out and mate with the only merman who can save her kind—the prophesied Lost Son of Triton. When Sirenia rescues injured Navy SEAL Byron Burke from drowning, she seals herself into his life debt. When the time comes to ask Byron for her freedom, her heart threatens to stand in the way of the last, best hope for her kind.

The Boy Next Door by Hannah Murray

Isabella Carelli isn't just looking for Mr. Right, she's looking for Mr. Tie Me Up And Do Me Right. In all the wrong places. Fortunately, the right place is right next door. And the boy next door is just about ready to make his move...

Devil in a Kilt by Nicole North

A trip to the Highland Games turns into a trip to the past when modern day Shauna MacRae touches Gavin MacTavish's 400-year-old claymore. She finds the *Devil in a Kilt* she's had erotic fantasies about for months. Can she break the curse imprisoning this shape-shifting laird and his clan before an evil witch sends Shauna back to her time and takes Gavin as her sex slave?

The Bet by Leigh Court

I can make a woman come using just my words... That outrageous claim by a very drunk Damian Hunt escalates into a high stakes wager between two friends: Damian bets his prized racehorse that he can do it... George Beringer gambles his London townhouse that he can't. George chooses his virginal sister, Claire, for the bet.

Contents

Heart Storm

※೨ჯ℃౨ઽ⁂

by Liane Gentry Skye

To My Reader:

A lifelong fascination with mermaids, a kayaking trip through the mangroves of Tarpon Bay and a snapshot sent to me by a friend provided the inspirations for *Heart Storm*. I hope you enjoy reading my story as much as I enjoyed writing it.

Chapter 1

Three years after his family's deaths, Lieutenant Byron Burke knew they'd insist he stop mourning and get on with living.

But he couldn't. Not with their killer still at large.

Wind whipped over the waves, coating his torso with sea spray. Standing his surfboard in the sand, his eyes narrowed, surveying the festering clouds.

A more cautious surfer would have deemed the waters off Skeleton's Graveyard too treacherous to navigate. The submerged network of shorn mangroves could impale a man, even on a calm day. With a hurricane threatening, the swells had churned into furious whitecaps.

In spite of years spent training as a Navy SEAL, he allowed his need to push caution to the wayside. His little brother Seth should have celebrated a birthday today. Bringing his killer to justice was the only present worthy of the boy who'd looked up to Byron as a hero.

Mind made up, he tucked the board beneath his arm and jogged toward the foaming surf. Paddling out toward the breaks, he wondered why every turn in his life hinged around this deadly stretch of water.

Here, the Burke's had rescued him as a child, plucking him from the storm surge before a Hurricane. News stories had focused on Byron's unique birthmark, which resembled a trident framed by a pair wings. Still, no family came forward to claim him. Though the trauma had rendered him mute, the Burke's had adopted him, loving him back to health.

Twenty years later, Byron had lost their killer in the exact same spot.

It can't be a coincidence.

Cutting through the swells, Byron riveted his focus on the past. Desperate to dredge up some previously missed clue, he forced himself to relive the worst night of his life.

He'd just returned stateside from Afghanistan. A drink with teammates after checking out at the command led to an eagerly parted pair of legs that went on for miles.

Temptation chased with tequila proved a deadly distraction.

Later, he stepped through his parent's front door just in time to witness the carnage. Tracking the assailant to the waterfront, he snared the bastard at the shoreline.

Digging his fingers into the bony cage of the man's trachea, Byron spun him around. Black eyes, soulless like a shark's crackled with a challenge Byron felt more than he heard.

"Kill me if you can."

Déjà vu slammed Byron to his knees. He'd looked into those bottomless eyes before.

Seizing that dizzying second of distraction, the killer broke free, diving into the inky breakwaters.

Though Byron spent hours scouring the swells, his efforts turned up nothing. A three-day manhunt consisting of police and every available member of his command failed to dredge up a single clue.

The man had simply vanished.

Just beyond the breakwaters, Byron's board bit into an angry swell. Setting his jaw against reeling emotions, he realized any *stranger* trying to navigate the graveyard at night would have ended up shredded shark bait. But the man's identity remained buried in the recesses of his memory, perhaps forever.

Plunging through the face of a twelve-foot wave, he popped out the back into a wicked rip current. Unseated, his board slammed into the back of his skull. Struggling to maintain consciousness, he reached out to recover his board just as another wave dragged him under. World dissolving to black, he couldn't shake the notion that he wasn't dying—he was going *home.*

Chapter 2

Sirenia had spent the better part of her morning tracking her sister's siren song to the mangroves that encircled Maidenhead Lagoon.

She finally found Arabeth sitting in a tangle of prop roots that jutted from the water to form a natural chair—the Wishing Throne, they'd dubbed it as youngsters. The sisters came here often to spill their troubles into the phosphorescent sea, begging their prayers drift from their cloistered home to seek Triton's divine ear.

"Has the morning sickness struck you already?" Sirenia asked.

Arabeth shook her head *no*, and blew out a quivering sigh.

"Then perhaps the rising storm troubles you?" Sirenia offered, leaping on long legs across the bog that stretched between herself and her older sibling.

"Neither." Arabeth bowed her head and swished her pale legs through the illuminated waters. Though glowing sea-life whirled away from the mermaid's ankles like waterborne fireflies, the glittering display did nothing to brighten her gaze. She squeezed her eyes shut and began to hum again. Her tune drifted on the wings of a rising mist, rolling out to sea on its vaporous billows.

Her sister's elegy caused Sirenia's heart to contract. "What brings you to sing such a miserable tune?" she asked, sliding her hands beneath the curtain of Arabeth's hair. Lifting a black curl to her lips, she kissed it in a customary show of deference.

Arabeth's recently consummated breeding moon would soon bring the inevitable news of her pregnancy, elevating her status to royalty. Sirenia would then become bound to the care and protection of her sister's child. Arabeth and her lover, Ba'at Rath, could then concentrate on pampered lives as their brood's only proven breeders in this generation.

"A child, Arabeth!" Sirenia crooned, pressing her cheek against her sister's. "We'll finally welcome a merling among us!" Sirenia dutifully kneaded the taut muscles of the older mermaid's shoulders. "I can hardly wait to hold him."

Arabeth lifted a shaking hand and placed it over Sirenia's larger one. "No, little sister, stop!" she commanded. Her frail shoulders reflected agony as they slumped closer toward the water. "Triton has not blessed me."

"Of course he has," Sirenia said.

Arabeth lifted her swollen eyes up to look at her sister's face. "Then explain why it is, little sister, that your breeder's mark is rising."

Sirenia's hand flew to her forehead to touch the dormant pearl of skin between her eyes. Remembering the years she'd spent searching her reflection for the phosphorescent sign that would prove her breedable, her heart rolled.

Stunned by her sister's insensitivity, Sirenia's brows fused. "You tease me as cruelly as Ba'at Rath himself. You know such a thing isn't possible. I'm a dominant. I was called to guard you, your young."

Arabeth's narrow jaw set in anger. "My time for lovers is over," she spat. "It is I who should be lifting your curls to my lips."

Sirenia's lips pursed with confusion. "I don't understand—the Elders witnessed your third mating with Ba'at Rath. Plans for the naming ceremony have already begun."

Arabeth yanked her legs from the water. Festering fin buds protruded from her ankles. "Ba'at Rath has spent my last chance to bear young."

A sharp gasp escaped Sirenia's lips. Unable to believe her eyes, she sank into the shimmering water beside Arabeth's legs. Reaching out an inquisitive finger, she slid it down the length of her sister's shin.

A rough rising of scales nicked her flesh. "But pregnant mermaids cannot surrender to the Call of the Waters."

"They can if their lover's seed falls shy," Arabeth whispered, voice brittle with emotion.

"But Ba'at Rath is—"

"A liar!" Sirenia's mother finished.

The crone mermaid, Mar-ala, crashed from the mangroves to join her daughters at the water's edge. Silver curls thrashed about her shoulders as she thrust an arm out to capture Sirenia's jaw. She cupped her daughter's chin, raising her to face to the verdant light. "Your rising mark confirms our fears," Mar-ala whispered. "Arabeth has exited her final moon as barren as the day she began it."

An agonized cry tore from Arabeth's throat. She slid from the Wishing Chair, moaning as she submerged herself in the waist deep water.

Mar-ala settled her hands firmly onto Sirenia's shoulders. "I can scarcely imagine by what wisdom Triton has appointed you our last hope for the future."

Sirenia dragged a hand through her unkempt mane as the implications of her mother's words washed over her. "I'm not the Chosen Daughter of Triton. Arabeth is."

"So we believed. But with Arabeth's moon wasted, you stand next in line."

"But I'm a dominant," Sirenia cried. "No man's seed can overcome my constitution." Her eyes scoured her mother's face for some sign that she'd be spared mating with Ba'at Rath. Nothing she saw in Mar-ala's troubled eyes brought her comfort.

Spinning around, she extended a hand to her more delicately wrought sibling. "Please, Arabeth," she cried, "get up. You are everything I am not. Mating, motherhood—these are your rights of submission. Not mine."

Arabeth buried her face in her hands and cried harder.

Sirenia hauled her sister onto quaking legs, gathering her close. "Never have I seen such a beautiful mer! You were designed by Triton to live a breeder's life. Fight this."

"I can't," Arabeth sobbed.

"You must!" Sirenia said, thumbing tears from her sister's eyes. "You are still young. You might conceive next time."

Arabeth wrenched herself from Sirenia's embrace and sank to her knees, surrendering to the Call of the Waters. "Are you really that simple, Sirenia? Can you not understand why there can be no next time?"

"I believe faith can make anything possible."

As if in answer, Arabeth's mottled tailfins unfurled and fanned out, spreading across the water's luminescent surface.

Desperate for intervention, Sirenia whipped around, facing Mar-ala. "Right this, Mother."

Tears beaded at the corners of Mar-ala's pale eyes. "Ba'at Rath's failure to impregnate your sister has wasted her third—and final—breeding moon. Because she has not conceived, she'll not have another."

"And you can rest assured Ba'at Rath will come sniffing your musk trail by nightfall," Arabeth hissed, lips stretching thinly across her teeth.

Guilt crashed over Sirenia as she endured Arabeth's expression of heartbreak. "Ba'at Rath finds me hideous."

"Ba'at Rath would screw a moray if it would insure him a son—and a throne," Arabeth spat, anger smudging her face into a mask of bitterness.

Sirenia shivered. She'd played witness to Ba'at Rath's idea of intimacy. Custom bound to witness Arabeth's first mating, she'd watched, horrified, as her sister endured his degrading intrusions. Not even the throes of passion-swell could check the tears that had streamed from Arabeth's eyes.

When it was over, Sirenia had spooned her sister's bruised body against her own. While Arabeth sobbed herself into the coma-like sleep of after-glow, Sirenia urged her to remain focused on the grand prize—the precious baby that would save their kind from extinction. "You will be revered as a queen, the savior of our kind."

Later, Sirenia had slipped away from Arabeth's side to answer the Call of the Waters. Fins flashing in the moonlight as they parted the lagoon's surface, she bathed herself clean, thanking Triton for sparing her such debauchery.

Now, I am next. A cry of disgust tore from her throat. Wrapping her arms over her breasts, she cringed against her rising fears.

"No!"

Mar-ala settled her hands onto Sirenia's shoulders, shaking her slightly. "You will stop this silliness, now! Your dawning moon obligates you to couple."

"I don't love Ba'at Rath." Scowling, Sirenia lifted her chin. "Nothing I allowed him to do to me during passion-swell could prevent my womb from spitting out his seed."

"You would risk our brood by indulging your heart?" Arabeth charged.

Before Sirenia could fire back a retort, a gale tore across the mangroves. A lifeless live oak snapped and splintered. The crackling deadwood swooned, crashing heavily to the ground. Something—a spooked animal perhaps—rustled in the sea grasses behind where the mermaids gathered.

"Shush!" Mar-ala whispered. Lifting her face to the wind, she scented the thick air. As her eyes swept the dense thickets, a colony of bats dropped from the rustling wall of vegetation and fled inland.

"Who's there?" Mar-ala demanded.

A heron snapped her head up from the shallows. The eel she'd won in her efforts plopped back into the water. The great bird stood motionless on one leg, wings readied to fly.

The wind died down, and the mangroves once again fell silent. The heron relaxed, dipping her beak back into the water.

Whatever threat the grasses had once concealed appeared to be gone.

"Do you think Ba'at Rath was watching us?" Bile seared Sirenia's throat as she imagined opening her untried sex to the merman's assault. "What if he already knows his seed fell shy?"

"Calm yourself," Mar-ala commanded. "Too much time has been squandered on Ba'at Rath." Seizing her youngest daughter's hand, she led her into the wind-whipped water to kneel next to Arabeth.

"Listen well, Sirenia," she whispered, glancing suspiciously over her shoulders to look back at the rustling mangroves. "Our future depends on you. Do you remember the story that you and Arabeth begged after as children? Of Triton's Lost Son?

Sirenia nodded, wondering why her mother would choose this moment to bring up a crib yarn.

"Ba'at Rath convinced your sister that he'd seen the carvings for himself—that they revealed that his birthmark proved him the Lost Son.

"He tricked her?" Brows slumping with sympathy, Sirenia slid her eyes toward her sister. "With a fairy tale."

Arabeth nodded and hung her head.

"The tale was created by the Ancient Mothers," Mar-ala rasped. "They passed the prophecy from mother to daughter, so that when the time of the Red Tides brought the Wasting Plague to pass, Triton's Chosen Daughter would know how to recognize the true mark of his Lost Son."

"I thought I was the Chosen Daughter," Arabeth cried, clasping Sirenia's hands into her own. "I believed my baby was destined to lead us into a new age. I believed it because Ba'at Rath said it was so. But I'm not her, Sirenia."

"*You* are, my child," Mar-ala said.

"N-no," Sirenia stammered, shaking her head so adamantly that the golden coils of her hair bounced before her eyes.

"Yes, you." Mar-ala cupped her hands on Sirenia's shoulders. With shaking fingers, she lifted one of Sirenia's ringlets to her lips, and kissed it in deference. Falling to her knees, she bowed her head before addressing her youngest daughter.

"Before this storm breaks, Sirenia, you must enter Open Waters and travel to the Mother's Mangrove. It is written that deep beneath her core, the ancient mothers have erected an underwater shrine. In that sacred place, they left carvings revealing the true mark of Triton's Lost Son. Find them. Memorize the mark, for it will lead you to the true Lost Son. Mate with him three times before your moon wanes, and you will bear his child, giving life to a new generation. Welcome his seed with a joyful heart, my rising queen, for therein lies our future."

How dare those yammering hags hold me accountable for Arabeth's withered womb! A fierce scowl sliced Ba'at Rath's ragged face as he repositioned himself behind the drape of a low hanging vine.

The last thing he'd expected when he'd sniffed Sirenia's musk trail, following her out into the mangroves, was news of the plot being hatched against him. He'd come here hoping to catch the mermaid alone with her first passion-swell, unable to deny her womb's yearning. He knew firsthand that any merman lucky enough to fall within her gaze at that moment would take the erotic ride of his life.

"So much effort, wasted," he spat. The same child's tale he'd used to woo Arabeth would now be used against him.

"No!" he growled under his breath.

He'd spent years—a lifetime—studying the ancient prophecies, methodically positioning himself to topple the matriarchy that had risen when the Red Tides came, weeding down the ranks of dominant males with their hideous, wasting plague.

He'd been so sure Arabeth was the one.

Wrong sister. Now, the women planned to send the overgrown mermaid searching for the one thing that could potentially threaten his goals—an outsider's seed. What if the dominant cow somehow managed to find proof that he'd lied—or worse, if she managed to find someone claiming to be the Lost Son, himself?

What if she conceived his child?

"My status will not be threatened by a gaggle of sea cows," Ba'at Rath croaked, fisting his hands against his rage.

So I will follow her, he thought. *Find a way, force her to acquiesce to my seed, proving myself the Lost Son, once and for all.*

The idea of tormenting the willful mermaid so she lacked the strength to resist conception amused him. He lifted his nose windward, inhaling the invitation of her musk—a heady combination of mossy earth and salty waters. Sliding a gnarled finger down his rising length, Ba'at Rath's excitement grew.

Once he got her away from Mar-ala's prying eyes, he'd only need hold Sirenia until she birthed. Then he could leave her—and her bloody afterbirth—to the sharks. Returning home with her child, he'd be coddled as a mourning husband—a heart-broken hero and an unchallenged king.

Perfection.

Chapter 3

When Byron came to, he was sprawled belly-up on his surfboard, sporting a hellacious headache. Slitting one gritty eye open, he couldn't tell if he'd been out for moments or days. All he could glean was that he wasn't alone. That much he could tell by the fact that a pair of velveteen lips worked against his.

Now this is my kind of Heaven, he thought, molding his mouth against hers.

The strange woman who sat straddling him raised her tousled head. Blue eyes flecked with bits of sunshine explored his. Twin furrows of confusion marred the sun-kissed expanse of her forehead, causing Byron to wonder if kissing was what she really had in mind.

As she appraised him, a bluish glow radiated from a raised mark situated between her eyes. He wanted to ask her—*are you an angel?* When he opened his mouth, brackish seawater dribbled out instead of the words that burned on the tip of his tongue.

Looping her suntanned arms under his shoulders, she groaned as she tugged their weight, forcing him to sit up. "That's right," she said in a halting voice. "Cough it out, pretty boy."

Every muscle in his body seized from want of oxygen. Lungs finally purged, he collapsed down again, sapped of strength. His body raked in lungful after burning lungful of air.

Guess, I'm alive, he thought.

"Lucky for you," she said, "I came along when I did."

At least, he *thought* she said that. But it was impossible. One, he hadn't spoken his thoughts out loud and two, her tantalizing lips hadn't moved.

Not one bit.

Judging by the pain pounding through his skull, he figured it quite possible that he was hallucinating all of this.

But as far as delusions go, things could be a helluva lot worse.

His statuesque savior was naked, save for the fact that his dog tags glittered like half-buried treasure from the shadow of her cleavage. She didn't appear affected by her nudity, and Byron sure wasn't going to complain about it.

"What are you doing out here?" the girl commanded.

The swing of her pink-tipped breasts charmed away any possibility of a coherent answer.

Her hands traveled the ridges of his gut, fingers skimming every crest and hollow, as if checking for wounds. Her thigh muscles flexed as her wide pelvis rocked in time with the current, causing the curls guarding her sex to capture glints of sunlight.

The tingling in Byron's groin helped him keep his grip on consciousness.

Gasping, she twirled her index finger in a lazy circle around the odd, mark that marred the hollow where his right pelvic bone sloped in toward the waistband of his low-riding cut-offs.

"You are a land-walker, yet you wear a mark of Triton," she said, blue eyes widening. "How can that be?"

"Birthmark." Byron's throat seized as the word scraped from his throat.

"Am I hurting you?" she asked, concern crimping her forehead. She shifted. Lifting her hips, golden curls parted to reveal tender, pink folds.

Byron's flesh sprang to attention, driving home the fact that he was not only alive—he was healthy enough to realize that only the worn fabric of his cutoffs denied him access to the sweet pussy hovering a hair's breadth over his groin.

A fiery blush spread across her lightly freckled face as his erection strained against the rigid seam of his cutoffs.

You're a pleasure I don't deserve, he thought.

"Shush", she whispered, smoothing back the damp curls that clung to his forehead. "There's another storm coming. We have to get you inland."

Leave me, he thought, steeling himself against the feral beauty of her features. *Forget you ever saw me.*

"If I leave, you'll die," she said. At least, he *thought* she did.

What was he thinking? No way could she read his thoughts but somehow she had answered him. Had she somehow *heard* his thoughts? Closing his eyes, he decided that his mind was definitely playing tricks on him. Perhaps he was delirious.

"Dead things draw sharks," she continued. "Then a hurricane will be the least of our worries. Anyhow, dragging you up from the bottom put me in your life debt. Triton shows no mercy to those who flee one of those."

If anyone was an expert in life-debts, it was Byron. If only he'd gone straight home after checking out with his command that night. Now, he'd never know if his brother Seth had cried out when the bullet penetrated his skull.

A groan of loss escaped his parched lips.

A driving wind whipped her hair into riotous curls."Save your strength," she said. Though her words came clipped, her eyes shone with something else— compassion.

A teardrop wound down the edge of her freckled nose. When it plopped onto Byron's forehead, she leaned forward to kiss it away. The gesture felt so tender that it left Byron to wonder again if she'd somehow truly heard his thoughts—and then felt his pain.

The points of the girl's nipples brushed up against his, reminding him that he was far from dead. "Now sit still and hush while I get you somewhere safe," he heard her say.

You smell like sex on the beach, he thought, grinning against his pain.

She gasped, jaw dropping in affront. "Well you smell like a banded rot barnacle."

Unsnapping his shorts, she slid her silken body down his burning length. Peeling the waterlogged denim off his hips, Byron's erection popped free. Her blue eyes met his, one pale brow arching with appreciation.

"You put Triton himself to shame!"

Sliding off the board's end, she lowered herself into the choppy water. Wadding Byron's cutoffs into a tight ball, she tossed them out to sea.

"You won't need these where we're going."

Resting her elbows on the end of the surfboard, she propped the elfish point of her chin onto her hands. "Rest now," she commanded.

Byron's head rolled sideways as she drove the long board through the angry waters with little effort. His burning eyes scanned the horizon for signs of land. Nothing save mile after mile of water surrounded them.

Crazy wench, he thought. *She'll get killed trying to save my ass.*

Before Byron could urge her again to forget him and save herself, she began singing in a language he'd never heard. Rings of blackness rolled at the edges of his vision. He closed his eyes, letting himself float on the strains of her haunting melody. That sweet song, paired with the roll of the ocean lulled him toward the forgetfulness he longed for.

He'd accomplished nothing by surfing Skeleton's Graveyard, except for putting another innocent life in danger.

We'll likely be dead by sundown, he thought, succumbing to the darkness.

Chapter 4

What in Triton's name was I thinking? Sirenia squinted against a rush of tears. Her impulsive nature had not only led her into trouble again—she'd also managed to indenture herself into a life debt.

To a land-walker, no less!

"Do. Not. Dally," she said. That was the urgent advice Mar-ala had offered earlier, while Sirenia slathered her arms with coconut oil, preparing a barrier against the dehydrating salt of the open waters. "Promise me again, Sirenia, that you will swim an *unbroken* trail to the Mother's Mangrove."

She had bristled as soon as Mar-ala spoke. "What could I possibly find in Open Waters more interesting than The Lost Son?" Deep down, she knew her history provided ample evidence to warrant concern. Too often, one impulsive investigation led her to the delighted discovery of another. More than a few times, she'd arrived home just in time to greet her outbound search party.

Sirenia shuddered, imagining the torment she'd face if she dragged this *stray* back to Maidenhead. The Elder's would likely banish her—and her land-walker—to Open Waters as food for the sharks. *And they'd be within their rights.*

By the time the emerald cap of the Mother's Mangrove crept above the horizon, she had devised a hundred reasons why she must take the human right back where she'd found him. "He'll likely die anyway," she tried, but each new glance at her human inspired a thousand fresh reasons why she must see him to safety.

Hours spent pushing the delirious man in front of her had taken its toll. Her stressed fins burned with exhaustion. Breasts heaving, she gulped against air running thicker than silt. A rushing school of sea jellies hastened past. Their agitated behavior mirrored the anxious prickling of her dorsal fins—all signs that the storm would break sooner than she'd hoped.

Riding out a hurricane was no big deal for a mermaid. Traveling alone, she could simply seek shelter below, in the arching network of prop roots that supported the Mother Mangrove. That's where she'd been going anyway, to seek the carvings Mar-ala had spoken of—before the land-walker had threatened her plans.

"Saving you, changes everything I *might* have done." Sirenia lifted her hand from the water, raking it through the curls that clung to the unconscious man's forehead. Even if she carried him to the deeps with her, sustaining him with breaths from her reservoir lung, he'd not survive long enough to weather the storm. He needed dry land. Shelter. Fresh water and plenty of nurturing. All requiring the one resource she couldn't afford—time.

"Why now?" Sirenia rolled her pleading stare up to the brooding sky. "If you had to drop a half-dead man into my arms, commit me to his life debt, couldn't he at least have been merkind?"

Lightening flared, leapfrogging the inky clouds. In its wake, thunder rolled, chasing a colony of gulls inland. The fine hairs at the back of Sirenia's neck bristled, and dread uncoiled in her gut. She felt that Triton himself was warning her that life debts—even to *humans*—could never go ignored.

A wailing wind lifted the wet coils of her hair, slapping them against the land-walker's angular face. The lush fans of his lashes fluttered against prominent cheekbones. Growling, his brows knit above glazed, golden eyes, creasing his forehead with agony.

"Shush, now," Sirenia said. She smoothed her palm against the human's cheek. He raged with fever. "We must get you to shelter and soon." Though logic bid her to get moving, concentrate on getting him to safety, her rebellious body vibrated with longing. She wanted to stop, admire, ruffling once more the rich, chestnut waves capping his forehead.

A fresh lightening bolt ignited the clouds, blazing a trail deep within the mangrove. The foreboding thunder that followed renewed Sirenia's sense of urgency, but such an overt expression of Triton's will did nothing to help her sprout the legs she'd need to navigate the mangrove—with her delirious land-walker in tow. She'd have to pause, invite her change to visit here—in full view of any predators that might lurk nearby.

Sweeping her fins deep, she puffed out a sigh when they rasped against the sandy sea-bottom. They'd reached the shallows. If she hurried, she might yet get the human to shore before she fell blinded to reason by passion-swell.

Drawing a deep breath, she closed her eyes, preparing to release herself from the water's call. Lower body thrumming with sensation, her change crept upon her. Barely able to move as fin and scale relinquished to flesh and bone, she curled the human's hand into her own so that the swirling rip currents would not drag him away.

The Lost Son should be half so beautiful, she thought, trolling her gaze along the muscled planes of the sleeping man Triton had seen fit to drop into her arms. Dipping her eyes to his beautiful man parts, her fist curled, and then clenched against the desire to touch him there. Breath catching in her throat, her ovaries began to thrum with the taut, aching need to mate—and soon.

Forcing her gaze back to the land-walker's angular face did little to assuage her growing desire. His lips were so sensual. Skimming her tongue over her teeth, she wondered what harm would be done if she nuzzled her cheek just once against the day's growth of stubble that coated his dimpled chin.

After all, he was barely conscious.

How would he ever know if she stopped to brush her palm across the curls that peppered his chest, tapering down to the chestnut tangles hugging his sex?

The idea of having her way with the human—claiming him without his knowledge—brought a moan grating across her lips. By Triton's sacred heart, she had told a lie when she said the land-walker's lips had tasted of rot barnacles. He'd tasted rich and spicy, more irresistible than the powerful aphrodisiacs mermen distilled from sea grapes to draw feminine attention their way.

"You're a complication I don't need right now." Her gaze raked over his sinuous body. Raising her hand to touch him, a ball of lightening dropped from the sky over her head, causing the fine hairs on her arms to stand on end.

"Hormones," she shouted to the Heavens, though her nipples peaked with anticipation. "It's just a hormone surge. Honest!"

Legs growing strong and firm beneath her, she knew Triton had warned her for the last time. She had to get the land-walker inland. Now, before passion-swell struck and she humped him senseless simply because he sported a convenient, and uncommonly bountiful, set of man parts.

As if animated by Sirenia's angst, Byron rolled off his board, grinning sloppily as he joined her in the water. "Skinny dipping time," he announced. Looping a chiseled arm around her shoulders, he crushed her close, belly flush to belly.

Before she could voice a protest, heat flared over her breasts as they flattened against his pecs.

Murmuring incoherent words in her ear, the land-walker rained feverish kisses down her neck, pausing to taste the hollow at the base of her throat. Unfamiliar sensations fanned out beneath her navel and her sex warmed with moisture. Wave after wave of heat crashed over her, pooling in her groin as the land-walker's mouth slicked a trail down the length of her belly.

Pausing to rim her navel with his tongue, his hand continued downward, slipping a gentle finger between the tingling folds of her sex. Need uncoiled in her womb, yanking a groan across her lips. "Please."

Laughter rumbled in his chest, teasing her. His enormous hands retreated, slowly slicking a wet trail up her abdomen. Palming her breasts, he cupped and squeezed, testing their weight.

"Such a pretty angel." Dropping his head, he captured a nipple lightly between his teeth. Twining a steely thigh around her narrow waist, the thick knob of his sex pulsed against her mons.

She wanted to answer him—"I'm no angel," but her breath caught as he dragged a fingertip around her clit. Heart galloping beneath her breasts, she could no longer resist the urgent demand of her passion-swell.

Twining her arms around his neck, she drew his weight down over her, succumbing to the call that surged through her veins. Legs threading around his lean hips, their entwined forms slipped beneath the foaming waters. Limbs knotted around limbs, they tumbled over one another in the shallow, foaming surf.

⁂

Right now, Sirenia didn't look like any dominant cow Ba'at Rath had ever seen. Knotted in the human's embrace, she performed like a siren born and raised only to breed.

He flattened himself against one of the jutting burls that guarded the entrance to the Mother's Mangrove. Forcing himself to swallow, he gulped down the bilious rage that had seized him the second he'd discovered Sirenia with the land-walker.

She belongs to me!

Sucking back the spittle that pooled against his teeth, he recognized that the object of Sirenia's lust was redheaded and hugely built. *Nothing but a lowly land-walker*, he thought *and certainly no real threat to my goals.*

He almost pitied the poor man. He didn't stand a chance of denying Sirenia the satisfaction she sought. Giant, human, animal, no male creature alive could resist the lusty assault of a mermaid swept up in passion-swell. Ba'at Rath bit back the laughter that boiled in his throat. He had seen more than one foolish human screw himself into a watery grave by indulging a horny mermaid's over-zealous attentions.

No matter, he thought. *It will be entertaining, watching this one hump himself to death.*

The fact that Sirenia looked delicate in the human's embrace testified to the man's enormous stature. Though the land-walker appeared wounded, Ba'at Rath felt loathe to engage any adversary who looked to outweigh him by a good forty pounds of rock-hard muscle. *No*, he thought, slipping deeper into the shallow water that hid the dim, recessed grotto, *better to wait.*

Watch.

Acquaint myself with my enemy's weaknesses.

Sirenia appeared dainty in the human's arms, casting her in a fresh light for Ba'at Rath.

Would it really be such a chore to spill my seed in her? She certainly seemed adept enough. Perhaps she was breedable after all—for a lover she chose freely.

Question is, he thought, peeling an urchin away from its rest on the burled roots, *how might I reveal myself to her in such a way that she will choose me, inviting my seed to trump that iron will of hers?*

Ba'at Rath cracked the urchin open, revealing the quivering flesh within. Sucking it into his mouth, he craned his long neck, settling in to watch, reaping useful clues from the passionate scene playing out before him.

Sirenia's mark cast a violet aura around her head, announcing her passion-swell. Rocking her hips up, her legs parted, revealing the folds of her sex to her lover.

The enormous human eased her onto her back across the water's foaming surface.

Choppy waters sluiced over her breasts, and Ba'at Rath watched the land-walker slide his hand down her body. Sirenia's head thrashed back and forth, whipping her hair across the furious swells.

Even from this distance, Ba'at Rath could hear the delighted cry that escaped her throat.

The unmistakable, almond aroma of her estrus permeated his nostrils. An answering tingle twitched in his groin, prompting him toward his own change, so desperately he yearned to take her himself.

By Triton's jewels, he wanted to be that human. He wanted to sprout legs right here and now, and sheathe himself inside Sirenia.

Too dangerous!

Should he succumb to the invitation of her season, allowing his change, he'd render himself vulnerable to attack. Once changed, his sex hormones would force him to challenge this unknown adversary before taking the satisfaction he wanted.

That risked injuries he could ill afford.

Biting his lip, he directed his focus away from his throbbing need and onto the pain. Though Sirenia's passion-wails rang in his ears, he riveted his attention toward his end goal.

Soon enough, Sirenia would have the child that would earn him a crown.

He need only bide his time.

Chapter 5

Dipping his head in for a taste, Byron lapped in lazy circles, rimming the taut junction of her folds. Her opening wept into his hand, staining the water's surface with ribbons of blue light.

"Now that's a good angel," he rasped, laughing. "Show me your halo!"

The bright rush of her fluid, so sweet and vaguely familiar, nearly pushed Byron over the edge. Raking in a deep breath, he steeled himself, delaying his own pleasure as she wrenched satisfaction from his fingers.

His last shred of logic insisted that he must be caught in some sort of wet dream gone 3D. He'd heard plenty of his teammates bragging about the hallucinations they'd experienced when they'd found themselves stressed by oxygen starvation. The way Byron figured, whatever remained of his body probably lay in the briny deep, dying if not already dead.

Oddly, he didn't feel too worried about his impending demise.

Yeah, he thought, grinning, *Drowning really is the only way to go.*

God, she felt so good inside, like melted butter slipping over his fingers. So what if she was only a figment? She certainly *looked* tangible enough, and her red-hot sex definitely felt like the real deal.

In fact, everything Byron had ever yearned for in a bed partner was right here, begging him to make love to her. Now.

My kind of woman, he thought.

His raging hormones didn't care whether she was real or not. His throbbing tip ached for her. He wanted to feel himself melting into those slick folds that promised delights he'd never conceived of.

By the looks of her, with her back arched and her hips grinding against his fingers, she was damn near primed, too.

Beautiful, he thought, slicking his fingers through the tangles that crested her mound. Judging by the muscles striating her thighs, she could easily open up a smoking can of whip-ass on him if she ever caught him with his guard down.

Her rasping moans urged him on as her tight sex girdled his fingers. The tiny after shocks from her first orgasm invited him deeper inside her wicked, hot core. Working a slow, rhythmic pressure across her internal nub, Byron slid his fingers in and out, rimming her opening with those shimmering, fragrant fluids.

"That's right, baby," he grated, "let's light your fire.."

Slicking liquid brightness around her swollen bud, he delighted in the way her hips rolled. Trembling with anticipation, he positioned his tip over her entrance.

Palming his buttocks, she shoved her hips higher, forcing him inside with one, savage thrust of hips.

"Ow!" she cried, tears gathering in her eyes as he tore past a muscular wall of resistance.

A virgin?

"Why didn't you tell me?" he crooned, lifting her. Drawing her close, he folded her in his arms to nuzzle the cascade of her hair. "I'd have been more careful, but…"

Before he could say more, her hips began to sway. Testing his length, she drew him deeper with each rolling motion. Her head dropped back. Her shocked whimpers of pain were soon replaced by purrs of pleasure.

Matching the rocking rhythm of her hips, Byron raised his upper body, watching her. Resting his gaze on her face, he delighted in each new rendering of ecstasy as it dawned in her expression.

Never had he felt a woman so tight, so ready and so hungry for him. Each time he dipped into that glowing warmth, he felt her radiance seep deeper into his soul, beating back the shadows he harbored there. He could not shake the growing feeling that he'd not only met his physical match—he'd also found a kindred spirit.

He grew more certain with each new spasm of her sex that everything in the world he needed to heal his heart lay right here, floating on her back in the break-waters, panting as she frenzied toward climax.

Wailing winds whipped the waters around them. His orgasm thundered through his veins, coursing into her creamy heat. A savage roar tore from his throat as she clenched, milking every drop of his seed into her center.

Dragging in a shuddering breath, he realized that everything he ever could have dreamed of from Heaven was his for the taking, right here, right now.

Nope, he thought, relishing the fading crests of a climax more intense than any he'd ever known. *I don't care if I ever wake up.*

A thunderclap shook the rain from the bulging clouds, dousing Byron with bracing water. The clash of sensations between the downpour and the warm hand fisting his cock yanked him from the throes of what he'd figured to be a wet dream.

What the hell?

Shivering against his rapidly dropping body temperature, his teeth began to chatter, chasing back the shadows of delirium.

Where am I?

Shaking the sea foam from his eyes, he felt sure they played tricks on him. He'd actually imagined that the woman, whose thighs were still vise-gripped around his hips, had somehow painted the water with light every time she came.

Helluva concept, he thought. But given the fact that a waterspout had just popped less than three clicks offshore, the best piece of tail he'd ever known would have to wait if she expected an encore.

They were in trouble.

Byron's eyes squinted into the slanting rain, assessing their surroundings. By the looks of it, they'd miraculously managed to beach themselves on a mangrove island. Not the best-case scenario, granted, but he could think of far worse places than a mangrove forest to hide out from a potentially killing storm.

Sharp branches and broken prop roots jutted from the whitecaps in an array far more intricate—and deadly—than Skeleton's Graveyard. It was a miracle he and *Glow Girl* hadn't impaled themselves as they'd tumbled through the shallows, oblivious to the danger raging around them.

Byron knew he could blame his problems on delirium, but what was her problem? She was insatiable!

Though he longed to drive his length full throttle back into her, he shook himself hard against the delirium that had blinded him to the advancing storm that would make land by nightfall.

"You shouldn't be out here," he said.

In answer, she drew herself upright, weaving her arms around his neck. Planting her lips to his, her tongue darted through his teeth.

Damn, but she was a wild thing, completely oblivious to the growing danger. A girl like her ought to be at home, tucked in her own bed. Perhaps entertaining her boyfriend during what promised to be one nasty storm...

Thanks to him, she'd likely die a senseless death if he didn't manage to drag her to safety—and fast. Realizing he might be facing his last chance in life to atone for the failures of his past, Byron unraveled her legs from his waist.

Before she could voice a protest, the pads of his index finger traveled down her swollen lips, shushing her.

Defiance sliced her forehead. Placing both palms on his chest, she shoved him back into the breakwater. Hooking her thigh across his groin, she straddled him.

Bolstering his shaky resolve, Byron sat up, lifting her off his groin so that she rested on her knees in the water, meeting him eye to eye.

"I will not let you die," he said, circling his arms around her. Rising to his feet, he lifted her up. "Not on my account. We have to get you inland."

Growling with impatience, she fell limp, slipping like butter through his arms. Snaking down his body, she stopped only when she'd sheathed him to the hilt in her soft mouth.

Moaning, Byron steeled his jaw against the flames that lapped at his core, sucking him back toward whatever delusions had brought them here. Tearing his attention away from the pleasure pooling in his groin, his entire body shuddered.

"Easy, Tiger," he said, hooking his fingers under her chin. Thumbs pressing gently against her Adam's apple, he knew she had little choice other than to swallow and gasp. Seizing the fleeting second of advantage, he released his regenerating hard-on from the seal of her lips.

"How 'bout a rain check, doll?" he asked, feeling more than a little disheartened. "It'll be you, me, and a nice patch of dry land."

"Seed me," she grated, lunging for him again. "Now!"

Byron squeezed his eyes shut, pushing back the fingers of dizziness that hovered at the edges of his vision. Damn, his head hurt.

Could it be possible that he was still hallucinating? He'd heard the words she spoke, true and clear. He felt sure of it.

She'd just asked him to *seed* her, but her lips hadn't moved.

Not so much as one millimeter.

Weird. Scooping her back up from the water, he snared her in the crook of his left arm. With his free hand, he reached out, slicking the wet tendrils from her forehead to get a better look at her face.

Unable to believe his eyes, he extended his index finger to touch the glowing nubbin situated dead center between her brows. Shooting a stream of air across his teeth, he let loose a low whistle.

"Are you for real?"

"Please. More."

Glow girl's lips *definitely* had not moved. Nothing beyond a feline growl had escaped her lips. But he'd *heard* the words.

No. He'd *felt* them.

Yes, he thought, *I'd swear it before God and everybody.*

He'd actually felt her voice, vibrating clear and true inside the cage of his skull.

He knew every word she was thinking.

Outrageous, he thought. *How could such a thing possibly be true?*

Maybe I'm dreaming.

Yes, that was the only rational explanation. Sinking a tooth into his lip, he tested the idea, certain that he wouldn't actually feel any pain.

He felt the hell out of it.

Impossible.

"Who are you?" he asked, cupping her angled jaw. He hitched up her chin, plundering that blue gaze for any hint of subterfuge or malice. He saw none of those.

"Better yet *what* the hell are you?"

Notching her chin still higher, she looked to Byron like the definition of royalty as she skewered him with her glare.

"I am Sirenia de Mar-ala, the chosen Daughter of Triton," she "said". Golden flecks danced in her eyes, twinkling like embers as Byron continued to hold her gaze.

"Go on," he said.

"I left my home in search of the Lost Son, for he alone can save my kind. Instead, I came across *you* in Open Waters and *foolishly* saved your life.

Byron fired a snort out his nose. "*You* saved *me*?" he asked, sliding his eyes from her face down to her feet and back up again. "I don't think so."

She puffed out a soft sigh, nodding. "You can choose to believe it or not, but Triton knows I speak the truth. So you can do whatever you want to me without fearing his wrath, for you own me."

"Huh?"

"I am bound to serve you for all Eternity, making you free to make love to me again." She set her jaw. "So just do it."

Her mouth didn't have to move for Byron to know... to feel... that she'd hissed those words.

"Daughter of Triton? Fated son?"

He didn't try to restrain the sarcasm lacing his voice. Everything about her hair-brained story defied reason.

"Well, thank you," he said, loosening his grip on her. "That certainly clears things right up."

Byron lifted his right hand, touching the aching, congealed gash where his surfboard had struck him on the back of the head earlier.

He winced. "Maybe I'm having a stroke?"

Instead of commenting, Sirenia dipped her burning gaze back to the vicinity of his cock. Dragging her tongue across her lower lip, she lunged for him.

Byron thrust his arms out to brace her shoulders, holding her at arm's length. "In case you haven't noticed, doll, there's a waterspout two clicks, due west, and headed our way," he said, spinning her around to face the water.

"So if you don't mind, Miss Sirenia De whoever, kindly douse your fires so I can rescue *your* horny ass."

"Excuse me," she said, whirling in his grasp, "but I've risked the extinction of everyone I love by preserving your lowly existence, and I'm completely capable of saving you again. And I will. Just as soon as you bless me."

"Bless you?" Byron asked.

"With. Your. Seed."

Shooting out a well-developed leg, she hooked him behind his knees. Before he could counter, she slammed him down onto his back into the silt at the surf's edge.

Wherever it was Glow Girl came from, it was becoming clear to Byron that she'd not accept any kind of rain check. As she reared her head back to wrap those succulent lips around him, he decided to feign compliance.

Snaking his hands down the sides of her neck, he could feel her pulse pounding beneath the pads of his fingers.

"That's right, baby," he whispered. Curling her into the crook of his arm, her neck nestled neatly between his bicep and forearm. Pressing firmly against her carotids, he applied a careful sleeper hold.

"Come on home to Daddy."

Sirenia's eyes fluttered, blue rolling to white before she collapsed into a heap on top of him. Scooping the unconscious girl up into his arms, Byron winced as his shoulder took her weight.

Determined to carry Glow Girl through every inch of this gnarled mangrove if that's what it took to save her, Byron stomped out of the surf, shouldering his way inside the dense wall of vegetation that composed the outer rim of the island.

"Forgive me, sweetheart, but as long as I draw breath," he whispered into the lush cascade of her hair, "I won't be adding your death to my list of sins."

Chapter 6

Deep beneath the Mother's Mangrove, the currents shivered against the storm pounding the land above. Phosphorescent sea life illuminated the cavernous hollows, infusing the water with an insipid light.

Ever mindful of his own welfare, Ba'at Rath had fled here to ride out the storm, leaving the sex-crazed lovers to their own devices. Sirenia's history had proven her resourceful and the fact that she'd traveled this far suggested Triton truly was watching over her. Ba'at Rath doubted even the vilest storm could harm her at this point, and he didn't care a squid's eye about the fate of her land-walker.

Determined to spend his time here to his advantage, he meandered through the intricate maze of roots, scouring the gnarled grottos for the carvings Mar-ala had alluded to.

Just one generation past, these catacombs had teemed with life. With their breeding moons spent, pregnant mermaids retreated to this remote sanctuary to raise their young, far from the intrusive activities of humans, who grew ever bolder in their destruction of the mangroves the mer-ken depended on for survival.

A mermaid's pregnancy was long and preparing her children to survive in an increasingly hostile world even longer. As the mer-ken's numbers dwindled, young mothers faced long, solitary confinements, with only their infants and their imaginations to vary the pattern of days.

With little to entertain themselves, the cloistered mothers began weaving romantic stories drawn from the ancient scriptures of Triton. Glyphic drawings etched onto the burls had preserved the prophecy of the Lost Son across countless eons.

In spite of the care, the women took to look after each other, more than a few mermaids had surrendered to deadly melancholia as they endured interminable separations from their mates. Reports of young mermaids consorting with humans began to reach the council.

Desperate to maintain the purity of their blood, the Council deemed that what mermaids remained fit to breed must conceive, birth and raise their young under their watch, with the assistance of a family appointed dominant—such as Sirenia.

The Council and its twelve dried up crones had never allowed Ba'at Rath to forget, for so much as a moment, that he and his long, lost brother were but taint-bloods, the bastard sons of a human man and their mother, a disgraced mermaid.

Only when Ba'at Rath shrewdly suggested to Council that his unique bloodline might have rendered him immune to the sperm-wasting sickness that plagued the purebloods, did his status increase in their esteem. That, paired with the rumor he'd so deftly planted in Arabeth's mind—that his birthmark proved him the Lost Son—had spread faster than the Red Tide.

I must admit, he thought, *using prophecy to lend credence to my claims was a particularly inspired moment of brilliance.*

He wasn't of a mind to relinquish so much as an inch of the ground he'd gained now. He need only be patient for a while longer.

Soon enough, he thought, *everything will change. Council will bow before me, begging me to spare their pathetic lives.*

After all, it was only his due. He'd spent a lifetime insuring it, and when his reign finally dawned—and dawn it would—his first act as king would be to cloister the Council here, in these catacombs, too far away to meddle with his rule.

Ba'at Rath scoured the tangled mazes, looking for the glyphs said to portend the mark of the prophesied king. *My mark,* he thought, bursting out into a high cavern.

By the looks of it, he'd finally found the place he sought.

Seashells and glittering bits of sand-polished glass paved a pathway that led to a roughly hewn altar. A triptych of flat rocks had been set upright on their ends to create a shrine that girdled an intricately whorled prop root. A mound of pearls encircled the root's base, each representing the prayer of the mermaid who had left it behind, a token of her petition before Triton.

A low growl gurgling in his throat, Ba'at Rath rushed to the makeshift shrine. He shivered with pleasure as his fingers traveled the glyphic carvings, plundering for the evidence that would finally prove that which he'd spent a lifetime manipulating into truth.

I am the chosen one, Triton's Lost Son. If what I have toiled so hard to insure becomes my divine path were not true, would not Triton have struck me down by now?

Now he would have irrefutable proof of his claim.

Over the years, Byron's command had sent him through some downright grueling survival schools, but no training in the world could have prepared him to weather a hurricane solo, much less with a glow-in-the-dark wet dream in tow.

Hurricane Blanco had wasted no time in unleashing his fury on the Mangrove. Always the realist, Byron quickly dismissed any thoughts of rescue on their dismally short list of assets. Even if anyone had witnessed his spill from his board back at Blackbeard's Cove, search efforts would have been suspended the moment the hurricane threatened landfall.

He had no clue where they'd washed up. Even if the mini-compass mounted on the band of his wristwatch still worked—which he doubted—it was too dark out to read the damn thing. They were on their own to ride out the storm as best they could.

Or more likely, die trying.

Moments stretched out like hours, and Byron felt like he'd already endured an eternity in Hell. His body screamed for mercy. Only the woman he held in his arms prevented him from diving into the densest thicket he could find, to live or die by Fate's hand.

But Glow Girl changed everything he might have done, left to his own devices.

She obligated him, and he would not let her die. Not on his watch!

Woody debris thrashed about his head, threatening his eyes. Bowing his head over hers, he tucked her face beneath his chin, sheltering her as best he could.

She lay so still. Too still. The sleeper hold he'd put on her had done exactly what he'd intended—dropped her into compliance. But she shouldn't have been out for more than a few seconds.

A minute at the most.

It felt like hours had passed. Sirenia hadn't so much as sighed.

A wind wailed across the mangrove, plastering him in wet vegetation. He could hear trees splintering, snapping. Felled limbs crashed around their heads like falling dominos.

Stopping to check her out wasn't an option.

Not yet.

Plodding onward, he sloshed through the root-choked waters, barely staying abreast of the storm's rushing surge. Without a single star to navigate by, he relied on his instincts to traverse the tangled network and its swirling tributaries. Coursing inland, he kept the winds to his back—always to his back.

The dense, outer walls of the mangrove finally dropped behind them. They would break the worst of the winds—for the moment. Seizing the tiny advantage, Byron paused to catch his breath and regroup.

Pain was all that kept him from passing out, giving in to exhaustion. While his spirit was more than willing to go on, he knew if they were to survive, he must somehow scale the wall of agony that threatened their progress.

Focus on something—anything—else.

Raising his head from hers, he saw that the mark between her eyes pulsed with a faint, lavender glow.

At least she isn't dead, he thought. It surprised him how much his heart sang with that knowledge. Sliding one hand to the base of her throat, he felt the frenetic pounding of her pulse beneath her skin.

She wasn't in shock, either. He grated out a relieved sigh.

She stirred slightly, burrowing her cheek into the well between his pecs. The smile that wrenched across his lips nearly took him to his knees with surprise.

I'm starting to care for her.

He couldn't let her die.

Though his leg muscles trembled beneath her weight, as long as she lived, he'd continue. At least until his body refused to cooperate.

Steeling his jaw against the agony rattling his bones, he dredged the depths of his reserves, scouring for any remaining shred of fortitude.

There wasn't much left.

Don't stop! Not yet.

Though each new step sucked him knee deep in churning silt, he preferred to die in the trying than give up now. Lunging forward to wrench his ankle from the muck, he knew he'd hit the wall.

He had nothing else left to give.

Barring a miracle, they would both die out here.

"Forgive me," he choked out, pressing his lips to the top of her head.

Stumbling, he lurched forward, crashing through a barbed wall of vegetation. Thorny branches clawed at his flesh, shredding it. Bursting out the other side, he sagged to his knees, nearly dropping the strange woman who'd been so willing to risk her life in exchange for another go-round with him.

For the moment, the rain had subsided some. *At least,* he thought, *until the next band hits.* Tentatively raising his head, he opened his eyes on a world unlike anything he'd ever seen.

Like a dreamscape, swirls of brightness came from both nowhere and everywhere. Raindrops pattered against the surface of the lagoon before him, piercing the water with daggers of light. Each droplet infused the water with the same bluish radiance that had oozed from Glow Girl when she'd climaxed.

Though he'd encountered phosphorescent pools in his previous travels, he'd never encountered a water-born lightshow as dramatic as this one.

Driving out a soft whistle, he gently dropped Sirenia to her feet, supporting her drowsy weight with one arm. Cupping the palm of his free hand, he lifted it from the waist deep water, raising a handful of the luminous liquid to his nose.

He inhaled, tentatively at first. The sultry fragrance of almonds and female reached his nose. *So sweet. Like her.*

Raising his hand, the liquid streamed in dazzling rivulets down his badly scratched forearm, assuaging the worst of his pain. When his hand fell, droplets trailed like diamonds from the ends of his fingers, dripping the worst of his misery into the phosphorescent pool.

Too practical to bother with questioning the miracle they so desperately needed, Byron moved toward a swelling rise of sand off to his right. There at least he could sit down, assess their surroundings. With her limp form leaning into his side for support, he planted one tentative foot in front of the other, testing the water's depth.

As their footfalls disturbed the lapping surf, the water responded like a living thing. Glowing concentric circles shivered across the lagoon, lighting the way to higher ground.

Struggling to wrap his mind around the notion he'd seen this place before, Byron turned in a slow circle, eyes sweeping, searching the battered terrain. Though unable to reckon why, he felt certain that if he stared hard enough into the darkness, the shadows would offer up the sanctuary they so desperately needed.

Narrowing his gaze, he scoured the undefined silhouettes of the surrounding shrub line.

Expecting.

His eyes stopped, latching onto what he'd inexplicably intuited was there—a shadow, nothing like the rest, jutting from the black backdrop. Unlike the irregular thickets of vegetation surrounding the lagoon, it boasted crisp, defined edges.

Right angles don't occur in nature.

How many times had his commanding officer drilled that into their heads during training? Whatever his eyes struggled to make sense of had been forged by human hands. The structure looked big—and strong.

Perhaps even strong enough to fend off a hurricane's blows.

Surely, he thought, gulping down his rising hopes, *my eyes are playing tricks on me.* Squeezing his lids shut, he lifted his face to the rain, letting the droplets sluice over his burning eyes. Licking the welcome moisture from his parched lips, he drew his leg back, slicing the water's surface with a kick. A shower of light spilled down in the direction of the shadow.

Grinning, his eyes confirmed the closest thing to a miracle he'd ever seen. He was looking at the battered stern of a wrecked ship—probably a galleon that some desperate pirate had driven high into the mangroves hundreds of years ago, trying to outsmart a storm.

"No way."

The sound of his voice provided the magic needed to reanimate his phosphorescent siren. She wound herself in the circle of his arms, rasping a kittenish purr into his ear.

For Byron, that sound meant one thing.

Glow Girl Gone Wild.

Before he could counter against her shifting weight, she'd threaded her arms around his neck. Clamping one leg and then the other around his hips, she snuggled her cheek against the deep curve where his neck dipped into his shoulder.

Then, falling still again, she began to snore.

Nothing in his realm of experience could account for the girl's vigorous reaction to a simple sleeper hold. *Could it be that she's just—wired differently?*

Before his mind could wrap fully around the notion, a brittle wind whipped a warning across the lagoon. Shaking the rain from his eyes, Byron filed away the suspicion that the woman whose gentle snores puffed against his neck might not be human.

A spray of leaves skittered across the water's surface, reminding him that another band of hellacious weather would soon make landfall.

He'd have to think about the mysteries surrounding Sirenia later.

It was time to dry her off and put her to bed before she got frisky again, demanding reserves he simply didn't have left to spend.

Somewhere off in the distance, a buffeting wind rumbled. The uncertain ground beneath Sirenia lurched, urging her toward wakefulness. Though her resting place pitched and groaned against each pounding gale, she was warm. Comfortable. Somewhere in the dim recesses of her mind, she knew she'd somehow managed to stumble onto shelter.

She was safe!

She smiled, relief flooding her heart as she snuggled deeper into the delicious heat swaddled around her. *Perhaps I might yet live long enough to find the Lost Son.*

Her world winding slowly back into focus, she began to see just how wrong everything about this place was. Her ears rang with the snaps and crackles of breaking wood, and the wet slapping of the tree limbs scuffed against the outer walls of the shelter.

Land sounds, she thought, sleepily. By the sound of it, the hurricane had already broken. For the life of her she could not reckon why she'd chosen to ride out such a dangerous storm on land.

Unless passion-swell struck me.

That's all that would have prevented her from summoning the Call of the Waters and hiding in the bottoms until the storm passed.

Peeling her way through layer after layer of murky awareness, Sirenia struggled to slit open her eyes.

Now, she stared wide-eyed into blackness. All she could glean for sure was that night had fallen. She guessed that much by the narrow band of stars that peeped through a ragged opening in the shelter's side. The scant patch of light stubbornly chased the coiling clouds that threatened to devour the heavens. Though she knew clear sky meant the storm's eye would soon make landfall, she also realized the danger was a far cry from finished.

It was still raining hard and the air ran so thick with brine that she could taste it.

But how did I get here?

Grating her tongue across her lips, she tasted the salty remnants of her swim through Open Waters as she'd rushed the land-walker toward safety.

The land-walker!

Memory filled in the details with a dizzying rush of images. Smiling, she recalled the lazy grin that melted across the land-walker's face when she'd straddled him on his long board. She wrenched out a moan and her fingers thrummed as she remembered grazing them over the burnished curls hugging his sex when she pulled off his clothing.

Her tongue tingled, recreating the salty taste of his lips as she'd pressed her mouth against his. Heat fanned across her breasts, urging them to points as she recalled trailing her fingers over his skin, checking for wounds. And then she'd found his mark—a trident, much like Ba'at Rath's. But framed by something else, a pair of soaring wings.

How could a human be marked by Triton's hand? Surely, it was some evil trick of the under gods. To distract her.

This land-walker could never be the Lost Son. He was human. And that made him forbidden.

But even that hadn't been enough to stop her from saving him.

The bitter truth of what she'd done yanked her fully into consciousness, forcing her to face the obligation her hasty rescue threatened.

Assuming the land-walker lived.

While her coconut oil barrier had extended her defenses against the brine, she'd heard tales from her mother that salt and humans did not mix.

"They're a delicate lot," Mar-ala had insisted, warning her daughters against consorting with humans. "It is one of their many weaknesses."

Judging by the warmth of the heavy arm draped around her shoulder, the supposedly delicate human had survived the storm's landfall just fine.

Pretty resilient for one of his kind. Wriggling to free her bottom from the toasty nest of his groin, she only managed to bury her butt deeper, so deep she could feel him—*and that magnificent sex*—stirring in the crevice between her cheeks.

He puffed out a soft sigh, its heat searing the skin at the nape of her neck. Curling his forearm tighter across her breasts, the growing evidence of his desire offered a hearty salutation against the small of her back.

So much for his death releasing me from life debt.

Immediately, her heart contracted with guilt. She'd never truly hope for any creature's demise but finding the Lost Son would have come far less complicated had she only closed her eyes.

Looked the other way.

Desperate circumstances had forced Mar-ala to entrust the brood's fate in Sirenia's care. Instead of finding the help she'd been sent for, Sirenia knew she'd done nothing but insure their extinction.

A mermaid with a logical nature—like Arabeth—would simply have swam on by, sidestepping the tangled obligations Sirenia had woven—at the worst possible time

Heat rushed to her cheeks as she considered what had first attracted her to the land-walker, urging her to help him. *That comely face, those sinuous muscles... his body is huge!*

And so is his sex.

Each of those had conspired, compelling her to save his life. For those particular details regarding humans, her mother had not prepared her.

But even that doesn't excuse me. A tremor rattled the length of the land-walker's body. Mindful of her obligation, she spooned herself completely in his molten embrace, offering her warmth as medicine to comfort his chill.

His thumb lathed across her nipple, rousing it to a point.

Deja vu melted over her in a sultry wave. The yearning began as a delicate tingling at the nape of her neck. Before she could gasp, an answering heat gathered in her loins. Squeezing her thighs together, she tried to restrain the rush of fluids that collected at her opening. Instead, she felt the raw, throbbing ache of internal muscles she'd never known existed.

Had she unleashed her passion-swell on the land-walker?

A slowly, spinning rewind of freeze frames flooded her consciousness.

They'd fought. That much, she remembered. Or had it been but a dream, those black-lashed, amber eyes looking so sincere as he deftly turned the tables on her, insisting it was *his* duty to save *her*?

She repressed a giggle, scoffing at the notion. *Imagine a human thinking he could take on a dominant mer and win!*

Sucking her lower lip between her teeth, she recalled how the land-walker's eyes had flashed, announcing his ruffled pride when she'd boasted that she'd rescued him. That certainly testified to his arrogance—something else her mother had warned her about.

But laying here in his arms, she had little choice than admit that the lowly land-walker had likely saved her life. That she was unable to remember anything else about how she got here proved that she'd been blinded to reason by passion-swell.

Now, she owed him her life. How that bore on her life debt, she had no idea. She could only hope that once she'd nursed him back to health, she could plead her case to him, make him see why he simply must release her to find the Lost Son.

"Cast your charms in a human's direction and he'll follow you to his death."

Something else her mother had advised her against.

Thanks, Mom.

Under normal circumstances, she'd prostrate herself before Council, begging them to help unwind this latest quagmire she'd invented.

But Council wasn't here.

Now it's just me and my land-walker, she thought.

Judging by the heat of his breath rushing against her skin and the way his body shuddered, his fever had returned with a vengeance.

If it didn't break by dawn, she'd have to make a dive to collect the makings of a healing broth. That meant yet more time spent away from her quest to locate—and mate with—the only merman who could offer her brood a tomorrow.

And all this before her breeder's moon ended.

I am obligated to serve him.

Teardrops pooled in her eyes. Squeezing her lids closed, she dammed them in the cage of her lashes, wondering how her twin commitments could possibly co-exist.

They can't.

She knew all too well the limitations of her own heart. Even if the Council were here, demanding it of her, she could not bring herself to let him die.

Not even at the expense of my own life.

The tears spilled over, winding in hot rivulets down her nose. Coursing to the end of her chin, they dribbled onto the land-walker's arm. A soft sob escaped her throat and he stirred, winding a steely thigh around her hips.

Groaning, he hitched himself up onto one arm so that his lips worked damply against her ear. "What's wrong with my Glow Girl? Did I hurt you when we made love?"

Made love?

The resonant timbres of his voice fully unlatched the floodgate. Erotic images pounded across her consciousness, washed in red tones—the crimson, blood-sight of her passion-swell.

A purr vibrated in her throat as her body responded to the memories, the carnal pleasures the human's sex had brought her.

She wanted more, so much more!

"What kind of spell have you worked on me?" he whispered, voice thick with desire. "I can't get enough of you."

His hand grazed the length of her belly, one finger threading slowly... too slowly... through the cap of curls at her mons.

"You're amazing," he rasped, flicking a fingertip over her clit. A deep chuckle vibrated through his throat as her hips bucked eagerly up to greet him.

Winding his fingers through the wet folds guarding her sex, he dipped boldly into the hot fluids beaded around her opening.

The memory of the climax that had seized her when she'd first impaled herself on his enormous sex shoved her to the precipice of a hormone surge.

"Triton forgive me," she prayed. Slipping around in the circle of his arms, she molded herself against him, offering up her healing warmth.

"Take me again, please, hurry."

Dipping his head, he captured her jutting nipple with his lips. He teased it with his teeth, wrenching a delighted yip from her.

Nipples pounding in time to her thudding heart, her rebellious libido roared. Pheromones surged, dimming her consciousness. Her vision heightened, pushing back the thick veil of the darkness, tingeing their surroundings in a sultry wash of red.

She must touch him, taste him. Have him once more.

Dear Triton.

The vanishing voice of her reason struggled valiantly to pray, to confess, redeeming her from her deviant desire for the land-walker's seed.

I have wandered so far from my call...

Her faithless nipples fully elongated, his fingers plunged into her. Wave after wave of sensation skittered through her sex as her muscles grasped at his knuckles, drawing two fingers and then three in deeper.

Worse, I have defiled myself.

Her hips pitched higher, and he wedged one thigh and then the second between her legs, parting her so wide that she could feel the sultry air rushing over her folds.

I've taken my pleasures from a human. The wavering voice of her conscience faded to nothingness beneath the thunderous roar of blood as it galloped through her veins.

Four fingers thrust high inside her. The walls of her sex clenched, forcing his broad digits to pile on top of each other. Working in, and then out, his thumb whorled in a maddening dance through her thrumming folds.

Releasing her nipple from the seal of his mouth, his tongue laved a path down the length of her. With his free hand, he spread her wider, warm tongue igniting a trail of fire around her clit.

Rocking her hips, she answered his pumping fingers, thrust for pounding thrust.

He bent his head low, lapping the fluids that seeped from her opening.

"You taste like Heaven," he drawled, hot breath rushing over her sex.

Her body had heeded no part of her mind's futile pleas. Need coursed through her, demanding the hot rush of his seed.

His burning gaze raked the terrain of her body. Riveting her eyes to his, she saw her own juices shimmering like gems on the corners of his lips.

A wicked flash of dimple twitched in his cheek as he drew her clit between his lips, again, suckling to the rhythm of the light that pulsated from her center.

Between one heartbeat and the next, her orgasm pooled, shoving her over the edge. All the longing, the want, every hunger she'd ever known converged, exploding into a head-banging rush of violet flames.

There would be no turning back now.

Darkness rolled at the edges of his vision, and for the second time that day, Byron fought to push back the encroaching wall of delirium. Riveting his gaze on the woman gyrating beneath his lips, the dizziness retreated. Moonlight framed her in a silver aura, polishing her pubic hair to a dull flame.

Breathing out a tremulous sigh, he brushed his lips across those springing curls. "I love watching you come," he whispered.

"Enter me, now," she demanded.

Driving his hands over the steep slope between her waist and hips, Byron palmed her generously rounded butt cheeks.

God, how he loved a woman packing curves. With the moonlight painting her hair silver as it streamed over her breasts, she reminded him of Botticelli's Venus come to life, all soft slopes and shadowy crevasses.

His erection jerked in agreement.

Her blue eyes captured his, and her unspoken plea sent the urgency of her need vibrating through his core. He experienced her longing like a living, breathing thing that had sprung to life inside him.

"Hurry!" Spreading her legs wider, she trailed her hand across her belly, and over her glowing mons, swirling her fingers through those luminous folds.

His pounding erection strained higher, harder. Even knowing good and well he was injured, his errant thoughts would not yield to the faint but persistent warnings from his inner warrior. Winding his hands beneath her butt, he cupped her cheeks and rolled the both of them over so that she sat straddling him.

Now that's how he liked his women. Wide open and ready for love.

She makes love like there's no tomorrow, he thought, grating out a gasp as she curled her fingers around his shaft. Weary as he was, he knew if he didn't bury himself inside her and soon, he might well... what?

Die?

Ask me if I care. Weaving his hands through the damp tendrils clinging to her nape, he pulled her lips down onto his—hard, not caring anymore whether he was gentle.

Her mouth felt lush as satin pillows. Parting her lips, she greeted him with an open mouth.

Weaving her tongue through his teeth, she softened the crushing edges of his kiss. She tasted of coconuts and salty water.

Paradise.

Somewhere off in the distance, thunder split open the sky.

They'd been running from a storm.

Hungry, greedy for more... *please, more...* he softened his jaw, deepening their union. Cupping one breast and then the other, her nipples pierced his palms with points of fire, filling them with their heat.

A terrible storm.

Slowing gathering his wits, his lips released hers and he raised his head to listen... to what?

Quiet.

Heaving a steadying sigh, he forced his gaze past the overwhelming sensations assaulting his body. Clamoring for something—anything—to focus on, he riveted his eyes to the moon.

Moonlight was good news. If the moon had risen, then the storm's eye wall was upon them.

Her hair fell forward, trailing down his belly, pooling in a silken crumple around his hips. Dipping her head, she traced her tongue along the throbbing veins lacing his erection.

Focus...

The remaining trickles of rainwater sluiced off the roof of the badly damaged galleon he'd found earlier.

Even as she sheathed him to the hilt in the damp cavern of her mouth, his conscience gnawed through the strumming waves of pleasure.

Just one more second, then he'd stop her.

She could have died out there...

He'd already endangered her enough.

Though he longed—needed—to sheathe himself inside her, celebrating the chain of little miracles that had conspired to bring them this far—he knew he couldn't.

Not yet.

The cautious operative in him yanked him back from the precipice of his orgasm, reminding him that dawn's first light could unleash a new world of troubles.

When she came up for air, he forced himself to pull away, ignoring the rampant pleasure bolting through his cock.

"Shh," he rasped, spending the last remnants of his willpower to resist her. Clamping his hands on her broad shoulders, he popped himself free and rolled way from her.

She looked pissed as hell.

"Patience, Glow Girl, he croaked. "I want to look at you."

"I need." This time she struggled to move her mouth as she spoke. "M-more."

"And you will have it." He grinned, considering her healthy enthusiasm for his lovemaking. "But first, we talk."

Grimacing, he raised himself up onto one elbow. A bolt of agony sliced through his head, nearly blinding him.

"So much for the theory I died and went to Heaven," he grumbled. Struggling to sit up, he shook off the delirium that threatened to encroach. "Last I heard death ends pain."

Reaching out an inquisitive finger, he traced the glowing nubbin situated between her eyes. It pulsed, sending shivers of warmth rippling through his flesh.

He grinned, understanding exactly what that raucous glow meant.

Wicked hot sex and lots of it.

His erection bucked in appreciation.

Seizing the encouragement, she flashed him one of the most contrived pouts he'd ever seen.

"Slow down, tiger," he joked, brushing his thumb across the curve of her lip. "First, you've got some explaining to do. And so do I."

Brushing the shining curtain of her hair off her face, he grazed his thumb across the fine brows capping the puddles of her eyes.

God, she's a striking creature.

Her hair looked much lighter now that she was dry, taming her appearance some. Fingering the errant tendrils that curved beneath her chin, he grinned, enjoying how they softened the fierce angles of her face.

"I came out here chasing the memory of a killer," he began, capturing her gaze with his. He was desperate for her to understand why he'd been so reckless with his life.

"Instead, I found you." Cupping her face in his hands, the glassy points of her pupils dilated, blue rings giving way to black. "I put you in danger. I'm sorry for that."

"No," she said in her choppy accent, chin rising in defiance. The corner of her mouth twitched toward a grin. "I found you, land-walker."

"Whatever."

While he knew she spoke the truth, his pride railed against the idea of any woman saving his ass. "You can try calling me by my name."

Offering his hand out to her, he expected she would lay hers inside of it, confirming his introduction. "Byron Burke. At your service."

Taking his hand as if to shake it, she lifted it to her mouth instead, tracing his lifeline with the tip of her tongue.

"Soon, lover," he whispered, pressing his face into her hair, inhaling the salty fragrance of her curls. "First tell me why you keep calling me land-walker."

"A land-walker is what you are. You are the land-walker," she added, corners of her mad dipping sadly, "who owns me."

"What?"

"By-ron Burke owns me." Tears pooling in the corners of her eyes, her pupils widened, threatening those inviting halos of blue.

Her stricken expression uprooted his heart. Twisted it. Had she only made love to him—offered up her virginity—because she assumed he'd demand it from her?

"Sweetheart," he said, holding her tormented gaze with his. "Where are you from that you could believe, in this day and age, that it's alright for a man to own you?"

Confusion furrowed her brow. "It is the way of Triton. When I saved you. I created a life-debt. I remain in your service unless—"

"Who is this Triton?" Hands curling to fists, his heartbeat quickened.

"Creator of all!"

"You mean like God? What kind of god would command you into slavery?"

"You don't understand. My world is not yours. There are rules." Grasping his hands in hers, she stood up. Eyes searching his, she urged him to follow.

For this, I haven't the words to tell you.

Byron rose, mind pregnant with images of glowing water. Remembering how standing in the phosphorescent lagoon outside had restored him earlier, he could think of nothing more soothing than bathing in its waters.

Legs trembling beneath him, he trudged along behind her, gnashing his teeth against the spasms that fired through every muscle in his body. Humiliation heated his cheeks when he staggered, legs threatening to give way beneath him.

"Please, let me help you," she offered, staggering only slightly as his immense weight leaned into her. "There is no shame in accepting help from one who is bound by Triton to offer it."

Too weary to argue, he allowed her to weave her strong arm around his shoulders Steadying him, she guided him through the gaping hole at the end of the galleon's stern.

Chapter 7

Ba'at Rath's eyes skidded across the low altar until they fell upon the mark he'd sought for so long. Joy leapt in his throat, and his fingernails scraped across the glyphs, chipping away many years accumulation of algae to reveal the carving in its entirety.

In disbelief, he squinted, convinced that his weary eyes played tricks on him. "Impossible!" he spat, teeth gnashing as if they were grinding bones.

So many years, wasted!

Slamming his head backward against the guarding triptych of stones, he relished the bright burst of pain that ripped through his consciousness. Tearing an incisor through his lip, a torrent of red gushed from his gaping maw. Opening his jaw wide, he spat forth a roar, giving a voice to the rage that railed through his veins.

Rolling his gaze downward to look once again, droplets of blood eked out between his parted lips, pooling in the nooks and crevices of the carvings that held the damning news. His entire life—*all of it*—had passed for naught.

His carefully orchestrated plans had failed.

How could such madness come to pass?

Because the truth I feared, even as a child, has finally come to fruition. I am not he... Triton's Lost Son.

Dragging his gaze back across the glyphs, he confirmed that the eroding image had indeed proved his fears. Though the scouring sands had nearly rendered it invisible, he could just make out the eagle's wings rising up behind the three-pronged staff of Triton.

The mark he'd toiled so long to behold was so like his own—nearly identical!

But not close enough!

Soon, Sirenia's journey would lead her here to behold this mark with her own eyes!

He closed his eyes, imagining her delighted reaction to his undoing.

"No!"

"I'll have no part of it!"

Slamming his body against the great stones, they tumbled outward. Clouds of silt fanned up from the seabed as the earth buckled beneath their enormous weight.

He'd spent so many long years swept up in the tedious business of insuring Triton's favor fell on him. At what point had it happened, when he'd actually come to believe himself ordained a king by default?

Because there was no one else left to inherit. Sinking to the bottom, he prostrated himself, wallowing in years of unspent bitterness. How many times had he seen the true mark with his own eyes—had even touched that winged trident depicted on the burls?

He had even felt that image pulsing beneath the curious curls of his own childish fingers. He had seen his mother's face light with joy as she marveled over the mark that was so like the one rendered by fate onto his own belly—and yet so different.

Curling his form into a fetal ball of woe, he realized how close he'd come to actually inheriting the Lost Son's prophesied glory. So close that he was bound to it through his own tainted bloodline.

Zane!

His lost twin's blasphemous name burned like bitter bile as it spewed past his lips. Zane had certainly been no more deserving of Triton's blessing than he was.

He, too, had been but a taint-blood.

From the moment the midwife had yanked the twins from their mother's bloody loins, the whispers began. Those rumors of the children's divine marks were all that saved the sullied infants from exile to Open Waters.

Ba'at Rath's head throbbed with images from the miserable childhood he'd spent with his brother under his mother's watchful, green eyes. Recalling the mermaid's haughty face heaped fuel on his fury. Eyes darting, he yearned for something— *anything*—on which to slake his anger.

Ripping a clot of barnacles from their roots, he captured them between his teeth, splintering them into shards of shell and flesh. The coppery thrill of blood streamed over his lips in rivulets of red—*red, like the precious hair sprouting from her favored son's head.*

Because Zane's appearance had reminded his mother of her taint-blooded lover, Serafel doted on the child so greatly that she seldom acknowledged that Ba'at Rath existed.

She'd taken perverse pride in the his brother's robust body, his titian coloring— features that never presented within the ranks of the purebloods—features that genetics and fate had denied Ba'at Rath.

Losing Zane had been easy—so easy that Ba'at Rath had since convinced himself that Triton had compelled him to lead the child out into a storm, beaching him on the shores of the Land-walkers, where he belonged.

Years later, when the Wasting Plague came, Ba'at Rath had gone back to finish the job he'd started. He had killed him as he slept in his bed.

If Triton had truly meant Zane to be the anointed one, the fertile one, would he not have stalled my hand to prevent his death?

Rolling onto his back in the muck, he plucked a bit of gristle from his teeth, considering his plight. Was the situation truly as abysmal as he'd first feared? After all, what need would a *dead* man have for Triton's grace?

Absolutely none!

So the truth, he thought, *is still yet malleable.*

For Triton has willed it.

Rasping his nails through the silt, his fingers scraped across a fractured lip of stone. Curling the shard into the grasp of his reedy fingers, he lifted himself to his knees to look down on the mark on the altar.

Then it struck him.

rippled over his lips. "Where I come from, pretty woman, we have a saying. You can't rape the willing."

The radiant pearl between her eyes shimmered, capturing Byron's attention. He'd never seen anything like it, at least not on any *human* woman. Save for that mark, she looked—and felt—much the same as any other woman he'd known. But what a difference one tiny button of tissue made. It changed in response to her moods, charting the course of her desire. He could even see the brilliant streaks of magenta dancing across the lagoon's surface echoed back at him in her mark.

As if she and the water were one.

The skeptic inside him objected, refusing to let his mind go there yet. But he couldn't shake off the notion that all of this was happening for a reason... that he was skirting around the edges of some pivotal connection.

"I braved that storm because I was looking for a killer," he said, brushing his thumb over the sweep of her jaw.

"My actions put you in danger, and if I'd had any idea."

Her gaze bore into his, the golden flecks in her irises winking back at him like little stars. "I know why you're here," she said. "I felt it when I found you... all of it. That's why I saved you. I felt *sorry* for you. But you didn't endanger me."

"The hell I didn't. We're buck naked in the middle of nowhere without so much as a Swiss Army knife between us."

"Byron, I'm not like you. I don't need the trappings of land-walkers. This place," she said, sweeping her gaze across the lagoon, "used to be my home. I'd be here even if I hadn't found you. Saved you."

A sob tore from her throat, her eyes shining with the tears that gathered there.

Confusion crimped Byron's brow. "I don't understand."

"I brought you here because I bound myself to you. And because I was already on my way here. Do you understand that much?"

Though the certainty of truth shone from her eyes, the warrior in him could not, would not stand down. How could anyone live for long in a remote location like this, much less such a captivating woman?

One who just happens to glow in the dark.

Like the water.

Perhaps sensing his doubts, Sirenia unwound herself from the tangle of his arms. Bowing her head toward the lagoon, her hair stirred its surface with shivers of light Cupping her hands, she filled them with the bright liquid. Carefully, so as not to spill, she turned back to face him. She stood so close to him that he could feel heat emanating from her mons as it brushed against his cock.

"This," she said, lifting the cup of her hands up to his lips, "is what keeps me alive, sustains what I am. Who I am."

All his questions, the endless years of ruthless training kept leading him back here. To the water. Now all he needed do was—

"Drink," she said. "It will help draw down your fever."

"Where I come from the first thing they taught me is don't drink the water."

"Then I guess you'll die from dehydration. Either way, just decide so I can get on with my journey before it's too late."

"Dehydration seems a kinder fate than shitting myself to death from drinking tainted water..."

She captured her twitching lower lip in her teeth, restraining the smile that threatened there. "I promise that you won't."

She didn't look much to Byron like a woman ready to back down. Not one inch. Her chin rose higher and her eyes crackled with challenge. "Drink or die, just hurry up and choose!"

"Stubborn wench," he grumbled. And how he loved that about her. Wrapping his fingers around her wrists, he bowed his head and drank, deeply. Swallowing, ribbons of warmth sluiced down his throat to pool in his belly. Sighing with relief, the pointed edges of his pain retreating to a bearable throb.

Turning her palms face up, he watched the light puddle within their crevices. Without thinking, he bent to place a kiss in the cup of each one.

Raising his head, he realized that for the first time in his life, his mind had surrendered to his heart. Wherever it was that fate took him after this day, he really didn't care as long as that destiny somehow included her.

"Perhaps," he said, shaking off the amazement that rose every time they communicated without words. "We found each other for a reason."

"That's impossible!" She dropped her head, cutting Byron off from the soft embrace of her gaze.

"For one who speaks so highly of divine interventions, you show little faith in them. Why?"

"I am not like you." She spoke aloud, and this time and her halting voice sounded husky with emotion.

"You can say that again." He smiled, remembering how light gushed from her sex every time she came.

Piercing him with her glare, she huffed out an exasperated sigh. "You don't understand. You are a land-walker. Your sex is forbidden and yet, I have bound myself to you!"

"Where I come from, we choose our own destinies."

"You're in my world, now. Here, whether you like it or not, Triton's word trumps all. So, I have to make you well. Because only then can I ask you to release me so I can bring his prophecy to pass."

"Question is, Rennie, just what would I be releasing you to?"

"Please. You have to stop."

"Why? Because you might 'fess up to the fact that none of this is accidental?"

"That will never happen." Striding backward, Sirenia waded out into the water until her breasts bobbed upon the lapping swells Lying on her back, she floated on the water's radiant surface. "Never!"

Byron's breath gauged her movements as her fierce backstrokes parted the swells with bands of light. Only when she'd reached the lagoon's center, did she fall still and begin to tread water. Though she had turned back around to face him, the back glow from the rising sun cast her expression into shadow. All he could hear was the rasping sound of her breath. He couldn't tell which emotion had won out, the tears or the anger.

"What I want By-ron?" she called out. "It doesn't matter. And it never will."

Popping her heart-shaped bottom above the water's surface, her buttocks gleamed in the spreading daylight. She kicked into the surface dive, thrusting her legs out behind her as she plunged into the deep water. Only a faintly shimmering trail of bubbles remained to mark the spot where she'd vanished.

"Go back to the boat, land-walker, before your strength ebbs," her voice called out inside his mind. "I don't know how long the glowing water will sustain one such as you."

"Where are you going?"

"To find a lasting cure for your sickness."

And mine, Sirenia thought, bitterly.

Squeezing her eyes closed, she settled into a bed of sea grass, conjuring Byron in her mind's eye as she'd just left him. He was so beautiful that sometimes it hurt just looking at him. The rising sun had ignited his hair into a corona of fire, casting the rest of his face into shadow. But she hadn't needed to see his expression to know what emotion resided there. She already knew.

She knew because she felt it, too.

Passion.

Mer-men did not experience it—or if they did, they seldom took the time to reveal it to their mates. But the land-walker—Byron—he sometimes seemed ruled by it. Sirenia had seen it for herself every time he raked his gaze over her.

He'd been ready to abandon himself to it.

No, to her.

She'd felt that passion pulsing deep within her body when he'd made frenzied love to her. She'd heard it in the throaty tangle of his voice every time he'd spoken her name.

Such passion! It had even emanated from his soulful eyes as they chased her across the lagoon. How those golden eyes had hungered.

For her.

And she for him. Even beyond the biological demands of her passion-swell.

That knowledge—that she yearned for him, yes, perhaps even loved him—brought so many emotions racing through her mind.

Pain.

Sadness.

But mostly sorrow.

Sorrow that he could not be possibly be the foretold one she sought. Sorrow that no matter how much she wanted it, she was not free to love him.

He is forbidden. That bitter truth was what had soured her sorrow into anger.

In the end, she'd chosen only to show him her anger, because dwelling on that emotion was the only way she could ever summon the wherewithal to leave him. And leave him she must. If she dared indulge her selfish heart by staying, she would risk unleashing another passion-swell on him. Then she'd conceive his child.

His child!

And then, her people would be doomed.

In spite of that, she yearned to turn back, slake herself again, dragging moans across his lips as his body tensed, filling her with his seed.

Her sex clenched, hard. Curling her hands to fists, she drove her nails into the beds of her palm, driving back the hunger that threatened.

Stop it! Now!

No matter how much her heart wished it, Byron was not, could never be, Triton's

Lost Son. That bitter knowledge lanced her heart to tatters.

These last hours in his arms had taught her why mer-ken mothers so vehemently urged their daughter to stay away from humans.

Land-walkers weren't just passionate.

They were persuasive.

Sirenia understood that now and that knowledge brought a sob grating across her lips.

Byron had convinced her that the feelings she'd denied since the very moment she first saw him lying on the ocean's floor were real.

I. Love. Him.

And now she had to go, find the healing mud that would draw back his fever, make him well. Only then could she make him see that if he truly loved her...

...Then he could only choose to let her go.

So she dove, but not only to get the healing mud from beneath the mangroves. She did it because she felt desperate to hide her turmoil from his penetrating gaze. Yes, she was running away, because she knew if she'd lingered for one more second, she'd have plastered herself to him like a hungry starfish on a mollusk's shell.

But plunging beneath the water's surface had backfired. The cool waters doused the flames of her anger, opening the door for all her sorrow, all her heart wrenching pain to return.

Threefold.

Why is it, she thought as she wove through the gnarled tunnels to stretch the distance between them, *that doing the right thing always hurts so much?*

Perhaps the hollow pain taking root in her heart was just punishment for her willfulness. She only had herself to blame for the well-deserved fate she'd carved out this day.

But Byron—he'd asked for none of this.

So why must he get hurt for simply being the victim of circumstance?

Nothing is accidental.

Isn't that what Triton mandated? That all these things were preordained in the cradle of creation?

"So tell me this, dear Triton," she cried, "why would you blaze a human with your sign, except to taunt me? How could you not know that I'd come to love him."

"Unless you meant me to?"

But that was impossible! Byron's hair was red and he possessed the immense build of a Titan. Those qualities never presented in the lines of the mer-ken.

There was also Byron's birthmark to contend with. Granted, he wore the sign of Triton, which was clearly a water sign. Even Ba'at Rath wore such a mark.

But Byron's trident blazed over the wings of a bird. A land sign.

The only other creature she'd heard of with such a mixed mark had been...

A taint-blooded child.

Born of both water and of land.

Ba'at Rath's *brother.*

But wasn't he dead? Hadn't Ba'at Rath himself reported the boy devoured by sharks years ago?

Could it be possible that Ba'at Rath's lies had begun even then?

Because of those lies, had Triton intervened, preserving the child for this preordained appointment? Did that explain why Byron had drawn strength from the glowing waters? Because mer-ken blood flowed in his veins?

Had Triton been smiling over her all this time, taking care to plant the Lost Son right beneath her nose?

Of course, he had.

"Nothing is accidental." Sirenia chanted the words like a mantra as she rushed through the dim grottoes. "All of this, everything under the sun has spun out since the beginning of time, exactly as Triton intended."

Her heart leapt and her spirits lightened as she navigated the catacombs, desperate to reach the ancient shrine Mar-ala had sent her to find.

Perhaps Byron could yet be the Lost Son.

And if he was, then the ancient glyphs would surely reveal it.

Chapter 8

The second Sirenia entered the water, Ba'at Rath knew it.

He knew it because he smelled her.

Snapping taut the length of sea grass he held stretched between his fists, he hitched his nose to the current and smiled thinly. *And so it begins.*

His attention to his labors wavered while his mind reeled against the aromatic assault of her musk. That decadent aroma told him everything he needed to know.

Sirenia had not yet conceived. Her seed remained ripe for the sowing.

All was not yet lost.

Had Ba'at Rath needed more proof that Triton had smiled in approval over his actions, it became evident in the fact that Sirenia had ventured into the water alone.

He knew that by the lack of a second scent.

Relief sluiced over him, the muscles in his shoulders unknotting. Perhaps he would not need to engage the land-walker after all.

The human might even be *dead.* If so, then Triton was indeed a merciful god!

My son may yet be conceived this day! Perhaps even on the very altar where I have inscribed my destiny.

The Divine approval Ba'at Rath had long hungered after barreled toward fruition. Lips twisting to a leer, his heart slammed against his ribs, though not from the heat of love.

Or even desire.

Rather, from the anticipation of her heartbreak.

Heartache. Such a potent aphrodisiac. Ba'at Rath wound the grass blade tightly around his index finger. The skin above it bulged, growing purple above the sharp edges that bit into his flesh.

Just as he'd suspected, the grasses were tough. They would make excellent bindings should Sirenia choose to fight, resisting the call of her passion-swell.

He almost hoped she would!

"No need to engage her just yet," he whispered, grating a hand over the piebald scales that concealed the place where his manhood would rise once he changed to his landlocked state.

She will need time to find the pretty trail you left for her.

Laughter rumbled wetly in his throat, a celebration of his own brilliance, recalling how he'd blazed the path to the shrine with the pearls he'd found heaped around its base.

Sirenia would not be able to resist their beauty.

What better way than a trail of spoiled prayers to turn a greedy mermaid's head my way?

Now he must remain patient, giving her sufficient time to savor the divine implications of the truth he'd left for her.

Then she would come looking for *him*.

Because she will have no other choice. Only then will I reveal myself.

Working several blades of the grass into slipknots, Ba'at Rath hitched them around his wrist.

He was ready, even if she resisted.

Concealing himself deep in the sea grasses, he summoned the paralyzing assault of his change. The air in his reservoir lung grew thin, his chest heaving in spasmodic gasps.

Time to do this thing or die trying, he thought.

Every cell in his body slammed together all at once. Come what may, there would be no turning back now.

The next time he left this place, he would appear every bit as human as the land-walker Sirenia so desired.

Byron Burke wasn't a man accustomed to relinquishing anything he truly wanted. What he wanted now was Sirenia de Mar-ala's heart, but never, for one moment, would he accept it under the bonds of servitude.

He wanted her to choose him freely. He would give anything to watch her chin hitching high with pride as she framed him in her gaze, acknowledging him as both her lover and her equal.

He'd never meant to overwhelm her with all his talk of free will. But he knew he had. He'd glimpsed it in the way her gaze hardened, the softness of sky giving way to the patina of metal.

Those eyes, they spoke volumes—about fear.

Byron grimaced, remembering how she'd looked back at him like a wild thing caught in a trap.

He could kick himself for making her feel that way.

Besides the hardness he'd seen, Sirenia had also had been fighting tears. He'd seen them pooling behind the golden fans of her lashes.

He knew then that he'd hurt her, frightened her and that knowledge gnawed at his heart. But her tears had told him what he yearned to know.

She cared for him, too.

A stiff breeze whipped across the water and with it came the lingering scent of her musk. Inhaling deeply, its almond essence pierced him with the memory of his skin sliding over hers. The beat of his heart picked up, pounding so hard against his ribs that when his hand flew up to settle on his chest, he could feel it racing beneath his palm.

I'll fix this. I have to.

But how?

All he knew was that the second she surfaced, he'd start over from the beginning. Make things right between them.

Sirenia was right about one thing. She wasn't at all like him.

Nor was she like any other woman he'd known. And he'd known—and bedded—plenty.

Like most young SEAL's, he'd sown the lion's share of wild oats. If it happened in bed between a man and a woman, he'd probably done it.

A dozen times over.

It had begun to bother him over the years that he never met a woman whose love-making didn't leave him feeling a bit—empty. Wondering, what else is there?

Finally, he came to accept that he might never find a woman capable of completing him. He'd always assumed it was some fundamental flaw in his own character. After a while, he made his peace with that. Then, after his family died, he never *wanted* to need someone, to risk feeling the pain of their loss.

Never!

Until today.

Even as the corners of his lips tugged toward a smile, the weary warrior within rebelled.

Stop it, Burke, before your heart gets you killed.

"Shut the hell up," he snapped. God, it felt good to silence that part of him. So good that he gave in to the laughter, that rumbled in his throat.

It felt right, every bit as right as waking up here, in this otherworldly place, with Sirenia wrapped in his arms. He felt like he'd finally found a home. Rather funny, considering he wasn't convinced that Sirenia was altogether human.

A soft mist rose off the lagoon's surface, and the humidity rolled in waves across the mangrove, growing thicker by the moment. Byron's ears popped, responding to the rapidly falling pressure. The storm's eye wall would pass soon. Then all hell would break loose.

Again.

Running through his usual assessments led him back to the realization that he and Sirenia were stranded, at least until this thing passed.

Fixing his gaze beyond the mist, he stared at the rapidly fading patch of water where she dove. Glancing down at his watch, anxiety prickled at the back of his neck. Sirenia was a strong swimmer, granted, but she was pushing toward a one and a half minute breath hold.

She needed to hurry and resurface so he could urge her back into the safety of the boat. Come what may, they were in this together...

...and God forgive him, he was almost glad that the backside of this Hurricane would soon force them into such close quarters.

Whatever was troubling her, they could work it out.

We have to because she fills up that hollow place in me.

The thought surprised him. He'd always assumed his sense of displacement— his loneliness—had to do with the circumstances surrounding his rescue. The day his parents had found him completely cut him off from any clues as to who he was, where he came from. He figured any biological relatives who gave a damn about his whereabouts would have scoured the ends of the earth to find him.

Nobody ever had.

At least, not until that night when his world exploded.

Byron shut his eyes against the memory of the assailant's face. Those black eyes—soulless as a shark's.

Kill me if you can. He'd heard those words vibrating inside his head that night, just as he could sometimes hear Sirenia's. Were she and the killer from the same, unnamed place, part of the same super-evolved species that could communicate without speaking?

This is outrageous!

What was even more outrageous was that the more time he spent in Sirenia's presence, the more often he could hear her thoughts.

Since his family's deaths, Byron had become watchful during his travels for anything that stirred a feeling of kinship. He'd hoped along the way, he'd experience a flicker of something that could pass for recognition—belonging.

He'd never failed to come up empty handed.

No, he thought. *Empty hearted.*

Until now.

Was it only the fever?

Or was that fluttering sensation that snatched his breath away every time she slid those blue eyes in his direction a symptom of something more—that he'd fallen in love with her?

Yes, he thought. *I do love her.*

But how could he feel good about that love without knowing whether she accepted it through choice, or obligation?

That answer would have to wait. The fog grew thicker by the second, so thick he could barely see his hand as he waved it in front of his face. Byron leapt to his feet, staggering against a fresh wave of dizziness.

She'd been under for well over two minutes. No matter how accomplished a diver she was, she definitely should have come up for air by now.

Rushing out into the hazy water, he dismissed any lingering fears that he might black out before he resurfaced.

I never should have let her go out there alone.

Ba'at Rath shivered and his bones rattled with misery.

The hormones that rendered a mermaid's body supple enough to enjoy painless birthing also gentled the way for her to shift comfortably between her two forms— unless she became landlocked by her breeding moon.

Mermen, on the other hand, enjoyed no such advantages.

For Ba'at Rath, summoning the change to his breedable form was an excruciating process. But necessary, if he expected to sprout the parts he needed to spawn a son. Curled on his side on the lagoon bottom, his mouth was agape with agony.

The horrific transmutation that he loathed had reached the point of no return, suspending him in a bone-crunching purgatory between the underwater self he preferred, and his legged self, which he loathed simply because it made him look so human.

Ba'at Rath could not move a muscle.

As crippled as his physical body was, his senses were hyper-aware. Each overexcited nerve ending broadcast a violent reaction to the slightest ripple in the sea grasses. Their blades lathed away the remaining scales that clung to his burning skin.

When the land-walker's immense form sliced through the lagoon's surface,

Ba'at Rath heard it tear through his head like an explosion. He could not squint to protect himself from the crimson light that illuminated the man's progress through the deep water. His eyes could only twitch right and then left, tracking the light that trailed in the wake of the human's fierce strokes. It collected about his shoulders like the fiery wings of an angel charging through a hell mouth.

When the land-walker's body arched into the bottom of his dive, his belly—and his birthmark—passed within inches of Ba'at Rath's horrified stare.

Zane lives!

And because Zane still lived, Ba'at Rath steeped in the realization that even if he mated with Sirenia a thousand times over, his seed would still fall shy.

There could only be one Lost Son.

And I am not he!

The heartsick merman could not voice the bellows of loss that boiled in his craw. He couldn't so much as shut his eyes against Zane's muscular arms as they sliced the water, tracking the remains of Sirenia's musk trail.

He could only plead his case in silence to a deity he'd spent a lifetime defying while Zane charged on toward the bright destiny he'd done nothing to earn.

Sirenia stood in the blue-tinged light before the fallen triptych of stones that had once guarded the low altar; she fisted her right hand and laid it over her pounding heart—a gesture symbolizing the highest show of respect between mermaids.

Tears prickled at her lashes as she swept her lids closed, bowing her head in reverence for the countless mothers whose hopes, heartaches and prayers had conspired to bring her here—to this fateful moment.

Uncurling her fingers, she revealed the single pearl she held cradled within the cup of her palm.

"Dearest Daughters of Triton" she offered, raising the gem to her lips, "if not for your efforts, all merkind would be lost. I fall before you with a humble heart, offering you my irrevocable promise."

Heart lifting with joy, she knelt, placing the pearl alongside the countless others heaped at the base of the altar.

"In your honor," she began, "I pledge myself, body, heart and soul to Triton's Lost Son, whose foretold mark you took the care to preserve here, in this very shrine."

"His name is Byron," she finished, unable to restrain the smile that curled at the edges of her lips. "And while he does not yet know his destiny, I am certain he is The One foretold by Triton."

Standing, Sirenia stepped forward, splaying her hands on the sacred altar. Butterflies fanned up from her belly as she realized that concealed somewhere in these ornate symbols was the mark that stood to re-direct the course of countless destinies.

Byron's mark, she thought, still barely able to believe her miraculous turn of luck. She'd entered Open Waters just yesterday, a habitual problem child to her people. Soon she would return to her brood, a triumphant woman in love and a brand new mother-in-waiting.

Even if Byron could not bring himself to stay with her forever, she would at least have a child sprung from his loins to love.

Hands dancing over the faded glyphs, her teeth chattered with anticipation. The pads of her fingers caressed each station along the broken trail of promises. What her eyes could not quite glean, she allowed memory to fill in. As her mouth murmured the words, her mind conjured Mar-ala's husky voice to recount the story of Triton's Lost Son just as she had first told it to Sirenia so many years past.

"Long before the mangroves provided our brood sanctuary from land-walkers, Merkind roamed open waters freely and without fear. During that time, Triton prophesied that when the tides ran red, a wasting plague would staunch the flow of the mermen's seed."

"When such signs pass, the last fertile mermaid will be sent forth to claim the heart of one conceived outside our brood. As Triton commanded from the Cradle of Creation, this chosen daughter will know The Lost Son by his sacred mark, as was preserved across the eons by the ancient mothers before her. Through their blessed union, a son shall be born and on that day the cup of souls shall come restored."

Sirenia's hand skidded over a crimson smear concealing the proof that would confirm Byron the Lost Son. Growling with impatience, she scraped her nails back and forth through the congealing mess. A red tinged cloud rose around her, permeating the water with the metallic stench of blood.

Realizing that the stain was fresh, perhaps only moments old, anxiety coiled in her gut. Harm had befallen someone here. Whipping her head around, her narrowed gaze swept the shadows for signs of movement.

The water remained undisturbed. Whatever—or whoever—had been hurt here appeared to be gone. But she still felt uneasy. She wanted to go back.

To Byron.

I can't leave here without proof that he is the one, she thought. Byron was a taint-blood, a fact that wouldn't sit well with members of Council who interpreted Triton's Scrolls literally. If she couldn't swear that she'd witnessed the mark with her own eyes—they'd never acknowledge Byron as the Lost Son. Given her history with the Council, Sirenia knew she must find the truth.

Satisfied no immediate threat lurked in the shadows, she summoned the tattered remains of her composure. Dropping her gaze, she returned to her task. Reaching out to brush away the last remnants of the stain, her hand hung frozen as the water beneath it cleared.

The mark depicted the three-pronged staff of Triton. But it also lacked the wings depicted on Byron's mark.

Jaw falling slack, shock stilled her heart. When it shuddered back to life, disbelief caused it to fall into her gut. Once fused, those emotions boiled in the pit of her belly as she realized that the merman she'd just sworn before the Ancient Mother's she'd accept...

In body...

In heart...

And yes, even in soul...

Was not Byron.

It was Ba'at Rath.

The scream gathered, rumbling deep in her core. When it tore across her lips, it rang through the water like a peal of thunder.

"No!"

Chapter 9

Reckless.

That was the only word Byron could think of to describe his own behavior. Any other man with his dive training would have heeded the voice of reason long before now, and broken for the surface.

Truth was, nothing he'd done since leaving Skeleton's Graveyard stood up to the demands of his training. He'd only managed to prove how hopelessly smudged the lines between bravery and cowardice really were.

He knew good and well no act of heroics had dragged him into the lagoon to find Sirenia.

No, he thought. *It was fear.*

Tracing her vanishing musk trail through the water, his arms quaked, his gut wrenched with the terror that he might not get to her in time. Yes, fear led him out here, but something else altogether caused him to kick prudence by the wayside and stay.

Love.

For Sirenia.

At this point, that love was all that kept him going.

Lungs scalding from want of oxygen, his heart pounded an urgent plea in his ears—*breathe!*

No way was he going cave in to the fear scalding his veins and run for the surface. Not until he held her in his arms. He intended to search for her right down to his last molecule of oxygen, if need be.

He'd lost enough loved ones, and he would not resurface into a world that didn't include her.

But what if she was already dead?

No, she still lives, he thought. He knew it, felt certain of it, because he could *hear* her.

The muffled sound of her heartbeat drummed off in the distance, echoing his. Though the very idea of it defied the laws of physics, he coursed on in the direction it emanated from—convinced he was closing in on her.

But close wasn't good enough!

A garbled scream reverberated through the water. With the world around him spinning toward blackness, he stroked against the ebbing currents so hard and fast that his muscles trembled. Rushing through a tunnel of twisted roots, he burst out into an arching cavern just as Sirenia came rushing toward him, mouth wide open and still screaming as if a great white shark snapped at her feet.

She slammed into his outstretched arms so hard that she knocked the last, scant gasp of wind from him. It spewed through his lips, streaming about their heads in a storm of bubbles. His jaw dropped, mouth agape, and lungs sucking for wind. Before the water could rush in to fill the excruciating void, Sirenia brought her mouth down on his.

Curling her hands behind his head, she tangled her fingers into the curls at his nape, molding so close against him that he could feel her heart slamming against his breastbone.

Joy washed over him, and his oxygen-starved body relaxed into her fierce embrace. Never in his life had he felt so happy to see another living soul. By God, if he had to die down here, then kissing her while fate counted down to his last, gasping second was exactly how he wanted to go.

He gave himself fully to her kiss and she seized the advantage, weaving her tongue through his teeth. He tasted a tinge of almonds coupled with the sharp tang of some other emotion as she filled him with her breath.

The raw ache in his lungs began to seep away. As she blew the life back into him, the truth behind her Herculean abilities in the water hovered about the edges of his mind.

How is she doing this?

It defied reason.

She defied reason.

Nobody could remain underwater for that long, except a mermaid.

Even if such a thing were possible, the woman in his arms was certainly no fish. She was one-hundred percent, red-blooded female. And right now, there was nothing more he wanted in the world than to kiss her, sating a longing that he couldn't put a name to as it crackled through his veins.

Splaying his hands across the small of her back, he molded her still closer against him. So close, he could feel the sobs that racked her body and the chill bumps that prickled beneath his touch.

She was frantic.

Hold me. First, he heard her voice moving through him and then he felt her need. He experienced them as vividly as if they were a living part of him. Capturing one more breath from her, he raised his head from the sanctuary of her lips. Cupping her face tightly between his palms, he slid one hand up to smooth back the frenzied tangles that hid her beautiful face from him.

Greedily, he gazed upon her. He redirected the question burning on his tongue to the front of his mind, hoping he could somehow cause her to experience his thoughts just as he could hers.

"Rennie, what happened?"

Hitching his palm beneath her chin, he turned her glittering gaze up to his, plundering her eyes for evidence of an answer. Even in the dim light, he couldn't miss the distress that stormed across her features. Her mouth contorted as her eyes darted back and forth across the shadows and another cry tore from her throat, piercing the water with a rush of bubbles.

He'd knew then that he'd do anything—yes, absolutely anything—if he could only chase that haunted expression away, forever. Squinting, he riveted his focus on the gnarled grottoes, sweeping the visible perimeter for signs of danger.

He saw nothing there to account for her panicked expression.

But he knew something had upset her. He'd tasted the sharp after-note of her turmoil as he drank the breath from her lips.

"Talk to me, damn it."

"Just hold me." Her voice broke mid-sentence in his mind, a short burst of unintelligible sobs. "Please."

Even though the blue rings of her irises had been swallowed by the black holes of her pupils, the nubbin between her eyes began to broadcast another emotion altogether.

Desire.

Her mark smoldered with it, and he felt an answering heat pooling in his groin. The water around them vibrated with her purple-hued aurora.

"Please", she repeated. Her flesh smoldered beneath his touch, telling him that this particular plea hadn't been born from fear.

"Make love to me." Again she pressed her lips to his, gifting him with a mouthful of air that he wasn't altogether certain he really needed.

He wanted to tell her, "No, not here. Not like this," but the words and the desire to make her hear them died in the same thought from which they were born.

What was happening to him?

Something deep inside his core sparked to life, blooming like a flower. It felt to him like her breath had carried a part of herself into him, transforming him. That budding gift took root and grew, lapping outward from the pit of his belly, urging him toward oneness—something he'd never known with any other woman.

Raining kisses down her face, his lips lit on every freckle as he worked a trail down to her mouth.

Dipping into her, she teased him with another small breath, sighing softly into his kisses. His knotted muscles relaxed as his strength grew, offering him the upper hand.

He didn't just take it.

He seized it.

Hands traveling the taut muscles of her back, his fingertips grazed each bony pearl of her spine until he splayed his hands, palming one buttock and then two. Curling his fingers into the warm crevice between her cheeks, he yanked her hard against him and his erection unfurled to greet her.

Splaying her legs wider, she hitched her thighs tight around his hipbones. Her trembling hand palmed his shaft, and she slicked his burning tip through her folds, separating, stretching.

Curling a tentative fingertip inside her tight nether-bud, Byron felt her muscles clench. Hips rocking, she worked him in deeper.

Stealing one last breath before he dropped his head, his mouth sought the peak of her nipple. Laving it with his tongue, his finger continued dipping in and out of her rear orifice, until his palm slapped lightly against her buttocks with each new stroke. Hot juices gushed from her sex, coating him with their heat and infusing the water with light.

There was nothing gentle in how she impaled herself on his cock. Hilting him fully, her mons slammed so hard against him that stars burst in the cage of his mind. The thin air supply only heightened his sensation, causing each nerve ending to thrill with sensation as her muscles girdled his thickness.

Orgasm gathering, he focused on her electric blue gaze. He wanted to see himself framed in her eyes as he shot his seed into her core.

"Look into my eyes, lover," his voice whispered in her mind. "See yourself as I see you. You look like an angel when you come. "

What Sirenia saw mirrored in the pools of his pupils brought a gasp to her lips. She saw herself as he must see her—beautiful—her face illuminated with pleasure.

Such pleasure!

Never had she dreamed her nether-hole could sing with such delight. By the time the knob of Byron's sex banged at the door to her womb, the threat of her climax had coiled tight. Arching against him, she met his motions at both of her openings, thrust for exquisite thrust.

Curling the fingers of one hand into the tangles of his hair, he slammed his mouth down over hers.

Whether he plundered her mouth from the biological demand for air or the raw hunger for sex didn't matter. She only wanted to kiss him back equally as hard and make love even harder.

Another scream gathered in her throat.

Bucking her hips, she matched Byron's aggressive down thrusts with equally ferocious upstrokes.

Raking her nails over the small of his back, she pulled him in deeper. His muscles seized in the same second her sex clenched around him. Together they dropped over the edge, just as their heads broke above the lagoon's storm-whipped surface.

When Ba'at Rath first heard Sirenia's screams, he knew that she'd completed her brief lesson in revisionist history.

Such a difference an hour makes, he thought. Earlier, he'd have greeted the news that Sirenia had come across the altered mark with relish. Now, those long anticipated wails of woe brought him no joy. Even if the brat lay down before him, legs spread and eager to honor the obligation the altered prophecy demanded, her compliance would do him no good.

Pleasures in a woman's sex he could fake.

Fertility, he could not.

To put it bluntly, a sea cucumber would have an easier time knocking her up.

No amount of mating with Sirenia would win him the son he needed to return home with, insuring his rise to power. Were it not for the bone-crunching paralysis that held him seized in the sea grass, he might have snorted out a bitter laugh, considering the dark melodrama in which he now found himself playing the buffoon's role.

Thanks to Zane.

I should have gone back that night—killed him with my own bare hands.

Instead, he could only lie here in the bitter bed of his own making, stewing on 'if only'. Years spent denying the Call of the Land had rendered his tissues far too tough to morph with ease and his landlocked state visited him with excruciating slowness. He couldn't even indulge in the luxury of shutting his eyes against the blasphemous sight of Sirenia casting her spell over Zane.

Unable to flee the loathsome stench of their sex, bitter tears burned in his eyes.

Forced to witness his brother seizing the fate that should have been his own, he began to understand that Sirenia would stop at nothing to get herself shot full with Zane's seed.

It was, simply put, her fate to do so.

A lifetime wasted. How many years had he squandered, working to insert himself into Triton's will?

Too many!

So why go on spending his energies for naught?

Could it be, he wondered, *that I've simply been trying too hard?*

What is the very worst that can happen now?

The inevitable answer wasted no time in making itself apparent. *She'll mate with Zane a third time, insuring the conception of the prophesied child.*

The very same event he'd spent thirty years working to circumvent.

Now here, he thought, allowing his mind the latitude to weave yet another plan, *is a novel idea.*

What if I let the prophecy play out, exactly as Triton foretold?

With the child conceived, what need would Triton have to meddle further in mortal affairs?

None!

With the prophecy enacted, surely Triton's divine attentions would turn to more pressing matters.

Sirenia would bear the child fate demanded she must.

Then Ba'at Rath would simply eliminate Zane and return to his original plan.

Neat.

Clean.

No further revisions needed.

The stark simplicity of it pleased him. *Greatly.*

All he need do now was wait for the child he'd conspired a lifetime to call his own, to spring from Zane's loins during Sirenia's next passion-swell.

Chapter 10

Sirenia understood now why Mar-ala had warned her against consorting with humans. They demanded far more from their women than a ready receptacle for their seed.

Humans insisted that their lovers feel pleasure and give it back in kind.

The first time she had slaked her passion-swell on Byron, she did so because her body hungered for seed. Any man's seed would have sated her—for a while.

The last time, she hungered for something far beyond the biological demand of passion-swell.

That time, she sought love.

Byron's love.

She wanted to wrap herself up in it, bask in its excruciating sweetness.

For soon—too soon—he would release her and be gone.

Triton's damnable prophecy would see to that. Then, she'd carry only the memory of love with her to her deathbed

A steady rain drummed against the hull of the galleon as it creaked against the wind. Sirenia lay curled in the circle of Byron's arms, so racked with heartache she could barely breathe.

Everything she could ever have dreamed of in a mate was lying right here beside her, sighing with contentment as his teeth nipped playfully at her earlobe.

Though she'd fled the lagoon without the healing mud she went in for, she could feel that Byron's skin no longer burned with fever. The healing effect of the glowing waters had followed him to land and for that, she should feel relieved.

But she didn't.

With his health restored, it was clear that Triton had cleared the way for Byron to choose. Now, he would either claim her in life-debt, or release her from it.

Somehow, she must convince him to let her go before her body succumbed to the heavy after-sleep of her passion-swell.

"I love you," he whispered, pulling her so close against him that she could feel his heart thumping against her back. "No matter what. I need you to tell me you know that."

"I do know," she murmured. Heart heavy with the knowledge that she'd soon tell him goodbye, she reached back with one trembling hand, smoothing her palm over the stubble that peppered his jaw. "I know you love me, Byron."

She'd not only seen the evidence of his love. She had felt it. When they'd coupled in the water, her spirit had bonded so tightly to his that she'd navigated the inner trappings of his heart. Byron—his loss, his heartache, and yes, even his love—was part of her now.

It always would be.

I love you, too, Byron.

But she couldn't risk telling him that.

Not now.

Not ever.

Not if she expected to free herself from him before her third passion-swell struck. If that happened, she knew she'd seduce him again, insuring she conceived his child.

His baby.

Her face contorted with grief. If she only she could, she'd barter her soul to bear a child sprung from his loins. *Dear Triton,* she prayed, clamoring to gather the badly tattered edges of her faith, *why would you taunt us so?*

For those few brief moments when she'd thought Byron to be Ba'at Rath's lost brother—everything, the way she'd felt so drawn to him and then so readily lost her heart to him—it all made perfect, cosmic sense.

Now, none of it did.

Triton knew she wanted more. More time, more love, more of the mind-boggling sensations Byron drove through her body. But no amount of wanting in the world would change the truth.

Triton's prophecy had divined no room for love in her world. She'd been doomed to mate with Ba'at Rath—a monster—since the beginning of time. Soon—very soon—she must go to him.

Mate with him.

Perhaps, she thought, *this is just punishment for my stubborn ways.*

"Where have you been all my life?" Byron's breath trailed a tingling path down the length of her neck and his voice was thick with fresh desire. Supporting his broad-shouldered frame on his elbow, he propped his head up on his hand. Peering down at her, his warm eyes simmered with emotion.

That smile, how it slew her. The edges of his face softened every time he flashed a grin her way, and even while her body ached with exhaustion, the sight of it caused her nipples to heat.

Gulping back the emotions that knotted her throat, she peeled her gaze away from his. She couldn't look at him, not if she intended to do Triton's bidding. Turning her head aside, she dodged his kiss so that his lips fell on her jaw instead of their intended target—her mouth.

"Byron," she began, struggling to speak aloud to make her intent unmistakable. Blinking hard, she fought to dam the tears puddling in her eyes. "We need to talk."

"Shush," he whispered, pressing his finger against her lips. Cradling her cheeks between his hands, she felt the rough evidence of the many scratches his hands had suffered in carrying her to safety.

"I know you want me to free you, Sirenia," he whispered. "But I can't..."

The sob she'd been struggling to hold back finally tore from her throat. "You don't understand."

"Let me finish," he ground out, eyes darkening to amber. "I can't let you go until I've said my piece."

This time when his hand captured her chin, she didn't try to argue. Realizing she could do nothing more to hide her tears, she lifted her head to peer into his eyes. Deep in her heart, she already knew that whatever words were coming her way would rise straight from the seat of his soul, and she wanted to be looking into his eyes when he said them. The memory of them would have to last a lifetime.

Unable to control herself, she tilted her head back further, pressing her lips against his. He kissed her so tenderly that she thought her heart might cleave in two. And then he broke the kiss, raising his head.

"Rennie," he began, dragging a hand through his mussed hair. "I came out here a lost man, chasing the past.

Swallowing audibly, he turned away and rattled out a sigh. When his gaze captured hers again, she saw that his eyes shone with wetness.

"Instead of the past, I found my future," he rasped, catching a stray tendril of hair between his fingers and tucking it behind her ear. "You have saved me in ways I didn't know I needed to be saved."

Her tears flowed unchecked, and she cupped his large hands between hers. Laying them out like the pages of a book, she bowed her head over the cradle of his palms, dropping a tear-soaked kiss into the cup of each one. Just as he once had hers.

Barely able to look him in the eyes, she veiled her lashes and forced herself to speak.

"I . Never. Meant. To hurt you."

"God damn it, Sirenia," Byron snapped. "Let me finish."

As soon as the words scraped past his lips, her stricken expression made him wish he could take them back. He'd never meant to sound so harsh, but she already looked like a woman trying to tell him goodbye.

Setting his jaw, he struggled to climb on top of his reeling emotions. He loved her. Completely. Come hell or high water, he was going to make sure that before this storm blew past, she understood that.

"I'm done living on a diet of bitterness and regret. I'm not letting you run away before I've told exactly how much you mean to me."

Freeing his hands from the trembling nest of hers, he brushed his thumbs across her face, sweeping back the damp curls that clung to her cheeks. Raking in a breath, he filled his eyes with her captivating face, wishing he could somehow memorize every nuance of it.

Her eyes shone like beacons as they peered up at him, and he saw that they brimmed with sadness. "I couldn't live with myself if I thought I did anything to put that haunted look in your eyes."

Her lips trembled, as if she were about to speak, but nothing came out save a strangled whimper.

Deep in his heart, Byron already knew two things.

She loved him.

And she was still searching for a way to tell him goodbye.

"B-Byron," she tried again.

Raising his hand, he motioned for her to let him finish. Heart pounding painfully in his throat, he started again. "Before I woke up in your arms, there was a place inside of me I thought had died. A place I thought could never be filled again."

Weaving his arms around her trembling shoulders, he tucked her head beneath his chin. "Rennie," he whispered, tangling his hands into the thick coils of her hair, "that place inside me is alive and well. Because of you."

"Now, if you can still stand here, look me straight in the eye and tell that you don't love me, then I swear to God, I'll give you what you want. I'll walk away."

I don't love you.

All she needed to do was utter those four, simple words and her life debt to Byron would be erased. All the problems she'd created in stopping to save him would finally end.

Neatly.

Cleanly.

No more drama.

But when did I ever do anything the easy way?

Sirenia would have found it easier to swallow a sea urchin than watch those four words register in his eyes as she spoke them.

Instead of scraping out the sentence that would buy her the freedom she needed to seek out Ba'at Rath and save her kind, her carefully dammed emotions burst. She realized she might never again see those warm eyes lit with emotion.

With love.

"I can't," she cried, fleeing to the far side of the galleon to stretch the distance between them.

But I have to.

Falling to her knees, huge, gulping sobs seized her. They came so hard and so fast that she couldn't draw breath.

In two strides, Byron was there on the floor with her, cradling her in his arms. Tucking her head into the well of his chest, he wrapped her in his arms and rocked her like a little child.

Like the baby we'll never have...

"Forgive me," he said, pressing his lips to the crown of her head. "You don't have to say it. Not now. Not ever. You're free..."

Sirenia felt the muscles in his jaw clench against her head, and already, she hated herself for what she'd done. Byron had absolutely no idea what he'd done to hurt her. He only wanted to end her pain.

Because he loves me.

She'd give anything to snare him in her arms and tell him there was nothing to forgive and that if it were up to her, freedom was the last thing in the world she'd ever ask for.

But the words wouldn't squeeze past the tangled knot in her throat. Nor could she grind out the four simple words that would have ended this, setting his heart... and hers... free forever.

Byron deserved the truth and that's exactly what she intended to give him. But how could a mermaid ever hope to pass such a complex message to a land-walker?

She couldn't possibly speak it, not with her mouth.

Squeezing her eyes shut, she concentrated on sending her message in the only way she knew how... with her mind.

Triton willing, he might actually hear her, understand her intent, even beyond his pain. Swinging her mind open to his, she shoved back the gray edges of exhaustion once more, telling him her story.

The birth of my kind began in a twinkle of Triton's eye, in the very cradle of time.

She told him—sent him—everything, except the one thing that might have caused him to consider staying.

She chose not to reveal how much she feared mating with Ba'at Rath.

It was information that would only hurt him.

"Tomorrow, I must summon him here and pledge my heart to him," she said, forcing the edges of her mouth to a tight smile. "Or my kind will die out."

Watching the play of emotions on his face as he processed her story, she saw disbelief, shock and bitterness.

Sometimes, she even thought she saw a hint of moisture pooling in his eyes.

Fixing her gaze on his, she steeled her heart for the worst. But she'd never once anticipated the soft smile that played on his lips.

Cutting his eyes away, he nodded slightly, letting her know that he got it, probably all of it.

For a long moment, he didn't speak. Nothing but their heartbeats punctuated the silence.

Nothing in the world could have prepared Sirenia for the way his golden irises dimmed, as if the very soul in him had fled. It was more than she could bear and the exhaustion took over, yanking her shaking knees out from under her.

Before she could fall to the floor, Byron had already scooped her up into his arms. He carried her to the corner of the galleon.

"Sleep now, my sweet siren," he murmured, settling her gently onto the floor. Spooning his giant body around hers, he tucked her firmly into the circle of his arms. "I understand now. And I swear to you, when you open your eyes, the sun will be shining and you will be free to love anyone your heart desires."

Only a coward wastes his time lamenting that which he has lost, Ba'at Rath thought, disentangling his pruned hands from their anchors in the sea grasses. Sinking his toes into the silt, he pushed away from the lagoon's bottom. As soon as his head broke the water's surface, a companion thought came bursting across his consciousness—a flash so brilliant he could only attribute it to rapture.

A hero, on the other hand, turns his attention to that which he might yet win.

Emerging at the water's edge, he struggled to his feet. Bending forward, his lips contorted as he forcibly clicked his displaced knee joints into place with his hands.

His change was complete. Now he had work to do

Lifting his face to the sun, he inhaled the almond-tinged fragrance of fertile female hanging on the breeze.

Checking the slipknots still hitched around his wrist, he smiled thinly. The time had come to assess the lay of the land. When the time came for Sirenia to conceive Zane's son, Ba'at Rath must remained poised to strike his brother down in an instant.

Chapter 11

"Tell it to us again? Please?"

In the dream, Sirenia was five-years old.

Her tailfins fluttered, agitating the water into a flurry of bubbles. She and Arabeth were begging Mar-ala to tell them another story. Not just any story—the story of Triton's Lost Son.

"Again?" her mother whimpered.

Sirenia flashed a contrived pout.

Unable to ignore her daughter's charm, Mar-ala's face yielded to a smile. "Only once more," she said. "But then off to bed with the both of you!"

Sirenia's fins settled like a blanket as she curled into the circle of Mar-ala's right arm.

"How will the Chosen Daughter know him?" she asked.

"She will recognize him by his mark..."

"What does it look like?"

"The Chosen Daughter will know the mark instinctively," Mar-ala continued. "Even should the evidence left in the shrine by the ancients be destroyed, the mark will haunt her very dreams."

"What if it could be me?" Sirenia whispered. Squeezing her eyes shut, she tried to visualize the mark.

"I think I can see it!" she whispered.

Arabeth scowled. "Triton would never anoint a mermaid who forgets the way home for chasing every whim that strikes her."

Bowing her head, Sirenia's cheeks heated. Arabeth had spoken the truth. Extending a chubby finger, she reached down into the silt, drawing what she imagined the mark to look like—a staff, like the one Triton carried, with three prongs.

Sitting back to consider her work, she saw that it did not yet satisfy her. Reaching down once more, she framed the staff with a pair of wings, like those of the great birds that soared over the waters as they flew toward the mainland—where the land-walkers lived.

Sirenia slammed into wakefulness, joyful tears streaming from her eyes. Just as Byron had promised when he rocked her to sleep, the horrors of the last days were finally over.

And yes, she was free now.

Free to love him.

Peeling her lids open, she saw soft rays of sun slanting through the holes in the galleon, and she could hear the happy water birds screeching as they fled the mangrove to fish in Open Waters.

Her dream memory had proven that she was exactly where Triton intended for her to end up all along—in the arms of the Lost Son.

Byron's arms.

Lips curling to a smile, she remembered that today would mark their third true mating. Thoughts of spending several lazy hours coupling with him sparked a fresh flicker of desire, and her womb contracted, forcing creamy fluid to trickle from her sex.

Already my body readies the way for his seed.

He would father their child today.

With Byron the Lost Son, someone had to have altered the mark in the shrine. Ba'at Rath was the only soul in the world who stood to benefit from such a vile act.

This meant the fresh bloodstain she'd seen had to be his.

He might even still be here, in the mangrove.

If the bitter merman had gone to such lengths to fool her, then he'd surely search her out soon, expecting to shoot her full with his hapless seed.

There was no telling how much he knew, or what he'd witnessed while he skulked along in her musk trail. But Sirenia doubted he'd act happy to see her in the arms of his supposed dead brother, regardless of what he knew. And she knew she could count on this—nothing Ba'at Rath intended would bode well for Byron or the baby they'd soon conceive.

"Byron, we're in trouble," she whispered. The hairs on the back of her neck prickled, and she grimaced, imagining that she could already smell the vile stench of the merman's breath.

"Byron?" she urged, shaking the arm that held her. They needed to get out of here fast, before her third passion swell struck, demanding a kind of time and attention she and Byron—Zane?—could scarcely afford right now.

Best, she thought, to *conceive this child in the watchful safety of Brood.*

"Byron, wake up!"

Sliding her hand up to ruffle his head as it cradled hers, her fingernail caught in the tangled snarls of his hair. Sifting it through her fingers, it felt longer—and much coarser—than she recalled.

Whipping her head around, her eyes didn't meet the welcoming gaze she'd come to love so dearly. Instead, she saw Ba'at Rath's dreadful leer scathing over her. His black eyes looked every bit as flinty as the jagged, stone blade that he held pressed against her throat.

"Good morning, sweet meat," he hissed.

"Fuck you," she retorted.

"Sorry to disappoint, my precious, but Triton has spared me that heinous chore," Ba'at Rath crooned into her ear. "However, I'm sure my brother will be more than willing to stand in for me by proxy."

Ba'at Rath pressed in harder with his blade. "Where is he?"

Sirenia forced a shrug. "I'm not your brother's keeper. I thought he was dead."

"Are you perhaps working on the assumption that I am blind? I saw you screwing him."

Hooking his thin fingers into her hair, he yanked it hard away from her face, forcing her up to a sitting position so that she sat facing him.

Sirenia swallowed her screams—she'd rather die than let Ba'at Rath have the satisfaction of knowing he'd frightened her.

Instead, she opened her mouth and began spinning a siren song. As she sang, she also prayed that the human part of Byron would not prevent him from understanding—and heeding—the subtle message she embedded in its words.

Wandering child of the sea, Triton's trumpet beckons you.

As her melody caught on the morning air, Ba'at Rath's spittle seared against her earlobe, lips working roughly against her ear. "You'll not hypnotize me with your siren-squalling."

Growling, he shoved her away from him. "The Council was right. You are a disgrace to our kind. Killing you will come easy."

Sirenia skewered him with her glare. Even knowing the danger such open loathing for Ba'at Rath invited, she also knew nobody she loved had a future if she failed to draw Byron back.

"Killing my brother will come even easier." Ba'at Rath's stare bore into Sirenia's, plundering for the faintest glimmer of fear.

Composing her face into a relaxed expression of serenity that she did not feel, she raised her voice another notch, singing all that much louder. *Wandering child of the sea, heed the ancient voice that rings.*

"No harm will come his way. Yet," Ba'at Rath continued, hitching his gnarled fingers beneath her chin, "for you do not wear the crimson mark of pregnancy."

Ba'at Rath stepped so close to Sirenia that she could feel his fetid breath rushing across her face. Winding his hands into the hair at the base of her skull, he drew her head back. "We need to get you knocked up, my dear."

Sirenia stopped her singing only long enough to spit at Ba'at Rath.

Wake up and remember who you are.

"As much as I loathe the sight of him," Ba'at Rath continued, circling once to stand behind her. "Zane is, for the time being, a necessary evil."

"You see, my precious," he hissed, trailing his blade along her jaw, "the two of you are going to give me the son fate denied me. "

"You'll have to kill me first," Sirenia spat, hating the pathetic way her voice trembled.

"Rest assured, you will die," he chortled. "Then I'll return home with your child, to be revered as a grieving widower—and Triton's Lost Son."

Lifting her hair with the weapon's crude point, he used it to tuck a few errant tendrils behind her ear.

"Since you won't tell where my surrogate has gotten off to," he crooned, "you've left me no choice but to rely on your screams to summon him."

Sirenia notched her chin higher. And she sang, *Claim your beloved as she has claimed you.*

"Perhaps I have not made myself clear," Ba'at Rath grated, voice brittle with rage. "What say I drag you out to the ocean and let the sharks have at you?"

"You're bluffing," she forced, voice thick with dread.

"Am I, now?" Riveting his focus, he planted images in her mind of exactly what forms of miseries he intended to inflict on her.

But still, she sang.

It is time to remember who you are.

Sirenia was awake now.

Byron knew it because he could hear her singing. Her haunting elegy reached out across the mangroves, grasping at his heart, and he knew as long as he lived, that mournful sound would follow him.

It's so hard to leave her.

But the more he learned of her—her kind—the more he realized he didn't belong here. No human did.

This was her world. Her future and her quest.

Not his.

Sirenia stood on the threshold of becoming a champion for her people—the kind of hero Byron wished he could have been for his own family.

He'd been too late to make a difference for them. Nothing he did in this life would ever change that fact. But Sirenia still stood a good chance of saving her kind.

He would not stand in her way.

But her song, how it beckoned him to just turn around. He knew he had to close his mind to it and keep moving. Otherwise, his resolve would weaken. He'd go rushing back to quench his desire for her one more time. He would not risk that

Sirenia's heart belonged to another. One of her own kind.

Unable to stop himself from glancing back before the narrow creek curved away from the lagoon, he stole a glimpse of the pool that Sirenia drew her strength from. From this vantage point, it looked like an alien world, but somehow, its light-dappled waters had come to feel like home.

Because of her, he thought.

She had healed the empty place inside of him. While his heart longed for it to be any other way, he knew his presence in her life would only strip the world of a future for her people.

Perhaps in time, he'd find comfort in doing the right thing. Sirenia would be able to offer a future to all those that she held dear.

It would have to be enough.

Traveling as fast as he could to spread a safe distance between them, he raced down the tributary that wound back toward the ocean. Moving into eyeshot of the shore, Byron noticed a gather of egrets coasting on an eastbound breeze.

Where there were mangroves, there was always land nearby.

The way he figured it, today was as good a day as any to return to the solitary life he'd left behind. All he needed to do was point himself east and put one arm in front of the other.

So why in the hell couldn't he bite the bullet, and do it?

Tilting his ear to the wind one last time, he opened himself to the penetrating tones of her melody. Something in her plaintive voice rang with such urgency that the hair on the nape of his neck prickled.

He turned around.

Could it be that Triton knows he has erred, anointing the wrong brother? Ba'at Rath believed it so, for the slightest of miracles had just smiled upon him.

Zane was coming.

Even now, Ba'at Rath could hear his brother splashing through the tributaries.

In the end, it hadn't mattered that Sirenia never screamed out. The sultry spell of her song must have been enough to reach her lover, seducing him back to her side.

Sniffing out more of her sex, no doubt, Ba'at Rath thought. He didn't let the idea perturb him, though. After all, Zane was exactly where he needed him—in the mangrove.

Now, my plan will begin to unfold.

Everything Ba'at Rath had witnessed suggested that one, particular trait had followed his brother into adulthood—an over-developed sense of heroics. Soon, the ever so predictable Lost Son would rush in to rescue his ladylove.

Laughter gurgled in Ba'at Rath's craw as he relished his unexpected reversal of fortune. Even now, he could hear the besotted fool crashing through the vegetation, shouting her name—"Sirenia!"

It was all too perfect!

"Answer him," Ba'at Rath commanded, raising his blade.

"Go ahead. Cut me," Sirenia spat through the cage of her teeth. "The blood-stench will eclipse my pheromones. No man would make love to me like that."

Her eyes simmered with hatred as she narrowed her gaze. Flashing him a syrupy smile, her eyes dropped to his groin. "Save a seedless sadist like yourself."

"I'll show you sadistic." Ba'at Rath grated. Growling with effort, he volleyed images portraying his gruesome intentions for Zane into her mind.

While the effort left his head pounding, his discomfort did not come without reward. Sirenia let loose the terrified scream he needed to lure Zane in their direction.

Launching one last image of him, presenting her squalling infant to Council as his own spawn, Sirenia's lashes fluttered, eyes rolling to white as she collapsed into a heap.

"So sorry, precious," he murmured. Clicking his tongue, he took a moment to gloat for over her inert form.

Now there, he thought, is the perfect mate.

Quiet.

Compliant.

And comatose with fear.

"Sweet dreams," he said, carving a wide berth as he stepped around her.

It was time to choreograph her next tryst with Zane. *By the sound of it,* he thought, turning his ear windward, *I've precious little time to spare.*

Unhitching one of the slipknots on his wrist, he bound Sirenia's ankles. But even as he yanked the knots tight, he worried the bindings might not hold her. The girl was a born fighter, packing almost as much strength as her muscle-bound lover.

Eyes cutting to the corner of the galleon, he saw some old fishing nets piled into the corner. Picking them up, he rushed back to Sirenia, heaving the rope mesh over her. Tucking several moldy loops over her hands and ankles, he felt reassured that even if she awoke, she'd not break free.

Brushing his hands, he stepped outside of the galleon. Scanning the lagoon, he saw that the currents had turned inland. The ebb tide was over. The rising tides would soon swell the debris-tangled tributaries, making them impossible to navigate for any but a native water dweller.

The whims of Triton still appeared to be working to his benefit.

Stomping toward the rushing water, his right leg punched, thigh-deep, into the mucking silt.

Quicksand, he thought, wrenching his leg free. It made each new footstep pregnant with the possibility for dire misfortune—for an unsuspecting victim.

Triton is, indeed, kind.

Waves of pleasure shuddering through him, Ba'at Rath wriggled free from the clinging silt. He could hear Zane splashing through the tributaries, bearing closer.

Wringing his hands, Ba'at Rath paced, considering the evidence he'd spent the last days collecting. He felt safe assuming two things about Zane.

The man possessed the strength of a giant octopus. Overtaking him by brute force did not enter the realm of possibility. Ba'at Rath needed a less confrontational method of dealing with his brother.

Ba'at Rath realized that Zane had likely spent a lifetime refusing the call of the water. With any luck at all, his brother had forgotten that he ever possessed the ability to invoke his change.

Yes, he thought, stroking his chin between his thumb and forefinger, *Sirenia fed Zane breath the entire time they were submerged.* The pair had gone at each other for some time, too. Certainly, long enough to prove that if his brother had known himself merkind, he'd have summoned his change.

That made drowning Zane the obvious answer. But how to do it, would defined the conclusion of Ba'at Rath's plan.

First, he must insure that Sirenia went into passion-swell, milking Zane dry of seed before his brother succumbed from lack of air.

An adrenaline surge. That would certainly provide the catalyst Ba'at Rath needed to tip Sirenia's hormones over the edge. And what better way to elicit adrenaline than through fear?

A deadly dip in the quicksand, perhaps?

Rushing back toward the wrecked galleon, Ba'at Rath's spied a rotted plank. It was both long enough and wide enough to hold Sirenia. Prying it from the mud, he dragged it back to the quicksand. It was enough to cover the pit from side to side, spanning it from end to end.

Squatting, he set stones under the ends of the plank to destabilize it. Finally, he stood, surveying his creation. The most decayed portion of the wood sat over the center of the quicksand. The slightest motion would cause the wood to splinter and break, causing anything sitting on top of it would plunge into the quicksand.

It would make a fine set of gallows. A rescue waiting for a hero!

Returning to the galleon, he hauled Sirenia over his shoulder, carrying the unconscious mermaid to his makeshift scaffold. Laying her on the ground, he freed her from the net—he would need it later.

He then rolled her carefully atop the unsteady platform. The wood crackled dangerously as it took her weight, but did not give way.

At this point, Ba'at Rath felt sure the contraption would hold until she came to, struggling. Then the rotted wood would split, spilling her into the quicksand. As she thrashed with fear, adrenaline would course through her veins, shoving her into passion swell.

"Sirenia, where are you?" Zane's shouts were laced with panic.

Ba'at Rath's nostrils twitched, detecting his brother's spicy scent. He was closing in fast. Soon he would scent Sirenia

And me, as well, Ba'at Rath thought.

The time for planning was over.

Utterly convinced that a kinder fate was heading his way, Ba'at Rath drew his hand back, slapping Sirenia with all his might.

"Rise and shine, sweetmeat."

His handprint blazed like a scarlet brand from the side of her cheek. Just as he'd hoped, her lids began to flutter. And not a moment to soon. Zane was so close that Ba'at Rath could hear him gasping for breath.

Panting, he retreated beneath the water, dragging the net behind him. He was wagering his entire future on a hunch. He felt sure that once Zane rescued Sirenia from the pit, he would bring her into the water to wash her clean of quicksand.

Already stoked on adrenaline from her dip in the quicksand, Sirenia's final passion-swell would break as soon as she scented the Lost Son. *She'll glue herself to him like barnacles on a ship's hull,* he thought, submerging himself deep beneath the vegetation-choked waters. With the tide rising fast, the swollen current would drag the couple under the surface.

Once impregnated, Sirenia would lose the ability to breathe for her lover underwater. Nor could she sustain herself long enough to make it to shore before the sleep of afterglow took her.

When she broke for air, Ba'at Rath would make his move. He would snag his brother in the net.

Gauging the direction of the strong current, he searched for a hiding place that would keep him near Zane and Sirenia. He spied a submerged tree, its limbs snaring all that floated toward it. The current would nudge them here. Nets readied, he concealed himself, waiting for the moment that Sirenia's mark turned crimson, announcing the prodigal child's conception.

Chapter 12

"Sirenia!"

Byron sensed a presence—tasted the sharp, masculine tang of it hanging on the wind.

Someone was there with her. Her lover, perhaps?

Bursting through the last brushy thicket, he stopped dead in his tracks. If the sight of Sirenia, struggling chest deep in quicksand wasn't enough to snap his heart in two, then the scarlet handprint blazing from her cheek finished the job.

The bastard had hurt her.

Not only that, he'd left her in grave danger.

"Is this how your Lost Son treats his women?" As soon as the words broke free, he saw the truth behind his accusation register in her eyes. And he hated himself for having uttered them.

"Baby, I'm sorry," he rasped, rushing toward her.

But if she'd heard him, she didn't answer—*couldn't* answer. Byron could see that she was terrified. Her pupils had all but disappeared in the glassy spheres of her irises. Her face contorted into a grimace as she struggled to escape the sand. Each new motion worked against her, sinking her several inches deeper into the reeking muck.

"Sirenia! Don't move!"

But she still didn't hear. Byron could tell it by the thrashing of her head. She wrenched it back and forth so violently that he worried her neck might snap. Her flailing only increased the sand's suction, sinking her deeper, shoulders and then neck.

Devouring the distance between them, he dropped to his knees, skidding as close to her as he could possibly get without falling in. Sprawling, belly flat to the ground, he reached out to cup her face between his hands.

"Look at me, baby," he croaked, forcing her to lock onto his eyes.

The startled points of her pupils found his and uncoiled. The quicksand was taking her down fast, threatening to devour the curve of her shoulder.

"B-Byron? I'm sorry," she said, eyes bright and puddling with tears. "I never meant to put you in danger."

"I never should have left you," he rasped. "But we're going to get you out. Just relax and stay still. Otherwise, you're going under, and I'm coming in after you."

"I'm scared."

"I know sweetheart," he said, sweeping her tears away with his fingertips. "But you'll be safe soon. Just focus on my eyes. And listen."

Though her pupils had widened some, panic still flashed in her eyes.

"I'm going to put my hand in here, now," he said, palm skimming over the sand. "Just sit still, sweetheart. The more you relax, the less the quicksand is going to grab at you. Blink if you understand."

Sirenia's lashes swept down, brushing the tops of her cheekbones. A few tears squeezed out and then she opened her eyes again, fastening her gaze to his.

"Just breathe, Rennie," he said. Holding her stare, he repeated the words like a prayer. "Breathe. And for the love of God, stay still."

While Sirenia inhaled, Byron plunged his hand into the sand near her neck. Running it along the slope of her submerged shoulder, he traveled down her quaking flesh until his fingers found the crevice where her arm joined her body. Hooking his hand beneath her armpit, he felt her relax. The sand shifted, releasing her from its crushing suction.

For the longest moment, they stayed there, him holding Sirenia wedged in the crook of his arm until bubbles of moisture began to rise to the top of the sand, buoying her upward.

"Gotcha!" Working his other hand down her other side, he hooked beneath her other arm.

"You smell so good," she said, lips nuzzling the side of his neck.

Byron smiled. He couldn't help it. He didn't need to see her mark to know exactly where her attentions were turning. He couldn't help chuckling as he pulled her even closer.

If Sirenia was feeling frisky, then perhaps the prodigal son hadn't seeded her yet. Ashamed, Byron cursed himself for how happy it made him feel that Sirenia may not yet have made love with another.

Knees drawn beneath his body, he pulled his weight back. Her shoulders popped free of the muck. Laying on the wet ground they both laughed as she rained sandy kisses over his face. But as soon as she lassoed her arms over his head, knotting them behind his neck, his mirth died.

She'd suffered a lot more than the stinging slap of an irate lover. She'd also been bound. And unless she'd somehow managed to sink her foretold sperm donor in the quicksand, the son of a bitch might still be out there somewhere.

Byron's heart thudded, matching the beat of hers as she lay panting on top of him. His emotions—the heart thundering fear of losing her, the raw anger that anyone would dare harm her, and the relief that she was finally safe in his arms— washed over him all at once.

Hands frantically working at the knots on her wrists and ankles, his heart seized, realizing that again, he'd left someone he loved alone and in danger. And he had a prickling, nagging feeling that the danger wasn't yet over.

Did he do this to you?

She nodded, her cheeks blanching.

"Why would he want to hurt you? Doesn't he need you as much as you need him?" Searching Sirenia's eyes, he probed for the answers he needed to make sense of what had just happened.

A sob tore from her throat. Casting her gaze on the ground, she hung her head. She hid behind the curtain of her hair like a woman deeply ashamed.

Byron's mind began to reel with rushing images of a merman's face. His consciousness exploded with guttural intrusion of it. That same cragged face had haunted his nightmares every single night since his family's murders.

Those eyes, so black. Soulless. Like a shark's.

None of this was accidental, Byron, her voice whispered in his mind.

"But why, Sirenia?" he searched her face hoping to discover the missing piece that might snap the disjointed puzzle of the last couple of days into place.

"Why me? My family?"

"Byron," she cried, rolling off him and onto her feet in one smooth motion. "Forget it. It's too dangerous. And you don't remember, so just go."

"Remember *what*?"

"Get away from me," she cried, backing away from him. "Just go, before you can't."

Sirenia spun away from him.

"The hell I will," he said, leaping up to lasso her with his arms.

But she didn't struggle, trying to run away, as he'd expected. Nor did she argue.

Instead, the stern line of her shoulders sagged, and the wind rushed out of her so hard and fast that he could feel the jagged release of it shuddering through her as he drew her against him.

Slipping around in the cage of his embrace, she tipped her face up toward his. Though tears carved gritty tracks on her face as they streamed from her eyes, her breeder's mark was glowing brighter then ever, and the gold flecks in her irises ignited, blue pools simmering with flames of desire.

"Make love to me," she demanded, eyes glazing with desire as her pink tongue darted out. Seductively rimming her lower lip, her scorching glance dropped to his groin.

"Shit," he swore. "Talk about bad timing."

In spite of his best intentions, he slammed his mouth down on hers. Byron swept her into his arms. The air sang with the aphrodisiac thrill of her sex. She twined her legs around his hips as he carried her toward the water, and he could feel her frantic heartbeat thudding in her mons.

His traitorous cock shot gunned to a pounding erection.

Her passion-swell had hit, snaring him in its dangerous spell. Lugging her further out into the tributary's chilly waters, he could already feel her silky juices. Gritting his teeth, he prayed he could summon the willpower to stand down, keeping his wits about him long enough for the cool water to douse her passions—preserve her fertility.

For the son of a bitch who did this to her.

Because nothing could change the fact that she still needed to mate with one of her kind or risk their extinction.

If she still has to mate with him, he thought, *then she'll do it under my guard.*

At least when it was over, he'd get the chance to choke the life out of the bastard with his bare hands.

After he got some answers.

Bracing his hands on her shoulders, Byron tried one last time to push her away, preserving her fertility for the merman who had killed his family.

Sirenia knew they were in danger. Just a moment ago, her legs had twitched with the desperate need to run, but suddenly, she couldn't remember exactly why she had wanted to escape in the first place. All she could think of was Byron, his scent, the straining rod of his sex as it parted the folds of her swollen nether lips.

She felt the bracing chill of the water lapping against her flesh, and she could taste the metallic bite of hesitation on his tongue as she had sucked it into her mouth. The water's frigid embrace made her gasp, but the effect was far too little, too late to dam the tidal wave of her hormone surge.

She'd passed the point of no return. Her entire world turned in on itself, imploding beneath the crushing weight of want. Now there was nothing that mattered, save this giant of a man, his enormous sex, her own hammering need.

Now he was pushing away from her, trying to deny her what her body most needed.

No!

Each cell in her body screamed with its own version of yearning, demanding satisfaction. Hooking her ankles together behind the small of his back, she threaded her fingers together at the nape of his neck.

Desperate to hold him—have him, she molded herself to his body. Hitching her hips higher, the swirling water closed over their heads. Her position left Byron no room to consider refusal.

Sirenia sheathed him in one fierce motion.

The force of her assault and the drag of the current slammed him back against the submerged trunk of a fallen tree. She held him there, penned between her straining thighs.

Riding him, her womb contracted into a tight knot and she felt her ovaries clenching, first the right and then the left. They burned in her core like volcanic stones, pushing their molten heat through to the mouth of her womb. Her need gathered, pooling in her groin until she felt so full with it that she could no longer endure the building peaks of pleasure.

Byron drew his hips back, stroking her with his full length. In, and then out, hard and then slow, over and over again. Meeting his thrusts, her internal muscles coiled and released, erupting in an explosion of musk that tinged the water with creamy bands of fragrant light.

She'd just ovulated.

He'd not be getting away from her now.

"Oh, God, baby no," Byron tried to protest. "It's not me you want." But she offered him her air just then and he had no choice but to take it. His hand found her breast, and the way it molded so perfectly into the cup of his hand caused the words to die before he could push them across the barrier of his mind into hers.

The light that rushed from her sex swept across his thighs in tingling trails, wrapping him in its erotic spell until it enveloped him in a silken layer of sensation.

There was nothing more than this woman, the taste of the breath she shared with him and the buttery grasp of her sex. All of that conspired against him, assaulting his senses until all he could think of was taking her again.

Dropping his head, he ran his tongue down the velvety slope of her breast until her nipple pearled. Seizing her taut areola in his mouth, he could feel her pulse drumming irregularly against his lips, could even hear the roar of her blood as it thrummed through her veins.

And then, returning to her mouth, he savored once more the decadent taste of her air.

Paradise.

Every nerve ending, each burning synapse buzzed with delight as his free hand slid down between them. Parting her, he stroked the swollen peak of tissue hidden beneath her golden tangles.

She voiced a needy groan of encouragement into his ear, then returned her mouth to his, exhaling her fragrance into him. Her hand trailed down his abdomen, cupping him, squeezing.

He needed more.

Stealing one last breath, he lifted her off his straining shaft, spinning her in his arms until her butt nested in his groin. Gently, he bent her over the submerged tree. He could see the up-thrust heart of her bottom and the illuminated folds of her sex. Sliding his hands beneath her hipbones, he plunged his full length back into her phosphorescent warmth.

Plowing deeper, he could feel her pulse pounding erratically in her core. Her taut, internal muscles contracted and pumped, drawing his burning tip in until it hammered at the doorway to her womb, demanding entrance.

Not until his orgasm bore down on him with a dizzying promise of ecstasy unlike anything he'd ever known did he realize how desperately he needed to breathe.

Ba'at Rath could barely stand it. The water reeked with the stain of their shared pleasures, and he had to bite back the urge to pounce on Zane, removing him from Sirenia before she conceived.

He yearned to screw her. Dominate her.

Soon enough, he'd take her for the sole sake of psychological domination but he'd not waste any care on insuring her pleasure. No, he much preferred to seek his thrills through the threat of pain, the raw scent of fear.

Ba'at Rath jerked spasmodically at his own flesh, watching transfixed, as the illuminated lovers frenzied toward climax. Twin expressions of ecstasy lit their faces as their bodies entwined in a glowing tangle of limbs.

Sirenia's beaming mark charted the arc of their pleasure, first blue and then purple. Her delighted shrieks pierced the water, and Zane threw his head back, teeth gritted and muscles straining against the threat of climax.

Their simultaneous roars of ecstasy rang in Ba'at Rath's ears, and Sirenia's mark infused the waters with the crimson announcement of her pregnancy.

Victory!

In the aftermath of her orgasm, Sirenia collapsed, falling slack in Zane's arms.

Ba'at Rath knew that the moment his future hinged on had arrived. Net still gathered in his arms, he sprang from his lair beneath the submerged tree. Triumphantly snaring his brother from behind, Ba'at Rath deftly tangled him in its loops.

Zane bellowed, slamming his head into Ba'at Rath's chest.

His brother had seized the slight advantage, and by pushing out with his feet, he shoved Sirenia toward the surface. Her eyes were wide with horror, and bubbles streamed from her mouth as her reservoir lung expelled its last burst of air.

Ba'at Rath knew Sirenia could breathe for her lover no more—not if she wanted her baby to live.

In spite of the pain that ripped through his chest, his lips stretched to a smile as he watched her surface to restore her oxygen.

Yes, he thought, watching the dappled surface of the water part as it received her.

God's do, indeed, err.

In the span of the same second, Byron plummeted from the mind-numbing summit of his orgasm into the red heat of rage. But even that lightening fast transition came too late to help him insure Sirenia's safety. The best he'd been able to do was shove Sirenia from the path of immediate harm, praying she'd have sense enough to save herself.

Save their baby!

Byron didn't have to lay eyes on his assailant to know that the same bastard he'd chased into the water three years ago had cast the net.

He could smell the fetid stench of his breath. Defying the net's cumbersome weight, Byron whipped around, targeting his attacker with his eyes. The same black-eyed murderer he'd lost in the breakwater so many years ago, glared back at him. He sat crouched on the water's floor, arms curled protectively over his wounded chest. His eyes flashed with the same, tired challenge.

Kill me if you can.

"Is that the only line you know?"

The merman's dour face contorted with hatred before he snarled and broke for the surface.

Byron ripped at the loops that held him. He knew now that the black-eyed beast was no man.

He was mer-kind.

Like Sirenia.

Like me?

Byron finally understood how he'd survived the long moments underwater without drawing breath. The convoluted mess of unanswered questions that had dogged him throughout his entire life found the only answer that made sense.

I am merkind, too. And I am in love with a mermaid.

Tracking Sirenia's fading light trail up to the water's mottled surface, his heart contracted.

She was up there. Pregnant and alone.

With the man who meant to kill them both.

Looping the netting over a sharp branch, Byron sawed frantically at the ropes that held his wrists. Though the net was old and fragile, and he peeled through the fraying ropes quickly, there were so many of them… too many to count.

Dammit! He had no time for this, not if he expected to reach Sirenia before that bastard did any harm to her. To their baby!

Straining so hard against the ropes that they chewed through his flesh, he realized he'd let down everyone who had ever counted on him when they needed him the most. Now, barring a miracle, he would fail Sirenia, too.

"No!" he roared. Rage hammered through his veins and his body burned with adrenaline. Deep in the well of his chest, ribs crackled, cartilage popping as his chest compressed. Gut heaving, fingers of blackness curled around the edges of his vision.

Waves of dread washed over him and he felt his bones turn to liquid.

Each screaming cell exploded. Pain razed along every nerve, sparking over each synapse, converging at the apex of his skull.

Bryon thought his head might split open—wished it *would* split open—anything just to make it stop.

Then the blackness advanced, taking him under.

"It's safe to remember who you are."

First, Byron heard the words spoken in Sirenia's halting cadence, but then he heard them repeated in his adoptive mother's slow drawl. Her familiar voice pierced the darkness, sliding over him like a comforting blanket. Aware he teetered on that magical cusp where dreams bleed into reality, he could not prevent his heart from leaping to his throat.

"Mom" he grated, knowing the second he allowed himself to turn around, his grip on reality would flee.

I owe her this moment, he thought. Seizing this last chance to become the dutiful son she truly deserved, Byron surrendered, allowing himself to become once more his mother's little boy.

He turned around.

His mother looked just the way his heart remembered, round face beaming as she held a stack of books against her heart.

Many days, she took Byron to work with her, at the island library. While she catalogued and filed, Byron sat curled up on the sill if a sun-lit gable overlooking Blackbeard's Cove. His eyes stayed riveted to the treacherous spot where he'd washed up during the hurricane.

The only thing that had followed him into his new life was the relentless obsession that if he lost sight of the water, he'd surely die.

Because his brother was still out there.

He'd left Byron with a warning that if he ever dared return to brood, their mother, Serafel, would be executed for favoring a child who was more human than mer-kind.

As the months ticked by, Byron remembered only that bitter betrayal, paired with heart-pounding horror every time he thought of his real mother.

Here, on land, he'd at least found refuge.

And now love.

He turned his thoughts away from the fading remnants of his old life.

"I thought we might choose a book for you to take home," his adopted mother said,, *her voice sounding thick and damp.* "You might find something in this one that will help you remember who you are."

His eyes lit as he saw the book she held out for his approval. Its cover depicted a grizzled old man, bearded and fierce.

He wore the crown of a king and the bottom fins of a great fish.

A merman! In his mighty fist, he held a three-pronged staff. A trident.

"What's his name?" his new mother asked, tapping on the book's cover with her index finger. *"Poseidon? Neptune?"*

"No," Byron said, speaking for the first time.

"Triton. God of the Water World and Father of all Merkind."

Eyes fluttering open, Byron finally understood the message Sirenia had buried in the siren song she'd spun out as he was leaving the mangrove.

He understood it because she had communicated her plea for him to return to her side in his native language. The ancient language of Triton.

He remembered who he was now, and he felt anxious to meet the destiny he'd spent a lifetime denying.

It was time to go home, reclaiming the future his brother had conspired to usurp. Not just from him. But from Sirenia and their child.

Their child!

His legs, that had been so hopelessly tangled in the nets, had morphed into the greenish-gold fins he'd felt so proud of as a boy. Unfurling them for the first time in twenty-five years, the tattered remains of the net fell away, freeing him to chase his claim to Sirenia's heart.

He squinted, searching the murky bottom until they fell on a pointed length of deadwood. Hefting it into his fist, he tested its weight. Satisfied that the barbed limb held enough bulk to fly true, he stripped the leaves from it. Pushing off the bottom, he broke for the surface.

Head above water, he sought out his brother. Ba'at Rath held Sirenia's arms wrenched behind her back.

Why wasn't she moving?

Her head was hanging too low for Byron to see her face. Could she even see him through the tangled shroud of her hair?

Then he remembered why it was that she sat so still and placid while Ba'at Rath bound her. She was sleeping off her after-glow.

Slipping silently across the water, Byron reached up, hitching several lengths of low hanging sea-grape vine around his wrist. Hefting himself up with one arm, he poised his spear over his shoulder.

Like the well-trained warrior he was, he waited for his target to move into range. Finally Ba'at Rath stood, stepping away from Sirenia to pick up another length of grass.

A dozen years spent training to be a hero had prepared Byron for this moment. Squinting, he honed in on his target—the small patch of skin just beneath and to the right of Ba'at Rath's left shoulder blade.

Byron drew his arm back, took his aim, and let her rip.

Chapter 13

Ba'at Rath wasn't quite dead when Byron dragged him by his hair through the tangled tributaries and out into the open water.

Byron was glad. Killing his brother would be far too easy. Considering what the bastard had done to Sirenia and to his adoptive family, Byron had a different ending in mind.

Triton could determine Ba'at Rath's fate.

Diving deep with his wounded brother in tow, Byron knew that even if the pathetic piece of shit lived, he'd never dare show his face around merkind again.

The Council would execute him on sight.

"I'm going to give you the same chance for survival you gave me when you left me for dead," Byron said.

Depositing Ba'at Rath belly flat on a coral bed, he yanked the spear free from his flesh. The wound began to bleed profusely, tingeing the water with the coppery stench of blood.

"Whatever pathetic bit of life you have left will be spent in fear."

Turning Ba'at Rath over on his back, Byron took satisfaction in the way his brother's obsidian eyes brimmed with horror. Tracking that soulless gaze up to the distant surface, Byron could just make out the streamlined silhouettes of some curious sharks circling lazily.

"Looks like sushi for dinner," he said.

Then, with a hearty flip of his fins, he left his brother in Triton's hands and raced back toward the mangrove where Sirenia waited.

Sirenia awoke with a start and shivered as she remembered what had happened. Fear for Byron's safety chewed at her belly. She fully expected to see Ba'at Rath leering down at her, eagerly waiting to inflict some new form of misery on her.

Instead of the loathsome face, she detested, she saw only a few water birds gliding overhead and heard the splash of a fish leaping in the lagoon.

The chill she'd felt earlier had subsided. In its place, delicious warmth enveloped her. A pair of strong arms held her tight, and the air no longer reeked with the fetid stench of evil.

It smelled clean and masculine. Spicy, like sweet moss and pine needles.

Like Byron.

Reaching her hand over her shoulder, her fingertips confirmed the crisp cap of hair that she'd come to love so dearly.

Byron's hair.

No, *Zane's* hair.

"So, we're even," he whispered, velvety lips nipping her earlobe. Turning in his arms to make sure she wasn't dreaming, his dimpled smile welcomed her back to the land of the living.

"Even? How's that?" she asked, cupping his face between her hands.

"Well." Byron grinned, grazing his fingertips along the slope of her breast. "Appears to me I just saved your life."

"So you did," she agreed, eyes widening to an expression of mock innocence. "Your point?"

Dipping his head down, he laved his tongue around her nipple, dragging a needy moan from her. "Well, you do know what that means."

"You're not going to hold me to that silly, old tradition," she whined, pulling his head back down to her breast.

"Oh, but it's written in stone, remember? I'm in your life debt, bound to serve you from sunup 'til sundown. Unless, of course, you choose to set me free.

"That will never happen," she insisted, knotting her legs around his waist.

"So tell me, my sweet mistress," he choked, thickly. "What's your first command?"

"Make love to me."

"Oh, so I'm going to be your sex slave?"

Nodding, she cupped her palms around his butt cheeks. "Funny thing about us mermaids. Pregnancy puts us in a permanent passion swell. Think you're man enough to keep up?"

"Nope," he rasped, entering her in one lusty thrust. "But I might just be mer-*man* enough."

About the Author:

Liane Gentry Skye was considered the girl most likely to become a nun in high school. Upon graduation, she wasted no time rewriting her destiny. Two marriages, one real life alpha hero and four beautiful babies later, she decided it wise to exchange her rhinestone thong for soccer mom sweats. These days, her walk on the wild side lives (mostly) in her imagination. Liane is a passionate advocate for persons with autism. Feel free to contact her at lianegentryskye@aol.com.

The Boy Next Door

by Hannah Murray

To My Reader:

Isabella and Jacob's story is full of laughs, love, and rope—a lot of rope. And boy, do they have fun with it! I hope you do, too.

Rope can be found in almost any home improvement or hardware store, but for good bondage rope, see the experts. Monk and his crew at **www.TwistedMonk. com** make the finest hemp bondage rope in the world, and they have some great resources for learning how to be safe and have fun with it. They and their love for their craft were the inspiration for this story… thanks, Monk.

Chapter 1

Jacob Hale was just getting started on the pile of work he'd brought home when he noticed the lights. Leaving his open case files on the table, he stepped up to his kitchen window and took a closer look over the fence at his neighbor's house. He'd seen Isa yesterday while he was getting his mail, and she'd asked him to look in on her cat while she was away for the weekend. So why then were there lights on in her bathroom? Flickering lights, like a flashlight.

"Hell," he muttered. Someone had broken in. He knew she had an alarm system—everyone in the neighborhood used the same monitoring company, and he knew it was a good one. And it wasn't a silent alarm, but rather was designed to scare off an intruder, and the fog horn of a siren could be heard for blocks. But someone was definitely in her house, and the alarm wasn't going off.

He quickly crossed to the back door, snagging his sidearm from where he'd placed it on the counter on arriving home. His private investigations business didn't often get involved in dangerous cases; he mostly handled cheating spouses and financial investigations these days, but he'd been a cop for ten years, and carrying a gun was a habit he just couldn't break.

The gun was kept loaded, but he checked the clip out of habit, drawing back the slide and ratcheting a bullet into the chamber as he crept out the back door on silent feet. He crossed through his yard and into Isa's, stepping up onto her back porch and testing the door. Locked. He frowned. It didn't make sense for an intruder to come in through the front door. It was too visible, too open. Her back yard backed up to the woods; it made much more sense to approach from that angle.

He heard the tinkle of glass breaking from inside the house, and shook his head. Probably a couple of dumb punks with too much time and not enough supervision. He grinned. At least he could scare the pants off of them, and have a little fun doing it. He kept his gun ready, just in case they were armed dumb punks, and crept around the front of the house to surprise them.

Isabella Carelli sank lower into the bathtub and glared at the bubbles that tickled her nose. She was supposed to be at her family's cottage on the shore by now, curled up in front of a romantic fire, drinking wine and making love, but no. She'd been dumped—again.

She felt herself getting pissed all over again just thinking about it. Of all the cowardly, slimy, lame ways to break up with someone—

She cut off the thought with a curse and picked up the bottle of wine. She'd had a glass, but the edge of the tub had been slick with spilled bubble bath and the delicate crystal had skidded right off, crashing with an almost musical tinkle onto the tile floor. She'd tossed a bath sheet over the shards of glass and switched to drinking straight from the bottle. It suited her mood.

The room flickered with the light of the dozen or so candles she'd lit, their soothing eucalyptus scent wafting in the air. At least it was supposed to be soothing; it really wasn't doing much to calm her ire. She took a sip of wine, hoping alcohol, bubbles, and a soothing mint mud mask would work where scent was failing. She closed her eyes, sank deeper into the tub, and tried to forget her day.

A plaintive meow reached her ears, and she opened one eye. Her enormous orange tabby was sitting on the edge of the tub by her feet, glaring at her in that unblinking and slightly disturbing fashion that only cats seemed to be able to pull off. "George," she sighed, "get down."

George stayed where he was, tail swishing against the side of the tub, and meowed again.

"You can't be hungry, I just fed you," she said, and picked her foot up out of the water to nudge him with her toe. He made a noise and shifted slightly, but otherwise stayed where he was.

"George, get down!" She poked him with her foot again, splashing him slightly this time, and he complied with a grumpy hiss. She watched him sashay his way across the room, lips twitching when he turned at the doorway to give her a haughty look before disappearing into the hallway.

She sighed, closing her eyes again and taking a deep breath in an effort to relax. Unfortunately, instead of serenity and calm, her mind filled with the memory of having her boyfriend break up with her—over the intercom, he couldn't even be bothered to come down from his apartment to talk to her! The fact that she'd been picking him up for a romantic getaway weekend was salt in an open wound, and she snarled out loud at the remembered humiliation.

"I'm sorry," she muttered out loud, her voice whiney and meek as she mimicked his words. "I just can't handle this. It's you, not me. You're a freak." She set the bottle down blindly on the edge of the tub with a clunk. "Fucker. I should have known this wouldn't work when he had to ask his freaking therapist if he could tie me up during sex."

She heard a shuffle across the room and sighed, picturing the cat sneaking up to the tub again. "George, get out!" She opened one eye, prepared to glare, and screamed bloody murder.

Jacob winced at her scream, his relief that she wasn't being robbed overshadowed by concern for his eardrums. For such a little thing, she had some pipes on her, he mused. He gave brief thought to announcing himself, to let her know it was only him, but it was too late—she was already in panic mode and reacting on pure instinct. She screamed louder, her voice going so shrill he was sure every dog in the neighborhood was now on high alert. He opened his mouth to call out, hoping calling her by name would break through the blind terror induced by seeing a man with a gun her in bathroom, but instead he found himself ducking as something came hurtling at his head.

He barely got clear of the first missile when the second came flying at him, clipping him on the side of the head and sending star bursts across his vision. "Help!" she screamed. "911! Call the police!"

Through the haze of pain he saw her kneeling in the tub, her nudity apparently forgotten as she picked up a shampoo bottle and winged it at him.

He had to credit her aim and her arm strength; he barely managed to deflect the bottle with his free hand before it could smash into his face. He saw her snatch up the matching bottle of conditioner and blurted out, "Isabella, for God's sake, it's me! Jacob!"

Isa already had her arm cocked back to fling the bottle, but that stopped her. "Jacob?" She paused, blinking water out of her eyes, and he stepped further into the room so she could see him better. He saw recognition dawn and let out the breath he'd been holding. Too soon.

"What is the *matter* with you?" she screamed, and let the conditioner bottle fly.

"Ow!" The bottle pinged off his forehead, and he glared at her. "What the hell did you do that for?"

"You scared me to death!" She shouted, shoving wet hair out of her eyes, and he suddenly grinned. He doubted she had any idea she was kneeling there, her only cover some sort of green paste on her face, giving him a full view of her lush, wet curves.

"What the hell are you doing, breaking into my house with—is that a gun?" Her eyes bugged out as she pointed to the pistol in his right hand.

"I thought someone was breaking in," he explained, keeping the gun down at his side. "You told me you were going to be out of town, and through all this—" he waved a hand at the glass brick that made up the wall behind the garden tub "—the flickering candles look remarkably like someone holding a flashlight. Like a burglar might? And I heard glass breaking. What was I supposed to think?"

"Oh. Oh, shit, I'm sorry." She winced, one hand coming up to cover her eyes and smearing green paste. *Yep*, he thought. *No idea she's naked.* "My plans got cancelled, and I broke a wine glass—did I hurt you?"

"Nah," he said, taking shameless advantage of her distraction to look his fill. She was all firm, lush curves, with full hips he knew would cradle him perfectly and lush breasts he was dying to get his hands on. Her nipples were wet from the water and puckered tight, and he imagined they'd look much the same after he finally got his mouth on her. He watched a trickle of bathwater wind its way from the underside of one breast, following it as it slid down the slight curve of her belly, detouring around her belly button before continuing down to disappear in the folds of her pussy.

Her bare pussy, he noted with a surge of lust. She either shaved or waxed, the lack of hair to shield her from his gaze making his gut tighten with desire. He imagined how she'd feel against his tongue, silky smooth and wet with her own passion, and had to suppress a shuddering groan at the thought.

He whipped his eyes back to meet hers as she dropped her hand. "You've got good aim, though," he continued easily, as though he hadn't been picturing her spread out like a buffet for his enjoyment. "If a burglar did break in here, he'd probably be lucky to get out alive."

She chuckled. "I played shortstop on my high school softball team."

"That would explain the aim." He fought a grin as she continued to kneel there, naked as a baby.

She shrugged, making her breasts bounce invitingly and causing his pulse to speed up. "I really am sorry. You scared me, and it's been a real pisser of a day," she said. Her voice went tight with anger, and he assumed that whatever had led up to the change in plans wasn't pleasant.

She suddenly shivered, the air in the bathroom cooling along with the bathwater, and he saw her face go slack with surprise as the light dawned.

"Holy shit," she breathed, looking down at herself in horror. She slapped one arm across her breasts, the other hand going to cover her exposed mound, and with a squeak, she fell back into the water and disappeared from view.

Jacob winced when he heard her head thump against the tub, but he didn't step any closer. "Are you all right?"

He heard a gurgling reply and grinned openly. "Tell me you're not drowning, Isa, so I don't have to come over and check for myself."

Instantly her head popped up over the edge of the tub. His grin widened when he saw her hair had come out of its clip, hanging half in her eyes as green water dripped off her face. "I'm fine," she sputtered. "Could you um... give me a few minutes? To get dressed?"

"Sure," he said. "I'll just wait for you in the kitchen."

"Thank you," she managed, her breath sighing out in relief, and he turned to go. He'd gone about four steps when he heard her agonized whisper, "Could this day get any worse?"

He grinned again as he continued down the hall to the kitchen. For him at least, the day had just gotten a whole lot better.

Chapter 2

Isa scrambled out of the tub as soon as she heard his footsteps fade down the hall, forgetting all about the broken glass and nearly slipping on the floor in her haste. "That'd put a cap on it," she muttered, her face burning with embarrassment. "I'll fall down, knock myself unconscious, and he'll have to come back and revive me. And then I'll just die of embarrassment and get it over with."

She shoved at the hair falling in her face, then stared at the green smear on her hand in horror. She dashed to the mirror over the sink, groaning when she saw what was left of her moisturizing mint mask sliding down her face. Uncaring what the paste would do to the towel, she grabbed it off the rack and wiped her face clean.

She poked her head out the door, making sure Jacob wasn't hovering in the hallway or standing where he could see her, then made the mad dash across the hall to her bedroom. She hastily dragged on a set of sweats, grabbed another hair clip off her dresser to tame the wet mess of her hair, then checked her appearance in the mirror.

"Not a total horror show," she muttered. At least her face wasn't green, and she wasn't naked any longer. She watched her cheeks turn pink as she remembered kneeling there in the tub, naked as a jay and oblivious, while Jacob stood there taking in the whole view.

Not that it mattered. He'd asked her out soon after she'd moved into the neighborhood, but he'd taken it well enough when she turned him down. He'd never given any indication since that he wasn't okay with maintaining their status quo as neighbors and friends, which was a good thing, even if she was madly attracted to him. If Joe, with his dark intensity and definite edge hadn't been okay with her kinky side, someone like Jacob was sure to freak right out over it. He was such an easy going, affable guy—she sure couldn't imagine him being masterful in the bedroom, or even knowing the difference between bondage rope and climbing rope. So it was best they keep on as neighbors and friends, even if he did set most of her bells and whistles to clanging.

"Just one of life's cruel ironies," she sighed. He was attracted to her, her panties started to squish whenever he smiled, but she was looking for kinky, and he wasn't it. She sighed again, made a face at herself in the mirror, and left the bedroom.

She detoured briefly to the bathroom to retrieve the bottle of wine—she had a feeling she was going to need it—then straightened her shoulders and headed down the hall to the kitchen.

She found Jacob sitting in her breakfast nook, both the gun and George on the table in front of him. The cat was purring like a motorboat under his stroking hands.

"You'll spoil him," she said mildly, nodding toward the cat. "He's not allowed on the table."

Jacob grinned and continued to scratch behind the tabby's ears. "Does he know that?"

Isa grimaced. "He knows, he just doesn't care. Watch. Bad kitty, get down!" George merely arched harder under Jacob's hand and smirked at her. "See?"

Jacob chuckled. "I see who's in charge around here."

Isa sighed. "Yeah, and it's not me." She glanced at the gun.

"Don't worry," he said, reading her mind. "I unloaded it. What are you drinking?"

"What? Oh!" She glanced at the bottle. "It's a really nice Pinot Grigio someone gave me. Would you like a glass?"

"Sure, that'd be great."

Grateful for something—anything!—to do, Isa retrieved a pair of glasses and carried them back to the dinette. She started to pour, then caught him looking at her with a bemused expression on his face. "Is something wrong?"

"No," he said, laughter coloring his voice. "But why does it say "juicy" across your ass?"

Isa laughed and poured out the wine. "I borrowed the sweats from my niece Jessica the last time I was at my sister's house. She's thirteen. Apparently advertising your ass as "juicy" is cool when you're thirteen." She handed Jacob a glass, then sat down across from him.

He took a sip. "This is nice." She nodded, taking a sip of her own wine. "You've been pretty scarce around here lately. Work keeping you busy?"

"I caught a big case," she explained. "A civil suit that could bring in a lot of money for the firm. They've made me lead counsel for it, so I've been putting in a lot of hours lately."

"Well, if you need any investigative work done on it, just let me know." He sipped his wine, watching her over the brim of the glass. "My calendar's pretty full these days, but if I can't handle it, I'm sure I could recommend someone who could."

She smiled. "Thanks, I'll remember that." She took another sip of wine and cast about for something, anything else to say.

"Nice rack, by the way."

Isa choked. "What?" she gasped, staring at him in shock.

He shrugged, broad shoulders shifting under the plain white t-shirt in a way that had her libido sitting up and taking notice. Again. "One of us had to say something."

She stared at him, pure shock keeping her mute for a full thirty seconds, then the laughter bubbled up. "I didn't even remember I was naked!" she managed between giggles.

"I could tell," he replied, green eyes dancing with mirth. "And I appreciated it."

"Well, you're welcome." She sighed, wiping away tears of mirth. "After the day I've had, I needed that laugh."

Jacob reached for the bottle to top off her glass. "Want to talk about it?"

"Oh, no," she said. "I mean, thanks. I really appreciate that, but you don't want to hear about my troubles."

He shrugged. "What are friends for? Sometimes it helps to talk it out."

Isa could feel her cheeks getting warm again. The thought of telling her very hunky neighbor that her boyfriend dumped her because she was too kinky was just... well, she couldn't do it. She shook her head.

He shrugged again. "Okay, but if you change your mind."

She smiled and picked up her wine. "Thanks."

Four glasses of wine later...

"It just sucks, you know?" She looked over at him from her upside down perch on the living room sofa. She lay with her back against the seat cushions, her legs up over the back and her head hanging down. "Dating is hard enough. Trying to find someone you're compatible with, that you have chemistry with."

"It's tough," he agreed, and drank from the bottle of water he'd gotten from her fridge. He must not be much of a wine drinker, she mused. He'd had one glass and switched to water.

She twisted around, giggling as the room swam lazily around her, until she was upright again. She shoved her hair out of her face and picked up her glass.

"Sometimes I think I should just give up," she sighed, and slumped back against the sofa cushions. "I should just put it all away, forget about it, and live a nice, sweet, normal vanilla life with a nice, sweet, normal vanilla guy."

"Vanilla?" he asked, and she looked up.

"Oops." She giggled. "I'm sort of rambling, aren't I?"

"A bit." He grinned, and she sighed.

"You're awful pretty, Jacob." She sat up, propped her wavering chin on her fist and gazed at him. "Do you shave your head?"

He grinned and ran a broad palm over his bare scalp. "Yeah. My hairline started to creep back in college, so shaving it is just easier."

"It's really hot," she said, and his grin broadened. Suddenly aware of what she was saying, she groaned. "I'm sorry. I can't seem to stop embarrassing myself tonight."

He laughed, the low chuckle vibrating down her spine. "I think it's charming."

She giggled again, and shook her finger at him in mock warning. "You know, if you weren't so nice..."

He raised an eyebrow. "Really? Nice as in... vanilla?"

"Oh boy," she said, and started to polish off her wine. She blinked in surprise when he nicked it neatly out of her hand. She watched him place it out of her reach on an end table with a sort of numb shock.

"I think you've had enough wine," he explained at her look of confusion. "What do you mean by vanilla?"

She frowned. "Are we getting personal? Because I'm going to need my wine if we're getting personal."

"Sweetie, I've seen you naked. We're already personal."

"Oh God," she groaned, and flopped back into the sofa cushions, covering her eyes with her hands as his chuckles rang in her ears. "Why do you have to keep bringing that up?"

"Hey, it was a great moment for me," he said. "I've been wondering what you look like naked ever since you moved in here. You have an amazing body."

She sat up at that, her hands flying off her eyes so she could see him. "Huh?"

He cocked his head, a gleam in his eye. "I said you have an amazing body."

That's what she thought he'd said. "I'm no skinny model, Jacob."

"Thank God," he said mildly, holding her disbelieving gaze with his. His eyes seemed to glitter like pale emeralds in the lamplight.

She cocked her head curiously, trying to ignore the curl of desire unfurling in her belly. "Most men like skinny models."

"Most men are morons, then," he replied. "A woman with lush curves—a woman like you—that's a lot sexier than getting poked by someone's rib bones."

She blinked, flabbergasted. "Geez."

He laughed. "That's all you have to say?"

She thought for a minute. "Pretty much."

He chuckled again. "Okay.

He kept staring at her, his gaze direct and unwavering, and the little curl of desire in her blood threatened to become a wave. "What were we talking about?" she asked desperately.

He grinned. "You were going to tell me what you meant by vanilla."

"No," she said carefully. "I'm pretty sure I wasn't."

He shrugged, the grin never leaving his face. "Okay, then let's get back to how fabulous your body is. Your breasts, for example, are particularly gorgeous. So full, with those tight little nipples that just beg to be sucked—"

"Okay, okay!" She held up a hand, covering her eyes with the other as if she could block out the picture he painted with his words. It didn't help that her nipples had tightened up and were now throbbing beneath her sweatshirt. "But gimme my wine back first."

She kept her eyes covered until she felt him put the wine glass in her outstretched hand, then took a fortifying gulp. Feeling braver with more alcohol in her system, she took her hand away, and immediately polished off the remaining liquid in the glass at the look on his face.

He raised an eyebrow. "Feel better?"

"Drunker, at least," she muttered. She gave a very unladylike belch, and his shoulders shook with silent laughter. "'Scuse me."

The laughter was evident in his voice when he spoke. "You going to tell me what vanilla means?"

She wracked her admittedly befuddled and impaired brain for a non-specific answer. "Plain."

He looked at her with reproach. "Come on, Isabella," he cajoled, her full name rolling off his tongue in a way that made her shiver. "Who had to ask his therapist if he could tie you up in bed?"

She frowned, confused. "Huh? Oh, that was Joe," she said, tipsy enough to not realize he'd overheard her muttering to herself in the tub. "He dumped me. He got spooked. Said I was 'too much'." She snorted, the wine making the words flow. "Wasn't like I asked him to put me on a meat hook and swing me around the room or anything. Just a little bondage, a slap on the ass once in a while, maybe a nipple clamp here and there. Was that too much to ask?" She shook her head, the room whirling. "I didn't think so, but maybe he's right. Maybe I'm 'too freaky'," she said, making quote marks with her fingers. She brought her wine glass to her mouth, frowning when she found it empty.

"Ah." Jacob drew the word out, and she looked up from her empty glass. He was looking at her with a knowing light in his eye. "You meant sexually vanilla."

She frowned. "Well, yeah."

"And you? You're not vanilla, are you Isabella?"

She sighed. "I tried to be," she murmured, her unfocused gaze completely missing the predatory and very interested gleam in his. "I really tried to be, but I have all these fantasies."

"What kind of fantasies?" he asked. His voice was a low murmur, unobtrusive, and she answered without thought.

"About being tied up," she said, wrapping her arms around herself in a hug. "Tied, pleasured, out of control." She sighed, feeling her body heat at the thought of it.

"Out of control?"

"Mmm. I like that," she said. She blinked, trying to bring his face into focus. His features were blurred, indistinct. "I like feeling out of control. It makes me feel free. Does that make sense?"

She thought she saw him smile. "Yes, it does."

"Oh. Good." She carefully set her wine glass on the coffee table. "Jacob?"

"Yes?"

"I have to pass out now," she informed him politely, then his blurry face disappeared into the darkness.

Chapter 3

Isa woke with a start, the previous night coming back to her in a rush. "Aw shit," she muttered. She was in her own bed, covered with the blanket she kept folded in her hope chest, and her head had that fuzzy, muddy feeling drinking too much wine always left her with.

She took a quick peek under the blanket, sighing with relief when she saw she still had on Jessica's sweats. "Thank God for small favors," she muttered. Unfortunately, other than the fuzziness, her head was clear and her memory intact. Which meant she remembered every detail of her wine-induced confessional.

She winced, her face flushing with mortification when she recalled the things that had come out of her mouth. "Oh, I'll never be able to look him in the eye again," she muttered, then froze in horror. Obviously he'd put her to bed—she'd passed out in the living room, after all—but was he still here?

She quickly scrambled out of bed, padding silently on bare feet out to the living room. She sagged with relief when she found it empty, then checked the kitchen for good measure. The only evidence that he'd been in the house at all was the extra wine glass next to the sink, and the empty water bottle in the recycling bin.

She said a silent prayer of thanksgiving that she didn't have to face Jacob yet and pulled a bottle of water from the refrigerator. She was slightly dehydrated from all the wine and guzzled the whole thing, feeling instantly better when she was finished. George came running into the kitchen, meowing for his breakfast, so she filled his dish before going back to the bedroom to change.

She moved by habit, changing quickly into running shorts and a sports bra. She pulled her hair back into a ponytail and tucked her spare house key into the tiny inner pocket of her shorts before heading to the back door. Her running shoes were set neatly aside, and she pulled them on quickly. She moved automatically through a series of stretches, purposefully blanking her mind and focusing on the stretch and pull of her muscles.

When she was sufficiently warmed up, she left the house and started towards the woods at a jog.

She set an easy pace, running along the well-worn path. It was barely six o'clock in the morning, and she had the popular jogging trail to herself. She was both grateful and disappointed for the solitude; grateful because she didn't want to have to talk to any of her friends this morning, and disappointed because the lack of distraction made it too easy for thoughts of the night before to come creeping in.

She thought of the highly personal information she'd let slip in her inebriated state and quickened her pace as though she could outrun her own behavior. She wasn't worried about Jacob telling anyone; if she'd learned anything about him in the six months they'd been neighbors, it was that he was unfailingly discreet. Discretion was his business—he could hardly be a successful private investigator if he made a habit of blabbing secrets. She'd never even heard him talk about any of his dates, and neither had any of the other women in the neighborhood. She knew because whenever any of them got together, he was always a hot topic of conversation.

No, she wasn't worried about him spilling her beans, but that didn't mean she was comfortable with him knowing her innermost desires.

She winced and ran harder. Part of the problem was she was still raw from Joe's rejection. As much as she understood that she was better off knowing now that he couldn't handle her needs, it still chaffed that he'd broken things off with her in such a cowardly manner. Knowing it was his problem and not hers didn't make her feel like less of an oddity, less of a freak.

And she didn't like the idea of Jacob thinking of her as a freak, too. Especially since he'd shown some definite interest after seeing her naked in the tub. She didn't think he'd sounded repulsed by her admissions last night, but the truth was she wasn't sure. She'd passed out pretty quickly after letting the cat out of the bag, so she really had no idea what his reaction was. But before that... .oh, there'd been definite interest.

She shivered, her skin popping out in goose bumps as she remembered the predatory gleam he'd had in his eye. He was attractive as hell, with his bald head, strong features and heavily muscled physique that she assumed came in handy in his work. The overall effect would have been intimidating if he'd been a dark and brooding sort, but his casual and affable humor made it easy to be comfortable around him. He laughed a lot, always had a smile and a teasing wink, making him adorably boyish despite his imposing physical presence. His personality was one of the things that had attracted her to him, but it was also the main reason she'd never gone out with him. How could someone so carefree and funny be intense enough in bed?

But last night, when the spark of interest had lit his eyes? Oh my, that had been intense. The humor was still there, the approachability unchanged, but the palpable sexual tension in the air had lent a dark edge to his normally easy going manner, and despite the wine induced haze, she'd felt the effect from her head all the way down to her toes, with a few interesting stops in between.

She mulled that over as she made the turn that would take her out of the woods and back through the neighborhood to her front door. She was definitely interested, and was seriously rethinking her original stance on dating her handsome neighbor. But without knowing how he felt about what she'd said, she was at a bit of a loss as to how to proceed. Should she wait for him to come to her and bring up the subject, or should she bite the bullet and seek him out?

She gnawed the inside of her cheek and slowed to a brisk walk, beginning her cool down routine a block from home while her brain continued to spin possibilities. There was the chance he wouldn't want to talk to her at all, that he'd be as freaked out as Joe had been and would start avoiding her altogether.

That thought depressed the heck out of her and she frowned, staring at the pavement as she turned to walk up her driveway. She was so caught up in thoughts of Jacob never speaking to her again that she didn't notice him sitting on her front stoop until she tripped over his feet.

She squealed and pitched forward, arms pin wheeling as she tried to catch her balance. He tried to move out of her way, but their legs tangled together and gravity conspired against her, and she collapsed in a heap on top of him.

"Shit!" he said.

"Fuck," she moaned.

"You okay?" he grunted.

She nodded, her head bumping into his sternum. "You?"

"Yeah, all good here."

"That's good," she mumbled. She didn't move, and after a moment he cleared his throat. She could feel his chest vibrate under her forehead.

"If you're okay, could you try moving? This isn't all that comfortable for me."

She took a fortifying breath and braced her hands on either side of his rib cage. "Okay." She pushed herself up, purposefully not looking at his face, and tried to slide off to the side. But her feet were still tangled up in his, and she lost her balance again, falling back into him with a thump.

"You know what?" he said, his voice strangled. He grasped her elbow and pushed it off of his stomach with a grunt. "You stay put. This time, I'll move."

She nodded again, embarrassment threatening to swallow her whole. It was getting to be a familiar feeling. "Okay."

She felt him wrap his arms around her, one hand coming up to cradle the back of her skull, then he tucked her in close and rolled them both over in one smooth move, and just like that she was under him.

They lay there for a moment in a sort of suspended animation, both of them barely breathing. Isa felt like she was having a hot flash, and the feel of his big hard body pressed into hers was making her stomach do cartwheels. She was still trying to get a grip on her rioting hormones when he suddenly shifted, pushing himself up on his arms and lifting the broad weight of his torso off her chest, and she stifled a gasp. The action pushed his lower body more firmly into hers, fitting neatly into the cradle of her hips. And with her legs in a sprawl from her fall, she got a very clear picture of just what he was hiding under those snug jeans.

And it pretty much settled the question of whether or not he was attracted to her.

He made a noise somewhere between a growl and a whimper, his eyes glittering and his mouth grim as held himself perfectly still. "I'm going to get up now."

She nodded. "That'd be good," she whispered, and braced herself.

He took a deep breath and pushed up and off her, gaining his feet in one swift move. She stayed where she was, in an awkward sprawl on her front porch, unable to move. Her hormones were clamoring at her to yank him back down, wrap her legs around him, and ride out the lust, and she was too busy telling them to shush to get up.

Jacob was having problems of his own. Isa was just lying there, arms and legs akimbo in what should not have been a sexy pose. But she was only wearing a running bra and shorts, and he could see her nipples poking up at him through the spandex. His dick was screaming at him to lay back down and bury himself in her, and he gritted his teeth against the urge.

"Are you hurt?" he managed, his teeth practically grinding.

"No, I'm okay," she said, her voice breathy and faint in a way that made his dick even harder, and he imagined it'd carry the imprint of his zipper if he stayed this way for much longer. She half pushed herself up on her elbows, thrusting her breasts forward, and he lost it.

She squealed in surprise as his hands closed over her upper arms and lifted her up. She dangled there, a full foot off the ground, and her stunned gaze flew to his face.

"Sorry," he muttered. "But I have to." And slammed his mouth down on hers.

Her mouth had fallen open in shock when he picked her up, and he took ruthless advantage, his tongue sweeping in to tangle with hers. That seemed to penetrate the fog of her surprise, and her hands came up to grip his t-shirt in her fists as she kissed him back.

He groaned, yanking her closer and wrapping his arms around her. Her pelvis nudged his, her legs automatically parting to allow for the hard jut of his cock. He tore his mouth from hers on a hiss, and her eyes popped open.

He knew how he must look. His jaw was clenched, his teeth practically grinding with the effort it took not to fuck her on the front porch. She cleared her throat. "So, I guess I didn't spook you last night, huh?" she managed.

He gave a harsh laugh. "No." He set her on her feet and took a step back, reaching up to peel her hands off his t-shirt. "Sorry. I didn't mean to get into this just yet."

"Oh. Okay."

"I stopped by to see if you were okay after last night." He bent down and picked up a mug from the edge of the porch. "I brought you a cup of coffee."

"Okay."

Despite the effort it was taking to rein in his raging libido, that got a small smile out of him. "Is that all you're going to say?"

She nodded. "Yeah."

He grinned. "Why don't you invite me in, Isa?"

She nodded again and turned blindly toward the door, fumbling the key out of the pocket of her shorts. "Okay."

He chuckled as she opened the door, following her into the narrow foyer that suddenly seemed a lot narrower. "I… I'm going to take a shower," she managed.

He nodded, his eyes twinkling at her as he tried not to laugh. "Okay. I'll wait in the kitchen." He winked and walked down the hall towards the kitchen, letting the chuckle loose when he heard her feet scramble down the hall.

She stood where she was until he disappeared into her breakfast nook, then suddenly burst into action, dashing down the hall and into the bathroom before the front door had swung shut.

She raced through her shower, soaping and scrubbing and shampooing as fast as she could. Barely taking the time to dry off, she wrapped her hair in a towel and dashed across the hall to the bedroom. She dug out a matching bra and panty set and yanked them on so fast she nearly tore the delicate mint green lace. She tugged on white shorts and a tank top that was slightly darker than the bra, slathered on moisturizer, then went to work on her hair.

Thankfully, having naturally curly hair made it fast and easy to do. She just rubbed her head briskly with the towel to soak up all the excess water, then squirted a blob of scrunching gel into her hands and finger combed it through the curls. She swiped at her lashes with the mascara wand, slicked on a layer of lip gloss, and she was ready to go.

She ducked into the closet for a pair of white canvas flats and was shoving her feet into them when she caught her reflection in the full-length mirror on the back of the closet door. She paused for a moment, a little startled at her reflection. Her eyes were sparkling, her cheeks flushed with color despite her lack of blusher, and her lips had a slight, knowing curve to them.

"Wow," she whispered, pressing a hand to her belly to quell the butterflies. She looked aroused; there was no way he could mistake the look in her eyes—or the thrust of her hardened nipples through the thin cotton of the tank top. "Okay, Isabella, get a grip." She took a deep breath and let it out slowly. "We don't have sex on the first date," she told her reflection. Then she remembered the very definite happy-to-see-her bulge in his jeans when he kissed her. "Okay, so we'll just try not to have sex with him until after at least one cup of coffee."

Happy with the compromise, she started to head out, but the trilling of her cell phone stopped her. Impatient, she crossed quickly to the bedside table where it sat charging and flipped it open. "Hello?"

"Isabella? Hi, it's me. Joe."

Stunned, Isa's mouth opened and closed without any sound emerging for a full five seconds before she managed a choked, "Joe?"

"How are you?"

She blinked. "Ah... I'm fine. How're you?" she asked, then winced. She didn't really care, but a lifetime of ingrained manners had the words coming out before she could stop them.

"Good, good. I wanted to make sure. You know, that you were okay. I worried that you weren't."

"Well, I am." Confused, she frowned at her reflection in the mirror, then leaned in closer. Was that a zit? Dammit, she had the finest man in six counties waiting in her kitchen, she couldn't have a zit!

She stopped examining her chin when she heard Joe say, "Okay, 'cause I was worried about you. You know, that you might be upset. And I wanted to tell you, I don't think you're a bad person or anything."

She winced. "I appreciate that, Joe. I don't think you're a bad person either." An insensitive jerk with no manners, she thought with an eye roll, but not necessarily bad.

"Well, of course you don't," he said, the baffled note in his voice unexpectedly tickling her funny bone so she had to stifle a giggle. "And I also wanted to say I hope we can be friends. Still. After everything, you know, that happened. I mean, I don't hold a grudge or anything."

"Sure, Joe, me neither." She said, startled to realize she meant it. Her venom of the night before had faded, disintegrating in the face of this new development with Jacob. She tapped her foot impatiently, anxious to get out to the kitchen and continue developing it. "Listen, I have to go."

"Oh. Okay, so we'll talk later. Maybe I can call you this week, just to make sure you're, you know, okay."

"Uh-huh, sure," she said absently. "Talk to you later." She clicked the phone closed on his stuttered goodbye, shaking her head. "I guess the world really is made for those with no self awareness," she muttered as she headed out of the bedroom.

Unfortunately, she wasn't one of them. She felt very self aware as she went down the hall, her hands fluttering nervously by her sides. She curled her fingers into fists, took a deep breath and strode into the kitchen.

Jacob was leaning up against her counter, drinking his cup of coffee and stroking her cat, who was on the counter next to the sink purring like a motorboat under his hands. She had a sudden visual of him stroking those hands over her bare flesh and felt like purring herself.

He grinned at her over the rim of the mug. "What I wouldn't give to know what's going on in your head right now."

She cleared her throat. "I thought that was my cup of coffee," she said, pointing to the cup in his hand.

He chuckled and passed the mug, turning it in his palm so the side he'd drunk from faced her. She lifted the cup to her lips, unable to resist watching him as she drank. The heat in his eyes nearly made her choke on the coffee.

"Good coffee," she said, her voice sounding like she was being strangled, and he grinned.

"So, how's your head after last night?"

She sipped coffee. "Fine. I don't really get hangovers, I just feel kind of fuzzy the morning after. The run took care of that."

"No hangovers, huh?" He was still stroking the cat, the loud purring echoing through the room. "So I assume that means you remember everything, too."

"Oh yeah," she said grimly. "I remember everything. Unfortunately."

The last word was said in a mutter, and he laughed. "Why unfortunately?"

She rolled her eyes. "Well, I'm embarrassed. I spilled my guts last night."

"Are you sorry you did?"

She looked up at that, her eyes flickering over his face as she tried to gauge his mood. His eyes were serious, his face impassive as he waited for her answer. "No," she said slowly. "I guess not. Especially in light of…" she gestured vaguely.

"The make out session on your front porch?"

Her mouth twisted wryly. "More like the dry hump on my front porch," she muttered, and watched his lips twitch with suppressed humor. "It doesn't bother you?"

"What, that you're kinky?" He shrugged. "Nope. Everybody has something they like that's a tad unusual. I had a girlfriend once who liked to pretend she was a jungle cat when we had sex."

Isa blinked. "What, she liked to growl?"

He nodded. "And scratch, and bite, and yowl."

Isa felt a grin tickle her lips. "I do all that as a human."

"Yeah, but do you lick your own genitals clean when you're done?"

Isa burst out laughing, nearly dropping the coffee cup. "Oh Jesus," she managed, blinking away tears of mirth. She looked up at his grinning face. "No, I don't. But I can't bend my body that way."

"Yeah, she was double jointed." He grinned at the memory, and she rolled her eyes again. "But my point is everybody's got something. There's nothing to be embarrassed about."

"I know, I'm sorry." She waved her hand. "I'm just not used to talking about this so frankly with a man. I mean, I talk about this with my friends, but it's something I'm always really careful about with guys."

He tilted his head, curious. "Why?"

"Well, I get one of two reactions. They either freak out, like in Joe's case. Or they're really into it, in a super creepy, super skeezy kind of way."

"Ah." He nodded. "Yeah, I can see that. Can I ask you a personal question?"

"Considering the topic under discussion, I don't see why not."

"Have you ever considered trying to date in the local kink community?"

"You mean the leather scene? BDSM? All that stuff? Sure," she said when he nodded. "That was worse."

"How do you mean?"

"Well, no one was put off by my kinky side, so that was a big plus. But the master/slave thing isn't for me, and jeez, everyone seemed to take it all so seriously! No one seemed to be having any fun."

His lips twitched. "Yeah, I can see that."

She shrugged. "It wasn't really that horrible, it just wasn't for me. I wasn't looking to swing, or to just play. I'm looking for a relationship, and I'm not big on being naked in public. It was just the wrong place for me, I wasn't comfortable." She frowned. "How do you know so much about it?"

He shrugged. "Before I answer that, I have another question."

"Okay," she agreed warily.

"When you first moved in, and I asked you out—was the reason you turned me down because I seem too vanilla?"

She took a deep breath. "Yeah."

He nodded, his expression unchanged. "Okay."

He didn't say anything else, and she hastened to explain. "It's not that I'm not attracted to you. I am. A lot. It's just… it's been really hard for me in the last year or so, trying to find someone who would be okay with this part of me. It's been especially hard for me when I find someone I'm really attracted to, and then I find out they can't deal with it." She shrugged, sheepish. "I know it's sort of cowardly."

"Little bit," he agreed.

"Well, I didn't know you," she protested, feeling a little persecuted. "And I'm pretty careful about who I talk to about this. For all I knew you could have been the neighborhood gossip, and my yen for bondage would end up being the main topic of conversation at the next neighborhood association meeting."

"Okay, I concede that point." He stopped stroking the cat, crossing both arms across his chest and pinning her with his gaze. George mrowed his discontent at being ignored and hopped off the counter. "But that was six months ago. You've had time to get to know me now. You know I don't sleep around, or talk about what goes on in my bedroom. So what's your excuse now?"

"Well, you're really happy."

He blinked. "Huh?"

She shifted her weight, trying to find a way to explain herself that wouldn't be insulting. "You're the boy next door, Jacob. You're fun, and kind, and sort of goofy sometimes. I just… couldn't see you being into anything like bondage, or kinky sex, or anything like that."

"Hmmm." He just kept looking at her. "So because I'm happy, and kind, I'm automatically vanilla."

"Nuts." She closed her eyes briefly, then forced herself to face him again. "I'm making a mess of this, and I'm sorry. It's just… every guy I've ever met who's into this kind of stuff has this intensity to them. An edge, a kind of darkness that you just don't have. So I really… I just assumed it wasn't your thing."

"Okay." He nodded. He was looking over her shoulder, at the table in the breakfast nook. She looked behind her, curious to see what was holding his attention, and saw George batting at something on the table.

"George, no," she said. Grateful for the distraction, she went over to shoo him away. "Bad George. You know you're not allowed on the table." She frowned when she reached the table, ignoring the cat's indignant hiss as she pushed him off. Confused, she fingered bundle of rope that lay there. "I didn't have this out," she murmured. Her bundles of rope were in the duffle bag she'd packed for her weekend with Joe. She turned back to Jacob. He was still leaning against the counter, watching her with an inscrutable intensity that made her chest feel tight.

"Did I get this out last night?" she asked, holding the neat bundle of crimson rope in her hands.

"No," he said. The little half smile he gave her made all the little hairs on her skin stand up. "That's mine."

Chapter 4

"Huh?" Isa blinked, not understanding. "It looks like mine." She twisted her head so she could see the front door, and yep, there was her overnight bag sitting right where she dropped it when she came home the night before. Still packed, with her rope still in it. "This is yours?"

Jacob walked toward her and took the rope from her hands. He released the knot on the bundle with a flick of his wrist, the rope spilling out to dangle from his fingertips, the ends pooling on the floor as it unraveled. She watched, transfixed, as he gathered it up again, running it through his fingers in a way that dried up all the spit in her mouth.

"It's mine," he said, his voice a low rumble. "You have some?"

"Ah…" She swallowed, forcing her eyes away from the way his hands kept stroking the rope and up to his face. Then she wished she hadn't—her happy, kind, humor filled neighbor was looking at her with a quiet intensity she'd never expected to see from him. "Yeah."

"Hemp rope, like this?"

She nodded. "It's even the same color."

His mouth twitched slightly, but the display of humor didn't detract from his intensity one bit, a feat that was making her increasingly nervous.

"Well, look at that. We have similar tastes." Her hand was still outstretched between them, palm up. He let the rope he was running through his hands trail over her wrist, raising goose bumps, and she shivered. He smiled slightly and did it again, then casually looped the rope around her wrist.

She swallowed heavily, her free hand coming up to hover between them, palm out as though she meant to keep him at arm's length. "What're you doing?"

Her voice quivered, and the slight smile on his face kicked up a notch. "Just playing with the rope," he said, his voice low. "I like to do that, you know. Play with rope."

"You do?" she managed. She knew she was breathing too fast, and tried to slow it down, but when she did that it only made her pulse thunder in her ears and she missed what he said. "What?"

"Yes," he repeated, "I do." He looped the rope around her other wrist, slowly, watching her face carefully, and she realized he was giving her the chance to protest. And she meant to, she really did. And she would. In a minute.

"I play with rope a lot," he continued, his emerald gaze so intent on her face she barely noticed when he looped the rope around both wrists again. "I like the feel of it."

Isa had to clear her throat twice before her voice would work. "Me too," she finally squeaked out, and he smiled.

"I thought you might," he drawled, the southern in his voice making her go over in gooseflesh. He'd stopped twining the rope around her wrists and was holding the ends between her hands, but she was so riveted by his voice she barely noticed. "Last night, hearing you talk about your fantasies? It was all I could do not to run home, grab my rope, and spend the whole night making all of them come true."

Holy shit! "Really?"

"Really." His eyes had gone darker, the sparkling green turning to a dark mossy shade. She had the slightly uncomfortable feeling that he could see past all her defenses and right into the heart of her. "Do you remember what you told me last night?"

She swallowed hard. "Yes."

One eyebrow went up, his eyes narrowing slightly. "What did you tell me, Isabella? What did you say your fantasy was?"

Oh my God, he wants me to say it out loud! "I... I said I wanted to be tied up."

"Yes. And you told me why, do you remember that?"

She nodded. "Because it makes me feel out of control."

"And you like that, don't you?" His voice had gone low and soft, so soft she almost had to strain to hear him. "You like feeling out of control, like anything could happen and you'd be powerless to stop it."

Isa's heart was beating so hard she was half afraid it would pound right out of her chest and land with a splat at his feet. "Yes," she whispered, so overwhelmingly turned on she could barely breathe.

"Are you attracted to me, Isa?" His hands were moving again as he spoke, passing the ends of the rope over and around the lines that connected her wrists once, twice, before tying them off in a knot.

She gulped. "Yes," she said, and looked down, away from the intensity in his gaze. Her eyes lit on her bound hands and she jolted at the sight. Her wrists were turned in, palms facing as though she was getting ready to clap, and the rope glowed bright red against her skin. She twisted her wrists experimentally. She could move with surprising ease, the rope shifting and pulling with her movements and yet still holding her snugly.

He gave the end of the rope he still held a tug, bringing her gaze flying back to his. He had one eyebrow raised, whether in expectation or question she wasn't sure.

"It's lovely, you know."

Her confusion must have shown on her face, and he elaborated. "Your skin, your hands, caught up in my rope." He tugged the line again, making her breath catch in her throat as her pulse quickened and her mouth went dry. He caught the quick dart of her tongue coming out to wet her lips, and the corners of his own mouth turned up in a slight smile that did nothing to quiet the hammer of her heart.

"How does it look to you, Isa?"

She didn't pretend not to understand what he meant. "Strange," she admitted, her voice a dark rasp. "I'm not used to it."

His gaze turned curious. "Not used to it how?"

She cleared her throat. "Well, I've been tied up before. But my hands were behind my back, or over my head. I've never… seen myself. You know?"

He hummed an agreement, his eyes never leaving hers. "How does it make you feel? Seeing yourself bound."

"Tight."

Both eyebrows went up at that. "Tight?"

She nodded, swallowing hard. "My chest, my stomach. Everything feels… tight."

"Ah." His face cleared, the confusion replaced with satisfaction. "Like you're wound up, waiting for something?"

She nodded, her breath easing out on a sigh of relief that he understood. The breath caught in her throat a moment later as he stepped closer, his feet bracketing hers and his torso pushing against chest. She instinctively moved back, then froze when she came up against the table.

Her eyes felt wide as saucers as she looked up at him, the slight, knowing smile on his face making the coil of tension in her abdomen wind even tighter. "There's nowhere to go, Isa," he whispered. His head came down alongside hers so he whispered right in her ear. "Nowhere to go," he repeated, his warm breath washing over her skin and making her shiver, "unless you want to." He paused for a moment, the only sound in the room the ragged sound of her breathing. "Do you want to go, Isa?"

She shook her head so violently she almost knocked into him. He pulled back slightly so she could see his eyes, the lust in their dark green depths filling her whole vision. "Say it, Isa," he commanded, his voice rough and unyielding. "Tell me you don't want to go."

"I don't want to go," she said, her voice barely a whisper and thready with need.

"That's good," he murmured, both soothing and enticing. "Now, what do you want?"

She stood mute, the words refusing to form. She was so excited she could barely think, her panties flooded with her own moisture and her nipples almost unbearably tight, and she could only think *more*. More of this feeling of being held, controlled, seduced, more of this dark stranger looking at her from the eyes of the boy next door.

He smiled at her, his face so close to hers their breath mingled. "Nothing to say?" he murmured. "Then why don't I tell you what I want?"

Oh, yes, Isa thought, and braced herself.

He kept his eyes on hers when he spoke, holding her still as surely as if he'd had her in shackles. "I want to use more of my rope on you. I have so much more rope, Isabella. I want to see it on you. There are so many different ways I want to tie you. Spread out, like a feast for my eyes, my mouth. My cock."

A hard shudder went through her as he pushed the cock in question against the soft flesh of her abdomen. She felt hyper sensitive, her skin tingling all over, and she writhed in his embrace as his words washed over her.

"Or curled up in a ball, arms bound to legs, feet to hands. You wouldn't be able to do anything except take what I want to give you."

She whimpered out loud at the image, her pussy clenching and pulsing with lust, and he growled at the sound.

"You like that, don't you Isa?" He tugged on her hands again, reminding her of her bonds. "You like the idea of being at my mercy, unable to keep me from doing whatever I want to that delectable little body of yours. Oh, the things I would do to you… shall I tell you?"

He didn't wait for her to answer, which was good considering the only word she was capable of uttering was "gah". The hand that wasn't holding her bound wrists came up to glide over her face, tracing her eyebrows, her nose, her lips. She boldly let her tongue flicker out to taste his skin, and his eyes darkened even further.

"If I had you bound," he went on, "helpless to keep me from touching you, I think I'd want to touch you here first." He laid his hand on her breast, the thin tank top and even thinner bra no barrier against the heat and pressure of him, and she jumped at the contact. She moved instinctively, her hands coming up and then jerking to a stop. He still held the ends of the rope in his hands, preventing her hands from rising any higher than her midriff, and the sudden reminder of being restrained was like a shot of whiskey on an empty stomach—it went straight to her head.

His hand lay unmoving on her breast as he tugged her hands back down, gently but firmly, watching her face carefully, and she realized he was giving her time to stop him. After a moment, when she made no further move to protest, he flexed his hand. She let her eyes drift shut and a moan escape her lips as his fingers squeezed her breast, already swollen and aching with desire. He rotated his palm slowly, rubbing her nipple against the fragile lace of her bra, and the moan became a whimper.

"So responsive," he murmured, his voice close to her ear again. "So firm and beautiful. I remember what these looked like yesterday, the water from your bath beading on the pink, hard tips. It made me want to curl my tongue around them and suck." He punctuated the words with a firm tug on the aching tip. She leaned into his touch, then let out a surprised yelp, eyes flying open as he twisted slightly, pinching the tender flesh deliciously. "And I wanted to nibble with my teeth."

Isa whimpered, her nipple throbbing in time with the pounding of her heart, her underwear soaked. "Oh Jesus," she whispered. "Yes."

"Yes?" he asked. His lips touched hers, the barest brush of skin against skin that left her yearning for more Much, much more. "Yes, what? What do you need, Isabella?"

"More," she moaned. Her hands flexed in their bonds, twisting and pulling against the grip of the rope. The delicious friction of it made her ache, and her whole body began to twist and flex against him.

"More?" he murmured. She felt him shift, his hand moving to grip the rope where it linked her wrists together, and in one swift move he'd leaned back, yanked her arms up and leaned back in to press her back against the table. He carried her arms up, over her head, bringing her wrists to rest behind her neck, elbows up by her ears.

She blinked, startled by the sudden shift in position, and gave her arms a testing flex. His hold was firm, and unlike before, unyielding—she had no room to maneuver. He pressed his body into hers from breast to knee, and with her hands no longer between them, she felt every firm, muscled inch of him.

"How much more, Isabella?" he growled. He nudged her knees apart, sliding his leg between hers and lifting her off her feet. With her arms bound she couldn't brace herself, and she let out a gasp as his hard thigh took her weight. She slid forward, away from the table and into him, his jeans rubbing against the sensitive, swollen folds of her pussy through the thin material of her shorts and panties. She groaned, her eyes drifting closed, and he let go of her wrists. Before she the sudden sense of freedom could register, he had grabbed hold of the trailing end the rope, wrapping his fist around it. He tugged hard, his fist tucked firmly in the small of her back, and the action arched her firmly into his chest.

"How much more?" he whispered. "This much more?" He slammed his mouth down on hers, his tongue driving past her lips to tangle deeply with hers. She returned the kiss eagerly, squirming, fighting to get closer. The friction on her clit was driving her crazy, the swollen little bud throbbing in time with the rapid beat of her heart, but it wasn't enough.

He tore his mouth from hers, his breath coming hard and fast. She whimpered and tried to recapture his lips, leaning forward only to be brought up short as he tightened his grip on her bonds. She whimpered again, frustration building along with desire, and he chuckled.

Her eyes flew open at the sound, the protest dying on her lips when she saw the look on his face. Despite the chuckle, he didn't look amused. He looked hungry, predatory, and she was the prey. His eyes traveled down her torso, and she looked down at herself, trying to see her body through his eyes.

Her back was bent slightly, the arch held by the position of her arms and the hold he had on the rope that bound her wrists. Her breasts were thrust high, straining against the confines of her tank top that had ridden up to expose the smooth expanse of her belly. Her hips were trapped against his, her legs dangling on either side of his jeans clad thigh. She looked, she thought, like a woman in serious lust.

Almost before she could complete thought, his free hand came up to rest on her exposed stomach. The muscles there quivered at the contact, clenching involuntarily under the weight of his hand. Against the pale skin of her stomach his hand looked impossibly big, hard where she was soft. It made her feel small and delicate, like he could pick her up and carry her around like a doll, and the thought of that was so arousing she nearly came right then.

"How much more?" he asked again. His hand slid up her torso, shoving the tank top up above her breasts. His eyes glittered with lust as he traced the edge of lace that barely restrained her flesh with callused fingertips.

"More," she hissed, and arched into his hand, aching for firmer contact.

He growled and shoved the delicate lace cup down and off one breast, baring the nipple to his hungry gaze. He wrapped his hand around the exposed flesh, plumping her breast up as he bent his head. He flicked his tongue over the rigid peak once, twice, then pulled back to blow cool air over the damp flesh.

Isa writhed with frustration, so aroused she could barely think. "More," she wailed, and lifting one leg to wrap around his hip for leverage, pushed herself up towards his mouth.

"You still want more?" he rumbled, his fist pushing hard against the small of her back, and his mouth descended on her aching breast. He didn't tease, but simply used his tongue to push her nipple against the roof of his mouth and sucked hard.

"Fuck," she whimpered, her hips rolling restlessly against him as the heat built with every tug of his mouth. "Yes, oh please more!"

He released her breast and moved to the other, shoving aside the lace cup and treating it to the same rough treatment. She moaned and cried and twisted against him, desperately seeking relief as lust rolled through her.

By the time he raised his head, her hips were bucking against him convulsively and she was straining against her bonds. She'd long ago stopped making sense, a constant stream of pleas and moans emanating from her lips as she fought for the orgasm that he was holding just out of reach.

"What do you want, Isa?" he asked. She didn't hear him, her head tossing mindlessly in lust. He fisted a hand in her hair, jerking her to a stop, and her eyes flew open in shock. "Tell me," he demanded, and her pussy clenched down at the command. "Tell me what you want."

"I want... I need..."

"Come on, baby. Tell me what you need and I'll give it to you." His voice was like dark velvet, a seduction she couldn't resist even if she wanted to.

"I need to come," she moaned. "Please make me come, please!"

"How close are you, hmmm?" he purred. He let go of her hair, his hand gliding down to her thigh to slip under the hem of her shorts. He teased, gliding one finger along the edge of her panties. "How wet are you?"

She hissed, arching hard when he slipped his finger under the panties, gliding through the pool of wetness to her opening and pushing inside with one hard motion. She cried out, her hips bucking and her pussy clamping down on the intruding finger.

"You're soaking wet," he murmured. He moved forward, pushing her butt against the edge of the table for support as he shoved the crotch of her shorts and panties aside. He worked another finger in beside the first. "Look how wet you are for me, Isabella. So wet, so hot, just from a little bondage and some foreplay." He pumped his fingers into her slowly, curling the tips up to tickle her g-spot on the in thrust and twisting them on the way out.

She went wild, hips pumping madly. Her eyes were wide and unfocussed, her entire being straining for the orgasm she could feel bearing down on her like a freight train. He shifted her suddenly, laying her back on the table, and she immediately wrapped both legs around his waist in an effort to gain more leverage. But he held her down, coming down on top of her and using his strength and weight to pin her to the table. With his fist still holding the rope in the small of her back she stayed arched, her breasts pushing up into his chest.

"Look at you," he repeated, his voice a near growl with his own arousal. "Such a little rope slut." He pressed his hand harder between her thighs, grinding his palm into her clit and rotating it as he pushed his fingers into her, high and hard, and the added stimulus was all she needed to fly shrieking into orgasm.

Long moments later Isa found the strength to speak. "Am I dead?"

She heard Jacob chuckle and pried her eyes open. He was standing over her, watching her intently and gently rubbing her wrists, bare but for the ligature marks.

"When did you take off the rope?"

"Just now," he murmured.

"Oh," she said, and he laughed softly at the disappointment in her voice.

"Sorry," he said. "You were a little out of it, so I thought it best to untie you."

"S'ok," she sighed, her eyes sliding closed with pleasure as he continued his massage, moving from her wrists to her upper arms and shoulders. She became aware of a slight stiffness in her shoulders and rotated them experimentally.

"Are your shoulders sore?" he asked, and she opened her eyes.

"A little bit," she admitted. "Nothing drastic."

"That's normal for the position you were in," he assured her. "How are you feeling otherwise?"

"Ah... pretty damn good." She gave him a sleepy grin. "How about you? You didn't...?"

He grinned back. "No, I didn't. Don't worry, we'll get to it." His grin widened at the startled look on her face. "You didn't think I was finished with you, did you?"

"Well... you untied me," she said. "I kind of figured you were done."

"For now, yes," he allowed. He slid his hands back down her arms to capture her hands and tug her into a sitting position. She looked down and immediately blushed; her tank top was still shoved up under her arms, the cups of her bra tugged down to expose her breasts, and her shorts were twisted to the side.

He chuckled at her blush and set about putting her back together, his hands stroking over her as he rearranged her clothes. She shivered, a little awed by how quickly her body responded to him, and of course he noticed.

"You're delicious," he murmured, his lips meeting hers in a tender kiss. "Are you sure you're all right?"

"I'm a little shaky," she admitted. "Kinda thirsty."

"Here, take a sip." He pressed a bottle of water into her hands, and she gratefully gulped the cool liquid.

"Any bad moments in there?" he asked, his hands stroking her arms, and she shook her head.

"Um... no, not really." She started to say something else, then stopped, concentrating on putting the cap back on the water bottle.

"What?" he asked.

She shook her head. "It's nothing, really. Just... when you called me a rope slut..."

"You didn't like that?"

"No, it's not that," she admitted, looking up at him through her lashes. "I did like it. I just didn't expect to."

"Ah," he grinned. "Well, I meant it as a compliment, not an insult."

"Well, I took it as a compliment," she said, blushing furiously, and he laughed.

"Good," he said, and kissed her again before helping her to slide off the table.

"Whoa," she said, clinging to him as her legs gave out on her. "Noodle knees."

"Here," he said, and stunned her completely by scooping her up into his arms and carrying her into the living room. She squeaked out a protest, which he ignored, and settled onto the sofa with her on his lap.

"What are your plans for the rest of the day?" he asked, and she blinked, the normalcy of the question taking her by surprise.

"Ah... well, I was going to call Nelson, see if he can meet me for lunch." She glanced at the clock on the wall. *How can it only be nine o'clock in the morning when so much has happened?* she wondered. Out loud, she said, "Other than that, nothing. Why?"

"I'd like to take you to dinner tonight."

"Oh," she said. "I'd like that." She nearly rolled her eyes at the insaneness of her response, but thankfully he didn't seem to notice how lame she was.

He smiled, pleasure in his expression. "Wonderful," he said, and kissed her again. She sighed with pleasure, sinking into the kiss, and when he lifted his head, she smiled up at him dreamily.

He shook his head at her. "Woman, you're trouble." He shifted her off his lap and stood, pressing one last kiss to her lips. "I'll come by for you around seven o'clock?"

She nodded, watched as he turned to go. When he reached door, she called out. "Jacob?" He turned, and she blushed again. "I just wanted to say... I really liked everything you did."

He smiled, slow and easy, but with a decidedly predatory gleam in his eye. "So did I," he murmured. "See you at seven."

"Right. Bye," she murmured. When the door closed behind him, she let out the breath she'd been holding and fell back against the sofa cushions. "Holy shit."

Chapter 5

"Holy shit!"

"Shhh! Keep it down, Nelson, I don't need the whole town to know about this!"

"Sorry!" her friend muttered. He leaned across the table, his dark brown eyes wide in his narrow face. Between the news about Joe dumping her and Jacob's sudden and intense interest, he was all but hyperventilating with excitement. "But seriously, Isa. Holy shit!"

"I know." Isa smiled up at the waiter as he refilled her iced tea, waiting until he was gone to speak again. "I can't believe I told you."

"I can't either!" Nelson's voice was climbing in volume, and Isa winced and shushed him again. "Sorry! But you never tell me anything good, it's like pulling teeth to get the slightest detail out of you."

"I'm a very private person," Isa protested.

"I know, that's what I mean. This guy must have really thrown you for a loop."

Isa rolled her eyes. "That's the understatement of the century."

Nelson shook his head, his carefully coifed and highlighted hair falling across his forehead. "To think, this whole time you've been looking for Mr. Tie-Me-Up-And-Do-Me, and the perfect candidate has been living right next door to you. Thank God the crazy one dumped you, otherwise you might never have known."

Isa rolled her eyes. "What a charming way of looking at it," she drawled, then re-membered. "Oh, and I can't believe I forgot to tell you that part! He called me."

"Who did?"

"Joe."

"No!" Nelson dropped his fork with a clatter. "The fucking nerve! What'd he say?"

Isa shrugged. "Something about hoping I was okay, that we could still be friends. It was right before Jacob dropped his little bomb on me, so it's a tich hazy."

"Still be friends." With a snort, Nelson picked up his forgotten fork. "What-ever."

She shrugged again. "I don't mind staying friendly. After everything that's happened, I realize I'm not that upset over him dumping me—I was more pissed than hurt."

Nelson continued eating. "Well, he saved you the trouble of dumping his sorry ass." He looked up and caught the rueful look on her face. "Oh, come on, darling. I know you, and you'd only have been able to put up with the lunatic fringe for another week, tops."

Isa frowned. "That's the second time you've called him crazy."

"Well darling, cleary he's bonkers. I mean, that business about him having to ask his therapist for permission to tie you up in bed? What is that about?"

"Will you hush?" Isa's face flamed as she glanced around the restaurant. Luckily the lunch rush was on, and the noise level was such that no one was paying attention to their conversation. She turned back to her friend. "You don't think he's really crazy, do you?"

Nelson was focused on his trout almandine and didn't look up. "I think he could benefit from a prescription or seven." He glanced up at her sound of distress and reached out to cover her hand with his. "Oh sweetie, don't worry. I don't think he's dangerous or anything, just that he's a couple of olives short of a martini."

She grinned at him. "I like cherries in my martinis."

He grimaced. "Wretched habit." He forked up more trout. "Anyway, my point is he did you a favor by taking himself out of the picture. If he hadn't, you'd never have gotten blitzed in front of Jacob, he never would have professed his kinky lust for you-"

"Kinky lust?"

"-And now that he has, you can concentrate on him and his heretofore undiscovered dark side." He waggled his eyebrows dramatically, and she laughed.

"Undiscovered is right. He's just such a fun, happy go lucky kind of guy, I never would have thought it of him."

Nelson shrugged. "I don't know why not. I mean, where is it written that if you're into this stuff, you need to act or be a certain way? Look at you. You're pretty happy go lucky yourself, and you're into it."

Isa shook her head. "I know, but…" She sighed. "Okay, so I was stereotyping."

"It's understandable," he soothed. "But now that you know you were doing it, you can stop. And have crazy monkey bondage sex with the hottie next door."

She laughed, pressing a hand to the butterflies in her stomach. "I sure hope so."

"Honey, after this afternoon, I think it's a given," he said dryly. He had a smear of sauce across his cheek.

Isa shook her head. "I don't know. You've got something…" she tapped her own cheek, and he wiped away the smear with a napkin. "I mean, I thought he'd throw me down on the rug and have at me right there, but he stopped." She shrugged.

"But you know he was interested, right? I mean, there was evidence of reciprocal attraction?"

Isa remembered the way his cock had felt like a brand against her hip when he'd leaned into her, a small smile curving her lips.

Nelson snorted. "That's a yes."

"Okay, but why did he stop?" She poked at her salad, spearing a grape tomato with her fork. "That's the part I don't get. If he was into me at all, wouldn't he have wanted to keep going?"

Nelson shrugged. "Maybe not. I mean, up until now your relationship has been strictly friendly, right? Neighbor to neighbor. So maybe this morning was a little bit of testing the waters. You know, dipping his toes in the shallow end before taking the plunge."

Isa chewed her tomato thoughtfully. "Maybe. Didn't feel too shallow, though. He was pretty much in deep and plunging by the end."

His mouth fell open. "Isabella Maria! I can't believe you said that!"

Isa's hands flew to her cheeks while Nelson roared with laughter. "I can't believe I'm telling you all this stuff."

Nelson chortled, his hands clasped together in glee. "I love this guy already. Pretty soon you'll be spilling all the juicy details without my even having to nag."

"Don't count on it," Isa warned, grinning.

"When are you meeting him for dinner?"

Isa forked up more salad. "Seven."

"Is he taking you somewhere, or are you staying in?"

Isa shook her head. "I don't know. He just said he'd be by at seven, I'm not sure what else he has planned."

"Hmm." Nelson tapped his fork against his chin thoughtfully, leaving behind flecks of fish. "What are you going to wear?"

Isa swallowed her mouthful of food. "No idea," she admitted. "I'm kind of stumped. I mean, if he's thinking to just stay in and throw a couple of steaks on the grill, I don't want to get too fancy. But I don't want to be too casual, because he could be planning to go out somewhere."

"You could just answer the door naked." He grinned, bobbing his perfectly groomed eyebrows again. "That'd set the tone."

Isa grinned back. "No. But I'm thinking a new outfit might be in order. How do you feel about skipping the movie and going shopping with me?"

"What do you have in mind?"

Isa sat back and tossed her napkin onto her empty plate. "Something girly. Flirty, but casual enough for an evening at home. Sundress?"

"Oooh, I know just the place." Nelson wiped his chin with his napkin and looked around for the waiter. "Check please!"

At six fifty, Isabella took a final check in the mirror. She'd spent nearly three hours shopping, hitting six different shops before finding something she liked, but it had been worth the effort. The dress was a pale blue cotton blend with a simple design of a square bodice with thin straps that left her shoulders bare. The waist was nipped in, flowing into a gathered skirt that came to just below her knees. She'd bought new underwear too, and had the delicate lace panties on under the dress. The straps of the dress were too thin to wear the matching bra, but the designer had taken that into account and built one into the bodice.

She twirled in front of the mirror, watching the skirt flair out then settle back into place. She'd strapped on a pair of thin heeled sandals to give herself a few more inches in height, and left her hair loose to curl down her back. She'd taken care with her makeup to make it look like she wasn't wearing makeup, so only the slightest hint of color warmed her lips and her eyes were enhanced with the barest touch of shadow and mascara.

"Not bad," she muttered, and spun around again. She bent to run her fingertips up the back of first one calf, then the other, testing for any hint of stubble. Satisfied with the job she'd done shaving, she poured a pool of scented lotion into her palm and massaged it into her legs, smoothing the excess down her arms when she was finished. She picked up a bottle of matching scent and dabbed it to her wrists and neck. A final fluff of her hair and she was ready.

The doorbell rang, and she looked at her watch. "Right on time," she muttered, and took a deep breath. "Okay, let's get this show on the road."

She left the bedroom, heels clicking on the hardwood floors as she made her way to the front door. She laid her hand on the doorknob, took one last deep breath which did nothing whatsoever to settle her nerves, and opened the door.

"Hi," she said, nerves giving way to pleasure as Jacob stepped into the doorway.

"Hi," he rumbled, and leaned in to press a warm kiss to her lips. "You look lovely."

"Thank you," she murmured. He was dressed in jeans, with a white button down shirt and a black jacket. His head gleamed freshly shaved, his goatee neatly trimmed. "You look nice too."

"Thank you." He smiled at her. "Are you hungry?"

"Starving." She grinned. "Just let me get my bag." She turned away to pick up her purse, and when she turned back he had stepped inside and shut the door behind him. She frowned. "Are we going out or staying in?"

"Going out," he said. "I made reservations at Sorentino's, if that's okay."

"I love that restaurant," she said.

"Great. But I wanted to talk for a minute before we left." He laid a hand on her shoulder. "How are you with everything that happened this morning?"

"Fine."

He raised an eyebrow. "I was kind of looking for a little more information than that, Isabella."

She laughed, embarrassed. "Sorry, I just… I'm not sure what you want to know."

"First, do you have any regrets?"

She shook her head. "No, none at all." She half smiled. "Well, maybe that we haven't done that sooner."

He grinned. "That would be my one regret. How are your wrists?"

"Fine," she said, lifting them up to show him. "You can't even see the marks any longer."

"That's good," he murmured, rubbing his thumbs along the fine bones in her wrists. He smiled as he felt her pulse jump. "And the things I was saying—how did all that make you feel?"

Her breath caught in her chest, and she shyly ducked her head to the side. He chuckled, catching her chin in his fingers and tilting her head up. "Come on, Isabella. If you don't tell me, I'll just have to assume you didn't like it and never do it again."

"I liked it," she blurted, then blushed at the speed of her answer. "It made me feel… dirty."

"In a good way?" he asked, his voice serious, and she found herself answering honestly.

"Yeah, in a good way. I didn't expect to, and I imagine if someone talked to me like that on the street they'd get a face full of pepper spray, but I really liked hearing you call me a slut. It made me feel... wanted. Desirable." She grimaced a little. "Does that make sense?"

"Sure it does," he said so easily she forgot to be embarrassed. "It's all about context." He was still rubbing her wrists in gentle, sure strokes that were slowly affecting her breathing. "Do you have any questions for me about what happened this afternoon?"

"Actually... why did you stop?"

He frowned. "What do you mean?"

"I mean, obviously you were aroused." She felt her own arousal rise as she remembered. "But you didn't make any move to..."

"Fuck you?" he suggested when she trailed off. She nodded. "It wasn't that I didn't want to, but I thought you might have been a little overwhelmed by everything that had already happened. I didn't want to push."

"Oh." She was quiet for a moment. "But you did want to?"

"I did, and do," he said, and used his grip on her wrists to tug her closer. He let go of her hands and wrapped one arm around her waist, putting his palm on the small of her back and pulling her lower body into his. "Feel that?" he murmured, pushing his hips into hers so she couldn't help but feel the solid ridge of his erection. She nodded again, her breathing growing shallow as he bent his head to hers.

"I've been like that since this morning," he whispered, his breath dancing over her skin as he brushed his lips over her temple, her cheek, the curve of her jaw. She felt his teeth nip delicately at the underside of her jaw, over her pulse, and swallowed convulsively. "I wanted nothing more than to fuck you, to sink my cock so deep into you that you'd feel me for days. Until you want me inside you as much as I want to be there." His tongue flicked out to soothe the marks left by his teeth. "And I will be. I will fuck you, Isabella."

She gulped. "When?"

He chuckled, the sound soft in her ear. "Soon," he promised. "Very, very soon. But first, I want to sit across from you in a lovely restaurant. I want to enjoy your delightful company, talk a few things over just to make sure we're on the same page. And drive you just a little bit crazy."

She giggled weakly. "Doing a good job of that already." Her new panties were already soaked through, rendering twenty-five dollars worth of French silk useless.

"Maybe you can take a little more, though." He pulled back to look at her face, his eyes intense. "What do you think?"

"I can sure try," she managed. His expression turned tender, and he carried one of her hands to his mouth to press a soft kiss to the palm.

"Good girl," he whispered, and she felt herself go gooey.

He let go of her hands, and pulling a bundle of black rope from his jacket pocket, lowered himself to one knee on the floor in front of her. He looked up with dark, mesmerizing eyes, and it occurred to her that despite his obviously subservient position, he didn't seem the least bit submissive.

She swallowed the lump in her throat. "What're you doing?"

He unraveled the rope, running the length of it through his fingers before laying it at her feet. "Let's see if I can make dinner a little more interesting," he murmured. She barely controlled an instinctive flinch when he wrapped his hands around her ankles. Was he going to tie her ankles? It was on the tip of her tongue to protest—how was she going to walk if he hobbled her feet? Besides, she might enjoy being on display for a lover, but she drew the line at being on display for the whole town.

But he slid his hands up, smoothing over her calves. His fingers danced behind her knees, making her wiggle. "Ticklish?" he murmured, and she nodded. He smiled a little at that, as though he were filing the information away for later use. His hands continued up, gliding over smooth thighs, up over her buttocks. She shivered as he hesitated, palming the cheeks of her ass for the briefest of moments before hooking his fingers in the sides of her panties.

"I want these off," he murmured. "Will you let me have them?"

"I'm not sure I can eat dinner without panties," she stammered.

"You'll get them back," he promised. He tugged, bringing the straps down her legs a few inches, then stopped. "Spread your legs for me, baby," he urged, and with a shaky breath, she obeyed.

With her thighs spread slightly he was able to draw the scrap of lace and silk down, past her knees to rest on her ankles. "Very nice," he murmured, and she wasn't sure if he was talking about her choice of underwear or her obedience.

He picked up the discarded rope, once again drawing it through his hands. She knew he was making sure there was nothing caught in the rough strands of hemp that would hurt her skin, like staples or splinters. She knew it, and yet still felt the anticipation build watching the coil glide through his hands.

He reached under her dress again, drawing the rope around her waist, letting it drag against her flesh in a way that raised goose bumps along her skin. He circled her waist once, twice, then drew the rope up between her legs.

"Easy," he murmured as she hissed out a breath. Her cheeks flushed and she trembled with growing arousal as he trailed his fingers through her damp slit, positioning the rope so it lay against the inside of her outer labia, then pulled it up to loop through the rope at her waist.

"Too tight?" he asked, and she shook her head. "Good," he said, holding her eyes with his. "If anything I'm doing is uncomfortable, I want you to tell me. You're going to be wearing this for a while."

"Okay," she whispered. He continued running winding the rope around her body under the cover of her skirt, going around her waist, up through her legs on the opposite side, and when he drew it back up to her waist she realized that the placement of the rope held the soft outer lips of her pussy apart. She felt exposed, vulnerable… and shockingly, achingly aroused.

"How does it feel?" he asked, running his palms in soothing circles over the tops of her thighs. "Any pinching or hurting?"

"No," she said, shifting her weight carefully from one leg to the other. She took a tentative step, intending to test the comfort of her bonds. When she came up short she looked down at her panties still tangled around her ankles.

He chuckled and began sliding her underwear back up her legs. He carefully positioned the delicate garment into place over the ropes that traversed her pelvis. Her breath caught as she felt the cool, slick silk settle over the exposed flesh of her cunt, held open by the rope. He caught the slight sound and trailed one finger over the damp patch of fabric, and smiled as her hips gave an involuntary surge.

Isa barely suppressed a whimper, panic and need a tangled mess in her chest. "I'm supposed to eat dinner like this?"

Jacob's fingers lingered between her thighs, giving her needy flesh one last caress before he drew his hands out from beneath her skirt. He smoothed it into place, running his hands around her waist as he stood. "For as long as you can stand it," he said. "How do you feel?"

"Exposed," she admitted, her cheeks flooding with heat. She looked down at her waist. "Can you see the rope through the dress? I don't really want the whole restaurant knowing what's going on here."

"Trust me, darling. I'd never put you on display like that. Unless you asked me to." He smiled guilelessly when she looked at him sharply. "Come on, take a look." He steered down the hall her to the bedroom. He leaned against the door jam as she studied her reflection in the antique stand mirror with a critical eye.

She looked, turning this way and that, but she couldn't see any hint of the ropes under the dress. The rope he'd used hadn't been overly thick, and it helped that the dress was lined—hell, she couldn't even see her nipples poking through, and God knew they were hard as pencil erasers at the moment.

She turned back to him with a slight smile that he answered with one of his own. "Okay?" he asked, and she nodded.

He held out a hand. "Then let's go to dinner."

She walked toward him, feeling the rope pull and tug at her with every step, and put her hand in his.

Chapter 6

The hostess at Sorentino's seated them as soon as they arrived, greeting them with a smile that to Isa's mind looked just a little too knowing. Which was ridiculous, she knew. She'd checked, hadn't she? The rope couldn't be seen though the dress. But with every step she took she was intensely, acutely aware of it. It hugged her body, holding her pussy lips slightly spread to allow her panties to slide and rub across her damp lips and swollen clit. It had only been twenty minutes since they'd left her house, and she already felt like she was going out of her mind.

Which, judging from the glint in Jacob's eye, was exactly the point.

He caught her looking up at him and smiled down at her. "How we doing?" he murmured. He laid his hand on the middle of her back, stroking in small circles in a way that would have been soothing if she wasn't already set to crawl out of her skin.

"Good," she said. "Just a little… wound up."

"Not too much?" he asked. She shook her head, and the corners of his mouth curled up in a half smile. "Good," he said. He lowered the hand on her back to her waist, gliding his palm along the rope through her dress. He traced it lightly, grasping at it through the dress to give it a tug.

She shivered, barely suppressing a gasp, and threw him the narrow eyed stare she usually saved for cross examining recalcitrant witnesses in court. Far from being intimidated, he chuckled richly and smiled at the hostess. "Thank you, this will be perfect," he assured her, and with a smile, she left them alone.

"Such a look you're giving me, darlin'," he drawled. He pulled out a chair, using the hand on her waist to guide her to her seat. He sat down across from her, watching with a decidedly predatory gleam as she wriggled in her seat, struggling to find a position that didn't remind her every second of her bondage. Something she quickly realized was impossible.

He waited until she'd stopped shifting, then raised an eyebrow. "Comfy?"

"Not even remotely," she admitted, and hid her face behind her menu when he laughed.

"Excellent," he purred, and the blatant satisfaction in his voice had her lowering the menu again.

"You're kind of a bastard, aren't you?" she teased, and was delighted to see the answering sparkle in his eyes.

"Oh, darlin', you have no idea." He was grinning openly, but the predatory gleam that made her stomach jump and her pussy clench was still there behind the humor.

Isa was saved from having to find something to say to that by the arrival of their waiter, Chuck. He went through the ritual of reciting the specials, and after considering them and consulting the menu once again, they both decided on the seafood pasta.

"What would you like to drink, Isa?" Jacob asked, and she looked up from her clenched fingers to find both Jacob and Chuck waiting for her answer.

"Oh. Nothing, actually. Just water for me." She smiled up at Chuck.

"I'll have a whiskey, neat," Jacob said, and handed over both of their menus. After Chuck had gone, he raised an eyebrow. "No alcohol?"

She shook her head. "The last thing I want to do is have to go to the bathroom in this."

He chuckled. "Smart girl. So," he leaned forward slightly, "we should talk a bit, I think, before we go much further."

Isa swallowed the sudden lump in her throat. "All right."

"How are you with everything we've done so far?"

She drew a deep breath. "Okay. I mean, this…" she indicated the restaurant, "…is a bit edgy for me. The public venue, I mean. I'm not an exhibitionist."

"Do you want to leave?" he asked, and she hastened to reassure him.

"No, it's fine. It's not too much, it's just closer to the edge then I thought I'd be going tonight, that's all." She smiled shyly. "I kind of like it—it's like having a secret."

He smiled, approval warming his voice. "Yes, it is. And I love that you're willing to push yourself." He reached for her hand and drew it to his lips for a kiss. "But I want you to know that anytime you want or need to call a halt, all you have to do is say so. I don't want you to do anything that isn't good for you. If you're not having fun, then I'm not having fun. Okay?"

She smiled. "Okay."

"Good. Now I'm not real big on protocol or formalities. I'm pretty much all about the pleasure, and that means whatever feels good, whatever feels right, that's what we'll do."

She frowned slightly. "What—" She cut herself off as Chuck delivered Jacob's whiskey. She waited for him to leave, then leaned in slightly. "What do you mean?"

He leaned forward. "I mean if you want to laugh, you can laugh. There's no rule against it. If you want to call me Sir, you can—if you want to call me a rat bastard son of a bitch, you can do that too."

She laughed, relaxing. "I don't think I'll be calling you names," she said.

"Oh, trust me darlin'," he said, his lips curled in a devil's grin. "You're going to be calling me every name you can think of by the time we're through, and I'll love it." His voice lowered intimately. "And so will you."

He sat back slightly while she floated on a fresh wave of lust. "So anytime you feel like something's going wrong, or in a direction you don't want to go, all you have to do is say so. Understood?"

She nodded. "Understood."

He smiled and kissed her hand again before picking up his drink. "Good. Now, tell me about this new case you're working on"

"Ah… my case? It's grueling," she admitted, adjusting to the abrupt verbal gear shift with only a little hitch. "We've got about forty witness depositions to slog through, although probably only about half of those will end up testifying. There's a mountain of information from the medical experts, from the cops. I've got four assistants who're just working on those."

"You have assistants?" he asked, and she grinned.

"I know. I'm trying not to let it go to my head, but delegating rocks."

He laughed, lifting his glass in a toast. "You're moving up."

"Moving up to move out," she said. "Hopefully the exposure of winning this case—and I will win—will give me enough juice to start my own practice."

"I didn't know you wanted to practice on your own," he said, and she shrugged.

"I like being my own boss," she said.

"It's an adventure." He grinned, and she laughed.

"Hopefully mine won't be quite as exciting as yours. I'm just a quiet, small town lawyer, not a hot shot private eye. That poodle-napping you worked last month was intense, I don't know if I could handle something like that."

"Hey, Mrs. Wilfred was beside herself with worry over little Lupé. She loves that dog, which is why her nephew was sure she'd pay the ransom."

Isa shook her head. "People are nuts."

"Honey, that's nothing." He went on to tell her about some of his more unusual cases, spinning the stories out as the waiter arrived with their food, and the meal passed quickly with pleasant conversation and laughter.

Anyone looking at them would think they were on a simple dinner date, but every time she shifted in her chair or crossed her legs, or even took a deep breath, Isa was reminded of the rope crisscrossing her waist and pelvis. Her pussy, held open by the rope, was soaking wet and pulsing in time with the beat of her heart, and with every movement the delicate silk of her panties scraped against the sensitive bud of her clit. Her entire body felt hyper-sensitive, so even the gentle air conditioning blowing across her skin was like a caress. It was making her jittery, and horny, and by the time Chuck asked them if they wanted any desert, she was ready to climb the walls.

"No thank you," she said, declining desert and coffee, and tried to control her erratic breathing.

"I'll have an espresso," Jacob said, his eyes on Isa's face. He waited for Chuck to walk away, then he said, "How are you doing over there?"

She breathed in carefully, trying to keep herself still, her hands in fists on the table. She wasn't sure if she could take her panties scraping over her clit anymore. She was on the ragged edge, afraid she'd explode if this went on much longer, and public orgasms were so not on her to do list. "If your intent was to drive me insane," she managed, "then I'm doing great."

He chuckled. "You've done great," he told her. "I wasn't sure how much time in those ropes you could take."

She took a deep breath, feeling the rope press harder into her flesh with the movement. "If you'd tied them much tighter, I'd probably be done by now," she admitted.

He smiled. "Well, I don't want you to be done quite yet. Is anything giving you any trouble right now?"

"My panties," she hissed.

"What about them?" he asked.

"They're driving me insane," she blurted, and he laughed. "The way I'm tied... .everything's exposed."

"I know," he murmured, and the lazy sensuality that he'd displayed all through dinner was suddenly much sharper, more intense. Darker, and she liked it. A lot. She could barely hear her voice over her own heartbeat when she spoke again. "They're scraping against me. Every time I move, every time I breathe..."

"Are you wet?" he murmured.

She laughed shakily. "Soaked," she said, her cheeks heating at the admission.

"If you keep your panties on, how much longer do you think you'll be able to stay in the rope?" he asked.

"I don't know," she said, her hands lifting helplessly, then falling back to the table. "I don't really have a frame of reference for being in public bondage. Probably ten minutes," she guessed.

"Well, I have plans beyond ten minutes, so we should do something to make you more comfortable."

Her body sagged slightly with relief. "Yes please," she sighed.

"So since your panties are causing you such discomfort, you should take them off."

Isa felt her jaw drop, and she started at him in shock. Take them off? Her underwear? In a restaurant? Was he crazy?

His eyebrows shot up, his mouth quirking in obvious amusement. "Problem?" he asked.

She blinked, struggling to focus her scattered thoughts enough to answer. She didn't know what she'd expected him to say; although now that she thought of it, taking her panties off was the logical move. But the idea of taking off her underwear in a restaurant had never occurred to her. She swallowed hard. "Here?"

He smiled slowly at her response, satisfaction and approval stamped on his features, and she felt an odd sense of pride that she'd pleased him.

"That would be charming," he murmured. "Absolutely charming. But perhaps that's a little too advanced. If you'd prefer, you can go to the ladies room instead. But of course you'll have to walk there."

And walking created friction, she realized. The reason she was taking the panties off in the first place. She chewed on her lower lip, the need for relief warring with the need for privacy. He was waiting patiently, watching her from across the table, and she realized he was going to leave the decision completely up to her.

The realization that he wanted her no matter what she decided gave her the courage to be bold. A quick glance around the restaurant confirmed that they were fairly well shielded from prying eyes; the tables immediately next to theirs had recently been vacated, and there weren't any wait staff currently nearby. She was seated facing the room, so the table would shield her lower body from almost everyone.

She thought frantically for a moment, trying to work out how best to do this. With a plan of attack in mind, she took a deep breath. "No, that's okay. I don't really feel like walking." He blinked, surprised, then his eyes widened with astonishment when she rose slightly, just lifting her butt off the seat.

She worked quickly, flipping the skirt of her dress up just enough to slide her hands under the dress. She hooked her thumbs in the sides of her panties in the same movement, and in the split second it took to sit back down, she had the under-wear off her hips and to the tops of her knees. She risked a quick look around the restaurant again, her cheeks stained with color as her bare bottom met the warm, soft leather of the seat cushion.

She turned back to Jacob, her heart hammering in her chest so loud she was surprised he couldn't hear it. He was watching her with a mix of shock, admiration and lust. "You're absolutely delightful," he murmured.

Isa barely choked back a hysterical giggle. "I'm terrified," she whispered. She could feel the panties resting on her legs just above her knees, and started shifting her legs, working them further down. She bit her lip in concentration, desperately trying to block the sensations that bombarded her pussy with every movement of her legs.

After what seemed like an eternity, she was finally able to get the delicate silk past her knees, and gravity took them the rest of the way down so they pooled at her ankles. She slipped her left foot out of its sandal and pulled free of the fabric. She started to do the same with her right foot, then stopped. The table cloth didn't go all the way to the floor, and she didn't want to leave her underwear in a puddle on the carpet for anyone to see. She bit her lip, unsure what do to now.

Jacob had been watching her with lazy arousal, but when she stopped moving his gaze sharpened. "What's wrong?"

She choked back another giggle. "Now that they're off, how do I get them off the floor without someone noticing?"

He bit the inside of his cheek to suppress his own smile. "Where are they now?"

"Still on my foot."

He tossed his napkin down and straightened in his chair. "Give me your foot."

Her eyes widened, and after a quick glance around, lifted her foot to his lap.

His fingers closed over her ankle, firm and warm, setting her heel on his knee. He began working the scrap of lace and silk over the heel of her shoe, taking his time, alternately tickling and stroking until she didn't know whether to laugh or sigh.

She was jerked out of her haze by the arrival of the waiter with Jacob's espresso, and tried to pull her foot from his lap. He held fast, keeping her foot on his knee as the waiter put down the coffee. She could have yanked free, but then Chuck the waiter wouldn't have any doubt as to what was going on under the table. She stayed put, face flaming, to wait it out.

"Will there be anything else, sir?" Chuck asked.

Jacob smiled. "No, thank you. Isa, do you want anything else?"

Both men turned to look at her, one expectant, the other amused. Jacob's fingers were dancing over her ankle, sending prickles of sensation up her leg. She cleared her throat. "No, I'm fine. Thank you."

Chuck smiled, either completely oblivious to the undercurrents of tension at the table or one hell of an actor. "Very good, ma'am."

Jacob's fingers kept moving over her skin, feather light, teasing, as he pulled the waiter's attention back to him. "I think we just need the check."

"I'll be back with that shortly," Chuck assured them, and hustled away.

"Oh my God." Isa sagged in her chair.

Jacob laughed, the rough sound dancing over her skin as surely as his fingers were. He quickly untangled the panties from around her shoe, tucking them discretely into his jacket pocket before picking up his espresso. "If you could have seen the look on your face."

She looked at him incredulously as she dragged her foot from his lap. "We almost got caught. I almost got caught, with my panties around my ankles."

"Yes," he said, watching her from over the rim of his cup. "How does that feel?"

"A little exciting," she admitted, reluctant arousal blooming at the thought. "But…"

"But… not really your thing, right?"

She sighed with relief. "Yes."

"What is your thing, Isabella?"

She blinked, confused by the question. "What do you mean?"

He shifted slightly in his chair, putting the coffee down and giving her his full attention. "I mean, what do you like? What do you like to feel, to experience, to do? What is it about bondage that appeals to you?"

She looked around quickly at the word 'bondage', but no one was paying them any attention. She looked back to find him watching her expectantly, waiting for her answer, and she struggled push past her instinctive embarrassment to put her needs into words.

"I like being restrained," she admitted. "I like having something to move against, to struggle against."

"That's what you like physically," he said, "and that's fine. But what else do you get out of it?"

Isa drew in a deep breath. "I like giving up control."

He smiled a bit, his eyes approving. "But it can be difficult, can't it—finding someone to give that control to." She nodded. "Someone you trust enough not to hurt you, to respect the limits you set." She nodded again. "Someone you want to be with."

"Yes," she whispered.

"So the question I have to ask now, Isa, is do you trust me not to hurt you?"

"Yes," she said, her voice firm and sure.

"Do you trust me not to violate any limits you set?"

"Yes," she said again. Her body was humming with anticipation, her excitement fed by the predatory gleam in his eyes.

"Do you want me, Isa?" His eyes were dark now, heavy lidded, and color rode high on his cheekbones. "Do you want to be with me? Will you trust me with your body tonight?"

Isa felt her breath catch in her chest, her whole body tightening at the idea of giving him control, free reign, of her body. "Yes," she whispered.

Chapter 7

It seemed to Isa that things moved lightning fast after that. Chuck came back with the check, and Jacob took care of it by the simple means of dropping a wad of cash on the table. She couldn't focus enough to discern how much it was—hell, she barely had the wit to remember to get her left shoe back on—but from the way Chuck's eyes had bulged with gratitude she assumed it was a substantial tip.

Then Jacob was standing, pulling out her chair for her and taking her hand in his as they left the restaurant. They walked to the car quickly, and she had to stifle the moans that wanted to erupt. She'd thought the friction of her panties rubbing against her swollen, needy flesh was torture, but the slight breeze that found its way under her dress as they walked was far worse. By the time they were in the car, racing towards home, she was hanging on by a thread.

He noticed, reaching a hand over to cover hers where they were clenched in her lap. "Are you all right?" he asked.

She shook her head hard, her hair whipping around and catching him in the face. "No," she managed to say between ragged breaths. "No, I'm not. I'm hot, and I can't breathe, and I need to come so badly I can fucking taste it, and you're not driving fast enough!"

His hand squeezed hers hard and laughter turned his voice into a rumble. "I'm sorry, I'm going as fast as I can."

"Just seriously, please hurry." She inhaled sharply, catching the scent of her own arousal mixed with his masculine scent, and groaned out loud. "I really need you to fuck me soon."

He stopped laughing at that, a growl rumbling up from his chest. "Hang on," he muttered, and put the pedal to the floor.

The twenty minute drive turned into ten, and then they were screeching to a halt in his driveway. "Stay," he muttered, and was out of the car, coming around to the passenger side before she could blink. He yanked open her door as she was unhooking her seatbelt, then simply lifted her out of the seat and into his arms.

Isa clung to his shoulders as he strode up the walk. He shifted her slightly to unlock the door, shutting it behind them with enough force to make the frame shake. As soon as they were inside, he set her on her feet, gathered her close, and slammed his mouth down on hers.

She moaned in relief, reveling in the contact she'd spent the whole evening yearning for. She clung to him, her arms curling up to twine around his neck as the kiss went on and on.

He raised his head after long moments, the only sound in the room the harshness of their breathing. "We need a bedroom."

She nodded, licking her lips and tasting him. "Now," she demanded.

"Now," he agreed. "Do you need to use the bathroom?"

She shook her head. "No."

"Good," he said. He put his hands on her shoulders and spun her around so she faced the hall. "Walk," he urged, and she did.

She'd been in his home before, but never down the long hall to the master bedroom. Part of her noticed the colorful art along the walls, the plush carpet that all but swallowed her feet, but they were just fleeting glimpses, vague impressions. Her entire focus was on the man behind her. She could feel him there, the heaviness of his hands on her shoulders, the heat radiating from his body. She tried to ease the tightness in her chest with a deep breath, and then they were in the bedroom.

"Wow," she blurted, her feet stumbling to a stop across the threshold. "That's a big bed."

He laughed behind her, and some of the tension went out of the air with the sound. The bed was big as a lake, covered in a dark copper spread that shimmered richly in the light from the hall. Jacob reached over and flipped a switch, and a series of recessed lights set around the perimeter came on, bathing the room in a soft, gentle glow. She had a moment to notice the wrought iron headboard and soak in the warm masculinity of the room, then he was turning her in his arms again.

He didn't take her mouth as she expected, but wrapped his fist in the tangled length of her hair and tugged her head back. A startled moan escaped her lips, and if she hadn't been so painfully aroused, she might have been a little frightened at the sharpness of the movement. As it was, it only fed the desire bubbling in her veins, like fanning a flame, and she met his fierce gaze boldly.

"Are you sure you want this?" he asked, his voice a husky rasp, and she realized up until now he'd been holding back, keeping his lust for her in check. She knew, sure as she knew her own name, that saying yes now would unleash the full force of his sexuality. Part of her trembled at the thought, but the other part of her, the deeply female part of her craved his possession. She needed it, more than food or drink or air, she needed at that moment to be his.

"Yes," she said, her voice as clear and strong as she could make it, which under the circumstances, wasn't much. "I'm sure."

She had about two seconds to savor the approval and hunger in his eyes before he moved. His free arm wrapped around her waist, lifting her into the air so her face was level with his. She clung to his shoulders for balance as he walked them toward the bed, stopping when her dangling legs bumped into the mattress. He set her on her feet and stepped back slightly.

"The dress," he said, his voice a rough vibration of sound that slid over her skin like a caress, leaving goose bumps in its wake. "Take it off."

She kicked off her shoes and reached for the zipper at the back of the dress, it never even occurred to her to object. She could feel her cheeks flushing; his gaze was so intent, so fierce on her that the urge to look away, to hide, was almost unbearable. But she wanted to see him, to see the lust and want on his face as she bared herself to him. So she kept her eyes up, locked on his, as she pulled the zipper down. The bodice loosened, falling away from her chest as she slowly pulled the zipper down. She tugged the zipper the last inch and let her arms drop to her sides, and the dress slid to the floor to pool at her feet.

He let out a low curse. "Jesus," he whispered. "Look at you."

She looked down at her body as though it belonged to someone else. She saw the rope, wound around her waist and through her legs, forming a frame for her sex. She could just see the swollen flesh of her cunt plumped up around the rope, flushed with heat and glistening in the light. He ran his hands lightly over her hips and across her stomach, making her muscles jump and quiver. He moved his fingers to the knot that lay just under her belly button, sliding two fingers against her skin to curl around the rope.

"I was going to take this off," he murmured. He tugged on the rope sharply, bringing her forward to collide against him. The rope tightened, digging into her swollen, aching flesh. She couldn't stop the whimper from escaping her lips, and his eyes sharpened at the sound.

"You like that," he said. He twisted his hand, tightening the rope even further and drawing her to her toes with a gasp. Her hands came up to clutch his jacket, her fingers curling into fists as he pulled her even higher.

Isa's head was spinning, and she couldn't make sense of the sensations rioting through her body. The pressure of the rope digging into the soft flesh of her cunt was both painful and arousing, and the combination was making her dizzy. She could feel moisture pooling between her legs; her thighs were slick with it, her clit pulsing, and all she could think was *again*.

"Yes," she whispered.

"Yes, what?" he replied, eyes glowing like emeralds in the dim light of the room, and she felt dark delight bloom as she realized what he was asking.

"Yes Sir," she whispered, using the title on impulse, and was rewarded by his growl of approval.

"I was looking for 'please', but I like that," he murmured, leaning down to tease her mouth. He flicked his tongue against her lip, darting in to taste her before sliding back out to nibble at the corners of her mouth. "I like that a lot." He trailed his mouth over the curve of her jaw and down her neck, nipping and licking his way to the hollow at the base of her throat. Her pulse beat frantically there, the rapid rush of blood under the skin betraying her excitement.

"I was going to take this off," he said again, tugging and pulling on the rope, making her whimper and burn, "but I think I'll leave it on. Are you okay with wearing it for a while longer?"

"Yuh huh," she managed faintly, her head spinning so much she barely heard the question.

She felt him smile against her throat as he picked her up again. The room spun crazily, and when it stopped she found herself flat on her back in the middle of the bed. He peeled her hands off his jacket, shedding it and tossing it across the room before leaning down for another kiss.

He pulled away panting. "Christ, you go to my head."

She laughed softly despite her own need. "That's fair, then. 'Cause I haven't had a coherent thought since this morning."

He grinned at her fiercely. "I don't need you to think, darlin'. Just feel." He drew her hands to his lips, pressed a kiss to each palm, then reached under the pillow next to her head and drew out two bundles of red rope.

"Oh good," she said, giggling even as she quivered with anticipation. "More rope."

He moved quickly, unraveling one of the bundles and quickly running it through his hands, then folded it in half. He lay her right hand on the bed, palm up, and with a few deft moves that she was too far gone to follow, had her wrist bound, a very neat and secure knot laying at the bottom of her upturned palm with the loose ends trailing up over her fingers.

He drew her arm out toward the corner of the bed. The bed was so large that even with her arm fully extended there was still a good two feet to the edge of the bed, but thanks to the wrought iron headboard, that didn't matter. He simply pulled her arm as straight as possible and tied the rope to the headboard.

"How does that feel?" he asked, and she flexed her arm experimentally. There was little play in the rope, just enough to bend her elbow slightly.

"It's good," she said, and wrapped her hand around the ropes running up her palm.

"Excellent," he murmured, and moved over to the other side. Her left arm was soon secured in the same fashion, and he sat back on his haunches at her side with a satisfied look on his face.

"Well," she drawled, feeling bold and saucy in her bonds, "now that you've got me here, what're you going to do with me?"

One eyebrow went up, his face fierce and unsmiling, and his eyes traveled slowly and deliberately over her bound form. Her nipples tightened even further under the heat of his gaze, her belly quivered beneath the rope crisscrossing it. She could feel her pussy dampen even further, and knew by the satisfied look that flashed across his eyes that he could see it.

She drew a shaky breath when he shifted, looming over her and stopping with his mouth a hair's breadth from hers. "What am I going to do with you?" he murmured. His breath washed over her skin, making her shiver as she felt him reach down and hook his hand through the rope traversing her pelvis. He yanked, jerking her hips up off the bed and making her cry out in shock. "Any fucking thing I want," he growled, and slammed his mouth down on hers.

She moaned into his mouth, frantic for the touch and taste of him. He held himself off her, bracing himself on his hands, and she moaned again in frustration. She lifted her legs to wrap them around his hips, to try and pull him down into her, but he caught her legs. He held them apart, pressing her knees into the mattress, making the muscles of her inner thighs stretch and burn and ache to have the weight of him pressing her down.

She wrenched her mouth from his. "Let me go," she panted.

He chuckled richly. "Oh no, darlin'. Now that I've got you here, I'm not letting you go for a good long while."

She made a helpless sound of frustration and tried once again to lift her legs, but he held firm. "Stay still," he ordered.

"No," she said, eyes flashing playful defiance. She twisted underneath him, wrenching her hips and straightening her legs, and she very nearly got her legs wrapped around him before he caught them. He forced them wide again, slamming them down on the bed with enough force to shake the bed frame, and she bared her teeth in a frustrated growl.

"Oh, somebody's unhappy," he chortled. "What's the matter, sweetheart? Things not going how you'd planned?" He laughed, delighted, when her hips twisted again and her legs flexed in his grip. "Oh, that's perfect. You just keep right on going, sweetie."

In a dim corner of her brain, a voice was calling out a warning. *It's a trap, that's what he wants you to do! Lay still!* She ignored it and lifted her body, pulling her knees up toward her chest. She felt a brief moment of elated triumph as her knees slid out of his grip, then blinked in startled surprised when he moved. He leaned his chest against her shins, pinning her knees to her chest and pressing her heels into the backs of her thighs. She grunted and tried to push him off, but with the weight of his broad chest pressing her down, she was well and truly pinned.

"You bastard," she muttered, trying not to giggle.

"Aw, you say the sweetest things," he purred. He reached up under the pillow and came up with another fistful of rope, this time in a vibrant purple.

"How much rope do you fucking have?" she blurted out.

He laughed. "Oh, you can't even imagine." He picked up the end of the rope, shaking the bundle free of its knot. She tried to buck under him, thinking to shake him loose while he was distracted. He merely settled his weight more fully onto her, pushing her legs even further back into her chest.

"Fucker," she muttered, and concentrated on taking shallow breaths.

He grinned. "I love it when you talk dirty," he said, and she laughed breathlessly with delight.

"Can you breathe down there?" he asked, and she gave brief thought to telling him no, that she couldn't. She knew he'd lift up if she did, giving her an advantage, but it seemed like cheating.

She nodded. "It's fine."

"Tell me if it's not, okay?" He waited for her answering nod. "Good. Now, let's see how much rope we can get on you."

He shifted his weight slightly so her right knee wasn't trapped against his chest and moved quickly. He wound the rope around her leg, binding her calf to her thigh with several passes of rope, then drawing the end between calf and thigh and cinching the rope together. She flexed her leg experimentally; she wasn't tied so tightly that her heel was trapped against the back of her thigh, so she had some room to shift, but it was now impossible to straighten her leg.

He bound the other leg just as securely, then sat back on his haunches. She twisted and flexed, testing her range of movement as he watched, grinning. She narrowed her eyes on him. "I can still move," she warned him, and he laughed.

"If I wanted you immobile, you'd be immobile," he informed her, and she believed him. He reached out with one hand to stroke down the length of her torso, from between her breasts to the glistening flesh of her pussy. With her legs pulled up she was wide open, fully on display, and she felt her face flush with heat as he looked at her.

"God, you're gorgeous," he muttered, his fingers petting over the smooth, damp flesh of her cunt. He stroked over the swollen folds once, twice, then delved into her with two fingers. She moaned, unable to keep her hips from surging up to meet his hand. He pulled nearly free and thrust again, pushing through the tight grip of her sheath to reach deep. She was so wet she squished as he pushed his fingers into her. The small noise echoing though the quiet of the room, and she flushed at the sound. The slight humiliation of being on display, of knowing she couldn't hide her body's reaction from him was unbearably arousing, and incredibly she found herself speeding toward orgasm.

He muttered a curse, indistinct and guttural; she barely heard it above the roaring in her ears as he ripped his fingers free of the clasp of her pussy. He stood, stripping his shirt off in one smooth motion, and her mouth went dry.

She'd seen him without his shirt on before, doing yard work or jogging through the neighborhood. The broad expanse of his chest was tanned, lightly sprinkled with tawny hair that was bleached by the sun, an intricately designed Celtic tattoo over his left pectoral muscle. His stomach rippled as he unbuckled his belt, drawing her eye downward, and she watched with breathless anticipation.

He didn't draw it out. His urgency matched hers, and he made quick work of the belt and pants, pushing everything down and off and kicking it to the side before climbing back up on the bed to once again perch between her spread knees.

Isa licked her lips, all her attention riveted on Jacob as he hovered over her. He was beautiful—muscled, with a hedonist's all over tan, and if what was between his legs was to be believed, part buffalo.

She watched, fascinated, as he wrapped one broad palm around his cock, giving the shaft a few lazy strokes. "Tease," she accused, her voice harsh with lust.

"You think this is teasing?" he rumbled, giving his cock another slow stroke. Moisture pearled on the tip, pooling there before splashing onto the bare skin of her thigh.

"Yes," she groaned in frustration, her hips twisting helplessly as she struggled in vain to get closer.

"You should brace yourself, honey," he warned, eyes glittering at her as he watched her twist and squirm under him. "If you think this is teasing—" he gave himself another firm stroke "—then this is going to kill you."

He slid down the bed until his broad shoulders were wedged between her knees, his face poised over her dripping cunt. He sent her an evil grin, then proceeded to drive her crazy.

It seemed as though he spent days between her legs, licking and nibbling and suckling until she thought she'd go out of her mind. He seemed to know a firm touch on her clit would send her flying over the edge, and he kept his touch frustratingly light, dancing around the tight bundle of nerves but never giving her what she needed. He covered every inch of her pussy, licking under and around the rope that still ran between her legs, using his tongue and teeth to add to the sweet torment, but never stayed in one place long enough for the tension to break. Instead it built and built until she thought it would tear her apart, and still he drew it out.

Isa groaned, mindless with lust and frustration, her head tossing on the pillow. "Please," she gasped, panting for air. She strained against her bonds, struggling to get closer in vain. "Please… need… fuck me." She knew on some level she was babbling incoherently, but she couldn't help it. She felt like her mind had shut down, and all that was left was her body and this throbbing, driving need he'd created in her.

He ignored her, continuing to tease and stroke and play with her pussy until she was sobbing out loud, a steady stream of pleas tumbling off her tongue. Her hips were surging of their own accord, frantically seeking the press of his body, the deep thrust of his cock and the orgasm that was hovering just out of her reach.

Desperate and frantic with need she cried out, the sound a shriek in the quiet of the room, and finally he lifted his face from her cunt. Then he was on his knees between her spread, bound legs, sheathing himself with a condom—she gave a brief prayer of thanks that one of them was thinking clearly—then his cock was in hand and he was aiming the broad head at her eager opening. She pushed up to meet him as he drove into her, the broad width of him tunneling through her clinging flesh, and she cried out in shock and relief as she finally felt the weight of him pressing her into the mattress.

He didn't pause, didn't give her time to adjust, and that was fine because if he'd stopped she might have found a way out of her ropes to strangle him with them. He began thrusting, pushing his body hard into hers, making the need climb even higher. She sobbed in relief, pushing her body up to meet the mad fury of his, wanting more and more and more until the tension and lust that had been clenched like a fist in her belly burst free. She cried out with the force of her orgasm, her cunt clenching in rhythmic spasms around his thrusting cock. He groaned as her muscles clamped down on him but didn't slow down, fucking her hard through her orgasm and drawing out the pleasure.

Her spasms had barely faded when he stiffened over her, the muscles in his neck cording with tension as he gritted his teeth, growling out his own pleasure as he came. The rhythmic pulse of his cock inside her was so erotic, so elementally sexual, she felt her body gather again and explode with him.

Chapter 8

The next few minutes passed in a haze for Isa. She roused herself when he pulled free of the clasp of her body, the delicious friction setting off minor orgasmic aftershocks that made her fingers tingle. Or maybe that was the ropes slowly cutting off her circulation; she couldn't tell.

She felt the mattress shift as he moved, then a tug on her right wrist and realized he was untying her hands. She opened her eyes and looked up to see him kneeling, still magnificently naked, next to her torso as he worked to free her hand. He got her free and began rubbing her fingers, looking down at her in concern.

"How're your hands?" he murmured.

"Fine," she sighed, curling her fingers to link with his. No tingle now, so it had probably been the aftershocks. He kissed the back of her hand, laying it on her stomach before moving off the bed to go around to the other side and work on her left hand.

He released her left hand quickly then removed the rest of the rope from her body, pulling her legs straight on the bed to restore normal circulation. He left her briefly to visit the bathroom and deal with the condom, then he was back, sliding up next to her and wrapping his arms around her.

"Doing okay?" he asked, his lips pressed to her temple.

She nodded. "I'm great," she murmured. "How're you?"

His low chuckle vibrated against her skin. "I'm great too," he said. "Cold?" he asked when she shivered lightly.

"A little," she sighed. "But I don't want to have to move to get under the covers."

"Don't move," he instructed, and this time she obeyed, watching through half closed eyes as he got up and crossed to the closet. He pulled a blanket off the shelf, shaking it out as he came back to the bed. She sighed with contentment as he spread it out, covering her up, then climbed underneath to cuddle her close.

"Hmmm." She closed her eyes again, turning into him to lay her head on his chest. "Jacob?"

"Hmm?"

"We're going to do this again, right?"

His hand swept up her back to curl around the back of her head. "Oh, I'm not done yet, darlin'. Bet on that."

"Good." She yawned and snuggled closer. "Neither am I."

The nose twitching scent of fresh brewed coffee wafted under her nose, and Isa sat up in bed so fast Jacob had to step back to avoid upending the breakfast tray all over the bed.

"Whoa," he said, the dishes on the tray rattling as they settled back into place. "You wake up fast."

"I smell coffee." Isa sat up straighter, the blanket falling to her lap unnoticed as she inhaled deeply. "And bacon, and.." she sniffed again. "Cinnamon rolls?"

He leaned down to kiss her soft mouth. "Good morning to you, too."

"Mmm." She smiled up at him. "Good morning. Can I have some coffee?"

He chuckled and set the tray down on the bed. He picked up a steaming mug of the dark brew and passed it over, and she inhaled the fragrant steam gratefully. She sipped, humming her approval at the rich taste, and watched as he removed the napkins covering the plates.

Scrambled eggs, crisp bacon and cinnamon rolls oozing with icing all but spilled off one plate. A huge bowl teemed with strawberries and blueberries, and a tall stack of buttermilk pancakes took up the other plate. She goggled at the sheer amount of food. "How many people are joining us for breakfast?"

"Just us," he said, settling himself on the bed next to her. She was momentarily distracted by the sight of him in low slung sweatpants and nothing else; the urge to lick the jut of his hipbones was almost as strong as her desire to taste the cinnamon rolls.

"I wasn't sure what you'd feel like eating, so I just made everything."

She laughed. "A man who can cook. How'd I get so lucky?"

"Don't get too excited," he warned ruefully. "This is pretty much the extent of my culinary talents."

Isa reached for a piece of bacon and bit in. "What about that big manly grill you've got on your back porch?" She grinned at him. "That's not just for show, is it?"

"Hell no," he rumbled, and draped a napkin over her lap. "Barbecue's a fine, Southern art, but it's not the same as cooking."

"This is true," she conceded. She polished off the slice of bacon and reached for another. "This is really good, though."

"Here." He handed her a fork and slid the tray between them. "Try the eggs."

She forked up a fluffy mouthful, moaning in delight as the flavor exploded on her tongue. "Oh, that's good. Onion?"

"And a little bit of dill," he admitted, sampling them himself. "I think it turned out good."

Isa's full mouth prevented her from agreeing, but he got the point when she proceeded to plow her way through most of the eggs, half the pancakes, one cinnamon roll and a handful of berries. He watched her put it away with something close to awe, and she finally noticed the look on his face.

"What?" she asked. "Do I have food on my face or something?"

"Now that you mention it," he said, reaching out to flick a speck of egg from the corner of her mouth. "Can I get you anything else? Maybe a salad bar, a side of beef perhaps?"

"Hey, gimme a break. I burned up a lot of calories last night."

"Yes, you did," he murmured. He lifted the tray, setting it on the floor before shifting closer and reaching out a hand. His fingers closed firmly over her bare breast and she gasped, startled. His eyes flew to hers, narrowed in concern. "Does that hurt?"

She gave a gasping laugh. "No," she managed, her nipple tight and tingling from his touch. "I just forgot I was sitting here mostly naked."

He chuckled. "I didn't forget." His fingers curled around her breast, cupping the heavy mound and scraping his thumb over the nipple. She let out a squealing moan and arched up into his touch.

"I'm still eating here, are you trying to distract me?"

"Is it working?" He leaned down and flicked his tongue over one aching peak. She let out a high pitched sound and clamped a hand on the back of his head, her fingers pressing into the smooth skin of his scalp and she all but climbed into his lap.

He lifted his head. "How did I overlook these last night?"

"What? My boobs?" She laughed breathlessly. "You were focusing on other stuff."

"True enough," he murmured. "But now that stuff is out of the way..." He bent his head again, intent on making up for lost time.

"Oh," she whispered, her breath catching with delight as he nibbled the underside of her breast. She flexed her fingers on his scalp, holding him to her.

"You're sensitive," he murmured, tracing her turgid nipple with a rough fingertip. He turned his finger, scraping her tender flesh with the edge of his fingernail, smiling as she stiffened and gasped. "Very sensitive."

"I know," she said. She shifted in his arms, pushing the blanket out of the way to climb into his lap. She stared up at him with wide eyes, her breath already quickened with arousal. "You're really good at this."

Jacob grinned. "Not bad for a vanilla guy, huh?"

She laughed. "You're not going to forget that, are you?"

"No. In fact, I think I ought to prove myself again." Her eyes went wide again as he yanked the blanket away and tossed it across the room.

"Well," she managed. "If you feel you must."

"I really love my life," Jacob drawled.

"Mine's starting to look pretty good," Isa said, her voice muffled by the comforter.

"Darlin', you should see it from this angle," he drawled, and sat back to admire his handiwork.

The tableau before him was straight out of his fantasies, the ones that had started the day Isa moved in next door to him. She was on her knees, her ankles tied to the bottom corners of the bed. He'd lashed her wrists together and then pulled them under her body and between her spread feet, tying the rope off on the footboard. The position held her shoulders pressed to the mattress and her ass in the air, and he couldn't resist running a hand over the curve of her hip.

"Um... it's not that I don't appreciate the ingenuity," Isa said, turning her face to the side and peering up at him from behind a curtain of hair. "But I'm feeling kind of exposed here."

"I know." He slid his hand around to her other hip. "I like looking at you like this, all spread out and helpless."

She made a soft, purring sound at that. "Well, when you put it that way, I like it too. But it does beg the question."

He was busy testing the firmness of her ass by gently squeezing and releasing the rounded cheeks. They were very firm. "What question is that?"

"Are you going to look all day, or fuck me?"

The question startled a laugh out of him. "Why Isabella, such language! What would your mother say?"

He saw her wince behind her hair. "Dude, are you trying to kill the mood? Don't mention my mother."

He was still chuckling. "Right. Good idea. But I can't let that kind of language slide. It's rude."

She snorted. "Rude. Right. I've got my ass so high in the air it's getting altitude sickness, and the word 'fuck' is just too crude."

"That's a dirty mouth you've got, darlin'. Maybe we should do something about that."

She snorted again. "Oh yeah? Like what?"

"Like this," he said, and brought his hand down on the curve of her ass with a crack.

Isa yelped. "Hey! Who said you could do that?"

"You did." He ran his hand over the bloom of red his hand had left on her cheek. "Don't you remember? A little bondage, may be a slap on the ass here or there."

Isa's voice was thick with suppressed laughter. "I don't think that qualifies as a negotiation, pal. I was drunk!"

"That's true," he allowed. "Strictly speaking, you didn't give your consent to a spanking. But since you're here…" he slapped the other cheek.

She was giggling openly now, her body shaking with it. He hid his own grin and put on his best big bad man voice. "You're laughing? This is funny?"

"Well, it does kind of tickle."

"Tickle?"

She laughed again, the sound bursting out of her at the outrage in his voice.

"Tickle?" he said again. "I'll show you tickle, woman!" He dug his fingers into her ribs, moving with her as she squealed and wriggled to get away. "Ah ha! Not so funny now, is it?"

She was laughing so hard she could barely breathe, her entire body moving and flexing against the ropes as she tried to evade his dancing fingers. "You asshole!" she managed to get out between gasps for air.

"Asshole? There's that mouth again," he rumbled and smacked her upturned ass, a little harder this time.

"Ah!" she gasped, her head coming up off the bed in shock. He rubbed his palm over her cheek, the sting from the initial blow fading into a spreading warmth. He repeated the action with the other cheek, and Isa moaned and dropped her head back to the mattress.

He peppered her cheeks with blows, pausing after each to rub and stroke, and soon she was writhing on the bed again. Jacob watched her body flex and strain against her bonds, his own hands stinging slightly from the repeated contact. His own lust was quickly reaching fever pitch, but he was having too much fun to cut things short.

He raised his hand for another smack, bringing his hand down flat and curling his fingers to dig into the muscle and watching for her reaction. A hissing growl rumbled out of her throat, her hips thrusting back into his hand.

He leaned over, curling himself around her body and pressing his hips into hers. She moaned as the worn cotton of his sweatpants made contact with the heated skin of her ass, and he ground himself into her. "Hey." He tangled his fist in her hair, turning her head to the side so he could see her eyes."You're not enjoying this, are you?" he said with mock fierceness, the laughter in his voice ruining the effect.

Her breath was coming fast, her cheeks flushed with color and her eyes sparkling with fire and laughter. "Oh no," she panted. He pressed into her harder, and she pushed back on a shuddering moan. "No, not enjoying this at all."

"Good," he muttered. Jesus, his dick was hard enough to drive nails, and if he didn't fuck her soon, he was going to embarrass himself by coming in his pants like a twelve year old. "Because it's punishment, you know. If you were enjoying it, I'd have to stop."

Her hair flew as she tossed her head. "No, you shouldn't stop," she protested. "Do your worst, I can take it."

He pressed his mouth to the shell of her ear, lust and laughter jockeying for position inside him. "Good girl," he whispered, catching the lobe between his teeth and tugging. She whimpered, her hips rolling against him, and lust pulled ahead.

He wrapped his arms around her, reaching under to cup her breasts and thumb the sensitive tips. She groaned, the sound vibrating through her as she tried to press herself hard into his hands. He teased and tweaked, alternating delicate strokes with a firmer touch, and he knew if the ropes hadn't held her immobile she would have been climbing the walls.

He gritted his teeth when she writhed again, her hips wiggling and pushing back at him, and he abruptly pushed away, rising to his feet and striding to the bathroom for a condom. He walked back into the room and around the bed so he was in her line of sight, tossing the condom on the mattress. He waited until her eyes, glazed and wide with lust, focused on him before tugging at the drawstring of his sweatpants and pushing them down. He watched her eyes flick down and widen even more.

He picked up the condom and was about to tear the wrapping with his teeth when she spoke.

"Wait," she said, her voice a mere whisper. She started to push up, but the rope binding her hands to the foot of the bed brought her up short. She whimpered in frustration, then began wiggling towards the foot of the bed. He watched as she scooted almost all the way down, until she had enough play in the rope holding her bound hands to the foot of the bed to push herself up. She licked her lips. "Here."

"What?"

Isa licked her lips, her eyes focused on his cock. "Come up here," she repeated, her voice dancing over his nerves like silk. "I want to taste you."

She's trying to kill me, he thought as he climbed on the bed to kneel in front of her. *But the joke's on her. If I have a heart attack, there won't be anyone to untie her.*

She leaned in, stroking her cheek over him. She didn't have enough play in the ropes to use her hands, so he held himself steady with one hand and cradled her head with the other. She looked up through a tangle of hair, and the heat and want in her gaze would have brought him to his knees if he hadn't already been there.

She kept her eyes locked on his face as she opened her mouth, flicking her tongue out to swipe over the head of his cock. Her groan echoed his and she did it again, lapping at the moisture that pooled there. She made a sound in her throat, like a purring growl, and opened her mouth.

Jacob groaned, fighting the urge to thrust as he watched his cock disappear into her mouth. Her lips stretched around his girth as she took him to the back of her throat, then pulled back. He hissed in a breath at the suction. "Christ, Isa. God, baby that feels amazing." He let go of his cock to tangle both hands in her hair and gently pushed his hips forward.

She squealed around his cock and sucked harder. His hands tightened in her hair in response, tugging at her scalp, and watched her eyes flare wide at the slight sting of pain. Then they drifted closed, and she began sucking in earnest, driving her mouth up and down his cock in a steady rhythm. For long moments the only sounds in the room were his harsh breathing and the slurping sounds of her mouth as she worked him, until he couldn't take it another minute.

He pulled her off him, ignoring her moans of protest to pull himself free. He groped for the condom and tore it open, climbing off the bed to circle behind her. He fumbled the condom on then got on his knees behind her. He slid a finger into her pussy, testing her readiness.

"You're so wet," he muttered. He brought the head of his cock to her opening, probing gently. "Are you ready for me, baby?"

Her answer was a guttural moan and a push of her hips. He held her steady with one hand on her hip, keeping her from thrusting back to impale herself on his cock. "Tell me, baby. I want to hear it."

"Yes, I'm ready," she moaned. "Please, I need you to fuck me."

"Fuck yes," he rumbled, and pushed forward.

Twin sounds of pleasure echoed in the air as he tunneled deep, moving steadily into her, not stopping until his hips were snug against hers and he was in her to the balls. He paused, as much to give himself time to adjust as her, then began moving.

The pace was slow, drawn out; he savored her. The hot clasp of her body around his cock, the smooth skin of her hips where he held her steady for his thrusts. He draped himself over her, pressing his lips to her shoulder, her neck, her back, savoring the taste of her skin. He breathed her in, filling his lungs with the spicy scent of her arousal.

He brought his hands under her again, lifting and squeezing her breasts and glorying in her cries of pleasure. She pushed her body into his, taking his thrusts and his touch and wordlessly begging for more. Time seemed to spin out as they drowned in each other, the room filling with the heat and sound and scent of their mating.

All too soon he could feel the urgency building, pushing him to drive, to thrust, to pound his way to completion, but he resisted it. She was begging, pleading with him to hurry, to finish it, to push her over the edge into oblivion and follow her there, but he didn't want it to end. So he drew it out until she was all but sobbing under him, her fingers digging into the bedspread under her, her hips pumping blindly in her search for release. He could feel the flutters begin, the tiny pulses deep within her pussy that signaled her impending release, and he couldn't wait anymore.

He gave in to the urge to drive, straightening up and grasping her hips for leverage as he began thrusting heavily. She cried out, in distress or relief he wasn't sure which, but he was beyond caring. He pumped and pounded, feeling his own body gather and tighten and strain for release, and suddenly it was on him. He stiffened, pumped once, twice more, and let out a roar as the room exploded around him.

Dimly he heard her cry out again, felt the hard clenching of her sheath around his spurting cock. The contractions of her cunt drew a roaring cry from his throat, the sensation making him feel as if his head would explode. He collapsed on top of her, shuddering and shaking in the aftermath as he tried to come back to Earth.

Chapter 9

Isa blinked hard and brought her thoughts back to the deposition in front of her. She had to get through these last half dozen before the end of the day if she had any hope of staying on schedule for trial, but her thoughts kept drifting back to Jacob and the innovative and mind bending method he'd used to wake her up that morning. She glanced at her wrists, smiling dreamily at the faint marks that were almost completely faded.

"Focus, Isabella," she muttered to herself. A quick glance at the clock told her it was almost lunch time, and on impulse she picked up the phone.

"Bandoli Spa, how may I help you?"

"Nelson, it's Isa."

"Darling, where have you been? I left half a dozen messages for you this weekend!"

"I was busy," she said, suppressed laughter making her lips twitch.

"Well, thank the gods, but did you forget that as best friend, it's my privilege to get the juicy details?"

She laughed. "Nelson, I never give you the details."

"But I never stop hoping," he answered. "If you're not calling to give me juicy details—and damn your soul for that—then what's up?"

"Do you have a break in your schedule for lunch?" she asked.

"Am I going to get any juicy details?" he countered.

"Actually, I'm feeling rather uncharacteristically chatty today," Isa drawled, then had to jerk the phone away from her ear at Nelson's squeal of glee.

"Yes! I'm clearing my schedule for a nice, long lunch, and you better plan on talking more than eating."

"That's a deal," she said, chuckling. "The café in half an hour?"

"Oh no," he said. "I'm not taking the chance on a public venue stifling your suddenly chatty mood. I'm ordering in Chinese, we're locking ourselves in a treatment room, and you're spilling your guts. I'll even give you a facial while we're at it."

"How can I pass that up?" she wondered. "I'll see you in half an hour."

She hung up the phone with a click and shuffled her files into a stack as she clicked the button on her intercom. "Julia, I'm going to head out for lunch."

"Okay," came the cheery voice of her young assistant. "You've got a call waiting on line two, want me to tell him you're already gone?"

"Him?"

"Yeah, him. Sounds kind of foxy, too."

"Um. I'll take it." She drew in a deep breath, then picked up the receiver.

"Isabella Carelli."

"How're you feeling this morning?"

Isa smiled. "A little tired, a little sore, but otherwise fine."

"Not too sore, I hope."

"No, nothing a hot bath won't cure."

"Good." His voice lowered intimately, brushing over her like a physical caress. "I was sorry you couldn't stay for breakfast this morning."

"Me too," she said with regret. "But this case... it's important."

"Of course it is," he murmured. "I understand."

She sighed with relief when she realized he wasn't upset at her mad scramble to leave that morning. "I was almost late as it was," she murmured, "but it was worth it."

"I'm glad to have made an impression," he rumbled, and she could hear the laughter ripe in his voice.

"Oh, you did that," she said. "I'm very, very impressed."

He laughed outright at her choice of words. "Glad to hear it. Listen, I wanted to tell you that I'm going to be heading out of town for a few days."

"Oh?" she managed, ruthlessly squelching the lurch of disappointment.

"I've got a cheating spouse who likes to travel, and since he's bringing his secretary along for the ride on this trip, I need to follow along and catch them in the act."

She grimaced. "Ugh. I'm glad I don't have your job."

He laughed ruefully. "It's definitely got its ugh moments, but it's a living."

"Well, good luck with the trip. I hope he cheats." She winced. "I guess."

He was laughing again. "Thanks. I was hoping to see you before I left. Are you free for dinner tonight?"

"I thought—you're not leaving today?" she asked, hope making her voice rise.

"I'm catching a flight in the morning," he said. "I thought I'd take you out for Chinese tonight."

"Actually, I'm going to have Chinese for lunch." She checked her watch, cursing at the time. "And I have to leave now or I'll be late and Nelson will have my head."

"I'd still like to take you out," he said. "I don't like the idea of not seeing you before I leave."

"Oh," she said, sounding to her own ears like the breathless heroine in some Victorian romance and not caring. "I'd like to see you too, but..." she looked at the stack of files on her desk. "I'm going to have to work a little late. I probably won't be home until around eight or eight thirty."

"That's okay," he said. "It'll give me time to pack before dinner. Why don't we plan on eight-thirty? I'll come to your place, and we can eat in instead of going out—I'll order Italian, since you're having Chinese for lunch."

"That sounds great," she said. "I'll see you then." She hung up the phone and, after checking to make sure her assistant wasn't hovering in the doorway, indulged in a purely girlish giggle and a spin of the desk chair.

Before the chair could come to a stop, she was leaping up and snagging her purse. Lunch beckoned, and for the first time in her adult romantic life, she couldn't wait to share the details of it with her best friend.

Isa pulled into her driveway that night at nine forty-five, exhaustion pulling at her. The deposition she'd had scheduled for late afternoon had run abysmally late, due to the witness's lack of desire to cooperate and his lawyer's objections to every question asked. She didn't think she'd worked so hard to get a simple yes or no answer out of someone in her entire career, and the experience had left her feeling tired, cranky, and not at all romantic.

She trudged up the driveway, rolling her shoulders to try to ease the tension knotting the muscles there. She'd called Jacob about an hour ago to tell him she would be late, but she'd gotten his voice mail, and she had no idea if he'd picked up the message or not. She glanced across her front lawn to his house; it was dark, the porch light the only illumination. "Probably gave up on me," she muttered, disappointment rising. She pulled out her cell phone to make sure she hadn't missed a call from him, and jumped a foot when it jangled in her hand.

"Hello?"

"Isa, it's Joe. How are you?"

Isa swallowed the hiss of annoyance. Why was he calling her? "As a matter of fact, Joe, I'm really tired. It's been kind of a long day."

"Oh. Well, have you eaten? I could pick you up, we could grab a late dinner." He sounded so eager, like a school boy with a crush, and she frowned.

"Uh, no thanks." She juggled her briefcase to fit her key into the lock. "I think I'm just going to heat up some soup and go to bed."

"Oh, okay. Well, maybe I'll call you later in the week, when you're not so tired, and we can do something." The eagerness was back in his voice, and she felt her confusion grow.

"I don't think that's a very good idea," she said. She finally got the key in the lock and pushed open the door. She kicked off her shoes with a sigh of relief and reached down to stroke George as he twined between her ankles.

"Why not?" Joe persisted, and alarm bells started to clang.

"Joe, did you forget we broke up?" she asked, too tired to dance around the point.

"No, but um… well… now that you mention it, I might have been a little hasty," he said, and she barely stifled a groan. "I talked to my therapist, and she thinks I ought to have given your… predilections… a chance. Explored them a bit. So I was thinking, maybe we could try—"

"No," she interrupted, and started towards the kitchen. "I think your first instinct was right; my "predilections" just weren't for you."

"Well, that's what I thought, but after talking to Fiona about it—"

"Who's Fiona?"

"My therapist. Anyway, Fiona thinks I might benefit from some sexual exploration."

Isa rolled her eyes and mentally cursed Fiona. "Joe, it's better if we make a clean break. You'll need to find someone else to explore sexually." She rounded the corner into the kitchen and stopped dead. Jacob stood at her stove in her Kiss the Cook apron, stirring a pot of something fragrant and sipping a glass of wine. He smiled when he saw her, a slow movement of his mouth that warmed his eyes and made her breath catch in her chest.

Joe was still chattering in her ear about Fiona and her suggestions for broadening his sexual horizons, but she'd stopped listening. "Joe, I gotta go," she said absently, and clicked the phone shut on his protest.

She crossed the kitchen, her belly tightening as he watched her. "What're you doing here?" she murmured.

"Making you dinner," he replied, and leaned down to brush her lips with his. She felt the contact all the way to her toes.

"Mmmm," she murmured, taking a sip of wine from the glass he pressed into her hand. "Italian?"

He shook his head, brushing one hand absently over her hair as he continued to stir. "It's so late I thought pasta wouldn't be the best choice," he explained. "Too heavy."

"So you made soup?" she asked, peering into the pot.

"Reheated," he corrected with a grin. "It's my sister's recipe, tomato basil. I like it so much she always makes a double batch and freezes one for me, so all I have to do is heat it up."

Isa inhaled the steam coming from the pot. "It smells fantastic," she said, smiling up at him. "You're going to spoil me."

"That's the idea," he said with a wink. "This is about done. Why don't you take your wine to the table, and I'll bring this in."

She turned to see her kitchen table already set. Twin tapered candles in her best silver candlesticks sat waiting to be lit, with a small bowl of lilacs perched between them. Despite her exhaustion, she sighed at the romantic gesture.

She took a seat as he came out of the kitchen, looking startlingly masculine in the apron with an oven mitt in the shape of a clown fish on his hand. As he ladled soup, she asked, "When did you do all this?"

"When I got your message," he said over his shoulder as he carried the pot back to the stove. He re-emerged sans apron and oven mitt and pulled out a pocket Bic to light the candles. "You left your alarm off, by the way." He glanced over at her as he sat down, one eyebrow raised at her look of confusion. "Didn't you wonder how I'd gotten in here?"

"Um, no." She winced. "I didn't even think about it. Oops."

"Yeah, oops. Don't do that again," he warned. "You have the alarm system for a reason, you should use it."

She shrugged. "I have the alarm system because it came with the house. I feel pretty safe here without it."

"Set it anyway," he said, the suggestion sounding suspiciously like an order.

She had her mouth open to ask him which it was, suggestion or order, when he asked, "How's the soup?"

She blinked down at her untouched bowl, then grinned. "I haven't tried it yet." She picked up her spoon and dug in, closing her eyes in pleasure as the flavor exploded on her tongue. "Yum!" She turned to look at him in surprise. "I didn't expect it to be so flavorful. I mean, it's tomato soup! What's in it?"

"I have no idea," he chuckled, spooning up soup. "From the name I would assume tomatoes, and basil, but the rest is a mystery."

"Well, your sister's a soup genius," Isa decided. She reached for the bread basket, then passed it to him.

"So I often tell her." He chose a hunk of bread then tucked back into his soup. "So how's the case going?"

"Oh, don't get me started," she muttered around a mouthful of food. "Today was a nightmare, and I have a lot of work ahead of me."

He topped off her wine. "You knew that though, right?"

She nodded. "Sure. But today was the first day I really got my hands into it, so it was a little overwhelming. But I'll get a handle on it."

He clinked her glass with his in an impromptu toast. "I'm sure you will."

Isa grinned. "Thanks." She looked back down at her bowl, surprised to see it empty. "Wow, I must have been hungrier than I thought."

"There's more if you want another bowl."

"Tempting, but no thanks. I can't sleep on an overly full stomach." She started to rise to clear her dishes, but he waved her back down, and she watched him clear the table with amusement.

"You really are going to spoil me, you know," she called after him as he took the dishes to the kitchen.

"I told you, that's the idea." He came back in and extended a hand, tugging her to her feet when she placed her hand in his. He smoothed her hair back from her face, his touch gentle and soothing, and she leaned into it with a sigh.

"You look tired," he murmured. "I should probably go, let you get some sleep."

"No," she protested, groaning with pleasure when his hands moved to her shoulders to knead and stroke away the tension that still lingered there. "You don't have to go."

"Are you sure?" he murmured. He pressed a kiss to one corner of her mouth, then the other, before settling fully on her lips.

Isa sighed with pleasure, curling into him and opening her mouth for his tongue. He rumbled a groan in answer, his arms tightening to lift her off her feet as he deepened the kiss.

She broke free with a gasp, curling her fingers into his hair to cradle his head as he nibbled along her collarbones. "Yeah, I'm really sure," she gasped. She tugged on his hair, bringing his head up so she could kiss him again. "Did you bring any rope?" she murmured against his mouth, and he chuckled.

"Lusty little thing, aren't you?" he teased, but his eyes were serious. "Are you sure you're not too tired?"

She swung her legs up to twine around his waist, her skirt sliding up to bunch at her hips as she settled her pussy against the growing ridge in his slacks. He caught his breath as she clenched her thighs on his hips, flexing against him, and she knew he could feel the wet heat of her through his clothes and her panties. "Pretty sure."

He started walking down the hall toward the bedroom. "I didn't bring any rope," he said, "but we can use yours."

"I don't have as much as you," she warned breathlessly. "Only about a hundred feet."

He grinned and winked. "I like a challenge."

"Fabulous," she sighed.

Chapter 10

On Friday afternoon Jacob was still trailing the cheating husband, and Isa was going insane. Slumped at her desk in the office, she stared out the window at the driving rain and thought with no little amount of hostility of Jacob's client. Was it really necessary to get more evidence on her louse of a husband? "I mean, he got pictures of them the first day, banging in the hotel cloak room, for God's sake," she muttered to herself, tapping her pencil impatiently. "Does she need pictures of them doing it everywhere else, too?"

"What're you talking about?"

Isa jumped as her assistant dropped a stack of folders on her desk. "Nothing," she stammered, and straightened in her chair. "What's all this?"

"Medical files for the class action. The interns have already been through them, highlighting the dates you asked for." She winced in sympathy when Isa dropped her head to the desk with a groan. "Oh, and that guy is on the phone again."

Isa's head whipped up. "Jacob? Which line?"

She was already reaching for the phone when Julia shook her head. "No, not that guy, the other one. The one that dropped by the other day when you were in court and acted all stoned."

Isa winced. "Joe. Jesus, what is wrong with him?"

"You ask me, he's a few fries short of a happy meal," Julia said. "Want me to get rid of him?"

Isa grimaced. "No, I'll do it."

"Line two," Julia said, shutting the door as she left.

Isa drew a deep breath, then picked up the receiver and engaged the line. "Joe."

"Isa, hi! I've been trying to call you all week, but you haven't called me back. I think that assistant of yours must be forgetting to give you your messages." He laughed, a high, wild sound that grated on her nerves.

"I got your messages," she said, keeping her voice even when she wanted to scream at him. "But I told you I thought it was best if we made a clean break of it."

"Sure, yeah, I know." He drew in a deep breath that did nothing to calm the mania in his voice. "But I've really been thinking that I made a big mistake. Our breakup was a mistake, and if you'd just let me take you to lunch and explain it to you—"

"It wasn't a mistake," she said firmly, then tried another tack. "You had very valid reasons for breaking up with me. We don't want the same things out of a relationship, and you were very wise to realize that. In fact, I should thank you for that. You saved us both a lot of heartache."

"But… I love you," he said plaintively, and she sighed.

"No, you don't," she said, forcing the words out between clenched teeth. "You don't love me. If you did, you never would have been able to break up with me like that. But that's okay, because now we're both free to seek out the relationships we truly want. And that's a good thing, Joe. A very good thing, don't you think?"

"I guess…"

"Trust me, it is," she said. "I want you to find someone special, someone you can really love and who can love you back."

"You're somebody special," he whined, and she stifled a scream.

"Thank you, Joe, I appreciate that. I think you're special too. But I'm not your somebody special."

"No, I guess not." He sounded confused, but he seemed to be getting the message, and she pressed on.

"And that's what you should be looking for, your somebody special. I wish you lots of luck with that, and I hope you find her."

"Okay. Thanks, Isa. I… .um, I hope you find somebody special too."

"Thank you," she murmured, pity creeping in. "I've got a lot of work, so I'm going to let you go now."

"Okay. Goodbye."

"Goodbye," she said, and hung up the phone with a click. "And good riddance."

Her office door opened and Julia stuck her head in. "Get rid of him?"

Isa stood and started to gather the files on her desk. "Hopefully for good. Poor guy, I think he's a little unbalanced."

Julia rolled her eyes. "I think he's completely nuts, but what do I know?" She watched Isa take her purse out of her desk. "Going out?"

"I'm going to take the rest of these files home to work," she said, slinging her purse over her shoulder and hefting the stack of folders. "I'll be at it most of the weekend anyway, I might as well get set up."

"If you're heading out, do you mind if I go home early?" Julia grinned, her blue eyes dancing. "I've got a hot date, and I could use a few extra hours to get ready."

Isa laughed. "Go ahead."

"Great! See you Monday!" And with a wave, she was gone.

Isa felt a twinge of envy as she headed out behind her assistant. She'd like to be heading home to pamper and perfume herself for a big date, but it looked like Mr. Cheating Asshole was going to keep Jacob on the road through the weekend. "I'll be cuddling up with you guys," she muttered, eyeing her armful of files with distaste. At least she'd be able to get a little ahead in her work, so when Jacob did come home she could spend some guilt free time with him.

"Until then, it's all you guys," she told the files, and headed out into the rain.

Half an hour later she had changed into comfortable sweats and was at her kitchen table, the files arranged in neat piles by date. Hands filled with a cup of coffee, a bright pink highlighter and a notepad, she used her knee to scoot the cat off her seat and was just sitting down to work when a bolt of lightning light up the darkened sky. Drawn to the flash, her eyes darted to the French doors leading to her back yard, and the coffee, highlighter and notepad flew into the air as she screamed.

Half a heartbeat later she was opening the back door. "Jacob!" She reached out, snagged his shirtfront and hauled him into the kitchen, slamming the door against the rain. "You scared me to death!" She blinked at him. "You look mad."

He tugged off the beat up fielders cap covering his head and shook it, spattering water on the floor and on George, who hissed his annoyance and darted under the table. "I haven't slept in forty-eight hours," he said grimly. "I finally convinced my client that still photos—and video—of her husband and his twenty-two year old assistant fucking their brains out in New York, Atlanta, and L.A. was plenty of evidence to get a divorce with, and under no circumstances was I going to follow them to Hong Kong. Where, if the phone tap can be believed, they're planning on enjoying the brothels."

Isa made a face and opened her mouth to speak, but he kept talking, watching her with fierce and hungry eyes as her blood began to pound.

"Then I spent half the night waiting stand-by for the red eye out of L.A., they lost my luggage, and I drove straight to your office in the worst traffic snarl I've ever seen—there was an eighteen wheeler jackknifed on the freeway—only to get there ten minutes after you'd gone. And on the way here, I got a speeding ticket."

She watched as he took a deep breath that, judging by the muscle jerking in his clenched jaw, did nothing to calm him down. "You went by my office?" she asked, and his face finally softened.

"I thought I'd find you hard at work, buried in an avalanche of briefs and depositions, and I could rescue you."

"I brought the avalanche home with me," she said, gesturing to the piles on the table. "But I could lay under it if you're going to dig me out."

His lips twitched, but he stayed where he was, a full arms length away. "God, I missed you."

She didn't move either. "I missed you, too."

His eyes were dark and wild, and focused on her with an intensity that made her want to trip him and beat him to the floor. "You have a lot of work to do?" he asked.

She glanced at the stacks of files, thought of all the medical reports, depositions and briefs she had to get through by Monday morning. "It can wait."

"Good. Because I can't." He reached out with one long arm to haul her in, and she met him halfway.

"Oh thank God," she breathed, and plastered herself against him, seeking his mouth with hers. "Touch me," she begged, frantically running her hands over his face, his head, before clutching at his shoulders to boost herself up against him. She heard him grunt at the impact, felt his arm come up under her hips to anchor her. She wrapped her legs around him, locking her ankles and grinding herself against the hard ridge of flesh behind his zipper. She heard him curse, felt the impact as he stumbled against the wall, and then they were on the floor.

"Ohmygosh!" She shoved her hair out of her eyes and pushed up, bracing her palms on his chest. "Are you okay?"

He was shaking with laughter. "You always seem to land on top of me," he managed between chuckles, and she smiled.

"I like being on top of you." She leaned down to kiss him again. "In fact," she murmured against his mouth, "on top of you is just where I want to be right now. So you just stay right there, and let me be on top."

She felt him smile against her mouth. "Does that mean you're in charge now?"

She quirked a brow and sat up, shifting her weight to settle square across his hips, and smiled smugly when he gasped. "Yeah," she whispered. "I'm in charge now."

She saw his lips twitch with amusement as she tugged his t-shirt free of his jeans and shoved it up to bare his flat belly. "Have I ever told you," she said conversationally, "how much I love your stomach?" She traced his belly button with the edge of one fingernail and watched, fascinated, as the muscles clenched. She glanced up at his face and smiled. The smirk had been replaced with a clenched jaw, and when she circled his belly button again she saw his Adam's apple bob in a hard swallow.

"No?" she went on when he didn't answer. "Well, I do. I can't even imagine the conditioning, the discipline it must have taken for you to get all this muscle." Spreading her fingers, she trailed them from his sternum to his waistband, watching the muscles ripple. His hips surged under her, the hard ridge of his confined cock pushing up, spreading her cunt open like the soft fleece of her sweats wasn't even there, and she couldn't swallow the moan.

Suddenly, teasing and tormenting him didn't seem important any longer. It'd been four days, four long, frustrating, lonely days since she'd been next to him, with him. Four days since he'd been inside her, and she didn't want to wait any longer.

She shoved at his t-shirt again. "Take this off," she ordered, and he lifted his shoulders off the ground to whip it over his head. She was leaning forward before he'd even settled back down, her mouth voracious. Slightly chilled by the rain, his skin warmed up quickly under her lips as she teased and licked and nibbled her way across the wide expanse of his chest. Her hands were busy unhooking his belt buckle, fighting with the button fly of the damp jeans. She scraped a nipple with the edge of her teeth as she shoved and tugged and pulled at the denim until she could work her hand in grasp his cock.

They both moaned as she found him hard and ready and already leaking pre come into her palm. She grasped him firmly, stroking down his length as she trailed her lips down his belly, tracing the faint line of hair that bisected his abdomen with her tongue. When she started nibbling along his hipbones and slid her hand from his shaft to his balls, cuddling them gently in her palm, he snarled something unintelligible and tangled his hands in her hair.

She smiled despite the slight pain as he tugged on her hair, trying to pull her head onto his cock. Power and lust mixed into a heady cocktail, swimming through her system and leaving her feeling slightly drunk. She lingered at his hip, fluttering her tongue delicately along the taut flesh as she pressed the tip of her middle finger just behind his balls and stroked. He growled, his fingers digging painfully into her scalp, and she lifted her head to stare at him.

He was out of control. His eyes were wild, his breath hissing out from behind clenched teeth as his hips surged and he rambled nonsensically. She might not have understood the words, but the tone was clear; pleading and imploring, he was all but begging her to take him into her mouth. *I did that*, she thought in awe. *He can't even talk, he wants me so badly.* The idea was so delicious, so absolutely amazing that all thoughts of drawing it out, of teasing him until he was mad for her flew right out of her head. She was suddenly desperate to taste him, to give to him the way he always seemed to give to her. She lowered her head, swirling her tongue around the crown of his cock, once, twice, delighting in his snarling curses before doing her best to swallow him whole.

"Oh God, baby." He found his words, and she savored them along with the taste and texture and heat of his cock as she worked her mouth up and down in a steady rhythm. "Yes, baby just like that. Take me, take all of me, you're so beautiful, I missed you so much." He rambled and moaned, pushing her hair away from face. She looked up to find his eyes locked on her mouth as she worked his cock with lips and tongue, and watching him watch her pushed her own lust past the point of no return.

She pulled her mouth off him with a pop and scrambled to her knees to tug frantically at the drawstring of her sweats. She fought them off, kicking her feet clear of the material, then yanked her shirt off. She turned back to find him fumbling a condom out of his pocket. He ripped it open with his teeth and had it on within seconds and was reaching for her, but she was already there, straddling his hips. She grasped the root of his penis in one hand, holding it steady, and bracing her other hand on his stomach, she lowered herself onto him.

Jacob's moan joined hers as her pussy shivered and pulsed around him, adjusting to his girth. She felt a slight pinch as her flesh stretched to accommodate him, but it only added to the pleasure, and without waiting for the feeling to fade she began to move.

The sounds of sex seemed to bounce off the walls. Moans and squeals and the slap of flesh on flesh echoed around them as she rode him for all she was worth. Her orgasm was bearing down on her with lightning speed; blowing him had aroused her as much as it had him, and neither of them was going to last very long. She leaned forward, curling her fingers into his shoulders, her hips picking up speed as she tugged him toward her.

"Kiss me." She licked her lips. "Please, I want you to mmmff!"

He dove into her mouth, his tongue delving deep as he raised his torso up off the floor. She moaned into his mouth, her nipples stabbing into his chest, her vision dimming as sensation sharpened. He slid one hand between their bodies, his fingers finding her clit with unerring accuracy, and she screamed into his mouth as the world exploded.

※❀⟨♡⟩❀※

She blinked her eyes open sometime later to find Jacob watching her.

"Hi," he said, smiling, and she smiled back.

"Hi yourself," she murmured. She looked around, slightly surprised to find herself in her own bed. "Did you carry me in here?" she asked.

"Guilty," he said, brushing her hair back from her face. "You feeling okay?"

"Mmmmm." She stretched her arms over hear head. "Wonderful. I missed this."

One dark brow went up. "This?" he asked, and the smile on her mouth faded.

"You," she whispered. "I missed you."

"I missed you too," he murmured. He brushed his mouth against hers lightly once, then settled in for a deeper kiss.

She wound her arms around his neck, suddenly anxious to be as close to him as possible, and he eased over her. She could feel the thrust of his cock against her hip, and felt desire flood back. Her hips arched up into his, and he pulled back slightly.

"You sure?" he murmured, and she nodded, her hands drawing his mouth back to hers. She felt him move, knew he was plucking a condom from the bedside table, and then he was sliding inside her once again.

She gasped, her body arching as his cock rasped against flesh already sensitive and swollen. "It's okay," she managed, answering the question before he had a chance to ask. "Just go slow, okay? I want it to last."

"Whatever you want," he murmured, his lips trailing from her mouth to her ear. "Whatever you want."

It seemed as though he made love to her for hours. He kept the rhythm slow and easy, sliding in and out of her slick flesh without haste. She felt surrounded by him, his focus solely on her, and the intensity of it would have been too much if she hadn't been just as absorbed in him. His mouth never left her; he stroked her with his lips, placing kisses over every bit of flesh he could reach, and when the constant friction and overwhelming sensuality that seemed to blanket the room became too much for them both, he swallowed her cry of release and gave her his in return.

She drifted off to sleep in his arms, her legs tangled with his and his heartbeat strong beneath her ear, and it occurred to her just before she slipped into unconsciousness that she'd be happy to end all her future days just like this.

Chapter 11

Isa woke the next morning to warm lips on her ear. "Wake up, sleepy head."

"Mmmm," she sighed, blinking her eyes open, then frowned as she saw he was dressed. At least in his jeans; at some point in the night she'd appropriated his shirt. "Are you leaving?"

He pressed a quick kiss to her mouth. "Only for a bit. I need to grab a shower."

"You can do that here," she protested, her mouth clinging to his.

"I need a shave too, and a change of clothes."

She sighed. "Okay," she mumbled, and he chuckled.

"I'll be back in an hour," he promised. "And I'll make you breakfast."

"Pancakes?" she said hopefully, and he chuckled again as her stomach rumbled.

"Pancakes," he said. "And omelets, because I'm starving."

"Me too," she admitted. "We probably should have had more for a midnight snack than Oreos and milk."

"No kidding," he said ruefully, and reached up to pluck something out of her hair. "And we probably shouldn't have had them in bed."

She giggled at the mushed cookie in his hand, and he kissed her again before straightening. "I'll be back in an hour," he said, and with a wink was out the door.

Isa sighed, stretching under the covers. She felt the gentle ache of muscles well used, and sighed again, then started as the phone on the bedside table buzzed. She glanced over at the display and smiled.

"Hello, Nelson."

"Hi honey. Listen, I know we were going to have lunch today, but I've got a bridal party booked into the salon for the full day treatment and I'm not going to be able to get away."

"That's okay," she said around a yawn. "I was going to call and cancel anyway."

"Planning on working all day?" he asked, and she giggled.

"No. Well, I was, and I'm going to do some work, but… Jacob got back last night."

"Oooh! More monkey rope sex! I've got five minutes before the maid of honor has to be paraffin waxed, so spill."

"Nope, no monkey rope sex," she said."

"What? What'd y'all do, play Parcheesi all night?"

Isa rolled her eyes. "No. We had sex. A lot of sex, actually," she said, remembering. "But no rope."

"Really? No kinky stuff?" She heard him whistle under his breath. "And how was that?"

She sighed and snuggled into the pillows. "Really good. Really wonderful actually," she allowed. "I really, really like him, Nelson. And I think he really likes me. He said he missed me," she said shyly.

Her friend gasped. "You're in love!" he squealed, and Isa sat up in bed.

"No, I'm not," she said firmly. "I can't be in love, people don't fall in love in a week. It takes longer than that."

"What do you mean, it takes longer than that?" Nelson scoffed at the notion. "It takes as long as it takes, darling. A week, a month, an hour. It happens when it happens, and honey, it's happened to you."

"Oh wow," she gulped. "What am I going to do?"

"Oh Christ," he muttered. "Here we go."

"I mean, what if he doesn't feel the same way? What if this is just a fling, and I'm just a convenient fuck? What if—?"

"Stop!"

Surprised, Isa shut her mouth.

"You're going to make yourself nuts," Nelson said, "and for no reason. Did he tell you he missed you?"

"Yes."

"Did he act like he missed you?"

"Yes," she said. "He went to my office yesterday when he got back into town, before he even came home. And he's coming back after he showers to make me pancakes."

"There you go," he said, triumph evident in his voice. "That doesn't sound like a guy just out for a convenient fuck to me. Does it sound that way to you?"

She smiled. "No."

"Then stop talking crazy." He huffed out a breath. "I swear, people in love are so irrational."

She laughed despite the clutch in her belly and kicked back the covers. "We have not yet established that anyone is in love," she said, padding down the hall to the kitchen. She needed coffee.

"Uh-huh," he muttered. "Just keep telling yourself that, doll. Meanwhile, I'm going to be really disappointed if you don't ask me to be a bridesmaid."

"I'll put you in lime green taffeta," she warned as she measured out coffee.

"Bitch," he said mildly, and she laughed.

"I love you, Nelson."

"I love you too, honey," he said. "Look, you know you like him, and that he likes you. So just let it happen, and don't worry so much. Enjoy it, for Christ's sake."

She drew a deep, cleansing breath. "Good advice"

"Damn right,"

She chuckled, then frowned when she heard the doorbell. She glanced at the clock; Jacob had barely been gone fifteen minutes. "You're so modest," she said as she headed for the front door.

"And wise," he said. "Don't forget wise."

"And wise," she agreed. "But I have to go now, oh wise and learned one, 'cause he's here."

"Didn't he just leave?"

"Guess he just can't keep his hands off me," she said, her body already flushed with anticipation as she reached for the front door. She opened it, the welcoming smile dying on her face. "Oh, shit."

"What, what is it? Did he show up naked? Is he on his knees with a big fat diamond in his hand? What?"

"No." Isa swallowed, her fingers tightening on the doorknob as she looked up into dark brown eyes. "It's Joe."

"Oh, shit."

"You look good, Isa."

She frowned at him as he made himself comfortable in her living room. "I saw you last Thursday. I look pretty much the same as I did then."

He had the grace to look sheepish, his dark hair falling across his forehead. "Yeah, but... you do. Look good." His eyes lingered on her legs, bare under Jacob's shirt, and she fought the urge to squirm. "Guess I got you out of bed, huh?"

"Something like that," she muttered. She crossed her arms over her breasts. "What do you want, Joe?"

He stood and walked towards her, taking her hands before she could move away. "I wanted to talk to you." He was looking very intense, and she tugged gently, trying to get her hands back, but he tightened his grip "I need to make you understand how I feel."

"Joe, we've been through this." She tugged at her hands again, but his grip held firm. "We broke up. To be specific, you broke up with me. How you feel is no longer my concern."

"Dammit, just listen!"

She winced as his fingers tightened painfully on hers, and she drew a careful breath. This was not looking good

"See, Fiona thinks that I thought I... well I didn't think I could give you what you were asking for, and that made me feel emasculated. I felt stripped of my manhood."

Ick, she thought.

"But you're really pretty, and I wanted to have sex with you, and if it's something you really need, then I can give it to you. It won't be so bad. I won't have to do it every day, will I?"

How charming, she thought. Out loud, she said, "You're not going to have to do it at all." His face lit with relief, and she quickly realized he'd taken that wrong. "Because we broke up," she said hurriedly. "We're not together anymore, so you don't have to worry about what I need. Isn't that nice?"

He was shaking his head. "No, we have to be together. It's right, you're right for me, I can feel it. We have to be together!"

"No, we don't," she said, appalled, and would have said more but he rolled right over her, his eyes wild, the pupils dilated so his irises all but disappeared.

"I talked with Fiona, and she thinks I need to find my manhood again, that you took it from me and I have to get it back. You have to give it back to me."

"I don't have it, Joe," she said, hoping like hell he could be reasoned with. If he couldn't, she might be in real trouble here.

She wrenched her hand free of his grip, wincing as his nails curled in to scrape the backs of her fingers "You look really tired. Why don't you go home, get some rest." She turned to open the door, then cried out in shock when she felt him latch onto her shoulders. He spun her around fast enough to have her hair whipping into her eyes, pushing her against the wall before she could squeak out a protest.

"No," he said, his face close enough for her to see the flecks of green in his brown eyes. His wild, unfocused, jittery eyes. "We are meant, you're meant for me."

Uh-oh. Isa swallowed hard. He was really nuts. Or high, she realized, looking at his dilated pupils. Either way, he was dangerous.

"Joe," she began, "don't you remember? You don't want to see me anymore. And that's okay," she soothed. "You don't have to prove anything."

"Yes, I do," he muttered, his eyes practically spinning in his head. "I have to prove my manhood."

"Ulp!" Isa tried to turn away, but he kissed her, grinding his mouth so hard on hers she could feel his teeth pressing into her. She wrenched her head to the side. "Joe, stop!"

"Just give me a chance," he begged. His mouth slid down her neck, and she winced. Jesus, he was drooling. She put her hands on his shoulders and pushed, knowing it wouldn't do any good.

"Joe, you have to stop, " she said, trying one more time. "This isn't right."

"It can be right," he babbled, slobbering over her neck. He pushed his hand inside the neck of her t-shirt, ripping the neckline as he fought his way inside. "Let me make it right."

Isa felt his hand—his cold, clammy hand—close over her breast. "Nope," she said grimly. "Sorry, that was it." She brought her knee up hard, connecting solidly with Joe's newly rediscovered manhood, and he dropped like a stone.

Her head came up at the sound of someone clearing his throat. Jacob was standing in the doorway, the back door open behind him, watching with narrowed eyes. She looked down at herself, the torn shirt hanging open to expose her breasts, and at Joe writhing and moaning on the floor. "Aw, crap."

"Am I interrupting something?" Jacob drawled.

❦❦(❁)❦❦

Three hours later the police had finally left, the paramedics had taken Joe in to the hospital for seventy-two hours of observation, and Isa and Jacob were finally alone in the living room.

"So, that was Joe," Jacob said. He was sitting in a chair, watching her with an unreadable expression.

"Yeah, that was Joe." She busied herself tidying up, gathering the coffee mugs she'd gotten out for the cops and stacking them on a tray.

"Tell me," he drawled, rising fluidly to his feet. "Were you planning on telling me that your ex-boyfriend was stalking you?"

"I wouldn't say he was stalking me," she muttered. "Bothering, maybe, but not stalking."

He rolled his eyes. "Bothering, then. Were you planning on telling me he was bothering you?"

She shrugged, eyeing him warily. "It didn't really occur to me."

"Oh really?" His eyes narrowed on her. "Well, from now on sweetheart, it better occur. If my girlfriend has some crazed lunatic "bothering" her, I want to know about it. Got it?"

"Got it," she said, her voice thin with surprise.

He frowned at her. "What?"

"Nothing," she said. She set down the tray, then looked up at him. "Girl-friend?"

His face cleared, and he stepped towards her. "Yeah, girlfriend. You got a problem with that?" he asked, sliding his arms around her waist to tug her close.

"No, no problem," she said, a shy smile curving her lips. "But I'm in my thir-ties, you know. I'm not really a girl anymore."

He grinned. "Woman-friend just doesn't have the same ring to it. I could call you my lover," he continued, eyes sparkling as she started to giggle. "Or my old lady."

"Hey!" She whacked his arm. "I'm not a girl, but I'm not a crone, either!"

"It's just an expression," he managed roaring with laughter as she tried to pinch him. "Okay, okay!" he said, wrestling her arms behind her back. "I won't call you my old lady. I'll just call you my woman," he said, pressing a kiss to her lips and teasing the corners of her mouth with his tongue. "What do you think of that?"

"That'll do," she sighed. She tugged her arms free to wrap around his neck and kissed him back.

He broke the kiss after a moment, cupping her face in his hands. "Sorry I didn't get around to tying you up last night," he murmured.

"Oh," she smiled at him. "I didn't mind."

"No?" he asked.

She shook her head. "Don't get me wrong, I like the rope. I love the rope, and I hope you never get tired of tying me up. But I liked that it was just us. No props, no bells and whistles. Just us." She winced, feeling foolish. "Is that okay?"

"Yeah," he murmured, stroking her cheeks with his thumbs. "It's very okay. I liked it too. And I like you, Isabella Carelli. In fact, I may be falling in love with you."

She swallowed past the tightness in her throat. "Me too," she managed. "Are we crazy? I mean, we've only known each other a week. Well, we knew each other before this, but we've only *known* each other for a week."

"I get your meaning," he said, chuckling again. "But I don't think it's crazy. There's no set amount of time we have to know each other before we can be in love. It happens when it happens."

Score one for Nelson, she thought with a smile. "I think you're right," she murmured, and lifted her face for his kiss.

"I'm a little worried, though." She looked at him quizzically. "Well, you said you liked it without the props."

"I did," she admitted, the twinkle in his eye tipping her off. He was up to something. "But it doesn't mean I don't like props sometimes, too."

"Oh good," he said, and reached into his pocket. "Because I brought you a present."

He held up a hand, something dangling from his fingertips to dance in the sunlight streaming in through the window. She reached up a hand to steady it, her eyes focusing, and she burst out laughing.

"What?" he said, lips twitching as she howled with laughter. He looked at the alligator nipple clamps dangling on a silver chain from his fingers. "I wanted to make sure I got to everything on your list. 'A little bondage, a smack on the ass once in a while, a—'"

"A nipple clamp here or there," she finished, still laughing. "God, I like laughing with you."

"If you're not having fun, then what's the point?" He fingered the buttons on the shirt she'd put on to replace the one Joe had torn. "Now, how about we see what can be done with your hundred feet of rope and these?"

She giggled. "Okay. But you have to catch me first." She danced lightly out of his reach.

One eyebrow went up, and his face took on that fierce look that made her nerves jitter and her breath catch in her chest. "Catch you? Woman, I've already got you."

"Maybe," she admitted, loving the look in his eye as he watched her, "But you still have to catch me." She ran down the hall, grinning when she heard the thundering footsteps of the boy next door, hot on her heels.

About the Author:

Hannah Murray is a self proclaimed hopeful romantic, who loves banana flavored Laffy Taffy and hates horror movies. She lives with a very large, very grumpy dog who pretty much runs the show. When not catering to his needs, she can usually be found reading, watching old British sitcoms and reruns of The Golden Girls, or doing anything else that allows her to put off the housework for one more day. She loves getting email from readers, and can be reached at Hannah@hannahmurray.net.

Devil in a Kilt

by Nicole North

To My Reader:

Who can resist a hunky Highlander in a kilt? Not me, and not Shauna MacRae who finds her erotic fantasies come to life when she travels almost 400 years into the past to the Highlands of Scotland and a cursed laird in need of her love. I hope you enjoy this adventure!

Chapter 1

North Carolina, present day

As a "born-again virgin," Shauna MacRae wanted to kick her own butt for indulging in the erotic fantasies that had ensnared her two months ago. If only she hadn't spied that sexy Highland hunk on the cover of a romance novel… She hadn't even read the book; at least she had some control. But the picture had spawned all kinds of erotic chaos deep in her psyche.

She tried to pry her eyes open and pay attention to what was going on in the Kelchner College faculty meeting, but the fantasy wouldn't release her. *He* wouldn't release her.

With hot breath, he murmured foreign words in her ear. *Gaelic.* The unusual sounds rolled off his tongue just before he flicked it against her neck. Warm, wet, tingling.

I'm a professor, dammit! I can't be caught daydreaming like a slacker student.

Fighting down languid arousal, she blinked herself back into reality. Distinguished Professor Longgrove paced at the front of the cafeteria expounding on his insurance gripes as he had been for the past hour.

Shauna's eyes closed and the delicious stranger dragged her back into her fantasies. Those devilish blue eyes of his could seduce her with one hot glance. The long straight scar that ran down the right side of his face from forehead to square jaw gave him a dangerous appeal. His sensual lips never smiled, but, hot damn, could he kiss with them.

He kissed her all over… kissed and licked and sucked… her nipples. They ached for his touch. With a tingling yearning, her crotch grew wet. She moaned.

The droning monotonous voice shut off and quietness surrounded her. Shauna catapulted back into reality and found quizzical eyes staring at her from every side. Professors' eyes—judgmental, patronizing. Amused? One or two bit back smiles.

Omigod, did I just moan in the middle of a faculty meeting?

She cleared her throat. "Sorry. Toothache." She rubbed her jaw. As the "new kid"—she'd been Assistant Professor of Psychology for less than a year—she had not yet been accepted into their tight, tenured ranks.

Matriarchal Dr. Munoz examined her over the red-framed reading glasses perched on the tip of her nose. "You should have a dentist examine it."

"Do you have dental insurance?" Longgrove asked.

Shauna nodded and rose. "If you'll excuse me, I think I'll go see if my dentist can fit me in," she mumbled and fled the room.

She ran to her car and sped across Asheville to her apartment, thankful the traffic was light this late in the day. Once inside her small economy, she dropped her bag and dove onto her bed.

Her eyes closed and she drifted, not to sleep, but back into her perpetual fantasy.

He was there, tracing insistent, slightly roughened fingertips over her sensitized skin. What should she name her imaginary lover?

Oh, who cared if he had a name? His body was all she needed.

She had been abstinent too long. After her first ghastly sexual experience at eighteen with a cocky college football player who did nothing but fumble, in the backseat of his car as well as on the field, she had avoided sex over the last few years, never becoming intimate with the men she'd dated. Avoiding sex hadn't been all that difficult, considering what shallow, egotistical losers she attracted. And now, pathetically, she'd become obsessed with a figment of her own imagination—a very hot, hungry, hypnotizing figment. She knew why. No man in existence could live up to this standard.

In her fantasy, her clothes disappeared. She lay naked before him in the low light. His wicked blue eyes scanned her body, halting briefly at her breasts then skimming down to her mound. There his gaze lingered. He pushed her legs apart and lay down to examine her at close distance. Scorching arousal burned through her. She squirmed.

Touch me. Lick me.

Leaning closer, he lapped at her with his tongue, eating her as if she were hot caramel cake.

Oooh yes, more.

Moaning, he parted her sex lips, slid his tongue deep inside her, then sucked at her clit.

She clutched the covers tightly in her fists. A bed-rattling orgasm rocketed through her. She tumbled through the erotic stratosphere, screaming. Before she was finished, he plunged his glorious cock inside her.

"Oh, yes. *Yes!*"

Her orgasm magnified and expanded into two, three. Even when the shudders ended, the pleasure continued as he pounded into her.

"More."

He gave her more, filling her, stretching her beyond her limits. He set a quickened pace, as if they were in some sort of race to see who could get in the most strokes. And with each frenzied, wet thrust, her pleasure escalated until she hurtled through the roof again.

The phone rang and she jerked awake, aching and wet, alone in the twilight filled room. Had she been asleep? She could almost smell him, musky male blended with sandalwood and lavender. And sex.

Blinking back the dream, she inhaled a deep breath and pressed the button of the cordless phone. "Hello?"

"Shauna? Are you okay?" The voice belonged to Amelia, a friend and professor of social work.

"Yes. Why?"

"How's your tooth?"

"Oh, fine. I came home, took a pain pill and went to bed."

"You aren't going to the dentist?"

"I'm sure they can't see me today. It's so late. I'll call tomorrow."

Shauna couldn't tell happily engaged Amelia about her dreams. She'd think she was in need of getting a life.

Which was exactly what she needed.

"I'm worried about you, Shauna. You seem to be in a fog half the time."

"Really?" Shit! She hadn't known anyone had noticed she spent so much time daydreaming about *him*.

"Are you seeing someone?" Amelia asked.

"No. Why?"

"I don't know. You seem like you're in love or something. You're not seeing a married man, are you?"

"Are you kidding? That would be stupid." But probably not as stupid as obsessing over a man who wasn't real.

After talking a few more minutes, she hung up the phone, rolled over in bed and closed her eyes.

The sexy scent of his skin settled over her like a fine mist. She loved the warmth of his big body lying next to hers. He covered her with a plaid woolen blanket and snuggled her against his chest.

She looked up into his eyes to ask his name, where she might really find him, but he started loving her all over again.

Scottish Highlands, 1621

Gavin MacTavish awoke from yet another sex dream. He hated dreams that made him lose control like a green lad. 'Slud, it had been too long since he'd had a woman.

But none wanted to lie with the devil.

He shoved himself out of bed. Naked, he stalked to the basin and washed himself with cold water.

He glanced out the window at the Highlands and the first faint trace of dawn peeking over the eastern mountains.

It won't be long.

A yell echoed from down the corridor, the ravings of a madman. His father. One day that would be Gavin, talking to ghosts and shadows. But likely when he sank to that level, he would have no roof over his head. Or else his sparse clan would lock him in the dungeon to die alone. Since he had no heir, his greedy, grasping cousin would become laird. His clan would rejoice when their devil laird was dead.

"Damnation! Alpin willna unseat me. The craven whoreson." Draping his plaid around his waist and holding it in place, Gavin strode from the bedchamber and down the corridor toward his father's room.

"There ye are, lad," Crocker said, his sparse gray hair sticking out in all directions. "Thanks be to God. He's a right lunatic this morn. Asking for ye, he is."

"What the devil is wrong with him?" Gavin stepped inside the chamber.

"I dinna kin."

"Gavin! Gavin!" his father screeched from the four-poster bed as his body writhed, his long gray hair tangled. "The lass. Ye must look for the lass. Ye must marry. For the sake of the clan. For the sake of yer very *soul*."

"What lass?" No lass for miles around would so much as glance in his direction. He used to have to drag them from his bed and send them on their way. Now, he couldn't pay one to give him an hour's pleasure.

He would like as not turn them to stone, or they would end up possessed by the devil, as he was thought to be.

Gavin waited for his father to tell him which lass he referred to, but the older man now lay still with his eyes closed, apparently asleep. Mayhap he'd meant the lass from Gavin's arousing dreams. But she wasn't real, and he'd never seen her face.

Fingers of dawn light gleamed over the mountains and Gavin's animal nature surged forth, beyond his control.

"Damnation! When will it end?"

He moved toward the open window, helpless to resist the call. Just as he reached it, a moment of pain sliced through him. His body transformed, and great glossy-black wings appeared where once he had arms, and talons on his feet. Taking flight from the window, he became one with the wind, the Highlands and the bright colors of dawn.

Chapter 2

"I will find him," Shauna muttered under her breath, the swirling wail of bagpipes at the Grandfather Mountain Highland Games in North Carolina covering her words. She gazed out at the kilted athletes on the gaming field. "Or someone like him." Hell, a halfway good-looking single man wearing a kilt would do. Someone to fulfill her fantasy, or more likely destroy it, banishing it once and for all so she could get her real life back.

She could scarcely get through teaching a class without *him* invading her mind, trying to lure her back to his sinful pleasures. She had spaced-out during one of her lectures recently and blurted out something stupid—*leave me alone*—in front of fifty college students. They'd all had a great laugh at that, especially since she'd been describing Freud's penis envy theory at the time.

A visit to a psychiatrist would've probably been a better idea than the Highland Games, but when she'd seen the advertisement, something had beckoned to her and she'd had a positive, uplifted feeling.

Though her ancestry was Scottish, she never attended Highland Games. She'd always thought them *uncool*. Something only her late grandmother had been interested in.

Not so. Men in kilts had an unexpected appeal, especially the ones with sexy, muscular legs.

"Shauna MacRae," a male voice called out.

She spun around, her gaze scanning the throng of kilted and costumed Scottish descendants moving along with her in the thoroughfare between the colorful clan tents. Who had called her name?

"Shauna MacRae." A man with a full white beard waved to her. He looked like Santa Claus in a blue and red tartan kilt and with a squat Balmoral hat perched on his head.

Who is he?

She cut her way through the crowd and arrived at the tent with the sign *Clan MacTavish* across the top. "Hi. Do I know you?"

He propped his hands on the table that separated them. "No, I don't imagine you do. I'm Ranald MacTavish. Pleased to meet you." A Scottish accent colored his words but she could easily understand him. He shook her hand. "I notice you're wearing Nessa's brooch."

"Oh. You knew my grandmother?" Shauna touched the aquamarine and platinum brooch that pinned a portion of her plaid *arisaid*, or traditional women's great kilt, to the shoulder of her white peasant blouse, both made by Grammy. Shauna missed her so much.

"Aye, a fine woman, she was. I was saddened to hear of her passing."

"Thank you. She always tried to convince me to come to the Highland Games with her, but I never did. I regret that now."

"Who is she talking to?" a man asked, passing behind her.

He and the woman with him stared at Shauna as if she needed committing to a mental hospital. *What is their problem?*

Thankfully they kept walking. A kilted man in the next tent turned his back and started whistling. She eyed Ranald. Was he a figment of her imagination like fantasy man?

"Are you real?" she whispered.

"Course, I'm real." He grinned and she didn't entirely believe him. "That's an ancient MacRae brooch, you know. It's supposed to have magical powers."

"You're kidding." She glanced down at it. "What kind of magical powers?"

"Legend says it will lead whoever wears it to their true love."

"Get real." Wait a minute. She'd retrieved the brooch from her safe-deposit box two months ago, just before the erotic dreams started. Maybe this brooch was to blame and not the book cover. Maybe the brooch made her *notice* the book cover. *All I have to do is return the brooch to the safe-deposit box and I'm fantasy-free again.*

"Ha! You've just helped me solve a problem. Thank you."

"What sort of problem?"

"Um, nothing you'd find interesting." Something flashed in the dimness of the tent behind Ranald and her gaze darted to it. A huge two-handed Highland sword sat on a stand. A light must have glinted off the blade.

"Ah, I see the sword has caught your eye."

"It's beautiful." And very large. Taller than her own five-feet-four.

Ranald moved away from the table and stood beside the sword. "You should see the detail."

She sidled around the table and joined him in the middle of the open-sided tent.

A few nicks and pits scarred the long dull steel blade. Spiral-carved, leather-wrapped wood formed the grip. The brass cross-hilt guard featured down-sloping arms with four tiny circles on the ends.

"Only a very strong warrior could successfully wield the *claidheamh dà làimh* in battle, and Gavin MacTavish was such a man," Ranald said.

"It's amazing. Is it authentic?"

Ranald's mischievous blue eyes twinkled. "Of course. It's nigh onto five-hundred years old. Would you like to hold it?"

Though she didn't like weapons and the violence they stood for, she did love antiques. Her hands itched to touch the hilt of this sword. She set down her backpack, rubbed her palms together and stepped forward. Then back. "Oh, no, I couldn't. I'm sure it's very valuable, and I might drop it."

"It's a sword, Shauna. It's seen many a rough day." He winked, lifted the sword out of the stand and offered it, hilt first, to her. "I imagine you'll regret it if you don't hold this important piece of history for at least a few seconds."

Shauna wiped her palms on her skirt. "All right. If you insist."

A wily smile spread across Ranald's face. "I daresay you will enjoy it."

She didn't see how holding a sword could be *that* enjoyable, but whatever....
She wrapped her hands around the grip and took the weapon. The weight of it
surprised her, and she could hardly keep the tip above the ground.

The world spun, a pain shot through her head, and a bang—like a gunshot—
exploded beside her ear.

She dropped the sword with a clang and grabbed her aching head. "Omigod!"
The sharp pain ebbed away by slow degrees.

A male voice—not Ranald's—growled something she didn't understand.

She opened her eyes, but blackness surrounded her. It had been midday. *Am
I blind?*

What had caused the pain? And the noise? Had Ranald shot her?

A few feet away, a candle flared to life and moved toward her. She gaped at the
dangerous, heavily-muscled giant with long, dark hair standing before her. He was
more than a foot taller than she.

"Omigod."

A straight white scar ran from his forehead to his jaw on the right side of his
face, but the injury hadn't affected his eye. His gaze pinned her to the spot. She
knew those eyes, pale aquamarine-blue with a darker rim around the outside of
the irises, surrounded by thick, dark lashes. He studied her and frowned with a
wicked, black slash of his brows.

Her fantasy lover was back.

"Not now! Very bad timing." She shook her head, trying to escape her daydreams.

He glanced at the sword on the floor, then back to her. "Ye think to kill me with
my own *claidheamh dà làimh*, do ye, lass?"

At first, she could hardly understand the words he'd rolled up in the thick Scottish burr, then finally decided most of them were English.

Huh? He never said things like that in her fantasies. In fact, he never spoke
English, only purred those Gaelic phrases that sounded so exotic and arousing.

"Explain yourself!" he demanded, sending her a glare such as she'd never
imagined.

"No, I—"

The candle's light glinted off the blade of a dagger in his other hand, and warmed
his sun-bronzed skin—dear God, he was completely naked just like in her dreams.
So why was he being such a bastard?

"This is the worst fantasy I've ever had." Blinking hard, she tugged tight at the
reins of her imagination but nothing happened.

"Who the devil are ye? And how'd ye get in this time o' night?"

In? In where? And how had night arrived so quickly? "Um." She shook her
head and glanced at the dim room surrounding them. "Where am I?"

"Ha. I'm no' daft. Ewan!" he roared, then glowered at her.

"What's going on?" she asked, but his only response was to narrow his gaze.
This isn't real.

Is it?

She backed up a step and her derriere bumped a stone wall. She splayed her
hands against it. Cold, hard stone. The rough texture rasped her fingertips. *I was
in an open-sided tent only moments ago.* Her gaze skipped about the room with
its darkened corners and landed on the large, four-poster bed sitting behind him.

The white sheets were twisted and thrown back. So inviting… if he wasn't being so damned surly. She smelled candle tallow and *him*—his musky, sandalwood and lavender scent.

He watched her like a falcon watches its prey before diving in for the kill. His danger was a bit exciting, but still… scary. A whispering feeling grew stronger in her. *This isn't a fantasy.*

"It can't be real," she muttered.

He watched her lips, then his gaze drifted down her body.

After a few seconds of chilling silence, during which she dared not move, the door opened and a short, burly man dragged himself into the room. "Aye, Gavin— er—m'laird. What's all the ruckus about?"

He was yet another confirmation this *wasn't* a fantasy.

"How are ye thinking she got in here?" Gavin demanded. Clearly, he was more pissed than she would've imagined to find a woman in his bedroom.

"I dinna ken. She didna walk past me. I woulda seen her."

"She tried to kill me with my own sword."

"No, no," Shauna said. "I wouldn't do something like that. I can barely lift the thing. I was only admiring it."

"Admirin' it?" Gavin's accent formed the words into a sharp question. "How did ye get it from the armory?"

"She's a Sassenach," Ewan sneered.

They thought she was English? How had she moved from the Highland Games in North Carolina to this… room with stone walls?

"Is this a castle?" she asked. "In Scotland?"

"Ye ken 'tis. Caithmore Castle. What's your name?"

"Shauna MacRae."

Ewan expelled a loud bellow, then spoke aside to the giant. "What d' ye think's the meaning o' this? The MacRae has sent one of his daughters as a peace of-ferin'?"

"He has no daughters. Maybe Wilona sent her. Or maybe she *is* Wilona. Best explain yourself afore I think ye're a form-changing witch."

"I'm not a witch, and I have no idea who Wilona is." Something was very wrong with this picture. There was no way in hell she'd conjured this from her imagination. Nor had she ever run into any modern Scots with accents this pronounced, but of course she hadn't been to Scotland either.

"What year is it?" Shauna asked.

Ewan guffawed.

Gavin's expression remained sour. "Sixteen-hundred and twenty-one."

Shauna's throat closed up, and she grew lightheaded. *1621?* "That's impossible!" *Time-travel doesn't exist.*

"Whoever sent her, they've sent a daft one." Ewan smiled, his brown eyes sparkling.

"I dinna think so." Gavin scrutinized her. "I'm thinking they've sent the most canny one. To throw me off my guard… and kill me." His square jaw hardened.

"No, I'm… a distant cousin… of the MacRae. From… the Colonies. I mean you no harm. I come in peace." There, she hoped that would placate him.

"Ye were sent for his bride, aye?" Ewan asked.

"Um." *Omigod. Bride?* Shauna's pulse thumped in her ears.

"I dinna trust her." Gavin set the candle on a nearby table, picked up the sword and handed it to Ewan. "Put this in the armory. Lock it up and haste ye back."

"Aye." Ewan scurried out the door with the long sword.

Gavin's intense gaze zeroed in on her. "Now, Shauna, is it?" Damn, what his accent did to her name, made it sound more exotic than it had a right to.

"Yes."

"Were ye sent to kill me or wed me? Or were ye just wantin' t' bed me?"

She sucked in a deep breath to calm her hip-hop heart rate. "Not bed," she blurted. *At least not now.* She glanced down at his cock. That thing could hurt someone. Even semi-erect it was impressive. But it hadn't hurt her in the fantasies. Quite the opposite.

"Of course no'. Ye wouldna be wanting to turn to stone."

Huh?

"Keep your hands where I can see 'em." He placed the dagger beside the candle on the table and moved forward, apparently oblivious to his own nudity.

But she wasn't. Holy codpiece, he was well-endowed.

Though danger emanated from him like the clean male scent of his skin, she didn't fear him. She almost felt she knew him. But she didn't. She barely knew his name.

He reached out and touched her face. Her skin tingled and heated. His gaze trailed over her face as if examining it. Then he stroked his warm, calloused fingers beneath her chin and down her throat. His touch was familiar, entrancing. Her body recognized him. Wanted him.

His expression eased, and his brows lifted. "I must search ye for weapons."

"I don't have any," she said, breathless as a ninny.

"Forgive me if I dinna believe ye." He placed his large hands on her shoulders, her blouse barely shielding her from his heat, and with a gentle grip, ran them down her arms and underneath them, firmly down the sides of her body, around her waist and back up between her breasts.

A storm tide of tingling sensation followed in the wake of his touch. Too intense, too real. No, this was no fantasy, and that scared the hell out of her.

"Stop it!" She shoved his hands away.

His eyes glinted. "Many a man has been sent to the hereafter with a *sgian dubh* that was hidden in a woman's bodice."

"They probably deserved it!"

Shauna grappled for control, but with Gavin's obvious superior strength, he won. Towering over her, he gripped both her wrists in one large hand and held them above her head.

I don't fear him. I don't. He's the one I've dreamed of. Why did her body tremble? Because of the invasion and his too-intimate touch, or because she craved his hands on her? She feared she would hand over control to him too easily. He was already a drug in her veins.

"Don't!" She glared up at his face, darkened by shadows.

"I willna hurt ye, lass," he said softly, then stroked his fingers down between her collar bones and into her cleavage.

His fingertips rasped over the sensitive skin of her breasts. So stimulating. Her traitorous nipples hardened.

Oh, this can't be happening! She hung suspended between fantasy and a reality more *real* than anything she had ever experienced.

She felt as though she'd been reunited with a long lost lover, her body heating with rising desire. But he wasn't anyone she actually knew.

He removed his hand, then caressed her waist all the way around the top of her skirt.

"Hmm, ye're no' wearing a corset," he murmured.

"So?"

Lifting a brow, he brought her arms down and knelt. He stroked his free hand from her calf up the inside of her bare thigh.

Arousal crashed into her. He ran his fingers all along both legs, top to bottom and over her hips.

"Let me take your boots off," he said in a husky voice. "So I can see if ye have any weapons inside."

She pulled her feet up, one at a time, while he yanked her suede leather ankle boots off. After he searched the inside, he released her, rose and turned away. But not before she noticed his heightened state of arousal. She'd thought he was large before...

How could she want him so intensely? Paralyzed, she ached for him. Tears pricking her eyes, she almost ran to him and begged him to throw her on the bed and take her.

Ewan burst through the door. Gavin grabbed a long white shirt off a chair and pulled it over his head. The voluminous garment reached to mid-thigh.

Gavin faced her, his wicked gaze turning into the evil eye. "I canna trust you until I find out why you were sent." He glanced at Ewan. "Take her to the dungeon."

Chapter 3

What a jerk!

"I can't believe it." The man of her dreams had relegated Shauna to the dark, creepy dungeon with only a candle, for hours. Many, many hours. Through the tiny aperture above the solid oak door, a bar of light shone from a torch in the stone corridor. The place smelled dank and musty, but she detected no scent of the death of the former inmates as she'd expected.

Earlier, the male cook, Crocker Loch, escorted by an armed guard, had brought her tough bread, mushy haggis and thick ale. Definitely part of the torture.

I didn't time travel. This had to be some grand prank someone was playing on her. Maybe Ashton Kutcher had *Punk'd* her. *I wish.* Unfortunately, she hadn't spotted any tiny cameras lurking about in the corners of the stone walls or beneath the wooden stool.

She pushed at the door, kicked it, but it wouldn't budge.

Stamping across the packed dirt floor, she growled.

Hours. A whole day had probably passed. And she'd had to use the disgusting chamber pot in the corner.

"Definitely not a fantasy, dammit!"

Okay, so… what if by some mind-warping stretch of the imagination, she had time-traveled? A cold chill latched onto her. How would she get back to the twenty-first century?

It had something to do with Gavin's sword, and maybe her brooch too. But he wouldn't trust her to touch the sword again anytime soon. He'd had Ewan lock it up. Somewhere. She had to find it, if she wanted to escape this hell-pit.

And Ranald—he'd known what would happen—had tricked her into holding the sword. "The cruel, manipulating Santa-wanna-be."

Yes, she'd sunk to conversing with herself. She'd never been both alone and awake this long before.

A key rattled in the rusty lock. Were they bringing her more food? Or had Gavin decided to free her? *Please, God.* The metal-studded wooden door screeched open by slow degrees.

Gavin appeared, fully clothed this time in a tartan great kilt, and placed a flaming torch in the wall holder. The sight of him… his fearsome height and broad shoulders, the horrid scar. His wicked, wonderful eyes that she could look into forever. She trembled deep inside.

Would he decide to trust her?

Gavin MacTavish studied the dark-haired woman before him, brave as any Scottish lass he'd ever encountered, though she'd been raised in the Colonies, or so she said. Her eyes met his without hesitation. That he liked, for most women were terrified of him. They thought him the devil's own son and had given him the nickname MacDeevil. Had she not heard of his reputation?

"The MacRae admitted to sending ye, and I've told him I'll accept his peace offering." He'd sent Ewan with a message.

When Gavin had mentioned her name to his father earlier, he'd gotten over-excited, yelling and screaming about her being *the one.*

Shauna frowned. "You're talking about me, aren't you? I'm a peace offering?"

Her accent and rhythm of speech were highly unusual and he had a hard time getting used to it.

"Aye, you. Ewan has gone to fetch the minister, and we'll be wed as soon as he returns in a few hours."

"*Wed?*" Her stunning eyes widened. Multifaceted like a gemstone. He thought they were green. Would he ever see them in the sunlight?

"Wait a sec. Let me catch up. So this MacRae dude said he'd sent me? Why would he say that?"

"Dinna try to lie or get out of it. I ken he sent ye. He wishes to break the curse, as do I, and he wants peace. He fears I will retaliate against his clan. As well, he fears and hates his sister-in-law, Wilona, for she threatens him at every turn."

"What curse? And who is Wilona?"

"Wilona MacRae, the witch with powers of darkness."

"Witch? Come on." She eyed him skeptically.

"Indeed. Do ye think ye can break the curse?"

"Yeah, I'm sure I could. *If I knew which curse you're referring to.*"

He didn't care for that shrewish tone she'd used.

"Dinna pretend to be daft. Even if ye are from the Colonies, surely the MacRae told ye about the curse."

"No. What would I have to do to break it?"

"Marrying me is the first step." He shrugged. "The rest is a mystery to all of us."

She did something strange with her eyes as if they were rolling around in her head.

Shauna appeared a good wife candidate. She didn't run screaming away from him as all other women did. Even if she didn't know the full details of the curse, she intrigued him with her courage and her beauty. Nay, she aroused him. The night before, when he'd searched her for a weapon, by the saints, he'd wanted to lift her against the wall, wrap her legs around his waist and drive into her.

"So, you're saying you want to marry me?" she asked.

"Aye, the sooner we wed the sooner the clan will return."

"Why?"

"'Tis a long story. The clan has been gone since last year because of the curse. My father says the curse will be broken when I wed."

"What sort of curse, exactly?"

"Upon the land, the crops, the cattle. 'Twas all forfeit. This year we pray for bountiful crops." He would keep the rest a secret for now.

"Why was a curse placed upon you and your clan?"

'Slud, he wished she would not ask so many questions. "Because Wilona believes I murdered her son."

"Omigod, you murdered someone?"

"Nay! He and four others ambushed my two friends and me as we were returning from town one night. We were but defending ourselves."

"Why would they attack you guys?"

"For the love of God," Gavin muttered. She asked more questions than any woman in the kingdom. "I have a cousin, Alpin MacTavish, who wishes to steal my title away and become chief of Clan MacTavish. James MacRae, who was Laird MacRae at the time, Wilona's son, was Alpin's best friend. He was the only one to die in the skirmish, though several received injuries."

He still couldn't believe his two good friends had abandoned him. But he understood; they'd been cursed as well because of him, and something like that was hard to forgive.

"I see. So if I agree to marry you, will you let me out of this stinking dungeon?"

He studied her. 'Twas easy to see through her guise. She would falsely agree to marry him in order to be free. Though she didn't appear to fear him like all the lasses about, she did not seem keen to wed with him either. Though that's what she'd been sent to do. Would she disobey her laird?

As long as he had her down here, she was fully under his control. And he wished to know if his fantasies about her would come close to reality. Though he'd never seen the woman's face in his erotic dreams, he suspected he'd dreamed of Shauna. How, he didn't know. The sound of her voice, the scent of her. The feeling that radiated through him when he touched her.

It had been many months, eight to be exact, since he had touched a real woman.

Arousal had stirred within him the instant he'd entered this cell, but now he was stone hard just from looking at her, talking to her.

"Before I answer, I wish ye to kiss me."

Her wide eyes openly searched his face. With a deep breath, she took a step forward. Damnation, but her courage magnified his desire.

Standing before him on tiptoes, she clutched the plaid gathered over his chest and tilted her head back. "I can't reach your lips way up there."

He bent toward her face but allowed her to do the kissing. He expected an innocent, flat peck. But when her lips met his, a tingle sizzled to his cock, and it jerked. She opened her mouth and flicked her tongue against his lips, between. Inside his mouth. Holy Mother Mary, this was no virgin. She kissed like the most expensive, highly trained courtesan in London, which he'd heard rumors about. Could make a man climax with only a kiss.

Before he knew what he was about, he picked her up, tight against his body. Her legs wrapped around his waist and her crotch pressed against his erection. Damn the clothing between them. He slid his tongue into her mouth as he wished to slide his cock inside her. She tasted of heaven and delicious, sinful oblivion. He couldn't draw away from her even should his life depend upon it.

She moaned and wiggled against him. 'Twas clear she was wanting a good swiving when she started yanking at his kilt. With one arm, he held her while they struggled to pull the clothing aside. But she was wearing some sort of lacy undergarment beneath her skirts. French? 'Haps this was a Colonial custom, covering a woman's privates in such a tempting way. He slipped his fingers beneath it and along her juicy slit. Between her swollen lips.

She cried out and seemed to hold her breath.

"Aye. Does that feel good?" She sure as the devil felt good to him. He hadn't touched anything so delightful in many a moon. He gently pushed his finger deep into her hot, wet passage. Tight, but no barrier. He didn't care whether she was virgin or no; he craved her.

"Yes," she whispered with a hot breath and kissed him, nibbled at his lips and chin. "Please."

Indeed this was the way a woman was supposed to respond to him. He felt a surge of victory, as if the curse had already been lifted.

He tugged the strip of lace aside and positioned himself to enter her. The hot moisture of her drenched the head of his cock as he nudged inside her tight opening. "Damnation!" He had thought her well experienced, but 'haps she wasn't. She was near tight as a virgin.

"God in heaven, lass, ye're squeezing the life out of me," he muttered, then realized he was speaking Gaelic.

She moaned and tightened her legs around him, impaling herself.

"Mmm, aye," he growled. Blissful heaven. Hot and wet and so tight he wanted to come now.

She gasped and panted. Her mouth devoured his. Her uninhibited arousal fired his own. Shivers chased over his skin. He held her against the wall and pumped himself up inside her, slowly at first, then with increasing speed and force. She cried out. Never had a joining been this pleasure-filled.

She tensed around him, grew still and held her breath. Abruptly she arched back and screamed, riding him like a woman possessed. "Yes, yes." She repeated over and over amid female growls and squeals.

He could endure no more of this delectable torture. The climax smashed into him with the force of a boulder. Nothing felt as good as pouring into her as rapture claimed him.

Amazed, he sucked in great gulps of the dank dungeon air, turned his face into her hair and inhaled her scent, like the freshest flowers.

I'll ne'er be letting ye go, lass. Ye're mine.

But nay, he would not tell her that. He would let her find out for herself if she ever tried to leave.

She pushed at his chest. Och! He had held her too long and too tightly. His cock was still firm and tingly when it slipped from her body. 'Haps he wanted her again. Indeed. He would never stop wanting her.

His kilt fell back into place, as did her skirts.

He watched with fascination as she tugged at her undergarments. That strip of flimsy lace still intrigued him. 'Haps it was a chastity belt, a useless one.

She cleared her throat and peered up at him, her skin still flushed. "I shouldn't have done that."

"And why no'?"

"My born-again virgin status has just been revoked."

"Ye were no' a virgin, lass. *Were ye?*"

"Of course not. I'm twenty-four years old. A born-again virgin is one who has sex, then swears it off for whatever reason."

A dark, unidentified emotion crawled through his chest. He'd known she wasn't a virgin; still, the thought of her with another man made him want to draw a sword and hunt down the whoreson. "How long ago did ye have sex and with who?"

"Forget the caveman possessiveness bit. It won't fly with me. To make a long story short, I was eighteen, the sex was awful and I haven't done it since."

"Until now?"

She nodded.

"Ye havena had sex in six years?"

"Congratulations, you can count."

He smirked. She thought she was so witty. "And what are ye, then, a professor at university?"

"Actually, I am."

He guffawed. She would provide him hot carnal pleasures and highly entertaining stories. What more could a man ask for?

"I like your delusions. 'Haps we are no' so different after all."

"Fine, don't believe me. I suppose you also won't believe I'm from the twenty-first century."

That was stretching it a bit. 'Haps she was a lunatic. "Dinna be telling anyone that. They will think us both fit for Bedlam."

"I knew you wouldn't." She blew out a breath, then froze. "You don't have any STDs, do you?"

He frowned. "What is this? STDs?"

"Sexually transmitted diseases."

"Nay! I have no diseases."

"Thank God. My friend Molly from high school had Chlamydia one time and it was a bitch."

He tried to follow her meaning, unsuccessfully. Whatever disease she was talking about was a female dog, or an immoral woman.

"I have no diseases," he said again, to be certain she understood. "Do you?"

"No."

He nodded. "Good. We will get on well in the bedchamber. I'm glad ye've agreed to marry me."

"Did I? I don't recall…"

They stared at each other for a long moment, battle of wills.

Chapter 4

"Um, yeah. Okay. I'll marry you."

Shauna crossed her fingers behind her back. Now, she had no doubt Gavin was her fantasy lover. Real sex with him was even more spectacular than her dreams had been. She was afraid she already wanted him again. But she had no intention of staying in seventeenth-century Scotland with the threat of a dungeon hanging over her head—er—under her feet if she wasn't an obedient wife.

Did her parents and sister even realize she was missing? Likely they wouldn't check on her until next weekend... four centuries in the future. *Argh!* No, her coworkers or boss would likely inquire about her when she didn't show up for her classes. If she couldn't escape this nightmare, she might never get to teach another class, or hole up in her tiny office again. From the time she was a child, she'd wanted to be a professor, Dr. MacRae. Even if her career was gone, she would miss her family most. Would she ever see Mom, Dad or Celia again?

"I am pleased. Come." Gavin led her from the cell and up the stone steps to the cluttered, dim great hall. She tried to concentrate on the present and an escape plan.

She now knew the full meaning of *filthy rushes.* The room looked like a huge horse stall with dirty hay-like stuff all over the floor. And who knew what was hiding in it?

"You know, you really should get this place cleaned up. I hope you don't expect your future *wife* to clean it."

"Nay. Of course no'. Ye shall be a lady."

Lady? Right. He was treating her like a prisoner, his own personal sex slave. Not that she had anything to complain about in that department, yet.

A huge man standing by the trestle table stopped and observed her.

"Clean up this hall, Finch," Gavin ordered. "Get these rushes out. My lady wants fresh ones."

"I'm a guard, no' a maid."

"I dinna care. I've just reassigned you."

The man quirked his brows, as if Gavin had lost his mind. Gavin in turn sent him a look reminiscent of the evil eye.

The man placed his sword on the table and set to work.

When Shauna and Gavin walked by a window, she realized it was night again. "You kept me in that freakin' dungeon all day. What kind of a fiancé are you?"

"A thousand apologies, but I couldna trust you." Gavin escorted her up the spiral stone staircase.

And maybe you still can't, yummy jerk. "Where are we going?"

"To see my father."

"You have a father?"

"Of course. Everyone does."

"I meant still alive."

"Aye."

"Then how are you the laird?"

"He ceded the title to me last year. Ye'll see why." Gavin pushed open the worn, heavy wooden door.

The dim light from one candle barely illuminated a large, ornate bed in one corner. A low moan came from within the bed-hangings.

"What's wrong with him?" Shauna whispered.

"We dinna ken. We think 'tis the curse. He was fine before it."

The man on the bed whipped his head toward them. His sharp, blue-eyed gaze speared hers much like Gavin's, except without a hint of sanity. He swallowed visibly.

"'Tis her," he whispered, his breathing harsh and picking up speed. "Tis her!" he screamed this time. "She's the one."

Shauna hid behind Gavin and peeped out, which wasn't like her at all. But good God, things here were weird. Getting herself under control, she forced her legs to move until she stood beside Gavin again.

"Da, this is Shauna MacRae. Shauna, Lunn MacTavish."

"Pleased to meet you, sir."

"Ye must marry that lass. No other. No other!" Lunn howled.

More talk of marriage? Jeepers. Exactly the kind of husband she wanted—lord of psychiatric patients and other assorted eccentrics. Why was *she* so all-fired important?

"Aye, Da, calm down."

"Do it, Gavin. Now. For the sake of the clan. Ye mustna waste any time."

"Why?" she blurted.

The two men stared at her as if she were an idiot.

"The curse, lass. The curse," Gavin's father chanted.

"Yeah, yeah." She released a long-suffering breath.

Now, where could she find that sword?

Minutes later, they passed several locked doors on their way back down to the great hall. How could she ask about Gavin's sword without looking suspicious? *By the way, where is the armory?* No, anyone she asked would surely tattle on her. There weren't that many people to ask anyway, all men. And all loyal to Gavin.

Quietness reigned except for the guard/maid raking the rushes into piles on the stone floor. She coughed against the thick dust floating through the air.

"Has Ewan returned yet with the minister?" Gavin asked him.

"Nay."

A fit of nerves seized her. "I'd like a warm bath in a private chamber," she told Gavin.

He lifted a brow, his gaze skittering down over her body.

"Please?" she asked. "So I will be prepared for the wedding."

"Very well. Finch, ye and Crocker prepare a bath in my chamber for the lady."

Finch let out a long breath and leaned on his wooden pitchfork. "Aye, m'laird."

Gavin glanced at Shauna. "That'll be sixteen buckets of water. 'Twill take a wee to heat."

She nodded. Good, she needed all the time she could buy.

"And tell Crocker to change the sheets on my bed," Gavin told Finch.

"Aye, m'laird." Finch headed toward the stairs.

Sheets. Hmm, what did the laird of sex have in mind? She knew. Dear God, she knew. Though she shouldn't indulge, she just might be persuaded. She sighed.

"Are there any women here?" she asked.

"Nay." He frowned.

"Why not?"

"The curse."

"Well then, why is Finch here, and Ewan and Crocker? And don't you dare say because they're men. What does that have to do with it?"

Gavin blinked hard and frowned. "Come, I'll show you." After tucking her hand around his elbow, he turned, took a torch from a wall holder and made for the wide wooden door leading outside.

He led her to a large boulder in the courtyard and motioned to it.

She placed her hands on her hips and pretended to be viewing an art nouveau piece. "Hmm. Interesting. Is it abstract?"

"'Tis a rock."

"I can see that. What's the significance?"

"They all think it used to be a woman."

"What?"

"Aye. Marilee was the last woman to warm my bed and ye see, two women say they witnessed her turning to stone as she left the morn after we—" He cleared his throat. "Because, it is said, she didna please me."

"That's ridiculous." Shauna tried to ignore the jealousy worming its way through her at the image of Marilee in his bed.

"Aye, I ken it well, but they believe it. And no one has seen Marilee since."

"Did the rock suddenly appear here?"

"I believe it rolled from up there one night." He pointed toward the hill that rose in elevation above the castle.

"How did it get over that wall?"

"I'm thinking it bounced and jumped it somehow. There was a bit of a slide above the wall at spring thaw last year."

"And that's why everyone left—because they think a woman turned into a rock?"

He glanced away. "Part of it. The crops failed, as I said. 'Twas a drought throughout the summer. And a disease killed most of the cattle and some of the people."

Why did she get the feeling he was holding something back?

Two men trotted through the open gate on foot.

"M'laird," Ewan gasped. "I found a priest. Reverend MacPherson was nowhere t' be found."

Gavin sighed. "Verra well."

The priest, a skinny man in black robes, drew himself to his five and a half feet height. He clutched a large ornate cross in a jittery hand and looked as if he might try to ward off Gavin with it.

Why did they all think him so evil?

"Are ye ready then, lass?" Gavin eyed her.

Dear God, her wedding. "You said I could have a bath first."

"No time. Ye smell lovely to me. Ye're face and hands are clean."

"You haven't even proposed." *You miserable lout.* How long could she stall? If she ran, would he catch her and throw her back in the dungeon?

"Ah, ye have romantic notions." He smiled. "You wish a formal proposal?"

She rolled her eyes. "Of course. What woman doesn't? And where is my ring?"

"I have it. So ye are no' averse to wedding me, then?"

"I'd prefer to wait until I get to know you better but you've threatened me with the dungeon."

"Aye, the dungeon." His eyes widened in mock evil like a cliché villain. "Ye dinna wish to go back there, do ye now?"

She wanted to kick him on his bare muscular legs beneath the kilt. But he was very large. And cursed.

She crossed her arms. "What do I get out of this deal?"

He observed her as if she'd lost her mind for a moment, then whispered in her ear, "A man to give ye such pleasure every night as ye had a while ago."

Her face heated but again the tingle of arousal simmered through her. He did have a point.

"And a dozen or so wee bairns."

"A dozen babies? Are you out of your freakin' mind?"

He smiled. "Okay, then. Half a dozen."

A knot formed in her stomach. She couldn't think about babies right now. She wanted to get back to the twenty-first century, hospitals, pain killers, and maybe two kids in the future. Normalcy. Thank God, she'd taken the three-month birth control inoculation a few days ago. She took the shots to prevent severe cramping. Who would have guessed she'd need it to prevent a time-traveling pregnancy?

"And ye're right, my mind is 'freaking' but ye shall get used to it."

What the hell is he talking about?

"I swear to you I am no' possessed. 'Tis but a rumor."

So the possession wasn't real but the curse was? What was the difference?

She had to get to that sword. *If I marry him and let him begin to trust me, I'll be able to get my hands on the sword sooner or later and it will take me back to the future. I won't be married to him then because he'll have been dead for several centuries.*

She couldn't imagine such a sexy and vital man dead. He deserved to live; he deserved happiness. Where had that thought come from? She barely knew the S.O.B.

She looked up into his gorgeous, fierce eyes. No, she knew him better than she wanted to admit. He'd inhabited her dreams for months. She knew he had a good heart, a compassionate soul. He was not evil, no matter what anyone said. No matter if the curse was real or not. She knew him. Her insides seized up every time she looked at him. And when those breath-stealing eyes fixed on her, she wanted to softly kiss his face all over, his entire delectable body.

"Verra well, lass." Gavin took her hand in his and dropped to one bended knee.

"Will ye do me the honor of becoming my bride, Shauna MacRae?"

Oh, dammit. No man had ever uttered those words to her... and maybe never would again. He wanted to marry her. Was it only because he wanted to break the curse? She needed more. She had to know he liked her a little, that she wasn't just convenient, in the wrong place at the right time.

"Why?" she asked.

His hopeful expression fell. "That's your answer?"

"No, but I need to know why." Marrying someone just to break a curse was unromantic and downright insulting to her. Real marriage or not, she didn't like feeling used.

He glanced behind himself to make sure the other men were not listening, then gazed up at her. "Ye're the loveliest lass I e'er laid eyes on. And I admire your bravery. Ye didna call me MacDeevil like the other lasses."

"Why would they call you that? Oh, I know, the curse."

"Even before the curse, some of them called me that. I'm a fearsome warrior in battle, and my scar frightens the wits out of 'em. Besides that, they say I have the evil eye."

She had to agree, sometimes the look coming from his eyes was rather intimidating. "I think your eyes are beautiful."

Shauna stroked her hand along Gavin's face in a tingling trail, over his scar, then traced his brow. No woman had ever touched him thus, with such care and tenderness.

"As well, I admire yer intelligence and canny wit."

Those feelings of arousal which overcame him in the dungeon returned—yet another reason he was more than willing to take her to wife. He had to have her in his bed, every night. Such pleasure would surely be beyond belief.

"Will ye marry me, then?" he asked and kissed her hand. *Please.*

"Oh, all right." She forced out a dry smile. "Yes."

He rose, pulled her to him and briefly kissed her lips. Not wise. He craved her, wanted to kiss, lick and stroke all her hidden places.

The way her lashes lowered and her eyes darkened further enchanted him.

But could he trust her not to slit his throat in the night with a *sgian dubh*?

Chapter 5

Shauna loved the warmth of Gavin's large, calloused hand surrounding hers almost as much as she'd loved his proposal. When he'd spoken his heart, there had been such honesty and hope in his eyes. He appeared to actually like her, not just want to use her. How could she betray him by leaving?

"Where would ye be wanting to say the vows? In the hall?"

The thought of that dirty, drab, dusty place made her cringe. She glanced around in the moonlight and spied a lovely hill not too far away, overlooking a loch that glistened and reflected the white orb in the midnight blue sky. "There." She pointed.

"Father," Gavin called to the priest and they all made their way through the gates and over the rocky ground to the crest of the hill. Ewan held the torch and stood as witness next to Gavin.

I can't believe I'm doing this.

The ceremony seemed ancient and unreal, some of the words spoken in Latin and some in Gaelic. Even Gavin's eyes seemed a figment of her dreams. But she'd pinched herself so many times since the ceremony began, she was sure to have bruises all over her arms.

The Highlands surrounding them were real. Gavin holding her hand was real. A shiver traveled through her from his heat, his possessive hold and the way he observed her with dark interest.

At the priest's prompting, Gavin slipped a band onto her finger, the gold already warmed by his hand. The ring glinted in the torchlight and fit her finger perfectly.

"I pronounce ye man and wife. Ye may kiss yer lovely bride."

Gavin bent and placed a hungry kiss of possession on her lips. A kiss that made her want to rip off his kilt and ravish his body here and now.

He picked her up and carried her toward the castle. She should have demanded that he put her down, but romantic idiot that she was, she loved this part. He was going to carry her all the way from the ceremony, over the threshold, and to his bedroom, she hoped—like a wanton fairy tale princess.

"The curse is broken!" he bellowed.

Ewan whooped and danced a jig behind them.

Once inside the hall, he repeated the declaration. "Go tell everyone in the village," he ordered Finch.

The hulking man sighed, dropped the two large empty water buckets and shuffled toward the exit. "There are but two old men there," he grumbled in a low tone.

Gavin carried her up to his chamber and set her on her feet. The wooden tub of steaming bath water called to her like a modern day hot tub.

"When the clan returns, we shall have a feast in your honor in the great hall." The look in his eyes almost broke her heart. Clearly he loved his clan very much and wanted them reunited. He believed she was the key. But what if she wasn't? What if he was kidding himself? And what would happen when she returned to the future?

"I give ye your privacy, m'lady, so ye may bathe. I'll bring food in a little while." He bowed and retreated from the room.

How could I have married him? How could I have married anyone so impulsively.

"Insanity. Self preservation. At least he's a gentleman... part of the time." Shauna removed her dress, bra and panties and sank into the tub of blissfully warm water. She picked up the weird, lumpy cake of soap from beside the tub and sniffed it. "Mmm, lavender." The scent was somewhat masculine and reminded her of him.

As she lathered her body with a soapy cloth, her mind drifted back to him and the sex they'd had in the dungeon. Phenomenal. He was big and commanding and so very hot. Strong enough to hold her aloft for several minutes while he power-drove himself into her. Whew! Okay, maybe she would have sex with him one more time before she looked for the sword. Just once. Maybe twice. Five times, dammit, and that was it.

After all, he had to trust her out of his sight for a while. And the more sex they had, the more he would trust her. Hmm, she liked that analogy, more sex equals more trust. She wanted all the trust she could get before she rocketed through that time-travel portal again, because in the future she'd go back to being Celibate Shauna.

No fun at all. And she would miss her dream lover.

When she'd scrubbed every inch of her body, she relaxed back, exhausted. The warm water made her sleepy, plus she'd missed a whole night of shut-eye in that damned dungeon. She started dreaming about illogical places to have sex, like on a golf course or on her desk in the college classroom. She couldn't tell whether her students were present or not. Suddenly she was teaching an abnormal psychology class.

A sound woke her, the slamming of a door. Gavin stood, watching her and holding a wooden tray loaded with food.

Abruptly she sat up, water sloshing onto the floor.

His gaze dipping to her bare breasts, he almost dropped the tray, righted it and set it on a bedside table. She searched beside the tub for a towel but found none.

The blue flame of his gaze returned to her breasts as he came toward her. "Move over, lass. I'm coming in."

"Really?" Well, the tub was huge, sure enough. He unfastened his belt, dropped his kilt and yanked his shirt over his head, all in less than five seconds. His erection bobbed and swayed as he removed his boots. A smile of pure witchcraft on his gorgeous but imperfect face, he sank into the water at one end of the tub while she rose onto her knees at the other.

"I would like for ye to bathe me," he purred as he reclined.

"Is that so?" *Bossy barbarian.*

"Aye. I'm wanting to feel your hands all over me."

"Hmm." She lifted a brow and watched him watching her. Waiting. Yes, she wanted her hands all over him. His defined muscles lured her to pet and stroke him.

His thick, dark lashes drifted low and his lips quirked.

She took up the cloth to lather it, slowly, while she made him wait. He lay in a vulnerable position, with her sitting between his thighs.

He trusts me. That realization didn't comfort her as she'd expected. Leaving him would cut her to the bone.

She shoved the prickly thought away and dragged the cloth over the hard curves of muscles that made up his chest. Leaning further over him, she brushed the cloth over his neck and face, then his shoulders, underarms and biceps.

His hands slid up from her waist, the water making their skin slick. He covered her breasts with his hands, then tweaked the hardened nipples.

"Mmm." He licked his lips.

She re-lathered the cloth and smoothed it over his muscular thighs on either side of her. Finally, she gathered her courage and rubbed the cloth along the length of his cock, hard as stone and lying against his belly. She stroked it up and down, the soap providing lubricant. He moaned but didn't move. His hands grasped the edge of the tub in restraint. She slid the cloth down again and cupped his testicles in her hands, caressed and massaged them.

"*Muire Mhàthair*," he gasped between clenched teeth.

She let the cloth drop from her hands and smoothed her bare palm up his erection again. She rinsed the soap off and lifted it so the head protruded from the water. Her fingers wouldn't even close around his cock and it looked too alpha and delicious to pass up. She kissed the wet tip and glanced up into his eyes.

His body jerked and stiffened. His hands on the edges of the tub tightened.

She opened her mouth and took the head inside, licking the satiny skin, stroking the shaft with her hand. Having never performed oral sex before, except in her fantasies, she had no clue if she was doing this right. But she always thought *Cosmo* gave pretty detailed instructions.

The flared satiny-smooth head felt so wonderful in her mouth, she ached for him. His ass muscles flexed and he gently thrust into her mouth. Guttural Gaelic words escaped his throat with harsh breaths. The only word she understood was Shauna. She sucked harder and stroked.

He grasped her to him, pulled her forward to lie on his chest and kissed her. His cock lay stiff beneath her belly in the water. His hands cupped her ass and squeezed her tight against him.

"By the saints! Ye turn me into a lunatic." He pulled her knees up and wedged his own legs between hers. With her thighs parted, he inched his fingers down her crack and dipped them between her sex lips.

A tingle raced through her and she arched.

"Hot. Wet." He devoured her mouth.

When he shifted, she felt the tip of his cock against her opening. So tempting. With his hand, he stroked it against her, teased her clit, let the head rest between her lips.

"Gavin," she moaned and pushed her hips toward him. He seemed intent on taking his own sweet time.

With much patience, he nudged inside her. Living, breathing pleasure. The tingling so intense she bore down on him.

"Please, Gavin." She lifted her upper body, placed her hands on his shoulders and rode him. Letting him slide almost all the way out, then plunging down on him again. Deep. Fast. Hard.

"Oh, aye, lass. *A shùgh mo chrìdhe*," he growled and lifted his head to lick at her nipples when they came near enough.

His slight thrusts mirrored her own, adding to the erotic friction.

"Hold on 'round my neck." Hands on the edge of the tub, he pushed himself up with her impaled on his cock. She crossed her ankles behind his back. His big hands cupped her ass, lifting her, stroking in and out as he crossed the floor. So delicious she couldn't think. His strength was another aphrodisiac. He lowered her upper body to his high bed.

Her skin drying in the cool air sent shivers over her skin even as an inferno blazed between them at their joined bodies.

"We'll get the bed wet," she gasped, not really caring, only wishing he'd continue what he was doing.

"I hope so." He lifted her foot and bit her ankle, gently. With a wicked grin, he pumped his hips harder. And harder still as he grazed his teeth over her lower calf.

"*Mo dia*," he muttered while he gazed into her eyes, his now gone mostly black, his lashes lowered, jaw clenched hard.

Hands over her head, Shauna clutched at the coverlet and arched her back, accepting him battering into her with intense pleasure. He was every inch the hard, fearsome warrior. Relentless and determined.

"Yes, Gavin!" She screamed though she didn't mean to.

"Like that, do ye? Like it when I fuck ye hard?"

"Yes! More."

She couldn't believe it when he actually did slam into her even harder and faster.

Tingles swirled around, she lost her breath and an orgasm plowed through her, long and drawn out.

She could do nothing but scream. Her awareness focused on his cock driving into her even as her inner muscles squeezed him, gripping onto him tightly, wanting to hold him forever.

He slowed to a more gentle rhythm and kissed her ankle. Trying to catch her breath, she opened her eyes, unable to believe what she'd just experienced—the most intense orgasm of her life.

When her gaze met his, he increased his pace again slightly. "Are ye ready for another, then?"

She shook her head. "I can't."

He smiled, lowered his body over hers and flicked her nipple with his tongue. Holding himself still deep inside her, he gently sucked at her hardened, tender nipple, then switched to the other, loving it with his lips.

She buried her hands in his midnight hair, ran them over his wide shoulders, unable to believe how beautiful, hot and sweet he was. Her inner muscles twitched, caressing him.

"Mmm. There canna be anything better than being married to a lusty wench."

She clutched his hair and made him look into her eyes. "I'm a lady, not a wench."

"Aye, ye are. A verra lusty lady. My wife. And dinna be forgetting it." He pushed her further across the bed and climbed up. Kneeling, he lifted her to sit straddling his thighs. She wrapped her arms around his neck. Face to face, gazing into her eyes, he lifted and lowered her. She nibbled on his lips, fearing she might be falling for him a little, considering the raw emotions cutting loose within her.

I can't fall for him. I can't.

After several minutes, he licked his thumb and stroked it back and forth across her clit. Licked it again, moaned and rubbed her clit, slow at first then faster as he plunged deep inside her. His wicked eyes dared her, challenged her to come again.

Incredible pleasure built and built. Compounded, magnified. She could do nothing but hang on and let the orgasm claim her. He controlled it; he controlled her, making the pleasure go on and on.

She was glad when he held her tightly, ground himself to the hilt and came inside her.

Oh, Gavin. She caressed his back, savoring the hard muscles and smooth hot skin. Savoring everything he was. Wishing....

How could she leave the only man who'd ever touched her soul?

Chapter 6

Before dawn, Gavin slipped from the bed where he'd gotten little sleep. He rubbed his stiff back and winced at his sore legs. He may not have bedded a woman in eight months, but he'd almost made up for it last night. Thank the heavens, Shauna was the lustiest lass he'd ever encountered. He grinned at his good fortune.

The faint glow from the window revealed only the outline of her form, still tangled among his sheets. Kissing her forehead, he wished he could light a candle and observe her for hours, but time was short. Dawn crept into his bones, spawning the urge to fly.

He wrapped a plaid around his waist, held it in place and exited the room. He bounded up the narrow stone steps to the battlements on the roof, five stories above the barren land. Dim light gleamed behind the rolling mountains in the east.

Maybe it wouldn't happen today. Maybe the lass had already broken the curse.

He glanced skyward. *Please.*

But he was too jaded to pray. Too cursed. No deity would hear the prayers of someone like him.

The ravings of a lunatic echoed from one of the windows below. The curse that caused his father's affliction hadn't been broken. A sinking feeling swooped in on Gavin, for he knew. *He knew.*

The first ember of dawn peeped over the mountain. He drew in a deep breath, held it and waited. Though he wished fervently for something else, he knew what would happen.

Piercing pain shot through his body. All his muscles contracted and shrank. The plaid dropped and with his altered body, Gavin soared from the ramparts with his black-feathered wings outstretched to catch the wind.

The deserted *barmkin*, the wall, the empty fields and barren hills all passed swiftly beneath him. His six-foot wingspan took him far and fast. With sharpened vision, his eyes scanned the ground a great distance below. No rabbits or mice scurried about. Even they feared him.

He glided down over the village his clan had once occupied. Now most of the cottages sat with moldering thatch and dim, dusty interiors, devoid of humanity. Some of his people had died of a plague and the rest fled to other towns and cities. He missed them.

He perched in a lone oak, its dead, drying limbs outstretched with no hope of leaves unfurling again. He had always loved this tree, had played in it and climbed it as a child. Now it was dead because of him.

His high-pitched screech echoed back at him. He was alone out here. All alone. Deserted silence surrounded him.

He missed her. *Shauna.* His wife, sleeping so beautifully in his bed. Warm and eager. More than anything, he wished to be a man lying beside her now. He'd thought she was the key. What had happened?

Flapping his wings, he launched himself into the air and propelled himself back to the castle. What would she think of him if she saw him in this form?

Drawing his wings in to stop the momentum, he lit again on the battlements. He hated the daytime for no one dared come near him. Even Ewan feared him in this form. He thought Gavin would rip him apart with sharp talons and hooked beak.

He would never be free of the curse.

Shauna woke, squinting against the sunlight streaming through the window. "Where am I?" She glanced around at the stone walls. "Oh yeah. Crap."

Last night's sex adventures sprang to mind. Gavin. Warmth purred through her. He was a giving, eager, very hot lover. She sat up.

"Gavin?"

Silence.

Seconds later, she thought she heard a yell in a distant part of the castle. His father? She listened but didn't hear it again. Arms and legs sore, she scooted toward the edge of the bed.

She needed to use a restroom in the worst way but dreaded entering the disgusting garderobe again. She'd rather go in the bushes. But she hadn't seen any bushes outside.

She dressed and cautiously opened the heavy oak door. Silence surrounding her, she slipped through rooms, along passageways. Once she'd used the closet-like garderobe, which thankfully had recently been scrubbed, she strode down the spiral stone staircase to the empty great hall, cleaner now minus the old rushes. Someone had scrubbed the stone floor there, as well.

Where is the kitchen? And food?

The room turned out to be down another level. The lyrics of a bawdy song, sung in a raspy thick burr, echoed off the vaulted stone ceiling.

The heavy-set man, Crocker Loch, jerked around and surveyed her with one dark eye and one milky, ruined eye. She hadn't noticed this about him before because it was usually night when she encountered him.

"M'lady?" He bowed a bit awkwardly.

"Good morning, Mr. Loch. Where is everyone?"

"Everyone?"

"Gavin and Ewan… people?"

He squinted his good eye and grimaced. "I've prepared ye a meal fit for a queen to break yer fast, m'lady. Have a seat in the great hall if ye would."

"I'd prefer to eat here if you don't mind."

"'Tis no' fittin', m'lady."

"Will Gavin not be dining with me?"

Crocker's bushy gray brow shot up. "No' likely."

"Where is he?" A shiver of delicious anticipation passed through her when she imagined looking into his eyes again now, after all their erotic activity of the night before. They connected in a way that made their physical bonding natural yet amazingly pleasurable.

"Canna rightly say where the MacTavish is. 'Haps touring about the lands, looking things o'er. He always rises at dawn."

Her stomach growling, she dragged a stool to the rough-hewn work table and Crocker set the loaded plate in front of her.

"Thanks. What is this?" She poked at a warm flat thing that looked almost like a pancake.

His eyes rounded. "Dinna ye ken what a bannock is, lass?"

"I've heard of them but never eaten one."

"Ewan said ye're a Sassenach, but I'm thinking ye're worse."

"I'm from the Colonies, in case you haven't heard. There's no haggis on here, is there?"

"Nay, but I can fetch ye some if ye want it."

"*No!*"

He drew himself up, looking a bit insulted. He pointed at her plate. "And that, m'lady, is bacon."

"I know what bacon is." She stuck a piece in her mouth and bit it. Slightly crispy, just the way she liked it. "Mmm." She hadn't realized how hungry she was. She crammed the rest of the piece into her mouth.

"Ye like that, aye?" He grinned and puffed up like a cocky rooster.

"It's delicious. You're an excellent cook."

"I thank ye, m'lady." He bowed, pleasure staining his face red.

"I thank you, too." She barely choked down a sip of the strong, lukewarm ale and pushed the pewter mug back. "Don't you have any fresh, clean water... or better yet, coffee?"

"Now, what would ye want with that when ye can have my own freshly brewed ale?"

That gawdawful stuff? She was afraid she might thirst to death in this century.

༠ৡ৻༽৶ৡ

Five hours later, Gavin still hadn't shown up. Shauna had secretly searched the castle and learned all she could about the layout. Many of the closed doors were unlocked, so she'd gone into the creepy, dim rooms to see if she could find Gavin's sword. No luck. But she had found plenty of yucky things, like dead rats and moldy straw mattresses with weeds growing out of them beneath windows.

This place had terrible feng shui and she intended to tell Gavin that next time she talked to him. When he wasn't seducing her. All this crap lying about in unused portions of the castle was probably causing his bad luck.

She'd also been fortunate enough to find some old dresses she would wash... sometime. She hated doing laundry, and the lack of anything but a rock to scrub the clothes on would be hell.

Three of the doors in the castle had been locked, and she suspected the sword was behind one of them.

Bastards.

From the way Ewan jingled when he walked, she knew he kept a large ring of keys on his person at all times. But how to get them... hmmm.

She wandered out onto the roof of the castle. The view from the battlements arrested her. The Highlands stretched out into the bluish-purple distance. Range after range of rugged, bare mountains, and in the valleys, glittering lochs that reflected the sky and mountains.

The eerie sensation that someone watched her chased away her awe. She swung around and found a large black bird sitting on a perch near the wall. She drew back.

The hooked beak and deadly talons told her this was a hawk, eagle or falcon of some sort. Glossy blue-black feathers and pale blue eyes. She frowned. She'd never seen a bird with blue eyes before, but then she wasn't a bird-watcher. This bird of prey seemed neither afraid of her nor aggressive; it just observed her, curiously.

"Hi, there." She felt ridiculous talking to a wild bird, but what the hell? She used to talk to her pets all the time when she was a kid.

The hawk tilted its head and studied her with sharp eyes.

"What are you doing hanging out up here? Are you someone's pet, or are you injured?" Cautiously, she moved toward him. "What's your name, huh?"

He lowered his head and eyed her. She had no idea why she thought it was a "he" but something about it seemed masculine.

She refused to venture too close. He might attack and sink those talons into her.

He jerked to attention as if he'd heard a noise. Flapping his wings slightly, he leapt to the edge of the battlements. Turning his head this way and that, he watched something on the ground. Maybe he'd spied a rabbit. Abruptly he dove off the roof and toward the courtyard. Staring after him, she held her breath, hoping he wouldn't crash. He zoomed over the heads of three people on horseback. A shriek echoed up. Wow, Gavin had an attack hawk on his staff.

Curious about the visitors, she ran back inside and down the stone steps.

"She's here. I know she's here!" yelled a voice from the entryway minutes later.

Hidden, Shauna froze on the spiral stone staircase and shivered at the gravelly female voice.

"I can feel her."

"Nay, m'lady," Ewan said.

"Ye lie. I shall find a fitting punishment for those who lie."

Shauna peered around the edge of the stairwell in time to see Ewan hold up a brass bell and a sprig of leaves in one hand and a thick candle in the other.

The woman standing in the portal instantly turned her head and locked her maniacal gaze on Shauna. "There." She pointed.

Heart pumping furiously, Shauna jumped back and flattened herself against the stone wall.

I'm not afraid. I'm not afraid. She's just a woman.

But there was something inexplicably frightening and powerful about that woman. Was she the witch who had cursed Gavin?

"Out! In the name of the Father, ye will leave our home!" Ewan shouted then slammed the door.

Silence. Shauna peered around the curved wall again. Ewan wilted into a heap on the floor and mopped his brow, the candle tumbled sideways and sputtered out.

Shauna descended the last few steps. "Who was that?"

"Wilona MacRae. The one who cursed Gavin."

"Are you all right?" She reached down a hand to help him up.

"Aye." He waved her off and pushed himself up. "Gavin willna be happy to hear of her visit."

"He should've been here. I don't understand why he leaves to tour the grounds every day."

Ewan lifted a brow, gave her a strange look and walked away.

"Weird little man," she muttered to the silence. Hell, everyone here was weird. And she was afraid it was rubbing off.

Late that night, Shauna awoke in bed alone, exhausted from the long and thorough episode of lovemaking Gavin had unleashed on her when he'd finally shown up just after dusk. The sheets beside her were still warm.

"Gavin?"

She sat up, intending to tell him the feng shui thing so he could have his guard clean the rest of this miserable castle but the candle sputtering on the bedside table showed the room to be empty. She rose, dressed and, carrying the candle, slipped into the corridor. Gavin's voice echoed from not too far away and she followed it.

"I thought she was the answer to our prayers. I thought she would break the curse."

"'Haps there hasna been time enough," Ewan said.

"I dinna ken what else to do," Gavin said in a low voice she had to strain to hear. "I dinna want her to find out what I am. If she does, she will fear me and leave like all the others."

"Has she ever seen ye in your other form?"

"Aye. She even talked to me, thinking I was someone's trained falcon."

Omigod! His other form? Someone's trained falcon?

He couldn't mean…

"But she didna ken that was me. 'Tis the only part of the curse she doesna know about. 'Haps Wilona strengthened the curse when she came here or cast a new one."

"Heaven help us. I warded her off as best I could."

"She willna give up. Keep a watchful eye out, as I will. Dinna open the door to her again."

"Aye."

"She's wanting Shauna. And if she gets her hands on the lass, she'll kill her."

Chapter 7

Omigod, he turns to a bird. A bird? No, that's crazy. Impossible. Shauna huddled under the covers, unmoving except for the occasional chill that had nothing to do with the room temperature. *I'll pretend to be in a deep, comatose sleep and he'll leave me alone.*

The bedchamber door opened and closed back. She dared not even breathe. With her head covered, she couldn't tell what he was doing. Undressing? A moment later, the bed jiggled as he climbed in and snuggled next to her.

"Ye're shivering. Are ye cold?"

"Omigod!" Unable to control her actions, she lunged from the bed as if catapulted, and backed into the corner.

"What's wrong, Shauna? Why are ye dressed?" Gavin lay in bed, uncovered to the waist, his muscled chest bare. He looked so *human*. No feathers sticking out of his ears. No talons on his fingers. No beak, only those sensual lips that knew how to kiss and nibble so sinfully well. But his eyes, beautiful blue, did resemble the hawk's eyes she'd seen on the roof.

"*What* are you?" she demanded.

He frowned. "A man. What are you?"

"I overheard what you said to Ewan. About the falcon. And your other form. What did you mean?"

"'Slud!" He shoved himself out of bed and covered his yummy nakedness with a long shirt. "I knew ye'd find out sooner or later. 'Tis the main part of the curse. At dawn, my physical form changes from a man to a hawk of unidentified species. And the opposite at dusk. This is why people believe I'm the devil incarnate."

"Ah." Though she swallowed hard, she still couldn't swallow this unbelievable info. "It's absurd. How can such a thing be possible? Are you a vampire?"

"Nay. Why are ye asking that? I change form. Some witches have the power to change form, ye ken. From human to a cat or whatever they desire. And they can change someone else too. One witch turned a man into a horse for a night, rode him to her destination, some twenty miles distant, then turned him back into a man in the morn. His hands were raw and bloody as proof. Another witch turned dice into swine and sent them to kill her neighbor's children. But she didna succeed."

"Get real," Shauna muttered.

"'Tis as real as can be. But likely ye willna believe it until ye see the proof."

"You're right. I have a Ph.D. in psychiatry, for Pete's sake. This is all in people's minds. Delusions."

"When I change into a hawk, 'tis no' in my mind, love. And in the morn, ye shall see for yerself."

She shivered. "I don't know if I want to watch. I might lose my grasp on reality like the rest of you."

"Indeed. Then ye shall fit in perfectly." He grinned, removed his shirt and lay down on top of the covers on his side, facing her, his arm propped beneath his head. What a pose. He knew what would convince her to forget their disagreement. His arousal grew as she watched. That's all he had to do to seduce her, let her see his delectable body for a few moments and she was nympho-putty.

But could she have sex with a man who claimed to be a bird during the day? What if he and the rest of his clan weren't delusional? What if he was a different species half the time?

A shiver passed through her.

When she watched his erection harden fully, point up toward his stomach and twitch once, calling to her, she could no longer ignore him.

Well, at least he was a man right now. A hot, gorgeous man. Her husband. It was her wifely duty to have sex with him. Hmmm.

Good excuse, Shauna!

Body already tingling, growing wet, she pulled her clothing off and joined him in bed. Slowly, she crawled over him and rested on his hard muscular body, his irresistible cock pressed beneath her stomach. His lips and tongue ate at hers and his hands stroked down her back to massage her ass. Yes, he was definitely a man, not a bird.

"Shauna." Someone shook her from a pleasant dream about a hot air balloon ride. "Shauna, 'tis time." Gavin's voice.

"Hmm? Time for what? It's still dark. I'm sleepy. Tired."

"Dawn is nigh. If ye wish to see me turn into a hawk, ye'd best open yer eyes."

"Oh, shit!"

Gavin snickered. "What a dirty mouth ye have."

She shoved the drowsiness away. Gavin turning into a hawk—just what she wanted to wake up to.

"Mother of all nightmares," she grumbled again and blinked up at him in the candlelight, squinting against the brightness. "Okay, shift. Get it over with so I can get some sleep."

"Ye break my heart with yer concern for my very immortal soul."

She sighed. "I'm sorry. I was just being a smartass. I care about your immortal soul."

"Indeed. I'm wanting to see yer smartarse now." He tried to flip her over.

"No. You're getting ready to shape-shift."

"No' for a few more minutes yet."

She let him turn her onto her stomach. He ran his fingers down her butt crack, then pushed her legs apart. A spark of arousal lit within her. She was such a sucker for him. He gently stroked the cheek of her ass and kissed it. "Lovely." And bit it. Hard.

"Ouch! Bastard!" She tried to roll over. When he wouldn't let her, she kicked him with her heel.

"Nay." He sat on his knees between her legs and lifted her butt into the air. She held on tight to her pillow, anticipation flooding her with moisture. She couldn't help but want him, even if they'd already made love three times during the night. He'd turned her into a sex fiend.

He pressed the head of his big cock against her sex lips, stroking, parting. A little thrust, lodging the head inside.

Her back arched, she wanted more and more. "Gavin."

"Mmm." His warm hands stroked over her, ate her up. He grasped her hips and pulled her back, pushing himself in another couple inches. "Mmm. *M'eudail.* Ye are a delight."

She moaned. "And you're freakin' awesome," she gasped.

He shoved himself fully into her. A stitch of pain grabbed onto her. She cried out.

"I'm sorry." He pulled out a bit, then gently thrust. Giving only pleasure for several long strokes.

She moaned. "Yes." At this moment, she wanted to stay with him forever, make love every night and early morning before dawn.

He slid his wet finger along her crack again, stroked it over her anus with concerted attention and firm pressure. A new sort of sensation tingled through her. Unfamiliar... but then she didn't have much experience.

"What are you up to? Stop it!" She reached a hand back to prevent his kinky move even though her curiosity peaked.

"Nay, wait." He pushed her hand away and inserted the tip of his finger into the tight opening.

She couldn't believe how that felt. Weird. Full. Erotic. Still she fought against it. She was not an anal sex person. Was she?

Growing wetter and arching up to meet him, she feared she might like this. Hmm.

"Relax," he murmured.

She was surprised to find she did want to relax and let him do whatever he wanted to her body, invade, tease and sensually torment any place he wished. He slowly, gently drew his finger in and out, even as he slid his cock deep inside her. The discomfort was gone and the pleasure intense.

"Gavin," she moaned.

He growled like a beast and thrust faster. "Aye, ye like that now, do ye?"

"No," she groaned.

"Liar. Ye love it. Admit it."

"No."

"Tell me or I'll stop." Pausing, he flicked his tongue against her back.

"I love it," she whispered.

"Aye, I knew it." He immediately rewarded her with more finger movements, deeper. "Someday I'm going to slide my cock into that wee hole."

"You're out of your... freakin' mind," she gasped, wanting to concentrate on each sensation he unleashed on her body.

A finger on his other hand busied itself on her wet, swollen clit, stroking back and forth like a tongue. So many intense feelings and erotic pleasures battering her from all angles. Within seconds, her orgasm smashed into her so hard she almost passed out. Her whole body tightened, convulsed, wrapping around and embracing the rapture. She thought she screamed and thrashed about, but her focus was on this man, what he did to her, how his soul fused with hers.

When she became aware again, he was still driving his cock into her, then abruptly shoved to the hilt and groaned. His hot semen shot into her, drenching her, and she loved it.

"Damnation!" He yanked himself away from her and climbed off the bed.

She turned over in time to see a grimace of pain cross his face as he staggered toward the window. Something weird happened, like a lightning bolt combined with a blurry mist and he emerged a large black falcon. Wings outspread, he sailed through the open window.

"Omigod!" She jumped up and ran to the window. In the dawn light, his elegant black form disappeared into the gray-white Highland mist over the mountains.

He hadn't been lying. She'd had sex with a bird-man. Hell, bird-man was her husband.

I shouldn't leave.

No, I have to get out of here, dammit.

Shauna had been having this argument with herself all morning. In the stone corridor, she silently peered around the corner. Ewan's nap time was just after the midday meal, and there he lay, snoring on his little cot next to that nook in the wall. Pulse thumping in her throat, she slipped forward a few feet during each snore. Though one part of her didn't like this plan, another part spurred her on. She'd never before realized two people resided inside her head. Talk about delusional. Schizophrenic!

Standing in front of Ewan, she waited. His keys were hooked onto his belt and it took all her strength not to grab them. During the next roar from his nose, she lifted the key ring with all the huge keys, detached it from his belt, and clasped them in her hands so they wouldn't jingle. He snorted and turned onto his side. She froze and waited while his nap resumed, then crept away.

The keys! The keys! She wanted to leap for joy but restrained herself. With the keys hidden in an old plaid she'd found, she sedately strolled about the rooms and corridors as she had the day before. Coming upon the door she most suspected of being the armory where Gavin's magical sword was kept, she glanced behind herself.

Silence.

Now which of the dozen keys fit this lock? She tried one after the other of the chunky bronze and iron keys. The rusty metal scraped and screeched. A key got stuck.

"Oh, crap," she muttered and yanked at the key. "Stupid piece of metal." It released with a loud rasp and she stumbled backward, almost losing her balance.

Finally, the eighth key fit and turned flawlessly.

Woohoo. She wanted to dance a Highland jig.

She pushed the door inward and the hinges let out a fierce screech.

"Oh, dammit," she whispered and rushed inside. The narrow slit windows allowed in minimal light. Dozens of weapons lined the walls and lay on tables.

Short, medium and long knives, most dull in color and nondescript. Swords of all sorts, basket-hilted, two-handed, and other designs.

"There it is." She froze, something weighing heavily in her chest and gnawing at her stomach. If she touched that sword, she'd never see Gavin again. She wouldn't get to look into his beautiful eyes or touch him. She would never find out what might develop between them, how deep their affection might grow. What if he was her one and only true love, and she left him four hundred years in the past?

On the other hand, she couldn't give up modern life, her family and career all because of a man who'd taken her prisoner, could she? Nothing about that said independence or feminism.

Studying the weapons, she tugged her hair back from her face, hoping that would help her think more clearly. It didn't.

Wait, several huge two-handed swords sat in the display. Which was the right one?

"Why, ye thieving lass!"

Shauna whirled. "Ewan."

"Aye! Caught ye, I did. Thought I was too daft to ken ye stole my keys. Give 'em to me." He snatched the metal ring from her hand, the keys jingling.

"Sorry." Unsure what to do, but determined not to lose this opportunity, she turned and quickly touched two of the nearest two-handed swords... with her fingertips. She winced, expecting pain.

Nothing happened.

"Dammit!" She didn't know whether she was disappointed or relieved.

"Get yer hands off 'em. Why the devil would ye be wanting a *claidheamh dà làimh* anyway? Ye are no' even strong enough to lift it." He grabbed her wrist and dragged her from the room.

Though she tried to dig her heels in, she was no match for him. The steward was strong for a little man.

"Come. I dinna want to hurt ye. Ye're going back to Gavin's bedchamber where ye'll stay the rest of the day, just as Gavin ordered."

"What do you mean?"

"He said if ye got out of line, to lock ye in the bedchamber."

"That jerk. Can I go to the bathroom first—er—I mean garderobe?"

"Nay, ye'll use the closestool. And ye'll be lucky if I bring ye any food, ye ungrateful wench."

"I'll tell Gavin you were showing me disrespect and manhandling me."

"I dinna care. Gavin will be more furious with ye than me. I'll be surprised if he doesna take a whip to ye," Ewan grumbled as he prodded her along toward her prison. "He should anyway."

"Like hell," she muttered.

"I married her and the curse still isna broken," Gavin growled, pacing from one side of his father's dim bedchamber to the other that night.

His da only gave him a vacant look from where he lay on the bed.

"Ye're no' helping."

"'Tis the lass," his father whispered as if in a daydream.

Gavin shook his head. "And now she's trying to steal weapons."

What was he going to do? The curse remained. His wife was unhappy and wanting to kill him. Watching him shift into a hawk had without doubt driven her over the edge. Why could she not accept him as he was? 'Twas all he wanted, a wife to pleasure… one who would look at him with adoring eyes and love him. *Love.* 'Twas too much to ask. He would never have that.

"She is the key." His father's feeble voice trembled. "Treat her kindly."

Kindly? "Devil take it. I should give her a good spanking." Naked.

Hmm.

"Nay. Love her, Gavin. Love her."

Chapter 8

I hate him!

At the sound of a key scraping and rattling in the door lock, Shauna turned from the smoldering blaze she'd built with peat in the fireplace. After being confined to this room and bored for many hours, she'd asked Ewan to bring her books to read but they were Latin, which she couldn't decipher. Boy, had she been wrong about Latin class being useless.

Gavin pushed the door open and entered with a tray of food. She ignored her gnawing stomach and glared at him. She would never stay with a man who kept her prisoner.

Gavin's expression remained dark as he set the tray down. "So, ye're still wanting to kill me."

"No, of course not! I would never do that. And you can't keep me prisoner!"

"Why did ye break into the armory?" His jaw hardened. The way he surveyed her, the expression on his gorgeous face, tight, serious and unhappy, she didn't like it. No matter the battle going on inside her, she wanted to please him, wanted to make him smile. Wanted to give him unreal sexual pleasure, as he'd given her, but now was not the time.

His frown deepened. "Shauna. The armory?"

She crossed her arms. "You wouldn't believe me if I told you."

"I might."

Studying him, she bit her nail. Could she trust him enough to tell him the truth? "You promise not to throw me in the dungeon again?"

He lifted a brow, his gaze turning sharp and menacing. "Aye."

"You swear? Upon your noble lairdly honor, or whatever?"

"Aye." He placed his hand over his heart. "I willna throw ye in the dungeon. Ye're my wife. What do ye take me for, a beast?" He glanced aside. "Dinna answer that."

The vulnerability in his eyes tore at her resolve. She wanted to hold him, stroke him and kiss his closed eyes. She wanted to strip the clothing from her beast-man, drag him to the bed and ravish him... because he was so precious.

But she couldn't.

"Okay, here's the thing," Shauna said. "I told you this once before and you didn't believe me. I'm from the future, from the beginning of the twenty-first century."

He chuckled, though she couldn't imagine why. Nothing about this was funny. But he did have a nice smile that made him even more appealing.

She firmed her resolve, determined not to fall under his spell until they'd hashed this out. "I'm glad you find that amusing. But if I can believe you turn into a falcon during the day, surely you can believe I'm from the future."

"I proved I shape-shift. Can ye prove ye're from the future?"

Hmm. Good question. If only she hadn't set down her backpack at the Highland Games before she'd picked up the sword, she would've had several modern things with her, including a cell phone and a camera. As it was, she only had her clothes and jewelry. Not even a watch, dammit. Grammy had handmade the blouse and the skirt.

"None, except some of my clothes are factory made, my panties and bra. And my boots."

"What is this panties? That strip of lace ye had over yer..." He glanced toward her crotch and she almost had the feeling he could see through her skirt.

"Yes."

"What is the purpose of it?"

"It's an undergarment. You know, like if I fall and my skirt goes over my head, people can't see my private parts. On the beaches where I'm from, it's all women wear on the bottom. And a bra on top. A bikini."

"Indeed? I would like to see ye clothed in such." His eyes darkened and his expression turned lusty. "Either ye are telling the truth or ye have an active imagination." His gaze searched her face. "Why did ye say ye were from the Colonies, then?"

"I'm from the United States, which is the nation the Colonies turn into in the late 1700s after the Revolutionary war."

"Indeed?"

"Yes, *indeed,* Your Majesty."

"I'm no' a king, so dinna mock me. Let me see your boot."

She took one off and handed it to him. He examined it. "'Tis a good cobbler who made these. Wait, this says *made in China.*"

She nodded.

"How can that be?"

"They were imported, as most of our shoes are."

"Why wouldn't these United States ye speak of make their own shoes?"

"It's a long story, free trade and all that."

He gave her boot back and she put it on.

"So why do ye want a sword if no' to kill me... or someone?"

"I was at a Highland Games when a man named Ranald MacTavish called me over to his clan tent. He said he knew my grandmother. He showed me your sword, suggested I hold it. When I did, there was a sharp pain in my head and a loud boom. I showed up here, in your bedroom, still holding your sword. Well, I dropped it. Anyway, you know the rest."

He stared at her with a disbelieving expression. "Someone had my sword four-hundred years in the future?"

"Yes."

"Ranald MacTavish? What did he look like?"

She described the Santa-wanna-be.

"Aye. Sounds like him." Gavin shook his head. "Ranald MacTavish was my uncle. He died about a decade ago."

"So, he was a figment of my imagination too. Or a ghost. No wonder people were staring at me like I was insane. They probably couldn't see him."

"And ye're thinking if ye hold my sword again, ye can travel back to the future."

She nodded.

"Ye want to leave," he said low tone.

She again spied the vulnerability behind his hard look. She wasn't afraid to answer, just afraid of disappointing him. Besides, she didn't really want to leave *him;* she wished she could take him with her because she'd like to explore and deepen their "relationship," even make it a real marriage. But his birdyness scared the bejesus out of her. Why couldn't he just be a normal man?

"I kenned when ye found out about the falcon part ye'd no' want to be married to me anymore. Ye fear me. Ye think I'm the devil, like everyone else does."

"No. I don't fear you nor think you're the devil. It's just so weird. And besides, you said if I married you the curse would be broken. But it isn't. You're still falcon-man. Maybe I'm not the right woman to break the curse."

"My father says ye are."

"What do you say?"

He observed her for a long fragile moment and shrugged. "I only ken that I want ye to stay. Ye've made my life not only bearable these last few days, but also happy. I've enjoyed talking to ye and... other things."

"Of course. It all comes down to sex."

"Nay. No' just the sex. Ye are a lovely and special woman. I never imagined or believed a fascinating woman such as you would be willing to marry me or that ye could even exist in real life. I thought ye were only a dream."

"A dream?" Wait a minute, what was he talking about?

"Aye, I confess, I had dreams of ye two or three times before ye showed up. I couldna see yer face, but after we made love, I kenned 'twas you." His eyes darkened. "That's another reason I think ye're the right woman."

"I had a lot of dreams of you. For two months, almost every night. And day. Daydreams. You almost took over my life completely before I came here. I thought I was losing my mind. Ranald said it had something to do with this magical MacRae brooch." Leaving out the bit about the legend of the brooch leading the wearer to her true love, she pointed to the piece of jewelry pinned to her blouse. "And, I believe, this brooch combined with my touching your sword is what brought me here."

He stepped closer and examined the brooch. "I think I've seen Wilona MacRae wearing this, or one like it."

"Really?"

"Aye."

"Do you think she's the one who made it magical?" Couldn't be. Since Wilona's powers were black magic, Shauna doubted the woman would create something that led to true love.

"I dinna ken." His gaze met hers at close range. "Explain these daydreams to me."

"They were sexy. Erotic. I could see you very clearly, your face, your eyes, your body. And the things you did—" She blew out a breath. "I stayed aroused all the time."

His lashes lowered a bit and he watched her with growing hunger. "And now?"

"Now... yes." Prickling warmth shivered through her. "When I look at you, I want you. I won't deny it."

"Yet, ye want to leave."

"I can't stay here just because of great sex." She let out an exasperated breath.

He studied her a long intense moment, and when he spoke his voice was low and deep. "'Haps what is between us is more than *great sex,* as ye call it."

Yes, maybe so. Maybe she was falling in love with him. And if so, going back to the future would be even more painful. If she stayed here, she'd be giving up everything she had—her family, her friends, her career, everything she'd worked so hard for—all in exchange for him. Was he worth that kind of sacrifice? What if he couldn't love her and grew tired of her? What if the curse was never broken? What if he continued to shift into a bird every day for the rest of their lives?

He touched her face and, in that instant, none of it mattered. She wanted to wipe that pained look from his eyes. She wanted the dark blue heat of his gaze flickering over her skin. She wanted him hot, hard and forcefully plundering her body. Making her feel things she'd never felt before him. Her pulse drummed in her ears. He inspired excitement in her, apart from sexual arousal. She wanted to gaze into his wicked eyes forever and never look away.

Stroking his lips across hers, he kissed her tenderly at first, but with rising intensity, licking between her lips, toying with her tongue. Her insides felt like warm, melting caramel. Oh God, she wanted him. She loved him. *No, no I don't.*

He paused, breathing hard, and pressed his forehead to hers. "Dinna be leaving me, Shauna. Promise me." His gaze delved into hers with a new fierceness.

The aching, thrilling sensation in her chest urged her to do anything he wanted—to please him, to make him happy. She stroked her hand over his face, his scratchy beard stubble and smoothed her fingers over the scar, wishing she could soothe his soul.

"I need ye, lass," he whispered. "I need ye here with me, even if the curse is never broken. I canna offer ye much, not the things ye had where ye came from, but I'll share with ye all I have. This castle is yours. Do with it what ye will. These lands, though barren, they're yours. Me, my body, my heart, all yours if ye'll have them. I've ne'er given a woman these things before."

She couldn't speak. What could she say to that? Her throat closed up.

"Every night I'll come back here and be with ye. I'll stay awake all night, giving ye pleasure, if 'tis what ye want. I'm a man. Even when I'm a falcon, I have the thoughts of a man. I understood every word ye said to me when ye saw me on the battlements. And I wouldna hurt ye for anything, so there's no reason to fear me. Promise me ye willna leave."

"I promise," she whispered, though she didn't know whether she was lying or not. They were the only words she could speak at that moment.

"Dinna lie to me, damn you." Gavin fused his lips to hers and devoured her mouth with erotic sweeps of his tongue. The hardness of his chest abraded her sensitive nipples. They ached for his touch. His fingers closed over one and tugged, almost painful, but not. She gasped into his mouth and yanked up his kilt.

She closed her fingers around his iron-hard cock, large and standing at attention.

Removing her hand, he growled, picked her up and dumped her on the bed.

When he drew near, she tugged at his clothing until he fell onto the bed. She rolled on top of him, shoved his kilt up and grasped his erection. She brushed her lips over it. He smelled clean and very male. She sucked the head into her mouth and made love to it with her tongue for a long moment.

"Mmm." He wrapped her hair around his fist and watched her with fascination and a dark frown.

Her devotion to him spurred her on. Stroking his long shaft with her hand, she couldn't get enough of the hard, smooth feel of him in her mouth. His potent masculine scent drove her mad. She squeezed the head with her tongue, then nibbled at it gently.

Abruptly he drew away, flipped her onto her back and snatched her skirt up. He shoved her legs wide, parted her sex lips and trailed his tongue between. He tugged at her pubic hair, exposing her clit fully and flicked it quickly with his tongue, over and over.

"Oh, Gavin!" A wave of burning-hot tingles swept through her and twisted into an orgasm. She was lost in several long seconds of insane pleasure. No thoughts, only sensations and Gavin.

When she opened her eyes, he was over her, driving his cock into her and capturing her mouth with his, the taste of sex on his lips. He pummeled her deep inside as if unable to control himself, his face fierce and hard with passion.

Each moment, she thought she might die with the intensity and the electrical pleasure. Before she knew it, her head hung off the far edge of the bed. Then she feared she'd fall. Her upper body slid down.

"Gavin!" She placed her hands on the floor but she didn't fall.

He had her thighs in a death lock and her skirt drifted toward her face. He didn't let up for long seconds.

Finally, he stopped and pulled her upward onto his lap, facing him. "Och, lass. I've ne'er... ye turn me into a rutting beast when you're in my bed. I want to do naught but take ye hard and fast and ne'er stop."

"Mmmm." Holding onto his broad shoulders and burying her hands in his long dark hair, she was dizzy for a moment but looking into his eyes at close range renewed her hunger. "Sounds like a plan."

He twitched inside her. "Are ye going to lie to me anymore?" he breathed against her mouth.

"Is this the punishment for it?" She grinned.

"Nay. I shall whip yer sweet arse with my bare hand." He smacked one cheek of her butt, gently, then caressed it. He lifted her up and down once slowly on his thick erection.

She pressed firmly against him, wanting him as deep as he would go. "I won't lie. I'm not lying. I want to stay with you." Truly she did. And she wanted to bite him at the same time she placed sweet, loving kisses over every inch of him.

He paused, his dark, pained gaze searching her eyes. "Aye," he whispered. "Stay with me always, Shauna."

Yes, I want to. But what if I can't?

Chapter 9

The next afternoon, as Gavin soared high above his estate, he spied his damnable cousin, Alpin MacTavish, riding toward the castle along with two armed men. *What the devil is he doing here?*

Gavin flew to the castle ahead of the men and let loose loud screeches to warn Ewan of the danger that approached, though his lack-witted steward was probably napping.

Gavin soared lower over his cousin's head. If only Gavin were bigger, he'd carry the whoreson off and drop him at the top of a high, craggy *ben*.

"Shoot it!" Alpin ordered.

The archer notched an arrow and aimed at Gavin. He quickly darted out of range and glided behind the castle. *Craven boar-pigs!* He'd see they were repaid in kind.

Gavin circled back around, and two arrows, one from each of his cousin's guards, shot toward him. Pulling his wings in, he dove toward Alpin. The imbecile screamed and fell off his mount.

Ah, a bit of sweet revenge.

Gavin lifted himself high into the air, far out of arrow range and watched them. He would make Alpin regret setting foot on MacTavish holdings, for he well knew Gavin was a black falcon during the day.

At the door of the castle, the men drew weapons and pushed past Ewan. 'Slud! Maybe he shouldn't have reassigned his one and only guard. Gavin sped toward the castle and his open bedchamber window. He glided in and perched on the windowsill.

A scream erupted, and he almost took back to the air.

Shauna.

She gawked at him and backed up a few inches.

I willna hurt ye, and ye ken it. He made a comforting sound and glanced toward the door. Still closed. He felt sorely trapped and vulnerable indoors when in bird form, but he would not let his despicable cousin harm her.

Using his wings for a soft landing, he leapt to the floor and stalked to the door. God's bones, it was unlocked. Slowly, so as not to frighten her, he moved toward Shauna, then glanced back at the door, turned his head sideways and tried to motion. He made a low whistling sound. Damnation! He hated not being able to speak words.

He ran toward the door again, leapt up and pecked at the bar. He couldn't move it with his beak. Looking at her again, he uttered the low sound.

"You want me to bar the door?"

He squawked, too loudly, but he couldn't contain his excitement. She'd understood him.

"Why?"

Oh, for pity's sake, he couldn't explain why. *Just do it!*

"You promised you would never hurt me."

Of course, I won't hurt you. I'm trying to protect you!

He perched on the windowsill again, away from her so she wouldn't feel he was a threat.

She crept forward and lowered the bar into place. "Are you happy now?"

He bobbed his head up and down.

She chuckled and her expression softened. "You're pretty smart, for a bird."

Ha. 'Tis no' amusing. He shook himself, fluffing his feathers.

"Silly. Can I pet you?"

Again, he bobbed his head, unable to believe someone wanted to touch him. "Don't bite me."

He moved his head side to side, his best attempt at a negative shake of the head. His animal side instinctively feared humans, even though he was one inside. But he knew Shauna wouldn't hurt him.

She approached him, her hand outstretched cautiously. He turned his sharp-hooked beak aside, away from her. Her fingers lightly stroked the feathers on the back of his neck. His animal instincts told him she was good, friendly. That she liked him and meant him no harm. He had not expected to sense that just from a touch.

Her palm smoothed over the broad feathers in his wings and he felt comforted. His every day in bird form was lonely, but Shauna could change that. He hated the weakness, the vulnerability he felt. Hated being under a witch's control.

"If I had one of those gauntlet things, I could carry you around. Although you do look pretty heavy."

Och! I'm a vicious predator. And I willna have my wife carrying me around like a lapdog or a wee bairn.

A knock sounded at the door and they both jumped.

Gavin gave a screech of warning.

Shauna stuck a finger in her ear. "Damn, you're loud. Who is it?" she called.

"Ewan."

She moved toward the door. Following her, Gavin leapt to the floor and grasped the back of her skirt in his beak.

Halting, she turned. "What are you doing? It's only Ewan."

Gavin shook his head and tugged at her skirt.

She frowned. "You don't want me to open the door?"

He repeated the negative gesture.

"I'm busy," she called out to Ewan.

A ruckus sounded in the hall and someone tried to open the door. "'Tis locked."

"Dinna ye have the key?" Alpin's silky deceptive voice.

"'Tis barred from inside. A key won't help."

"*Dògan!*"

"Who is out there with him?" Shauna whispered.

Gavin cocked his head sideways. Did she honestly expect him to answer?

"Besides, Gavin is in there with her," Ewan said. "Didna ye hear him? He will rip the flesh from yer bones."

"Bah! I'm not afraid of the wee birdie. I have an arrow with his name on it. Gavin will be happy to know I've reported to the authorities that he's a magician, practicing the black arts, turning himself into a bird. And ye, wee man, had best tread softly or ye'll find yerself in the dungeon once this castle is mine. What a heap of rubble 'tis turning into. I shall restore it to the former glory of our ancestors."

Over my dead body, ye whoreson.

But that was exactly what Alpin intended, for Gavin's body to be dead.

A loud groaning cry awoke Shauna. She hadn't remembered falling asleep, only that she'd been petting Gavin's feathers. In the twilight, she bolted upright in bed to find Gavin in human form, naked, bent over the foot of the bed. A tremble shook him. Inhaling a breath, he straightened, all his glorious muscles flexing and stretching as if he'd been hunched in one position too long.

"God's wounds!"

"Does that hurt?"

"Aye. Like a second of getting yer whole body ripped apart and put back together."

She jumped up and took him into her arms, stroked his back. "I'm so sorry. I want to break the curse. Tell me how."

"I dinna ken. I wish I did." Holding her, he kissed her forehead, her cheek, her neck. "I thank ye for no' fearing me, for listening to me and locking the door. 'Twas Alpin, my greedy outlaw of a cousin. He hasna left yet. I'm thinking he wants to confront me."

"Why?"

"He wants the castle, the estate, and my title. The whoreson, he shall regret coming here and forcing his way inside."

Gavin opened a trunk, dragged out clean clothes and dressed. She loved the way he looked in his kilt, all gorgeous, brave and bit barbaric. Excited chills covered her.

"Ye'll stay here while I go talk to him. Bar the door after I leave." He started out.

"Wait." She caught up with him and reached up for a kiss. A delicious kiss, like a midnight snack of rich, hot fudge cake and ice cream, something that had to be devoured slowly and each taste savored.

"*Iosa is Muire Mhàthair!*" he growled and pulled away. "Ye're dangerous as a siren, stealing my focus that way. I'll be back in a trice. Wait for me in bed, naked." He exited, then stuck his head back in. "When I return, I expect ye to unbar the door for me wearing naught."

"You can dream." She winked and smiled at his fearsome glare that promised sexy retribution. Having no desire to meet this evil cousin who'd wanted to barge in on her, Shauna secured the door behind him. She hoped Gavin would be all right.

Minutes later, as she paced from one side of the room to the other, sounds of clashing metal and men's shouts reached her ears.

"Crap! What is that?"

A sword fight? Gavin could be hurt. She ran to the door, threw the bar aside and rushed into the corridor. She silently crept down the spiral stone stairwell, stopped in the shadows and peered out into the great hall. The tables, holding several lit candles, had been pushed against the wall. Gavin and a tall, light-haired stranger—probably Alpin—circled each other, swords drawn, on the wide expanse of the stone floor.

Gavin did not have his huge magical two-handed sword. Instead he used a normal-sized basket-hilted sword, as did his cousin.

The two launched into noisy swordplay again, slashing and thrusting and blocking. Neither was able to make a cut with that onslaught. Both drew back and moved with deliberate calculation and skill, holding their tempers firmly in check. Gavin's malicious, taunting smile told her he was actually enjoying himself.

Alpin's gaze lit on her. "Is that her?"

Dammit, she'd thought she was hidden in the shadows.

Gavin quickly glanced at her, but returned his gaze to Alpin, stealthily placing himself between them, though they were some distance apart.

"M'lady, return to the bedchamber forthwith."

She did not care for his bossy, hard tone.

"But Gavin, I wish to meet yer new bride. 'Tis the reason I came. Truce, hmm?" Alpin held his sword aloft, then shoved it into his scabbard.

Gavin did not sheath his sword, but held it at his side. "Nay." He strode toward Shauna, half his attention still on his cousin. "Go upstairs," he demanded in a low but forceful voice. "I told ye to stay in the chamber."

"Excuse me for worrying about you. I heard the sword fight and wanted to make sure you were okay."

"Ye have little confidence in me," he snapped.

"Bastard," she whispered under her breath, hoping Gavin heard it but not his cousin. She climbed the stairs toward the bedchamber, but in the upstairs corridor, she paused. Gavin must have gotten the sword from the armory. Maybe he'd left the door unlocked. She didn't want to leave him, but this might be her only chance to return to the future and her real life. She was starting to miss it. Missed being able to drop by Mom's and Dad's to see what weird new dessert she'd cooked up. She always enjoyed sitting around the kitchen island on bar stools gossiping with her mom and sister, discussing said sister's eventful love life, having to whisper when Dad was nearby.

Should I or shouldn't I go back to the future? She would just see if the door was open. It didn't mean she had to touch the sword.

Taking a candle from the wall sconce, she tiptoed toward the armory. But when she arrived, she found the door locked as always.

Dammit. Though she had determined to let fate decide the outcome, she was still irritated to find the door locked. She wanted control of her own destiny; the decision was her right.

She stamped back to the bedchamber and barred the door. What kind of instrument would pick the armory lock? Not that she had ever picked a lock in her life, except for her sister's diary many years ago so she could learn all her dirty secrets. Could the same principal apply?

After searching the room, she realized nothing here could be used to pick a large lock. She'd need a small, keen-bladed knife and Gavin would never trust her with such a weapon.

A spoon handle might work. Hmm. Tomorrow morning at breakfast, she'd slip the silver spoon into her pocket when Crocker wasn't looking.

Now, she definitely felt like a prisoner trying to escape.

Chapter 10

After another bout of swordplay, Alpin left with only a slice in his shirt and a shallow nick to his upper right arm. Gavin did not wish to kill the man outright. Such a thing would hurt his beloved aunt too much. As youths, he and Alpin had been friends and always practiced swordplay together. Sometime after they had become men, Alpin had grown bitter and jealous of Gavin, more and more each year.

He did not want Shauna near Alpin. No telling what the viper would do. That was why he'd ordered her back to his bedchamber. Though lovely, luscious and intriguing, the wayward wench wouldn't listen to a thing he said or obey him, though *obey* had been in the marriage vows. She always wanted to make her own decisions, some of which were daft and dangerous.

Gavin tried to open his bedchamber door but found it barred. Good, at least she'd obeyed him finally. Would she open the door naked, as he'd asked?

Anticipation tingling through him, he knocked. "Shauna, 'tis me."

No response.

With a balled fist, he pounded on the door. "Shauna? Are ye asleep?"

"Find yourself a new place to sleep, butt-munch," she called back.

"What?"

"I don't like bossy, demanding, inconsiderate men who order me around in front of company as if I'm a schnauzer."

"What the devil are ye talking about? Shauna, open the door."

"No."

He disliked her petulant tone. He envisioned her bottom lip plumped out in a pout. He'd like to lick it, suck on it until she moaned.

"I didna ken ye were such a weak woman."

"Weak? I am not weak!"

"Sounds that way to me, what with the way you're whining."

Something thumped against the door. Gavin smiled.

Wood banged against metal as she lifted the bar and yanked the door open.

"I am not weak!" Her fiery green eyes burned into his.

Wrapping his arms around her, he lifted her and barged inside the room. Amid her kicking and throwing punches, he slammed the door back. She tried to land a knee to his groin but he jerked aside just in time. He turned her about and captured her hands behind her back. "Are ye wanting to be locked in the dungeon again? Or would ye rather be tied to my bed? I much prefer the latter."

She glared back at him. "If you had left the armory open, I would be gone back home by now."

"Indeed?" The sensation of icy lake water trickled through him. The glimpse into how he'd feel if she left him near overwhelmed him. The hollow loneliness. Stark. Empty.

He released her.

She nodded and backed away from him.

"'Tis exactly why I didna leave the door unlocked. I kenned ye were lying even though ye swore 'twas the truth." That realization tasted like poison. She could never love him.

"So you're keeping me prisoner?"

"Ye are my wife but, sadly, I canna trust ye. Open yer eyes, Shauna. Ye were sent here for a purpose. Else why did you travel through time when ye touched *my* sword—if what ye told me is true?"

She averted her gaze.

"Ye ken I'm right. Ye were sent for me, for my wife and to break the curse. Ye are mine."

Her sharp glower lifted. "I'm not a piece of property to be owned. You are keeping me a prisoner in your time and ordering me about like a slave in front of your cousin. I deserve some respect."

His stomach ached. "Aside from yer habit of lying, I respect ye. But 'tis my duty to protect you. I didna want Alpin to get near you. He canna be trusted. And I canna show weakness before him. I dinna wish him to ken I care about ye or he will scheme a way to take advantage."

"You don't care about me."

"Aye, I do." More than he wanted her to know at the moment. More than even he could fathom.

"Only because you think I can magically break the curse. I can't! You still turn into a hawk every morning. Is that the way it's going to be for the rest of our lives? Will our children be bird babies? Or are we two different species with incompatible DNA?"

Babies? "An heir. That's it." A chill raced through him.

"What are you talking about?"

"I must get ye with my heir. Once a bairn grows in yer belly, the curse will be broken." Dear God, that had to be the answer.

She scowled. "Are you insane? What would that have to do with it?"

"Ye shall see."

"Well, lucky for me I took a birth control shot a couple weeks before I came here."

"What is this?" He hated it when she talked about things he didn't understand.

"An inoculation that keeps me from getting pregnant for three months."

"In truth?"

"Yes."

"*Iosa is Muire Mhàthair!* 'Tis no wonder the curse isna broken! Damnation! Why would ye use this remedy if ye are no' in the habit of bedding men? Or did ye lie about that too?" He wanted to throw something out the window.

"It reduces my severe cramps, if you must know!"

He frowned. "Cramps?"

"Don't know much about women, do you?"

"I ken enough." Damn the wench. He hated showing his ignorance. And he hated that she could prevent him from planting his seed within her. "So this medicine lasts for three months?"

"Yes."

"I wish ye had told me before."

"So now you no longer want to be married to me, right?" She crossed her arms.

He easily saw the pain behind her glare. Was the woman completely daft?

"Nay! I like being married to you."

"All you want is someone to break the curse and give you an heir. Selfish jerk. How do you think I feel? I was ripped from my regular life and everything familiar. I've lost my family and friends, my career, the hobbies I enjoyed, my warm comfortable apartment, my car, my clean bathroom—all because you need your curse broken. Why am I the only one who has to give up everything? I know. To you a woman is something to be owned like a dog or a sheep. Let me tell you something, Buster, it isn't like that where I'm from!"

"I dinna think ye a dog or a sheep."

"Bull! You said 'you're mine' like you own me."

"Ye are my wife. Do ye deny it?"

"No, but that doesn't make me a piece of property."

"I never said ye were property. Ye're far more valuable than any property that could be owned."

"Yeah, I'm valuable 'cause I'm a curse-breaker, or at least that's the rumor." She stalked away toward the fireplace.

He followed, turned her to face him and lifted her against the wall so she'd have to look directly into his eyes. He hated the churning emotions inside him. Why couldn't she understand? "Listen, lass! I never wanted anyone for a wife before I met ye. Ye are like no one else. When I say ye're valuable, I mean ye're a treasure to me. No' like silver and gold. No' because of the curse. *M'eudail. Mo dia*, why canna ye understand?"

She kissed him hard and all thoughts left his head. They struggled amidst the tangled clothes and seconds later he again knew bliss as he slid inside her hot, wet depths. Nay, he could not think while he took her. This sublime peak of all his experiences required his entire focus. He wished he could make love to her all night without stopping. He wished he could show her what she meant to him. How he couldn't breathe without her now. "Shauna." *Ye are mine and I am yours.* Damn her for forcing him to depend on her. If she left, he had naught—no life, no purpose, no existence.

The next day, Shauna sat beside Gavin's father's bed reading from one of the two English books they had. History written in a cumbersome old style. At times, Lunn watched her as if he understood each word, other times he rested with his eyes closed. Either way, her voice seemed to calm him. And now, with his breathing deep and even, he'd gone to sleep.

At breakfast, she'd slipped a silver spoon into her pocket, then hidden it under her bed. She hadn't yet decided whether or not to use it to try and pick the armory lock. The incredible night of lovemaking Gavin had given her had weakened her resolve. *I want to go back to the future and take him with me.* But he would never choose that. He took the responsibility for his ill father and his clan seriously.

A crying noise outside the window caught Shauna's attention. She paused in her reading and listened but was unable to identify the weird sound. She rose and approached the castle window. A lamb waddled about, far below and outside the walls.

"Oh, where is your mama?" she whispered so as not to wake Gavin's father.

The tiny white creature turned and limped a short distance, blood on its hip, and tried to mouth some grass.

"It's hurt." Shauna put down the book and tiptoed into the corridor, past the sleeping Ewan on a tilted back chair, and down the staircase.

Finch sprawled on one of the tables in the great hall, his snores echoing off the high ceiling. Shauna unlocked the entry door and crept outside. By the time she unfastened the *barmkin* gate latch, the lamb was several yards distant, scuttling this way and that. What had injured the poor baby?

Dodging the short scrubby plants, she ran forward. When the lamb saw her, it sped away with a limping trot.

"I won't hurt you."

A loud whistle-screech echoed above her head. A great black hawk with an incredible wingspan, soaring and circling like the grim reaper.

"Gavin!" she yelled up at him. "Did you hurt this lamb?"

He screeched again.

While she'd paused to glare at him the lamb was getting away. It wouldn't last long on its own, so small and frail. It couldn't be more than a few days old. But what did she know about lambs and sheep? Maybe Crocker had some milk she could feed it.

"Where is the herd, Gavin?" she called. "I'll try to find its mama."

He screeched and headed toward the castle, flapping his wings.

"No! Bastard." He probably wanted the lamb for a meal. Did he catch animals and eat them raw like a regular bird of prey? "Sadistic vulture!" She chased the lamb, running faster over the rocky ground. Her feet tangled in a low-growing plant and she tripped. She landed on her knee and pain shot up her leg. "Ouch!" She tumbled, screaming, down an embankment, rocks bruising and scraping her arms, her legs.

At last, she slid to a halt amid a pile of rocks. "Dammit!" Her hands were bloody and every part of her body ached. Lying there, she stared up at the sky, the early afternoon sun almost blinding her. Gavin circled, lower, then folded his wings and dove at something off to the side.

"What the hell is he doing, trying to kill himself... or attack the lamb?"

She squirmed around and pushed herself to her feet in time to see Gavin collide with a man's head. The poor sot flopped to the ground. Two other kilted men flailed about, trying to ward Gavin off with their swords.

"No!"

With powerful wing strokes, Gavin lifted back toward the sky. They hadn't hurt him. But what was the dispute? And who were they? Thankfully, Wilona wasn't with them, nor was Alpin. Maybe they were MacTavish clansmen returning to the village. But if so, why would Gavin attack them? No, clearly they were bad news.

She had to get back to the castle.

The men headed toward her, quickly. With purpose. The stones shifted beneath her feet and she staggered. She couldn't escape up the rocky embankment.

"Hello, lassie."

"Who are you?" She glanced around trying to locate the lamb but didn't see it. "Did you see an injured lamb?"

"Nay. Come and we shall help ye."

She did not trust their smirks but saw no way out of this rocky pit without walking past them.

"Thank you, but I'll be fine. I don't need your help."

"Are ye the new Lady MacTavish, then? We'd heard the MacTavish had married but we didna ken ye'd be so bonny."

She didn't buy their ridiculous sweet talk in the least.

"No, I'm only her maid."

The men laughed. Dammit, she was no better at lying than they were.

"Back up and give me room. I'm going back to the castle. I don't know what you have in mind, but Laird MacTavish is watching our every move."

The men grinned and glanced up toward Gavin soaring in a circle over them.

"He will rip the flesh from your bones!" she said, mimicking Ewan. "He has not a speck of pity or mercy in his heart."

The outlaws' tall, skinny leader bared brown broken teeth in a grin while they inched closer in unison. Even at ten feet away, she smelled their stench.

She bent, picked up a rock and threw it at them. The leader dodged and it flew past his shoulder. "Back off!" She picked up two more fist-sized rocks and waited.

Overhead, Gavin soared lower, screeching out warnings. He dove toward the men again but they ducked to the ground.

"*A mhic an uilc!*" one of the men yelled.

She didn't know what the hell that meant, but she darted past them and threw the rock at the same time.

One of the men surged up, chased after her and grabbed her skirt. She kicked him but he wouldn't let go. Before she could shed her skirt and take off, his friends joined him. One clasped her wrist in his vice-like hand. The more she fought, the harder they held her. *Dear God, what will they do to me?*

Chapter 11

An outlaw clutched each of Shauna's wrists and their leader followed behind with a sword at her back. "Coming with us, ye are."

"Why? Where are you taking me?"

"Ye'll be knowing that when ye get there."

"Turn me loose!" She twisted, trying to dislodge their hands. Why hadn't she taken karate when it had been offered at the college?

"Gavin!" He still flapped his wings above them. Now she knew the disadvantage of being married to a bird. Why didn't he get all his hawk friends together and do a replay of *The Birds*?

She stumbled over a rock and if not for the men's hands strangling her arms, she would've fallen, which she would've preferred.

"Had pity on the poor wee lamb, did ye, lass?"

"If you guys hurt it, so help me!"

"Nay, we wouldna hurt Lady Wilona." They laughed.

"Lady Wilona? The lamb was her? She shifts into a lamb?" How freaking bizarre. *I'm the most gullible person on earth. I should've suspected.*

The leader smiled.

"Do you work for that wicked witch?"

Their eyes widened. "Dinna be calling her that or ye won't last long."

"Why did she send you after me? If she thinks I broke the curse, I didn't. I'm not a threat to her. As you can see, Gavin's still a bird during the day."

"We dinna give orders; we just follow them."

They neared a stand of bushes where four horses waited, tethered. Gavin's cousin Alpin stepped from behind one of them.

Oh, dear God! Why had she not felt any true fear until now? Drowned in disbelief? Numb? In shock?

"'Tis a pleasure to see ye again, m'lady." He'd tied his dirty blond hair back in a ponytail that revealed his long, lean face. His smarmy grin made her want to gag.

"So you're behind this? Gavin will come after you. You know he's a better swordsman."

Alpin lifted a brow and his smile disappeared.

"Why?" she asked. "What do you hope to gain?"

"I'm the only one here who gets to ask questions."

"You can't just kidnap me. It's illegal. You'll be hanged, drawn and quartered."

"Hardly. Ye will be a guest."

"A prisoner, you mean."

"Nay. Hospitality is of great importance here in the Highlands."

"Gavin will stop you."

Alpin glanced up at Gavin's black form in the sky. "He doesna worry me."

Two of the men pushed her up into the saddle and tied her hands together.

"I've never ridden a horse before." The animal beneath her kicked rocks and snorted. "What if I fall off?"

The men laughed. Cryptically. Probably save them from having to kill her themselves. And avoid the hangman's noose.

Oh shit! What if that was their plan?

She didn't like pain but decided it was time to do something drastic. Before they tied her hands to the saddle, she slid off the left side. One of the men caught her and tried to shove her back into place. She kicked and screamed. The horse bolted a few yards away, leaving her flailing half on the ground and half in the man's arms.

"Damnation!" he grumbled.

She continued her struggle and high-pitched screams, hoping to scare the horses away and maybe get someone's attention.

"Gag her," Alpin ordered, stalking forward with a strip of cloth.

Gavin sailed from behind and dive-bombed him. Alpin stumbled and fell to his knees in the rocks. He shouted in Gaelic, rose and slung his sword about like a fly-swatter, almost flaying one of his men in the process. Gavin flapped away then circled back toward the man she was struggling with.

His eyes grew big and he ducked behind her, using her as a shield. She curled away, trying to expose him. Big black wings brushed softly against her but she couldn't see what was happening behind her.

Her captor squalled like a terrified child and released her.

"Get it off me! Get it off me!"

Pushing to her feet, Shauna stumbled away. She glanced back to see the damage. Gavin's talons sank into the man's bloody arm and he pecked at his head. Going after his eyes? Ugh! Alpin ran into the fray with his sword.

"Gavin! Watch out!" she yelled.

He launched into the air just in time to avoid the tip of the weapon. She dashed back toward Caithmore Castle that loomed in the distance, the tall towers easy to see. Her hands were tied in front of her and she couldn't move as quickly as she wanted over the rough terrain.

"Come back, wench!" Alpin and one of his uninjured cohorts chased after her.

"Dammit!" Her feet wouldn't move fast enough. Unable to see the rocks beneath the scrubby plants and heather, she stumbled too many times. She fell amongst the rocks, scraping her hands, bruising her knees. What could she do? Even if she got up, she couldn't escape them. They'd kill her. She cried out and tears wet her cheeks.

"I want to go home!"

The two men yanked her up by her arms and pain shot through her shoulders.

"Ouch! You bastards! Gavin is *so* going to make you regret this one day real soon. And I'll help him."

"Hold your tongue, whore!" Alpin growled.

"I'm not a whore! I'm Gavin's wife!"

Wow, why did it feel so good to say that? Did that mean she *liked* being his wife?

"I'm Lady MacTavish, you idiots. That means I'm part of the aristocracy now. And you're just a couple of lowlife dimwits. Even you, Alpin. You're just a greedy outlaw who is so jealous of Gavin you'd do anything to take away what he has. If you hurt me any worse than you already have, there'll be hell to pay! They put criminals to death in all kinds of torturous ways these days, don't they? Hanging, beheading, drawn and quartered. That's gotta hurt."

"Shut your mouth!"

"Yeah, I know you don't want to hear it, but it's time to face facts, boys. Your boss-lady is not going to protect you when the authorities come to claim your moldy, stinky hides and string them up from a tree. Your rotting corpses will be hanging off a bridge somewhere and the crows will have a feast. It would be much better to release me now, let me go back home and I won't turn you in."

"What say ye, Master Alpin?" the lower ranking minion asked, his eyes wide.

"Are ye an imbecile? Nay! Take her back to the horses, Harv."

"I think you are the imbecile, Alpin."

"I said shut yer gob." He slapped her cheek.

Her head jerked to the side and a pain shot through her neck. "Ouch! You son of a bitch!"

"I have something to shut ye up."

Oh really? Crap! What was he going to do now? Maybe she'd screwed up. Adrenaline fueling her, she struggled several more times to get away. But they hung on tight, like a couple of leeches.

"Put her on my horse," Alpin ordered. Two of his men threw her over the front of the saddle, stomach down, tied her on and Alpin got on behind her.

As the horse trotted over the rocky ground, the saddle jabbed sharply into her stomach.

"You'll pay for this, I grant you!" she yelled but her voice vibrated so much Alpin probably didn't understand her. He and his men certainly didn't slow. When they reached a worn trail, they sped the horses up into a gallop. Pains shot through her abdomen.

Where was Gavin? She didn't hear him whistling overhead anymore. Facing the ground as it whizzed by, she couldn't look up into the sky to see if he was following.

Don't leave me, Gavin, please.

Suddenly she just felt like crying. Tears burned her eyes and dripped onto the rapidly passing dirt.

I'm sorry I couldn't break the curse. I wanted to. But I guess everyone put too much faith in me.

From far above, Gavin helplessly watched Alpin the bastard and his three men take Shauna closer and closer to Wilona MacRae's lair several miles from his own home. He was afraid if he spooked the horses with his nearness they might bolt and hurt Shauna.

If he hurts her, I willna rest until I have my revenge.

The sun hung over the western mountains. She had already been in their clutches several hours. Only a couple more until he'd turn into a man again. But not soon enough. He followed the party on horseback until they disappeared inside the Raeglen Castle walls, then he circled back. He couldn't shift here, unarmed, naked and without reinforcements.

The sun crept lower and lower. Pumping his wings as powerfully as he could, he flew back toward Caithmore Castle.

At dusk, Shauna's captors dragged her from the horse in the graveled bailey of a small gray castle. Pains shot through her stomach and her joints. She swayed, dizzy from being upside down so long. Finally, her eyes focused on two flaming torches flanking the castle entrance and the woman standing between. Alpin pushed her forward while Harv held a torch nearby.

"So this is the lass who thinks she can break the curse." Wilona's raspy voice, combined with the chill wind, made Shauna shiver. Not because of the sound, but what lay beneath it and the haughty look in her eye. Towering over Shauna by several inches, Wilona glared down at her. Her braided and coiled red-gold hair gleamed in the torchlight.

"I haven't broken the curse, so I'm no threat to you," Shauna said, flexing her tied, numb hands, trying to regain the feeling.

Wilona produced a tight-lipped, malicious grin. "Indeed, ye are no threat to me—at least ye willna be for long."

Shauna's attention shrank to one unreal, heart-stopping thought. "You intend to kill me?"

"Aye."

"But why? I *cannot* break the curse." Why was everyone in this century so unreasonable?

Wilona laughed. "Ye really dinna understand, do you?"

"Understand what?"

"What breaks the curse."

Shauna shook her head.

"Love. True love given and returned in equal parts, with complete trust and without reservation."

"Oh." Well, there was the problem then. Shauna had feared she was falling in love with Gavin, but she had not given her love without reservation. She didn't yet know if she wanted to stay in this century. And obviously, Gavin didn't trust her either, with good reason.

"I used that in the curse because I assumed no woman would again go near enough to Gavin the Devil to fall in love with him," Wilona said. "I underestimated him and whatever powers he used to find you in a distant land. As for the curse, either ye dinna love Gavin yet, or he doesna love you. But given time, it could happen. I canna risk that. Take her inside," she ordered her guards.

Shauna glanced up at the twilight. If Gavin hadn't already shifted, he would soon. Was he here? Did he care enough to rescue her? *Please God.*

Alpin shoved her forward. She stumbled, her pulse spiking, then regained her footing. She hated the way they laughed at her. The guards directed her into the great hall, smaller than Gavin's and empty of people. A few torches and candles revealed tables and benches. The scents of smoke and herbs hung in the air.

Minutes later, Shauna stood alone before Wilona in what she assumed was a parlor, a small room with ancient chairs and tables. One guard stood inside the door.

Wilona sank into a comfy-looking chair and eyed Shauna with speculation for long minutes. Was she devising a method of death? Shauna glanced around for a weapon. The heavy silver candlestick on a nearby table looked promising.

"I've seen what he does to you," Wilona said.

"What?"

"Aye." Wilona's eyes lit up. "I have a crystal ball that shows me whatever I want to see. Even your bedsport with the devil's spawn."

"You watched?"

"Indeed."

"Pervert," Shauna mumbled, a shiver passing through her.

"You enjoy him far too much, and he you."

"No such thing as enjoying someone *too* much. He's good in bed." Shauna shrugged. "That isn't my fault."

Wilona grinned. "Nay, but it shows me he could fall in love with you. And it makes me wish I was twenty years younger. Or at least fifteen. I'd take him prisoner and make him my sex slave." She tapped a fingernail to her lip. "Hmm, maybe I will anyway."

Shauna wanted to punch the woman's beige teeth out. "Why didn't you do that to start with, instead of cursing him?"

"Because I hated him after he killed my son. I still hate him. But I now find him... interesting. I would like to bed him and torture him at the same time."

You will not! Nausea latched onto Shauna.

"But I'm not sure his fine member would stand up as well for me as it does for you. What do you think?"

"I think you're a bitch!"

Wilona's eyes narrowed. "Hold her," she calmly told the guard, then stood. Footsteps pounded behind Shauna. She dodged out of the way, but large hands gripped her shoulders and held her in place.

Chapter 12

Through the gloaming, Gavin rode toward RaeGlen Castle with a two-handed Highland sword strapped to his back. He intended to put the vicious weapon to good use in the midst of Wilona's men. Kicking his large warhorse to a greater speed, he glanced back at Ewan and Finch, trying to keep up on their smaller mounts. Two men was all he had. He shook his head. It would take a miracle to win against Wilona, Alpin and their larger force.

The horses winded, they drew up on a hill overlooking RaeGlen. Likely Wilona had guards posted some distance from the walls. Within the torchlight, he counted numerous guards. Engaging them in a skirmish would be certain suicide.

"Do ye have a plan, m'laird?" Ewan asked.

Gavin glanced aside at him and Finch. His two friends. He'd left Crocker to care for his father.

A plan?

"Aye, here's the plan. We are sorely outnumbered. We willna fight. I'll give myself up, get inside. Then I can have a chance at rescuing Shauna."

"Give yourself up?" Ewan's mouth hung open.

"Aye. Charging in there to fight will only get us all three killed for naught. Wilona has at least thirty men. My main concern is Shauna, and you men. Go back to Caithmore."

"Nay," Finch said. "Ye canna mean it m'laird."

"Aye, I do. And ye will obey my orders. I'll save Shauna's life. If I lose my own in the process, so be it." *Without her I have naught to live for anyway.*

"Ewan, Finch, I appreciate the two of ye and your years of service to me and my father. Ye're good men. Take care of my father." Gavin rode away from them. After a few seconds he glanced back and didn't see them following. Good.

Minutes later, he approached the gates. Guards converged on him. He dismounted and held his hands aloft in surrender. A guard quickly relieved him of his two-handed sword and searched him.

Another guard tied his hands behind his back and shoved him through the opening gates and into the *barmkin*.

Alpin trotted down the steps, a grin on his face. "I kenned ye'd come for your lady love."

"I shall kill ye if 'tis the last thing I do," Gavin said.

"Such bold promises, cousin? And ye with yer hands tied." Alpin laughed. "By the by, once ye are dead and your title and lands mine, your wife will also be mine, though I willna be marrying her." He chuckled again.

"And the devil shall haunt ye."

Alpin's smile fell as the guards shoved Gavin toward the entrance.

Three armored warriors escorted Gavin into the great hall, his hands tied behind his back and his long, dark hair wild about his face. Shauna's stomach clenched and her bound arms and legs trembled. Her face still stung from the slaps Wilona had given her earlier.

The guards positioned Gavin a few feet from her.

"Are ye well, Shauna? Did they hurt ye?" Gavin's concerned blue eyes locked on hers and she found reassurance there.

"I'm okay. Why did you let yourself get caught?" she whispered. She wanted to yell at Gavin or maybe choke him a little.

He winked and she melted inside. His presence comforted her, but at the same time she feared for his safety more than her own.

"Welcome, Gavin," Wilona purred and ran her hungry gaze over him. "I'm so glad ye've come."

"What do ye want?" he asked. "Let Shauna go to safety, away from Alpin, and I will do anything ye wish."

"No!" Shauna said.

Wilona smiled and addressed the guards. "Take him to the prepared room and strip him."

"What are you going to do to him?" Her blood felt like ice as she watched the guards lead Gavin away.

"Hold your tongue!" Wilona snapped.

Shauna's hands fisted. She wanted to take them to the witch and pound her into the stone floor.

She held her breath and prayed they wouldn't hurt Gavin.

When the men had finished with Gavin, Wilona instructed them to do the same with her. She would get to see Gavin. Eagerly she strode before the guards toward "the room."

"I'll strip myself, thank you," Shauna said outside the door. She glared at the guard as he cut the rope from her wrists. Was Gavin behind the door? Was he okay? Was Wilona going to torture them naked?

The bulky guard, a foot taller than Shauna, lifted a brow and held out his hand.

"Turn your back."

"Nay. Strip or I'll enjoy doing it for ye."

"Back away then."

He took two steps back, folded his arms and waited, his attention riveted on her.

"Can't you look at the ceiling or something? Jerk."

His gaze slipped up to the ceiling, but next time she glanced at him, he was again observing her. She wanted to snatch his sword and do something violent with it.

Ignoring him, she took off each article of clothing and dropped it to the floor. She glowered at him and his gaze slid down her. Nausea filling her, she covered her breasts and mound with arm and hand.

"Voyeuristic bastard," she muttered.

He chuckled, unlocked the door and shoved her inside.

Standing naked just beyond the door, Gavin caught her.

"Gavin, you're okay?" She ran her hands over his chest, his face, his arms.

"Aye." He frowned. "Are ye hurt? What did they do to you?"

"Nothing. That freaky guard watched me undress."

"What happened to your face? 'Tis red on this side." He carefully touched her cheek.

"Wilona slapped me. What do you think she's up to?"

"I dinna ken. But I will have my revenge, against both her and Alpin." He kissed her cheek where it burned.

Shauna stroked his face in return, savoring the warmth and prickliness of his jaw. "Wilona said she might like to keep you as a sex slave prisoner."

"In truth?" He grimaced.

"She also said she had a crystal ball where she'd watched us have sex."

"Ah. It makes perfect sense now."

Shauna followed his gaze around the room which contained nothing but two torches, a bathtub full of water and a bare, lumpy mattress on a small bed.

"What?"

"She's wanting to watch us, in person this time. I wager there's a spy hole in one of these walls."

"You're kidding. You mean I'll be the equivalent of a seventeenth-century porn star?"

"What is a 'porn star?'"

"Someone who people watch having sex."

His brows lifted. "There is such a thing where you come from? And you know about it?"

"Of course. But I've never wanted to *be* one."

"Nor do I wish to be a sex slave to a witch of the Dark Arts."

The door squeaked open and Wilona stepped into the room with a guard. Shauna again tried to cover herself. Stepping in front of her, Gavin seemed unconcerned about his nudity. Shauna craned her neck around his shoulder. The witch looked him up and down with lustful eyes, though Gavin didn't have a hard-on at the moment. Shauna wanted to give her a good karate chop to the neck, hard enough to behead her.

"Ye have guessed your reason for being here, alone in this room. If ye perform to my satisfaction, I shall let Shauna live another day."

"Evil bitch," Gavin growled.

"Indeed, I am. In particular, I enjoyed watching the way you two bathed each other." She grinned and walked out. The door slammed.

"Where is she watching from?" Shauna whispered. "And is she the only person watching?"

"I dinna ken." His gaze searched the walls one more time then landed on her. "At least our task isna a terrible one."

Shauna gasped. "I don't want to be watched."

"Nor do I, but it canna be prevented at the moment. Come."

"Why didn't you bring an army to help you?"

"What army? The clan is gone, scattered to the winds. I have two men, besides my cook, as ye ken. Wilona has thirty, at least. Her brother-in-law has a hundred more."

"I thought I was part of some sort of twisted peace agreement."

"Aye, with the MacRae but no' with Wilona. Though I now know he was lying; he didna send you. He canna be trusted either."

Gavin led her to the wooden tub and helped her inside. The water warmed her chilled limbs but nothing could warm her chilled psyche. "What are we going to do? How will we escape?" she whispered.

"Shh. We will discuss it later, when we have more privacy." He sank down into the water with her, much as they had in their other bath. But this time, she wasn't aroused.

"If it helps, pretend we are in my room."

She nodded.

"Wet your hair and I shall wash it."

She dunked her hair beneath the water, then sat between his thighs with her back to him. With gentle hands he worked the soap over her hair and massaged her scalp. She relaxed, absorbing the sensuality of the moment. The clean herbal scent of the soap, the heat of the water, his caressing fingers.

What if this was the last time they could be together like this? The full impact of how much Gavin meant to her now pressed in on her. At some point during all the sex and power struggle, she had come to love him and need him—something she didn't want to happen. He'd become a necessary part of her life.

When she rinsed, it was his turn. She tried to put the scary thoughts from her mind and enjoy washing his hair.

She suspected Gavin was stalling, delaying anything sexual as long as possible and she was thankful. His eyes were eloquent with emotion and regret. She felt the same. Despite the times she'd wanted to go back to the future, she had never truly wanted to leave him. He was her sweet, fierce beast of a warrior, so strong and tough, yet vulnerable. He'd needed her.

Gavin lathered a cloth and washed her from her face down her body, with slow movements. When she rinsed her hair and upper body, he pressed a chaste, loving kiss to her lips, then focused on his task. He wasn't trying to seduce her, but he did anyway, especially when he dragged the cloth between her legs and she yearned for him.

"Sit back."

Once she did, he lifted each of her feet in turn and washed them and her legs.

She was almost glad when it was her turn to bathe him. Though this situation sucked, nothing was better than exploring his body. She stroked a clean soapy cloth over him from head to toe in much the same way he had done her. She tried to ignore his growing erection bobbing in and out of the water, but that was impossible.

Clearly Wilona wanted to watch Shauna perform oral sex on Gavin again, otherwise why bother indulging them with the bath? Should she appease the witch by giving her what she wanted or anger her?

Lying back in the tub, Gavin watched her beneath half-lowered lashes, his pale eyes grown dark.

"Do you want me to?" she whispered.

"'Tis up to you." His tiny wicked grin told her what he wanted.

She stroked her fingers up and down his rigid, wet cock.

His breath caught.

With one hand she lifted his yummy member and kissed the tip.

"Mmm," he breathed out softly.

In her other hand, she cradled and massaged his testicles beneath the water. She opened her mouth over the head of his cock and took it inside.

His body jerked and he made a deep but restrained growling sound.

She trailed her tongue around the head, then gobbled him up again, taking him to the back of her throat. She sucked hard and firmly stroked her hand up and down his shaft.

Moaning, he fisted his hands on the tub's edge.

She treated him to what she hoped was erotic torture for several long minutes. Abruptly, he grasped her shoulders and lifted her.

"'Tis all I can take," he whispered and kissed her, flicking his tongue inside her mouth where his cock had been only seconds ago. The move spurred her arousal.

"Stand," he said.

"Why?" She glanced around, suddenly shy about being so exposed.

"Ye'll see. Put one foot outside the tub."

Once she stood, he motioned her forward. "Move up here."

She inched upward, closer to his head. He ran his hands up her wet legs and pulled her near, rose up and kissed her inner thighs. He pushed her sex lips apart and flicked his tongue over her. He slid his forceful hot tongue into her slit several times, then wiggled it against her clit. She wanted to sink to her knees in bliss. Her legs trembled and she spread them wider. Throwing her head back, she massaged her breasts and plucked at her hardened nipples.

"Mmm, aye." He intensified his licking, then sucked fiercely at her clit as he slid a finger inside her.

"Gavin," she gasped.

"Aye." He slid two fingers inside her, tugged at her pubic hair and licked her clit harder. It felt swollen to twice its normal size. He used firm, fast strokes that drove her mad.

"Gavin!" She was afraid if she came, she'd fall and hurt herself.

"Hold onto my shoulder."

She did but when the orgasm hit, she wasn't sure whether she was falling or flying. She only felt his hands and his mouth on her as pleasure ripped through her with trembling fury.

When she became aware, she was sprawled across his lap in the tub and trying to catch her breath.

Grinning, he turned her so she would straddle his lap.

Holding her above the water, he positioned his dick, poised to enter her. He stroked it between her nether lips and she suddenly had the mad urge to suck him again. Instead, he coated the head with her juices and thrust inside her.

A small pain made her cry out. He paused and focused his attention on her nipples, gently licking and kissing them. Her arousal grew and she opened to receive him, sliding down on him. He flexed his hips, driving himself deeper and growling.

"Your cunny's so hot and tight and sweet," he whispered and massaged her ass. He rolled his hips, withdrawing an inch and pushing deep again. He sucked harder at her nipples. "*Boidheach leannan.*"

Holding onto his wide, muscular shoulders, she rode him for several long seconds. He reached up for a kiss and she tasted her own sex juices on his lips and tongue. She wanted him even more.

"Turn around," he said.

"Why?"

"They're wanting a show; we'll give them one."

"Are you insane?"

"Aye, I believe I am." He grinned. "Trust me."

Looking at him askance, she lifted off him and turned her back to him. She lay back against his hard chest and he spread her thighs over his. She placed her feet on each side of the tub.

"Guide my cock into you," he whispered in her ear.

She placed the head at her entrance, wanting him badly she arched her back. He gently thrust upward, imbedding himself inside her halfway.

"More," she whispered.

"Mmm." He pushed deeper. His hand slipped downward to brush over her mound, and lower still to trace her lips spread around his sliding cock, stroking the wetness over her clit.

He licked his finger then returned it to her clit. "Mmm." He moaned against her ear. "Ye taste like honey."

She ran her hands into his wet hair and held on around his neck. His strokes grew harder, deeper and faster and she felt like a ship tossed upon a stormy ocean. He controlled everything about her, the physical sensations, her emotions. Nothing existed but him and his connection to her. What he could give her.

Her eyes closed. His hot, harsh breaths in her ear, the scent of their sex and a maelstrom of erotic sensations bombarding her body, that was all she knew. That and her feelings, for each stroke not only drove her arousal another notch toward the peak but also heightened her love for Gavin. Deepened her devotion to him. It wasn't only his body driving into her but his soul penetrating hers, wrapping around her and capturing her heart firmly once and for all.

"I love you!" she gasped just as her orgasm claimed her. She screamed and the wave of ecstasy carried her up and flipped her over.

"*Tha gràdh agam ort,*" Gavin growled into her ear just before he shuddered against her, into her. He gave her two final strokes and stilled. "*A shùgh mo chrìdhe.*" He held her tightly to him and kissed her cheek. "Never have I been so thankful for anything as I am to have ye as my wife," he murmured in her ear.

"Oh, Gavin." She turned and kissed his lips.

"Hold on." Withdrawing and repositioning her, he lifted her with one arm around her hips and pushed himself from the tub.

Cool water slid down Gavin's legs. He carried Shauna to the bed and lay her upon it, hating the lack of covers. He wanted privacy for them now, but they wouldn't have it this night. He turned her to face him and drew her against his chest. She shivered.

"Are ye cold?" he asked, loving the emotion in her green eyes. He still couldn't believe what she'd confessed to him moments ago.

"A little."

"Damn her for not even giving us a blanket to cover up with." He put his arms around her, trying to share some of his body heat.

"What do you think she'll do to us?"

"I dinna ken but if this is my last night on earth, there is no way I'd rather spend it than with you."

Tears appeared in her eyes. "I feel the same way." She stroked his face.

"I wish ye hadna followed the injured lamb. I tried to warn you."

"I didn't know. I can't stand to see an innocent animal like that in pain. I'm sorry, but I have a heart."

He smoothed her dark, wet hair back from her face. "Aye, well. I have one too, which is why she's going to hurt me now worse than ever."

"What does that mean?"

"It means I love ye, lass. And I would do anything to keep ye from being harmed in any way."

"I love you too. And I never wanted to leave you, not really." Tears slid from the corners of her eyes, and by the look in them, he knew she was telling the truth. She kissed him and he rolled partially over her, returning the kiss, hoping to show her how much she meant to him.

"Make love to me, Gavin. Show me how much you love me."

"Aye, I will."

He intended to put on a good performance so Shauna's life would be spared. He knew the evil bitch's plan—to take him as a sex slave hostage and to kill Shauna, or give her to Alpin. That would be worse because the bastard would likely rape her repeatedly then kill her. But none of that was going to happen. Though he loved Shauna more than anything, including his clan, his lands, or Scotland itself, he was going to send her away from him, back to her home many centuries away.

Chapter 13

Shauna awoke abruptly and opened her eyes. Gavin's sleeping face was the first thing she saw. Gorgeous. She pushed long strands of his dark hair back from his face. The warmth of her love flowed through her. Remembering they were in Wilona's clutches, she watched him for a long moment savoring the way he looked in the morning sunlight.

Sunlight? Her gaze flew to the barred window.

"It's daytime," she gasped and ran her hand down Gavin's arm.

"Hmm?" He stirred.

"Gavin, wake up. It's past dawn and you didn't shift into a bird. The curse is broken."

His eyes sprang open and he stared down at his body, the window, then at her. Wide-eyed, he swallowed hard. "Ye broke the curse."

"We did. With our love. Love given and received in equal parts, without reservation."

"She told ye this?"

"Yes."

The door burst open and the big hairy guard entered. "Rise and shine, love birds. The lady wishes to see ye both in the hall."

Gavin shielded her from the guard's lustful gaze. "Bring us our clothing."

"Ye're no' the laird here, sirah." He waited a long moment, then motioned another man forward who held their clothes in his arms. He dumped them into a heap on the floor, gawked at Gavin and Shauna as if they were circus performers, then left.

The guard chuckled and closed the door on the way out.

"What's she going to do now?" Shauna asked.

Gavin shook his head and got up. They both dressed in silence. Her stomach ached, both from hunger and nerves.

Gavin took her into his arms, embraced her and buried his face in her hair. "I love ye, Shauna. Dinna be forgetting it no matter what."

"I won't. But you're scaring me. You said we'd get out of this."

"I ken it. And I will try to get us out of it. But no matter what happens or where ye are, remember how much I love ye."

She nodded, tears burning her eyes. It couldn't be over; it couldn't end like this. Could it?

After giving her a soft, lingering kiss, Gavin stepped away from her and rapped on the door. The guard opened it.

"I would speak with your lady alone."

"What are you doing?" Shauna latched her fingers on his plaid. "Gavin?"

"I will be back forthwith." Kissing her, he pried her fingers off and left with the guard.

In the great hall an hour later, all Wilona's men and several of her servants grew silent and stared at Gavin and Shauna. Alpin, standing not far from Wilona, looked as if he were on the verge of drooling. If she didn't know better, she'd think they'd all watched her and Gavin have sex via hidden camera on a big screen TV. But that was impossible. Still, there could've been more than one spy hole. Her face burned. She met Wilona's gaze straight on, hoping her hatred for the woman came through clearly.

"Come." She motioned them to stand before her high table, cluttered with dishes and the remains of breakfast.

"Gavin, ye have pleased me greatly with your virile… impressive performance last night." Her lustful eyes devoured him before they switched to Shauna with cutting intensity. "Shauna, ye are no longer needed here. Gavin has requested that ye magically be sent back where ye came from, far away from here. The Colonies."

"Nay!" Alpin yelped.

"Hold your tongue, lack-wit," Wilona said, then returned her attention to Shauna. "It suits me to send you elsewhere, because I dinna want to be accused of murder." Smiling, she motioned at something to their left.

A guard held a large, two-handed Highland sword, the one Shauna had searched for since she'd arrived in this century. He offered her the grip.

"Hold Gavin's sword," Wilona ordered.

Shauna already wore the brooch, and the sword would complete the magical combination to launch her back to the twenty-first century. Every muscle in Shauna's body tightened. "No."

"What do you mean, *no?*" she seethed.

"No, I won't do it. I'm not leaving."

"Shauna," Gavin said in a low, desperate voice. "Touch the sword. Ye wanted to anyway."

"I did before, but now I don't." Her throat ached and she could barely get the words out past the constriction. "I love you and I can't live without you."

"Shauna," he growled then whispered close to her ear. "She or Alpin will kill ye if ye dinna go. I'd rather ye live in your own time than die now. I want ye to be safe."

She shook her head. Tears scalded her eyes and dripped from her lashes. "I can't leave you. We broke the curse because we love each other. Do you realize how strong and true our love is?"

"Aye." Pain glinted in his eyes. "I know it, lass."

"I'd rather die than leave you."

"Damnation! Dinna say that." He squeezed his eyes closed then glared at the guard who held his sword. He waved him closer.

She backed away. "Don't try to force me, Gavin! I make my own decisions."

The guard neared, holding the sword below the hilt. The grip was bare and waiting for her to grasp it in both hands as she had at the Highland Games so long ago.

Her throat closed up and she shook her head again. "I can't." She unpinned the brooch, dropped it to the floor and kicked it beneath the table. Even if he forced her to touch the weapon, without the brooch, nothing would happen. She hoped.

"By the saints, Shauna. This is your way out!" Gavin yelled, snatched the sword from the guard and wielded it as it was meant to be, in two large hands by a man of superior strength.

She dropped to the floor. He swung the blade around and the guard ducked, while the circle around them widened. The people yelled and pushed backward. Swords slid from scabbards.

"Disarm him!" Wilona ordered. "But dinna injure him."

Shauna hardly dared breathe. How could Gavin fight against so many and win?

Backed into a corner with her behind him, he fought off the guards and soldiers one by one, killing some and wounding others.

Two large windows shattered and armored warriors swung through on ropes. More men poured up the staircase from outside, and down from the top floors.

"Stay behind me, lass," Gavin ordered and moved forward.

A man with a sword charged Gavin and he swung the huge sword. She closed her eyes before she could see whether the strike decapitated the man. Hunching down, she crept to the side to try and find a weapon. She yanked a dagger from the back of a man's belt while he fought off enemies.

"Alpin!" Gavin shouted.

She peered out to find his cousin standing behind the table near Wilona, his wild eyes searching about the room, his mouth agape.

Wilona pointed at him. Shauna could barely hear the words the witch chanted over all the shouts and clanging swords.

"Horse and hattock! Ye shall go into a mouse, and I shall go into a raven. With sorrow and *sych* and *meickle* care...."

Gavin charged them, but their bodies disappeared. Two puffs of smoke billowed up. A black raven swooped down, plucked the mouse up by the tail and flew out the broken window.

Shauna ran forward. "Omigod! They're getting away!"

"I no longer have wings, love," Gavin said over the din.

"And I'm glad."

"They will turn up, eventually."

"Who are these warriors helping us?"

Gavin grinned. "My father's men."

"You're kidding. How? Where did your father get men?"

The noisy battle died down and a proud, silver-haired man stepped into the hall as if he owned it. He looked incredibly familiar.

"Who is that?"

"My father." Gavin appeared awestruck for a moment.

"Wow! He looks thirty years younger."

Gavin yanked her from the floor and held her aloft as if she were an oversized rag doll. "The curse is broken."

"So the curse really was his problem?"

"Aye." The joy on Gavin's face filled her eyes with tears.

"Gavin!" his father called. "Bring yer bride and come now."

Setting her to her feet, he led her between the rows of his father's men who'd disarmed Wilona's guards and now held them back.

"Father." Gavin approached the older man, both their faces aglow, and pulled him into a bear hug. "Ha ha," they roared. How could this be the same gaunt, drawn man who'd looked like he was in his eighties only yesterday? Now he was a hale and hearty man in his fifties. Gavin went on to shake the hands of the men surrounding them. He called each of his clansmen by name, though some of them hung back with cautious eyes.

"Shauna lass," Gavin's father, Lunn, said, "Ye have saved our lives and that of our clan. For that I thank ye and owe ye a grand debt." He picked her up and whirled her around.

Though she laughed, tears burned her eyes. She had never done something this important, that meant so much to so many, by her mere presence. Actually, because she'd fallen in love with Gavin, but that had been easy.

"And I thank ye for reading to me. I enjoyed the history lesson." Lunn smiled.

"Come. We shall go home," Gavin said.

❦❧

A week later, Shauna and Gavin sat in the midst of their crowded wedding feast, underway in Caithmore Castle hall. Voices, laughter and music echoed around them. Most of the clan had returned and others were on their way.

Shauna unwrapped a plaid cloth from one of their gifts, a large book. *Omigod, how can it be?* The same hand-bound manuscript of Scottish folklore her father had in his collection. It had to be a different copy, didn't it? Though it now looked far newer, many things about this book were the same as the one she'd paged through with reverence as a child. She had begged to look at it over and over. The hand-drawn pictures had enchanted her. Her father had finally allowed it if she promised to wear the special gloves he'd given her to turn the fragile pages.

Noticing Gavin was engaged in conversation with one of the other men, she bit her lip and slipped away with the book to the library. This was her only link to her modern day family, the one she'd never see again. Though she knew she was desecrating a priceless ancient text, she scribbled a message on the blank back page with a quill dipped in ink.

"Argh! I'll never learn to write with these things."

Dear Mom, Dad and Celia, if you find this and understand it, that means you remember me. The year is 1621 and I live in Scotland with my new husband, Gavin MacTavish. I have found the love of a lifetime with him. I never dreamed that such a man existed (well actually I did) but who knew I would love him so much I couldn't live without him. Please know that I'm well and happier than ever. I love all of you and I'll miss you forever. Shauna MacRae MacTavish.

"What are ye doing?" Gavin padded into the room. "The clan is wondering where their beautiful lady slipped off to."

"But you weren't?"

"Aye, I was. I see ye like the book my father gave ye."

"Your father?"

"He said he wanted to give ye that because he enjoyed ye reading to him when he was sick. But the book ye'd read then was dry history. This one is more entertaining."

"Yes, it is, and I love it."

"What are ye scribing?"

Suddenly self-conscious, she lifted a top corner of the page. "Um, just a note. It isn't dry yet."

Circling behind her, he leaned down, looked over her shoulder and read it. Well, she couldn't hide the note from him, didn't want to really. She would no longer hide anything from him.

Gavin's gaze lingered near the bottom of the page. Swallowing hard, he lifted his gaze to hers, then straightened.

She couldn't interpret his expression. Did he think her crazy?

"My father owns this book in the twenty-first century. It's been a part of my life since I was a child, and I thought since my father will one day have this book, I can leave him a note in it about what happened to me."

"Ye are staying with me. Forever," Gavin whispered as if he hadn't truly believed she would until this moment.

"Of course. I love you."

"And I love you, beyond anything ye can imagine. Ye possess my heart and soul. And if no' for you—" He shook his head.

She stood and took him into her arms. He drew her close and kissed her.

"None of that now!" Gavin's father burst through the door. "'Tis time for a dance!"

"I came to tell ye, a returning clansman spotted Wilona and Alpin near Loch Ness," Gavin said as they followed Lunn from the room.

Shauna strained to hear Gavin over the music and laughter in the great hall. "In human form?"

"Aye, and traveling deeper into the Highlands. I've sent missives to two friends that live in the area who were also cursed. I dinna ken whether their curses are broken yet, but I'm hoping they will find her and stop her."

"Maybe she'll take Alpin for her sex slave."

Gavin chuckled.

"And I'll take you for mine." She tugged at his arm and kissed his cheek.

"I'm no' going to argue with that." He grinned and yanked her close for a dance. He kissed her while his hands busied themselves on her butt.

"Stop it." She tugged his hands upward.

The hall grew quiet. She was afraid to look around, but she did anyway. A hundred smiling faces greeted her. A raucous cheer went up along with whistles and whoops.

"To Chief and Lady MacTavish!"

His father, standing nearby, also raised his wine.

She faced Gavin, smiling. "I'm glad your clan came back."

"I told ye they'd love you. But no' as much as I do," Gavin murmured in her ear.

He captured her lips in a possessive, driving kiss. When he picked her up, carried her from the hall and up the stairs amid the clan's cheers, she wanted to punch him.

"Isn't this rude, leaving our guests that way?"

"'Tis better than bedding ye in front of them, dinna ye think?"

She actually punched him this time. And he laughed.

About the Author:

Nicole North lives with her husband in the beautiful Blue Ridge Mountains, but wishes she lived in the Scottish Highlands at least half the year. Though she holds a degree in psychology, writing romance is her first love. Devil in a Kilt *is her first published work. Please visit her website at www.nicolenorth.com and drop her a line. She loves hearing from readers.*

The Bet

by Leigh Court

To My Reader:

What happens when a boring winter's night prompts two best friends to make an outrageous wager? The stakes run so high that losing simply can't be contemplated! There's just one unexpected twist, and her name is Claire...

Chapter 1

"I can make a woman come using just my mouth."

Damian Hunt, Viscount Atherton, leaned back in his club chair after delivering that salacious pronouncement. He and George had been drinking heavily for the past two hours, but what else was there to do to keep the boredom at bay on a cold winter's night? Tucked away here at the Atherton country estate, they'd already discussed horses and politics—the only other thing of interest to a man was sex.

"What's so impressive about that?" George slurred, inching his chair closer to the roaring fire in the hearth. "Cunnilingus has always been one of my favorite activities. Works like a charm every time. Sends a woman right over the edge."

Damian gave him a slow smile. "Oh, but I'm not talking about using my mouth on her. I'm talking about making a woman come using just the power of my *words.*"

"*What?*" George nearly dropped his wineglass. "Balderdash! You may have a well-deserved reputation as a ladies' man, but it's impossible to make a woman climax using just words."

Damian took a deep swallow of his wine. His outrageous claim had certainly succeeded in perking up the conversation, but just how far was he willing to take it?

Oh, maybe just a bit farther.

"Care to place a small wager on that?"

George stared at him, as if silently debating Damian's abilities, and then obviously dismissed them with a shake of his head. "Why, I'll place a *large* wager on it, you arrogant bastard. My London townhouse says you can't do it!"

Damian's eyebrow quirked, and he held up his wineglass in salute. "I've always admired your house in town."

"Admire it as much as you like. You'll never—" George frowned. "Wait a minute. Have you ever *made* a woman come using just words?"

"Well, no." Damian admitted. "But I'm certain I can do it."

"Hah!" George obviously felt some measure of reassurance at Damian's response.

"So." Damian put down his wineglass. "The wager is your London house. Now we need to name the woman. How about Marie-Thérèse D'Auberge? I have a fancy for something French."

"Oh no you don't, you slick-tongued devil. That woman is so highly sexed she could climax from a man just looking at her! No. If I stand to lose my house, then we'll have to make this a true challenge. *I'll* be the one to pick the woman." George stroked his chin thoughtfully. "Hmm…."

"Well, get on with it," Damian said impatiently. "How hard can it be? We know practically every woman in London."

"And have bedded them."

"True."

George smiled slowly. "Which is why the woman in our wager must be a virgin."

"A *virgin?*" Damian bolted upright in his chair. "The devil you say!"

"It's perfect, don't you see? The ultimate challenge for the ultimate rake."

"A virgin wouldn't even know what the hell I was talking about!"

"Now, now, I'm sure you can be very, er, *descriptive*, shall we say. And I know just the girl for our purposes."

"Bloody hell." Damian scowled. What had started out as a vain boast was quickly turning unsavory. "Who?"

"Claire."

"*Your younger sister?*" Damian couldn't believe his ears. Even for the notoriously disreputable George Beringer, the suggestion was beyond the pale.

"Come on, man. There'd be no harm done there. She's almost one-and-twenty, practically on the shelf." George shrugged. "No man's ever even made an offer for her."

"But she's—"

"A prude. Prim and proper to a fault. And, sexually, a block of ice."

"She's a *lady*." Damian's face darkened. What the hell was George thinking? It was a brother's obligation to protect his sister, not offer her up for some puerile bet. "I may be a rake, George, but I'm no seducer of innocents."

"Ah, but that's the beauty of it, don't you see? You *wouldn't* be seducing her, not literally. Even if she does eventually marry, she'll still be as innocent on her wedding day as she was when she came into this world."

Damian stared hard at George. In their childhood, he knew George had always thought of Claire as an annoying tag-along, a nuisance, a familial irritation, but perhaps he didn't realize until just now how deeply George's resentment ran.

"She may technically still be a virgin, but after I'm through with her she will no longer be *innocent*, George. Pick another woman."

George tilted his head and cocked an eyebrow. "What is it, you old sod?" he goaded. "Worried that you can't do it, after your fine boast?"

"I can do it," Damian growled. "Just pick another woman."

"No. It's either Claire, or you forfeit the wager. And if you forfeit, I believe it's only fair that I get to claim a prize of equal value to my townhouse."

Damian gritted his teeth. How had this situation gotten so completely out of hand? "What would you want?"

George tapped a finger against his lips, considering. "I'll take Thunder."

"*Bloody hell!* My new horse?"

They'd spent more than half an hour tonight discussing Damian's recent purchase of the stallion and his hopes for a win at Ascot this year. George knew full well he would never part with the horse. Aside from its value, it was too much his pride and joy.

"He'll make a fine addition to my stable," George observed.

"You will never get your hands on that horse," Damian vowed.

George took a swig of his wine and smiled wickedly. "Then I take it we have a bet?"

Chapter 2

"I need to speak with you, George," Claire said stiffly, pulling on her gloves and straightening her hat in the entryway of the Beringer's London townhouse. She rarely saw her brother these days unless they happened to pass each other going in or out of the house.

George glanced briefly at the small envelope she pulled from her reticule.

"It's an invitation from Viscount Atherton," he said. "I received one myself."

"Yes. I've opened it. But it's impossible for me to accept."

George let out a small sound. "Have a care, my dear. An invitation like this doesn't come too often to one such as you. He's the son of an earl, don't forget."

Claire recoiled slightly at George's cruel implication. It was true she was something of a social recluse, but that was only because she was determined never to acquire a reputation like her brother's—that of a wastrel of the first order. George was a hard drinking, loose living, gambling man-about-town who lived a life, in Claire's opinion, of pointless self-indulgence. As a result, Claire was very careful about the engagements she chose to accept, only agreeing to those that came from the best families. Trouble was, it seemed her efforts to hold herself completely above reproach had resulted in acquiring a certain reputation of her own—that of a social snob. The invitations she *did* receive these days were few and far between.

"You know," George added. "Damian mentioned he *particularly* wants you to come this weekend."

That remark brought Claire up short. She certainly didn't travel in the same low social circles as George and his friends, so she'd convinced herself the invitation had been sent because Damian was probably in need of an extra body to make up the numbers, a companion for George, so that this house party wouldn't be a woman short.

Claire bit her lip.

She was surprised that Damian Hunt even remembered her, though he was often on *her* mind. It had been almost nine years since she'd been a young girl with a mad crush on the future Earl of Northrup, following both him and her brother around the Beringer estate like a puppy whenever he'd visited, just to be close to the handsome, blue-eyed, black-haired Damian.

He'd been a heartbreaker even at age seventeen.

Since then, she'd seen him only from afar, but had often heard his name connected with George's, usually in some scandalous vein. Damian's notorious reputation should have been enough to cool her secret ardor, but, ironically, it wasn't. She wondered if his dissolute ways had taken a toll on his dramatic good looks and found herself hoping it might be true. After all, if he had grown fat and florid, perhaps she could finally lay this silly crush she had on him to rest.

Here is your opportunity to find out.

"Who else will be there?" Claire inquired, hoping her voice sounded casual.

"Damian didn't consult me on the guest list, but he may have mentioned his sister."

That answer put Claire in a quandary. Despite his wicked reputation, Damian's rank would always make him socially acceptable. But how could she agree to go without knowing exactly who else would be there? And yet how could she refuse when her burning curiosity over Damian was tempting her to accept? On one hand, she was too protective of her reputation to risk any hint of scandal, but on the other, if Damian's sister would be there—

Of course. That must be the reason for Damian's invitation. It was not personal at all. Damian was simply looking for a guest of similar quality to make his sister feel comfortable.

Silly girl, to think he'd actually want to see you. Still, it was the perfect pretext to spend the weekend in his company.

"All right."

"What?" George said, leaning in.

"I said I'll go," Claire acknowledged tightly, desperately hoping she was reading the situation correctly. "But right now I'm late for a lecture at the Royal Geographical Society. They have a speaker today who will be talking about India, and the lives of the native peoples there. It should be fascinating."

"Indians?" George's jaw dropped. "Honestly, Claire, it's beyond me how a woman of your caliber could find that sort of thing interesting. It shows an unnatural interest in—*heathens*—as well as an unflattering streak of independence in you. It's no wonder you're not married."

"And it's no wonder, brother, that with an attitude like *that* you're considered a conceited, smug, narrow-minded bigot," Claire bristled. "Now if you'll excuse me...."

She swept past him, out the front door of their townhouse.

⁂ᘓⱤⱤᘔ⁂

Damian scowled at his reflection in the looking glass as his valet worked to dress him, wondering for the hundredth time how he'd gotten himself into this mess.

I can make a woman come using just my mouth.

Oh, right. His own big mouth had gotten him into it, and now it looked like his, er, *mouth*, was going to have to get him out of it.

"Bloody hell."

"Something wrong, sir?" The valet looked up in surprise. "Isn't this the waistcoat you ordered?"

"Don't fuss, Jenkins," Damian growled, tugging at his shirt cuffs. "You know how I hate it when you fuss over me."

"Guests tonight, sir." Jenkins brushed a piece of unseen lint from Damian's shoulder.

"Hmm." Damian cocked an eyebrow, assessing the folds of his cravat. "Did they arrive all right?"

"I have it from Andrews that the Beringers arrived at four. Master George was taken to the gold bed chamber, while Miss Beringer was shown to the room next to yours, as you requested."

"Good."

The valet indicated the chair next to him, over which two jackets were draped. "Your brown coat or the green?"

Damian paused. He was dressing for seduction tonight, and there was one coat in particular that always seemed to work well with the ladies. "The blue."

Jenkins frowned. "The blue, sir?"

"Yes. The blue." Damian had often been told that the deep cobalt color brought out the startling sapphire of his eyes.

"Very good, sir." Jenkins gathered up the rejected coats. "I'll return in a moment."

Damian nodded, and then turned back to the mirror. He glanced at his mouth—at his lips, in particular—and frowned. *I can make a woman come using only my words.* Good lord. Just how bored had he been when he'd made that outrageous claim? And how in the world had it turned into a bet, a challenge to his virile masculine abilities?

He'd been half-expecting Claire to turn down his invitation. In fact, he was quite sure George must have had a hand in securing her agreement. Why else would a prim and proper virgin agree to visit the home of a known rake?

He might be a skilled seducer of women, but up to now he'd always drawn the line at despoiling virgins.

I will not lose my best horse over this.

"Damn," he sighed resignedly. "Damn, damn, damn."

What would Claire Beringer look like after all these years? He remembered a coltish twelve-year-old, all gangly arms and legs, with dirty blond braids and freckles on her nose. Not much potential there and certainly not his type at all. He preferred a woman with curves, lush feminine flesh he could wrap his fingers around and sink his hard body into.

And yet, there had been something endearing about her back then. While George had obviously thought of her merely as a nuisance trailing after them, Damian had often enjoyed teasing her or offering her the odd compliment in order to coax a shy smile from her lips. He distinctly remembered that she had two charming dimples at the corners of her mouth when she smiled. In fact, he'd *liked* making Claire smile and had been flattered by her attention and obvious hero worship.

But that was years ago. She'd grown up to become a prude and he'd grown up to become a philanderer. And what she looked like physically now didn't matter. This was to be a seduction of the mind, not the body, and Damian knew what few men realized—that the mind was the most powerful sexual organ of all.

He needed to give Claire Beringer an oral orgasm. Literally. Using words. He'd let her imagination do his work for him, and her body's response would follow.

Jenkins returned with his jacket, and Damian turned to slip his arms into the sleeves and glanced again at the mirror. He made a striking picture, if he did say so himself. Crisp, white lawn shirt topped with a gold brocade waistcoat and a velvet cobalt coat. Midnight black hair and sapphire blue eyes. A sensual curve to the mouth.

If Claire wasn't halfway to an orgasm just at the mere sight of him, he'd be very surprised indeed. After all, he was Damian Hunt, renowned seducer of women.

An innocent virgin wouldn't stand a chance against his talent.

An innocent virgin....

Damian inhaled sharply, then pushed his qualms aside and straightened his spine.

I will not lose my best horse over this.

Chapter 3

Damian was pouring himself a scotch from the drawing room sideboard when his butler, Andrews, appeared in the doorway. "Mister George Beringer and Miss Beringer, sir."

Damian took a quick swallow of the amber liquid and turned to greet his guests. He gave George a curt nod, but he nearly choked on his drink when his eyes came to rest on Claire.

Far from the plain young woman he'd envisioned, she was a beauty of the first water. Her girlish, straw-colored pigtails had turned into a lustrous, honey-hued waterfall of curls. Her once-gangly body had developed voluptuous curves in all the right places, which her dress clearly accentuated. And her young, timid face had matured into the features of a striking woman, with no hint of a freckle anywhere.

Damian blinked to make sure the sight of her wasn't simply wishful thinking on his part, but when he opened his eyes, the extraordinary vision of Claire remained.

He smiled broadly.

"Welcome to my house, Miss Beringer," he said, taking her hand in both of his and bringing it to his lips. His eyes swept appreciatively over her. "What a beautiful woman you've become, Claire. May I call you Claire? I'm certain you'll let me, since we've known each other practically forever. I'm almost speechless before such beauty."

"Far from speechless, it seems," George mumbled, low.

Damian shot him a glare. He knew he was blathering, but he'd prepared this flattering speech to charm a plain, drab, dowdy virgin. With Claire, he found he actually meant the words, and he suddenly felt immensely confident about the bet. It would be easy to seduce such a luscious piece of femininity.

But instead of blushing prettily over his effusive compliments—as any young virgin would—Claire firmly withdrew her hand from his, and arched one eyebrow.

"You simply can't help yourself, can you?"

Damian was taken aback. "I beg your pardon?"

"I am well aware of your reputation as a ladies' man, my lord—"

"Damian," he corrected.

"*My lord,*" she said sternly, insisting on decorum. "But your charms and flatteries won't work on me, I'm afraid."

"*Claire.*"

Either man could have uttered the word, but it was George who'd said it, with obvious horror at her rudeness. Damian, on the other hand, simply smiled.

"Aha! Here I was wondering how on earth it could be true that no man has yet made an offer for you, but it's all clear now. You have the face of an angel but the tongue of a wasp. Can't you accept an honest compliment?"

Claire's smile was sugary sweet. "Have you ever given one, my lord?"

"*Claire!*"

That was George sounding mortified again, but this time Damian actually threw back his head and laughed. It was rare that a woman could hoist him on his own petard.

"Touché. It seems my reputation precedes me." He took a step back and bowed deeply from the waist. "Please, Miss Beringer, I'd like to start again. We are old friends, you and I, isn't that so? Let's put aside the usual superficial platitudes and simply enjoy each other's company this weekend. *Honestly.* Agreed?"

Claire looked from him to her brother. She seemed to consider for a moment, and then nodded.

"Very well."

Damian gave her his most dazzling smile, and noted that she went oddly pale at the sight of it.

"But only if you agree to behave yourself," she amended quickly.

"I'm afraid I can only promise to behave *honestly.* As we agreed." He gave her a wry shake of his head, then straightened. "Well then. Shall we drink on it? George?"

"A scotch," George grunted. "And make it a double. I need something to steady my nerves after that unseemly little confrontation."

Damian turned to the sideboard and picked up a crystal tumbler. "Claire? A touch of sherry, perhaps?"

"Thank you, no. I never drink."

Damian sighed. A waspish tongue and a teetotaler as well? His confidence in the bet was beginning to falter a bit. He poured a double scotch for George, and decided he could use one as well. He handed a glass to his friend, raising his own in salute.

"One moment, my lord," Claire said with a frown, effectively halting his drink on the way to his lips. "Surely we should wait for your sister."

Damian's eyebrow lifted curiously. "What?"

"Your sister," Claire repeated. "Wouldn't it be courteous to wait for Lady Sarah to come down and join us before you start to imbibe?"

Damian opened his mouth to speak, but caught sight of George gesticulating behind Claire's head. Damian's eyes widened in surprise. So that was how George had convinced her to come this weekend, the lying bastard!

"I'm afraid Sarah had to cancel. Yes. Unfortunately, her carriage lost a wheel in the snow as she was starting out, and she deemed the roads too unsafe to continue. She sent word earlier."

Claire paled. "And the other guests?"

Damian shook his head. "There are no other guests. It will be just the three of us."

Claire gasped and wheeled around to her brother. "We must leave at once, George. It isn't proper that I should be alone here in this house for an entire weekend with two men."

George snorted. "The devil you say. We just got here. We're not going anywhere."

"George—"

"Calm down, Claire. I'm your brother, a proper chaperone. Besides, you've known Damian all your life. What harm could it possibly cause your reputation to visit an old family friend?"

"George, please—"

"We're not going anywhere." Putting an end to the argument, George upended his drink with a firm snap of his wrist.

She turned to Damian. "My lord, I would sincerely appreciate it if you could provide me with one of your carriages to take me home."

He sighed deeply. "I'm sorry, my dear. Sarah had it right. The roads are too dangerous to travel in this weather. Now that you're here, safe and warm, I couldn't possibly let you head back out into the elements, especially since darkness has fallen. It would be treacherous."

He could sense her obvious agitation in her rapid breathing, an action which pushed her full breasts dangerously close to the neckline of her gown. His eyes riveted on the sight, at the rhythmic motion of her luscious flesh rising and falling, and his fingers itched to reach out and take advantage of that blatant opportunity.

Words, Damian. You are only allowed to use your words *on her. Remember the bet.*

He pulled his eyes away from the tantalizing display and up to rest on her face, where he could read her unspoken thoughts clearly. *Treacherous out there, perhaps, but equally treacherous here.*

Little did she know.

Claire idly dragged a spoon through the cockle soup sitting in front of her. She'd hardly touched it because her mind was too busy wrestling with her frantic thoughts.

Damian was seated at the head of the dining table with George on his left. She was positioned on Damian's right, but luckily, he was deep in conversation with her brother, which gave her time to collect herself and silently regroup.

How on earth was she going to get through this weekend?

George seemed determined that she should stay, but maybe Damian would reconsider lending her a carriage tomorrow morning. Surely he would agree that being alone with two notorious rakes for an entire weekend might well ruin her reputation.

If only he knew just how *seriously* she was in jeopardy....

Dear lord, when she'd entered the drawing room with George earlier, she'd nearly been struck dumb by the sight of Damian, looking even more the perfection of physical male beauty than she'd remembered. His deep blue eyes were as hypnotic as ever, his striking face seemed chiseled by some artist's hand, and when he'd turned his dazzling smile on her she'd actually felt weak in the knees.

He'd grown in height as well as stature since the last time she'd seen him. He was now a full head taller than George, and she couldn't help but notice how his brocade waistcoat hugged a broad chest, his blue coat stretched across muscular arms, and his snug trousers accentuated firm legs.

Claire swallowed hard and stirred her soup again. Yes, she could clearly see how dangerous it would be for any woman to be around Damian Hunt for long. He was the sort of man who could make a woman forget about her reputation altogether, even one as intent on protecting that reputation as *she* was.

Thank goodness he now thought of her as a shrewish termagant with a wasp's tongue. That should keep him a safe distance away.

Still, if only he'd *meant* his flattering words.

Lovely. Beautiful. The face of an angel.

No, no, no. She couldn't possibly still be pining after him, could she? Despite what he was? She felt herself turning scarlet at the thought.

"What's the matter, Claire? You look flushed." She jumped as Damian turned the full force of his attention on her. "Is the soup too hot?"

"N-no," she managed shakily. "The soup is perfectly fine."

"I thought we should start with something to warm you after your long trip, but if it's not to your liking, Andrews can bring the next course."

"No, please, I'm fine." If there was one thing Claire hated more than being the center of attention, it was causing a fuss. She quickly shoved a spoonful of the fish broth into her mouth. Unfortunately, she hadn't blown on it first, and the soup now threatened to burn her tongue. Gasping, she reached for her glass of water.

Damian grasped the glass and passed it over to her. She gulped it down thankfully, but the water went down the wrong way, and a fit of coughing brought Damian to her rescue a second time, hand poised behind her back, gallantly offering to—

"Don't touch me," she managed to wheeze.

He snatched his palm away, a frown on his face. Long, awkward moments passed before her breathing finally slowed to normal.

"Good God, Claire, what was all that about?" George tutted when the crisis was over, his annoyance evident in his tone.

An embarrassed heat threatened to rise in her cheeks again, but to her relief, she saw Damian scowl at her brother. He turned to her with a look of genuine concern on his face.

"Won't you have a sip of wine? It might help soothe your nerves after that unfortunate episode."

No, no, don't let him be sincerely nice to me. I couldn't resist that. Like I nearly couldn't resist the thought of having his hand on my back.

His warm palm in contact with her body. Those long, elegant fingers caressing—

Stop it, Claire!

"I told you I never drink," she snapped.

Damian frowned again, then shrugged. "Well, at least you've recovered. Will you tell us why you were so flushed? I hope you're not feeling ill."

She shook her head.

He quirked an eyebrow and gave her a teasing smile. "Surely you weren't thinking about *me* and blushing red like that, were you?"

Dear lord, he'd hit the nail right on the head, but she could never, ever let him know he still affected her that way. Despite her resolve, though, heat flamed her cheeks again.

"You're such a provocateur," she accused, hoping to put dripping disdain into her every word.

"So true," he agreed with a nod. "My only interest in the status quo is to *upset* it, I'm afraid. It's much more fun that way."

"Well, I for one will take you up on that offer of more wine," George said, proffering his glass with a bored wave. "Will there be any sport tomorrow?"

The rest of the meal passed mostly in silence, broken only by the occasional pleasantry, until finally dessert was done.

"Excellent meal, Damian. What do you say? Shall it be cards or billiards this evening?" George pushed his chair back from the table and laced his hands over his stomach.

"Cards, George." Damian shot Claire a glance. "Whist, perhaps. That's much more a lady's game."

"Not this lady, I'm afraid," Claire responded, laying her napkin on the table. "Thank you for the meal, my lord, but cards promote gambling, and I loathe gambling."

Damian sighed. "I'm rapidly becoming acquainted with the long list of things you loathe: alcohol, gambling, dishonest compliments, calling me by my given name, and any risk to your reputation. But tell me, Claire, there must be something you actually *enjoy*?"

"I enjoy many things," she bristled. Did she really come off as such a straight-laced, boring, stick-in-the-mud? "For instance, I enjoy broadening my mind by the reading of books."

George made an exasperated sound, but Damian smiled broadly. "Wonderful! Then perhaps you'd care to spend a few minutes in my library? I would dearly love to hear your opinion of it."

"Er—" Claire had intended to politely excuse herself and retire to her room, but considering how many times—and in how many ways—she had insulted Damian already tonight, it seemed churlish to add another demerit to that list he was keeping. Besides, she suddenly found herself curious to see what kind of reading material a man like Damian Hunt kept in his library. "Very well."

"Excellent." Damian moved behind her chair. "Andrews!"

The butler appeared immediately in the doorway. "Yes sir?"

"Show Miss Beringer to the library."

"Certainly, sir."

Damian pulled out her chair and politely handed her to her feet. "I'll give you half an hour, and then I look forward to hearing your opinion of my collection."

"All right." Claire frowned. What was Damian up to? He seemed too eager about this, but there was no way she could get out of the commitment now. She followed Andrews out of the room.

Damian watched her go, and then threw himself back down into his own chair. He heaved a sigh and looked at George.

George took another generous gulp of his wine. "I know. If she were any more rigid she'd have a stick up her—"

"George, that's your sister you're talking about."

"The devil take her! I'd pay up now if I were you, Damian. There's no way you can win this bet, not even with your talent with the ladies."

Damian was inclined to agree. He'd never in his life met a woman as priggish as Claire Beringer. Still….

"Did you see how she blushed when I asked her if she was thinking of me?"

George snorted. "She was more likely red with *outrage*, you bastard. No, it's hopeless for you. You should sign Thunder over to me right now, so we can just forget about Claire and enjoy the rest of the weekend."

"Not yet." *Not with my best horse at stake.* Besides, Damian Hunt was not a man to give up when he was determined to pursue a lady, and he had one potential ace up his sleeve.

Claire had gone to his *library.*

Chapter 4

Claire stared at the rows and rows of books in front of her. History, art, geography, philosophy, economics, law, social commentary, classical fiction. Who knew that a ne'er-do-well like Damian Hunt would have such depth and breadth of interest?

She frowned. Could she possibly have misjudged him? Was there actually a serious man behind that mask of flippancy and sinful beauty?

Impossible. His idleness and dissolute reputation were well known. It was more likely he'd just amassed this collection as a sop to his vanity, to impress his visitors. Or possibly he'd inherited the volumes.

Still, it was an extraordinary collection. She drew her finger idly across the spines of the books in front of her. There was the ancient military treatise, *The Art of War,* by Sun Tzu, and the deep philosophy of *The Republic* by Plato. Homer's historic recounting of the Trojan War in *The Iliad* held a spot, and even the modern fiction called *Great Expectations*, by Charles Dickens. A very diverse assortment indeed, and she found she wouldn't mind perusing any one of these books.

Her own personal favorites were books on the history and culture of peoples and countries of the world. At the moment, she was particularly fascinated with India because of the British rule there. Did Damian have any books on India here in his collection?

She stood on tiptoe to be able to read the titles on the shelf above, and let out an excited squeal when her gaze came to rest on a travelogue called *Goa and the Blue Mountains*, by Richard Francis Burton. Not only was it about a particular region of India, but it was authored by the very man she'd heard lecture at the National Geographical Society last week.

She excitedly pulled the book off the shelf and settled herself into a comfortable club chair. For the first time since she'd arrived at Atherton House, she found herself smiling. There was a fire blazing in the hearth, she had a tantalizing new book in her hands, and she was blissfully alone to enjoy it.

Within minutes, she was immersed in the history of India's smallest state, and surprised to learn that Portuguese merchants had landed in Goa in the fifteenth century, and held it even to this day. It wasn't under British rule at all.

Fascinating.

She eagerly flipped the page, wanting to learn more about the people themselves.

"Ah, Ruffian Dick."

Claire looked up. Damian was standing in the doorway, his hip negligently propped against the doorframe and his muscular arms crossed over his broad chest. He was the epitome of casual male grace—relaxed, yet utterly refined in his elegance.

"Pardon?" She shifted in her chair.

"I've been standing here for several minutes, but you've been thoroughly engrossed in that book. Do you realize that when you're concentrating on something, you suck your bottom lip into your mouth? It's quite alluring."

She felt herself flush. He was an incorrigible flirt, and since it was obvious he was patently incapable of controlling himself, she decided the best thing to do was to ignore his comments completely.

As if any woman could ignore Damian Hunt!

"I didn't see you there, my lord," she said, coolly polite. "The book is quite absorbing."

Damian pushed himself off the doorframe and came into the room.

"Don't apologize. Ruffian Dick tends to have that effect on people."

She frowned. "Ruffian—"

He indicated the book in her lap. "Richard Burton. Some call him Ruffian Dick because of his lack of respect for authority and his tendency to buck convention. I, on the other hand, prefer to think of him as a fearless adventurer with the courage to live by his own rules. A man's man." He paused, and his eyes took on a faraway look. "I envy him greatly."

Claire frowned. That look of longing on Damian's face did not quite equate with the frivolous reprobate she knew him to be. Since Damian had everything he could possibly want—wealth, a title, devastating good looks, women at his beck and call—why would he envy some ordinary army captain?

"Mark my words," he said. "The Queen will knight him before long, and then everyone will realize what a service he's done the world with his writing, exploring and soldiering."

"I heard him speak last week at the Royal Geographical Society."

Damian's eyebrows shot up. "Did you now?"

"Yes. He was very charismatic. Unfortunately, George did not approve. I have what my brother considers an unseemly interest in the natives of India, but in truth, I enjoy learning about all foreign cultures. Some of them are so incredibly different from our own."

"As a matter of fact, the study of alien civilizations is a particular passion of mine. Perhaps we can have a discussion this weekend about which ones you find most fascinating."

Claire paused. Damian wanted to hear her views on foreign cultures? Well, that was very flattering. It wasn't often a man expressed interest in a woman's intellectual opinion. Perhaps she was right when she'd wondered earlier upon seeing his books if she'd misjudged Damian. "You're curious about my opinions?"

"Of course. It's rare to find a woman more interested in improving her mind than her embroidery stitches. I admire you for it."

He gave her a little bow. Since he was standing in front of her club chair, the movement brought his face down almost level with hers, and for a brief moment, his black-haired, blue-eyed perfection was mere inches from her face. She literally had to squeeze her hand into a fist to stop her fingers from reaching out to stroke his cheek.

The instinct left her speechless.

Her heart had always harbored a secret spot for him, but her head had always managed to overrule that silly girl crush, especially considering how Damian Hunt had turned out. But now, with the possibility of something to admire about him, her heart was urging her head to reconsider the situation.

Thank goodness Damian seemed oblivious to her internal dilemma. He straightened and waved a hand toward the bookshelves.

"So. Do you approve of my library?"

She released a breath she hadn't realized she'd been holding. "Yes. It's a remarkable collection. I can't imagine anyone who would *not* approve of it."

"Ah, but *your* praise, I suspect, is not easily given, and therefore more valuable when it is."

Claire bit her lip. There it was again—his subtle reprimand of her high-handed behavior this evening. She supposed she *had* been a bit pompous since she'd arrived, and found that she didn't want him to think too poorly of her, didn't want him to misjudge her, especially considering that she may have misjudged him.

"I—I am not *so* bad, my lord."

"I have no doubt." He graced her with one of his magnificent smiles. "But then, neither am I. For instance, here we are having a pleasant, *honest* conversation. It's not so difficult, is it?"

Her own smile hovered at the corners of her mouth. "I suppose not."

He took a step closer and swept the length of her body with a glance. "Then let me be clear about one thing. I was being completely *honest* in my observation earlier that you've become a beautiful young woman, Claire."

Thank goodness she was seated, or her legs would surely have given out. There was no mistaking the intense look in Damian's eye. This wasn't idle flattery. He did *honestly* find her attractive.

Incredible.

He turned on his heel and casually walked to his desk. "You say you are interested in learning about foreign cultures, especially India. That you enjoy broadening your mind with the reading of books."

She turned in her chair to follow his movement, and tilted her head curiously. What an odd direction to take the conversation after his fervent declaration about her beauty!

"Yes. What of it?"

"I, too, am fascinated by the people of India." He rummaged around on his desk until he found a sheaf of papers, bound together with string, which he held up. "This, I believe, is Captain Burton's greatest work. It's certainly his most personal. A topic that has long fascinated him."

Claire eyed the bundle with interest. "What is it?"

"A translation of writings from the fourth century, of a celibate Indian scholar called Vatsyayana, about his people's most basic beliefs and practices. It's called the *Kama Sutra*."

"It sounds intriguing."

He came back to stand next to her chair. "Very few people have been given a copy of this. In fact, it's only in private circulation amongst the members of a certain society to which I belong. But I hope you'll find it interesting. I hope it will broaden your mind."

"With an introduction like that, I can hardly wait to read it."

He gave her an enigmatic smile and handed her the bundle.

"Captain Burton has taken it upon himself to sketch versions of some classic Indian artwork and sculptures, some of which illustrate the text. Perhaps you'll find the drawings even more illuminating than his words."

Claire frowned at Damian's cryptic comment, but eagerly took the pages from his hand. She turned to the opening paragraph. *Study of the Shastras.*

"In the beginning, the Lord of Beings created men and women," she read aloud, then glanced up at Damian curiously.

"Go on."

She scanned the page. "—laid down rules for their existence... seduction... love play... sexual union...."

With every phrase that caught her eye, an awful suspicion dawned on Claire, until the words on the page stuck in her throat. In a panic, she started flipping through the loosely bound papers, glancing at the illustrations. Here was a half-naked woman, her breasts exposed and the tips of her nipples erect, staring in obvious anticipation at a lover. Then came a man with a hand between a young girl's thighs, eagerly watching another naked waif dancing for his enjoyment. Then a woman with her legs spread open wide, waiting to be impaled by—

Claire gasped. The images provoked an immediate and unfamiliar response in her own body. Her breathing sped up, her nipples tingled beneath her corset, and there was the oddest sensation between her legs.

Claire snapped the pages shut, feeling righteous indignation burning her face a bright crimson. She threw the bound sheaf at Damian in disgust, but the bundle missed its target and ended up at his feet.

"How—how *dare* you show me that!"

Damian calmly bent to pick up the pages. "Yes, it *is* about sexual congress, Claire. Apparently the Indians are far more open about it than we as Queen Victoria's subjects are. But the book also gives great insights into the Indian psyche and the everyday lives of its people. It talks about how to be a good citizen and the importance of virtuous living, as well as giving advice regarding men and women in relationships."

"Get it out my sight this instant, you-you—"

"Isn't this what you're interested in?" Damian set the book down on the small round side table next to her chair. "To learn about the ethos of a foreign people? A culture radically different to our own?"

"You are *despicable*, my lord. Nothing but a lecherous Lothario. I would appreciate it if you would leave the room this instant."

"You disappoint me, Claire. I actually believed you when you said you enjoy broadening your mind, but clearly you're not the intellectual you portray yourself to be." Damian sighed deeply then straightened. "Very well. The library is yours."

With that, Damian turned and left.

Claire jumped up from her chair, the travelogue on Goa tumbling from her lap. She grabbed it roughly and slammed it down on top of the odious *Kama Sutra*. She didn't even want the thing in her line of sight.

She began to pace the room. How *dare* Damian try to trick her into looking at that salacious book, to descend to his base level! He was truly a scoundrel, a cad. And his comment about her being beautiful? Good lord, that was most likely a

feint, intended to get her to lower her guard, revise her sour opinion of him, a trick so that he could slip in this disgusting book and see if he could entice her with it. He probably hadn't meant his remark at all.

It's rare to find a woman more interested in improving her mind than her embroidery stitches. I admire you for it.

Had that compliment been a lie as well? Ironically, that one would hurt even more than his other. To find a man who would value her for her intellect would be gratifying indeed. She stopped abruptly in her pacing.

You disappoint me, Claire. I actually believed you when you said you enjoy broadening your mind.

She blew out a maddened breath and threw herself back down onto the club chair.

His salacious behavior aside, was there any chance Damian was right? For all her eagerness to learn about the world and its peoples, could she truly be as small-minded, as judgmental as he claimed when it came to certain subjects? Alcohol, gambling, and now this.

She glanced at the side table. She gingerly picked up the book on Goa, and stared at the bound sheaf of pages underneath.

Indians are far more open about sexual congress than we....

Claire shivered slightly. What little she'd seen from those pictures hinted that the text might be even more explicit. Explicit, but educational. And that scared her even more. What virgin wouldn't leap at the chance to know the secrets about what really went on between a man and a woman?

The images in the pictures flashed through her brain.

Did a man really have a piece of flesh between his legs as enormous as the drawing she'd seen? What exactly did he do with it?

Did a woman actually bare her breasts for a man's enjoyment? How would he pleasure himself with them?

The thought of all that hidden knowledge mere inches from her fingertips made her hands shake and a bead of sweat break out on her brow.

"Damian said the book talks about the everyday lives of the Indian people," she reasoned aloud. "That's what I'm truly interested in."

Yes, but the everyday lives of its people obviously included sexual union.

A virgin should not know certain things!

"Nonsense," she said, trying to convince herself. "Knowledge is never a bad thing."

Besides, at the rate she was going, it was almost certain she'd end up an old maid, never to have firsthand experience of marital relations. This might be her only opportunity to learn about what she'd be missing.

Her heart began to race as she stood, laid the Goa book on top of the *Kama Sutra* to cover it, and then picked up both and nestled them gingerly in the crook of her arm. She'd just take these upstairs to her room tonight—there'd be no chance Damian would ever find out, because she'd return them first thing in the morning, long before he woke.

She took a deep breath. Damian must never know she'd borrowed this *Kama Sutra*. Despite his contention that it revealed far more information than just instruction in sexual congress, it would surely be the end of her precious reputation if he discovered she'd read it.

Several hours later, George stomped into the library on Damian's heels.

"Bloody hell, why all the fuss and bother?" he grumbled. "Why couldn't we simply have had our brandy in the drawing room?"

Damian's eyes immediately went to the small round table between the two club chairs near the fireplace. It was empty. His pulse gave an excited leap, but he shifted his gaze in the direction of his desk.

"I wanted a change of scenery," he said with forced nonchalance. "You beat me so soundly in cards tonight that I felt a desperate need to get out of that room."

George laughed. "Your pockets a bit lighter, are they? Serves you right. The game only had half your attention. I should have realized it sooner and doubled my bets."

Yes, Damian's mind had been otherwise occupied. He'd been pondering on the very pleasant surprise he'd experienced over Claire's keen interest and knowledge of India, indeed, of her apparent curiosity of the world at large. A rare trait in a woman of his acquaintance.

And now this. Another surprise.

Damian swept his desktop with a glance. There was no sign of Burton's book anywhere. His pulse kicked up another notch.

"Right you are, George. Luck was not with me tonight." He craned his neck to steal a covert glance at the waste basket, but it was empty. She hadn't thrown it in the trash, despite her outrage.

Had his plan worked? Had Claire taken the lure of the *Kama Sutra* after all?

"Luck is not with you *this weekend*," George corrected. "There's no earthly way you're going to win the bet we made over Claire."

Damian clapped George on the back. "Don't order the hay for my horse just yet. Now, how about that drink?"

Chapter 5

At her dressing table, Claire took an inordinate amount of time getting ready for bed, her gaze constantly straying to the bound bundle of pages lying next to the pillow on her bed.

Seduction... love play... sexual union.

Oh, my. Despite how much she coveted that information, how on earth was she ever going to gather the courage to open those pages?

A half-naked woman, breasts exposed, staring in obvious anticipation at a lover.

Her body was doing strange things again. Her nipples felt incredibly sensitive where they rubbed up against the thick cotton of her nightgown, and she moved her hand self-consciously to cup her right breast. She rarely touched herself like this—especially not after her mother had caught her as a curious seven-year-old and told her that touching herself was something a lady *never* did—but those pictures seemed to have unleashed some inner demon inside her, some curious imp she didn't recognize.

Curiosity killed the cat.

She jerked her hand away from her breast. Maybe if she only read the text of the *Kama Sutra*, and avoided the drawings.

Yes, words were clinical and staid, unlike pictures, which could incite the imagination. She only wanted the *information* that the book contained. Facts and figures about what went on between a man and a woman. Surely she'd be safe if she only read the words.

She purposely gave her hair one hundred strokes with the brush, feeling her breathing slow and a tenuous calm settle over her during the familiar routine. Yes, that was better. She was certain she could open that book with equanimity now.

Crossing the room to the bed, she climbed up onto the mattress. She took a deep, steadying breath, and reached for the book.

Opening it to the index, she saw the tome was divided into seven parts. *Book One: Study of the Shastras... Study of Arts, Sciences... Man About Town.*

She bit her lip. As revelatory as those pages might be about the lives of Indians, tonight she was interested in only one thing.

Book Two: Love Play and Sexual Union.

She flipped to that section.

"Oh, dear," she whispered, reading the individual headings aloud. "The Kiss. The Embrace. The Bite. Striking. Sexual Vigor and Intensity. Oral Congress."

An odd tingle swept through her body, and she swallowed hard. Kissing and embracing she could understand as being part of a relationship between a man and woman, but the rest she wasn't even sure she could envision. Would a man actually bite or strike a woman while in the throes of passion? And what was oral congress, if not kissing?

Good lord, had it suddenly gotten hotter in here? She leaned back against her headboard, and unbuttoned the high-necked collar of her nightgown in order to let the air cool her skin. After a moment, she decided to unbutton her gown all the way to the waist, leaving it parted just an inch. After all, there was no one here to see or judge her wanton action.

Taking another deep breath, she began to read aloud.

"Kissing Spots," she began. "The places for kissing are the forehead, eyes, cheeks, lips, throat, bosom and the interior of the mouth."

Bosom? Forehead, cheeks and lips she could see, possibly even the throat and the eyes if a woman was particularly dear to a man, but her bosom? That seemed scandalous in the extreme.

Still, the idea induced her left hand to slip underneath the edge of her gown to cradle her right breast again. This time, the feel of skin on skin, without the barrier of her nightgown in between, was incredibly stimulating. Her nipple puckered, and her finger came up to rub back and forth against the taut tip, sending little lightning bolts of pleasure shooting through her body.

She arched her head back into her pillow, enjoying each sharp jolt. Did an Englishman kiss a woman on her bosom? And what about on her sensitive nipples? Her finger felt so good here, what would a man's lips feel like?

Claire shocked herself at the thought, and she sat up straight.

No. She couldn't imagine an Englishman engaged in so improper an activity. It was probably a national trait, something only Indian men did.

And speaking of that, how was a man supposed to kiss the interior of a woman's mouth, for heaven's sake? No woman could possibly open her mouth wide enough for a man to get his lips in there!

She was beginning to wonder if Captain Burton's translation abilities were not quite as proficient as he thought.

"But I should read on in order to make a proper determination."

She flipped past the section marked *The Embrace*. There could be nothing particularly revealing about two people hugging each other, could there? She stopped, though, with fingers trembling, at the part marked *Sexual Union*.

"Oh, my," Claire said softly. "Am I really ready for this?"

Too late. Next to the chapter heading, Captain Burton had sketched a very detailed picture of a man and a woman *joined*. Shown from the side, the woman was kneeling, but arched back on her hands, blatantly offering her naked body to the man, who was also kneeling, spearing between her thighs with his—

Don't look at the pictures!

Claire gasped and her eyes flew to the text.

"Man is divided into three classes, according to the size of his *lingam*, or phallus." She swallowed hard. "A woman, too, according to the depth of her *yoni*, or vagina."

Good lord. Here it was in black and white. The answer to all her questions. She flipped forward several pages.

"After inserting the *lingam* into the *yoni*, the man performs certain actions—"

Claire closed the book with a snap, fanning herself briskly with her hand. She squeezed her legs together tightly, feeling an unfamiliar pressure in her own *yoni.*

So. A man has an organ between his legs that he sticks into a woman's body during sexual union.

Her own body shivered at the thought, and her hand drifted down the opening of her nightgown, past her waist, to slip under the thick cotton at the juncture of her thighs. The women in those pictures had been portrayed as having an opening, a slit by which the man entered her. Claire had never touched herself here, at least never more than to give herself a brisk wash during her bath, but now her fingers tangled in her tight curls, sliding through them gently to explore the secrets beneath. She seemed to be wet. Shocking! But perhaps the dampness might help with the experiment she had in mind.

She had to discover if her body was made the same way as the women in those pictures.

She slowly investigated herself. Yes, she did have an opening. She inserted one finger inside herself, imagining it was a man's *lingam.*

She glanced sideways at the book. She'd learned what she'd sought, the details of what went on between a man and woman. Did she really need to know any more?

Yes. Her inner devil rose up to demand more. When would she ever have another opportunity like this? She should take advantage of it!

She slowly withdrew her finger and then tentatively opened the book again, picking a page at random.

"A man must first arouse the woman by ardent love play, and then vigorously commence the sex act so that she reaches the climax earlier or simultaneously with him."

The climax? She frowned and scanned more of the text. *Pleasure... passion... amorous movements.* Yes, it seemed the act being described was enjoyable for both the man and the woman, in spite of the uncomfortable-looking position of the woman in that picture.

Maybe there were better examples of the act.

Despite her resolve not to look at the pictures, she quickly turned the page. There was a woman with her legs bent up toward her ears, *yoni* deliberately exposed, ready to take a man's huge *lingam.* Another of a woman straddling a man's lap, ready to lower herself onto his thick organ. Yet another of a woman on hands and knees, the man impaling her from behind.

How did people possibly invent these positions?

And then there was the picture she'd seen earlier, of the man with his hand between one woman's legs while watching a second naked waif dancing for his pleasure.

One man with two women?

She quickly scanned Burton's translation of Vatsyayana's text.

When a man enjoys two women at the same time, this is known as a united congress. When a man enjoys many women together, this is referred to as the congress of a herd of cows.

Sure enough, the next picture showed a man with—Claire counted them—*six* women!

She dropped the book as if it were on fire. She'd learned more than enough about sexual congress for one night—frankly, more than enough, period. And somehow her logical reason for opening the book in the first place now seemed terribly unsound.

Be careful what you wish for....

A loud noise from the room next door startled her. Heart racing, she clutched the two sides of her open nightgown and held them tightly together, an embarrassed heat flaming her face. Pulling back the bed covers, she quickly scooted under them and yanked the sheet up to her chin.

There were voices now, low and muted, but above the pounding of her heart she could clearly make out Damian's deep rumble, along with that of another man. She listened closely. She couldn't be sure, but they seemed to be discussing clothes. Was the man Damian's valet?

In a panic, Claire looked toward the wall the voices were coming through. There was a door there that she hadn't really paid too much attention to before. Dear lord, was Damian's bedroom beyond that door? He obviously was occupying the main apartment of the house, but was her room the one intended for use by the lady of the house?

And does that possibly mean the connecting door is unlocked?

Claire hastily fastened all her buttons, and then snuck out of bed as quietly as she could. Short of jiggling the door handle to make sure it was locked—which Damian surely would notice—Claire did the only other thing she could think of. She picked up the dressing chair, tiptoed as quietly as she could to the door, and propped the chair next to it. That way, if Damian was tempted to use the door in the middle of the night—for whatever nefarious purpose—she'd have adequate warning when the chair tipped over or Damian toppled over it.

A floorboard creaked loudly under her foot, and Claire heard the voices next door abruptly stop. She froze in place, but after a moment, the voices resumed. Relief washed through her, and she scurried the few feet to her bed.

This whole situation was uncomfortable in the extreme. Not to mention highly improper.

Why on earth had Damian put her in the room next to his? George was a respectable distance down the hall, so why wasn't she? Perhaps Damian had wanted to provide her with the best accommodations he could offer, and he'd believed this room was it.

Nevertheless, it was shockingly inappropriate for her to be here.

Claire listened closely and could still hear the voices next door. If indeed that was Damian's valet in there with him, he would no doubt be helping Damian out of his clothes and dressing him for bed.

Damian without his clothes.

Claire shivered at an image of a naked Damian Hunt. Broad shoulders, muscular arms, powerful chest and firm legs, all in the flesh.

And what about Damian's *lingam*? Would it be as long and thick as those illustrations she'd seen tonight?

She swallowed hard, picturing Damian doing to her what some of the men in those images had been doing to the women.

These are not appropriate thoughts for a virgin!

Appalled at herself, Claire let out a dismayed groan, punched her pillow, and turned onto her side in the bed. She purposely put her back to the connecting door, as if that could stop her from thinking of Damian. But she could no more keep the scandalous thoughts from flooding her mind than she could erase everything she'd seen and read in the *Kama Sutra*.

Good lord. How was she expected to get any sleep tonight with Damian just a few feet away in the next room? He was so close. Close enough to—

Stop it, Claire!

Pulling the pillow over her head, she knew she was in for a fitful night.

Damian put a finger to his lips to silence his valet, Jenkins. If he wasn't mistaken, that was Claire he'd just heard, letting out a loud, exasperated sound.

Good. If she was feeling sexually frustrated, it meant his plan was working.

She'd taken the lure of the *Kama Sutra*, and now he wanted the images she'd seen in it to haunt her all night long.

He glanced at the blue coat his valet had just helped him remove. Obviously his first thoughts had been wrong about Claire. She hadn't been halfway to an orgasm just seeing him dressed in all his finery. His pride had been slightly pricked by that, but he'd quickly adapted his tactics, and she'd finally bit at the hook of the *Kama Sutra*.

And by purposely making noise just now, intentionally speaking too loudly to his valet, Damian had let Claire blatantly know that he was here in the next room. Close by. Scandalously, improperly, dangerously near her.

With any luck, he'd weigh heavily on her mind tonight, hopefully even starring in her frustrated fantasies.

As she would star in his.

He frowned. No. This plan of his was designed to win his bet with George, nothing more.

Ironically, George couldn't have picked a more dangerous virgin. If there was one thing Damian found more attractive than a beautiful woman, it was an intelligent one. But while Claire Beringer might be everything he admired in a woman, she was simply a means to an end. And after she spent a night dreaming about the *Kama Sutra*, he was confident she'd be desperate for him to say the magic words that would put her out of her carnal misery and give her a release from her sexual frustration.

I can make a woman come using just the power of my words.

He smiled. Yes, this was going to be a pleasure. For both of them.

Chapter 6

As she'd expected, Claire spent a restless night. The clock on the mantle read 7:45 when she finally gave up on sleep altogether.

She shivered beneath the covers. The room was freezing. It was too early even for the maids to have come in to start the fire.

Turning onto her side, she pulled the covers tighter around her. She felt tense, on edge, with an unfamiliar sort of gnawing inside her. Sighing, she stared at the door that connected her room to Damian's. It had been thoughts of him coming through that door that had preyed on her mind both asleep and awake last night.

But apparently those thoughts hadn't all been unwelcome. In her brief moments of slumber, it seems she'd willingly let Damian do whatever wicked things he'd wanted to her body. He'd stripped her naked like the women in the pictures, and run his hands intimately over her breasts and between her legs. Then he'd peeled the clothes slowly from his own body, giving her the luscious glimpse of bare skin she'd only imagined yesterday.

He'd been magnificent—long, lean, and muscled. Everything she'd expected. Except that she was still technically imagining it. It had been a dream, after all.

Or a nightmare. The images had startled her awake, flaming her face with guilt and embarrassment.

And yet every time she managed to get back to sleep, the dream would continue. With an impossibly huge phallus, Damian had impaled her like the women in the drawings. From the front. From behind. With her on his lap.

She had screamed in her dreams, but she wasn't sure it had necessarily been from terror.

Now that she was awake, she imagined she could still feel the lingering pressure of his fingers on her body. Long, silky fingers, stroking her. Good lord, what would his hands really feel like on her naked skin? A scandalous part of her longed to know, even though she was mortified to admit it.

She threw back the covers, breathing hard, her hand landing on the *Kama Sutra*. The book still lay on top of the bedspread where she had dropped it abruptly last night after viewing that salacious picture of the man with six women.

The book. Yes, this book was the source of her current agitation, not Damian. Everything would be all right if she could just get rid of the book. Out of sight, out of mind. Once the book was safely back in Damian's library, she could get her wayward thoughts back under her usual rigid control.

A low knock came from the direction of the door. Claire gasped out loud and quickly pulled the covers back up to her chin, hauling the book with her. Was her dream coming true?

He wouldn't dare! She stared at the connecting door in a strange mixture of dread and anticipation, refusing to answer.

But she'd been mistaken. It was the door to the hall that opened to reveal the scullery maid, who'd come to light the morning fire.

"Beggin' your pardon, miss," she apologized, obviously surprised to find Claire awake. "I'll just be a minute."

The girl knelt in front of the fireplace and busily swept out the ashes from last night before laying a new fire.

Claire's mind raced. "Tell me, what time does your master rise?"

The girl bobbed her head. "Usually never before noon, miss."

"Good. Can you send me a lady's maid?" Normally, Claire would have brought her own lady's maid, but given Damian's notorious reputation as a womanizer, she was certain he'd have one employed on his staff.

"Right now, miss? At this hour?"

"Yes."

"Very well, miss." The maid rose from in front of the fire and dropped a quick curtsy before scurrying from the room.

Within ten minutes, the woman appeared. She was older than Claire expected, and seemed a tad nervous, wiping the palms of her hands on her apron.

"Er—I'm Sarah, miss. We, er, we don't often have ladies here, but I'll try to serve you best I can."

Claire stared at the woman. It was rare to have a lady here? What about Damian's notorious reputation?

She frowned. Perhaps his usual routine was to seduce his conquests at their own homes. Claire had no idea how these things worked, after all. Or, could she possibly have misjudged his profligacy, like she'd misjudged his seriousness, given the depth and breadth of his library?

No. His reputation with the ladies was common knowledge. And look how he was behaving with *her!*

"Er—will you have a bath, miss?"

Claire pulled herself out of her thoughts. There was nothing she longed for more than a bath to wash away all her shameful visions of last night, but there was something more important to do.

"I'll have a bath this afternoon. Right now I'd like you to help me dress and do my hair. *Quickly.*"

"Yes, miss."

The maid worked as fast as she could, readying Claire in half-an-hour. Once Sarah had gone, Claire listened carefully for any noise or movement coming from the direction of Damian's bedroom. All was quiet. He was probably dead to the world after a long night of drinking and gambling. Making a small tsking sound, she glanced at herself in the dressing table mirror, and frowned.

Two of her buttons were misbuttoned, and one wayward curl was already coming undone from her bun. What was Sarah's real job? Was she the cook, perhaps? Oh, well. Claire had certainly looked better, but given the urgency of her errand, her appearance took second place. She could put herself to rights as soon as her mission was accomplished.

Crossing to her bed, she reached under the covers to extract the *Kama Sutra.*

She tucked the book under her arm, and at the last minute, remembered to pick up the book on Goa as well.

She silently let herself out of the room, crept quietly down the staircase, and began to breathe easier the farther away from Damian's room she got. At the library door, she paused. Where to put the books? Damian had conspicuously picked up the *Kama Sutra* and laid it on the side table by her chair after she'd thrown it at his feet last night, so she'd better return it to that exact spot if she didn't want him to know she'd borrowed it.

She crossed the room and placed the bound sheaf of papers carefully on the side table. Now, what to do about the Goa book? It had been in her lap when Damian left her, so she felt confident in placing that one back on its proper shelf.

She sighed in relief after successfully returning the books, but then frowned when her stomach let out a loud growl. She was famished. It was no surprise, really. She'd barely touched her dinner last night.

Hmm. If she ate something now, she might be lucky enough to avoid seeing Damian this morning altogether.

But where would the kitchen be? She decided to retrace last night's steps to the dining room. The kitchen must be somewhere close to that.

Unfortunately, as soon as she rounded the dining room doorway, she spotted the very man she'd hoped to dodge seated at the table, teacup in hand, reading placidly from the morning gazette.

�֍ֿֿ⟨ᵔ⌣ᵔ⟩֎ᵎ

Damian looked up from his newspaper to see Claire standing in the doorway. It was exactly as he'd planned, although he'd been waiting more than an hour for her anticipated arrival.

By her disheveled appearance he could clearly tell she'd dressed in a hurry, probably hoping to avoid precisely this little scenario.

"Good morning, Claire. I hope you slept well."

He almost laughed at the flustered look on her face, as if she were a child who'd just been caught with her hand in the cookie jar.

"I didn't think—um—the servants said—" She took a deep breath and straightened her shoulders. "Good morning, my lord."

He gave her his best smile and waved a hand at the chair next to him. "Please. Come in."

She didn't want to. He could see that clearly. But he wasn't about to miss this opportunity.

"Andrews!"

The butler appeared instantly behind her in the doorway. "Yes, sir?"

"Bring Miss Beringer a cup of tea."

"Certainly, sir."

Damian knew Claire had no option now but to join him, although from her rigid stance he feared he might have to pry her fingers from the door jamb. He stood politely and held out a chair for her.

She stared at him for a long moment, as if desperately trying to find an argument against it, then sighed deeply and crossed the room to take a seat.

Damian reseated himself and looked nonchalantly back at his newspaper. He needed to put her at ease before he began his planned verbal assault.

"It seems a factory chimney collapsed at Bradford yesterday. One boy was rescued, but several people are dead. Tragedy."

Claire took a sip of water from the glass next to her plate. "I've read that factory chimneys—and especially mine chimneys—are by their very nature dangerous things, my lord."

"And why is that, pray tell?" Damian gave her an indulgent look.

"Because subsidence from the removal of the minerals in the earth beneath them can cause the chimneys to sink or collapse. Something should be done to improve the system."

Damian's eyebrows shot up in surprise. He didn't know many *men* who could address the plight of factory workers with such depth of knowledge, much less a *woman*. He felt that strange sensation rising up again—a deep respect for her mind.

No, no. This wouldn't do at all. He needed to hold her at arm's length if he planned to casually seduce her in order to win his bet with George.

Luckily, Andrews appeared at that moment with Claire's tea, giving Damian a moment to regroup.

As soon as the butler left the room, Damian cleared his throat. If he delayed any longer, he feared he might lose his resolve.

"You know, Claire, your little lecture on broadening the mind inspired me to read last night. Unfortunately, when I went to the library to retrieve my favorite bedtime material, I couldn't find the book where I'd left it. Not on the table, nor on my desk, nor on the shelf. You didn't happen to see the *Kama Sutra*, did you?"

He saw her blanch, and squirm slightly in her chair. "I—um—well, yes, as a matter of fact. I accidentally picked it up along with my copy of *Goa and the Blue Mountains* last night."

"Is that so?" Damian murmured. "And tell me, was your mind broadened by the experience?"

"Don't be absurd," she snapped. "I didn't actually *read* it. I put it aside as soon as I realized I had it."

"I don't actually *read* it myself," Damian admitted with a slow smile. "I mostly like to look at the pictures. They give me pleasant dreams."

Claire blushed scarlet and Damian knew she *had* examined the book!

"My favorite," he continued, pushing to see how far she'd let him go, "is the one of the man with six women. Did you happen to notice that one? Imagine! One lovely lady spreading her feminine lips for his eager mouth. One impaling herself on his stiff cock. Both his hands exploring the treasure between the thighs of two nearby women, while the lucky devil's big toes diddle with—"

"Damian!"

He chuckled. "Yes, I supposed we should be on a first-name basis after a discussion like this. Tell me, Claire, which was your favorite picture?"

She was breathing so hard he thought she might hyperventilate, or perhaps pop her remaining buttons. Was that indignation she was feeling, or, hopefully, some measure of sexual excitement? Either way, the sight of her heaving bosom was eliciting a growing response in his own body. At least it was, until she suddenly picked up her water glass, threw the contents in his face, and bolted from the room.

He smiled wryly, and calmly picked up his napkin to dab at his nose.

"Andrews!"

The butler again appeared in the doorway, his eyebrows reaching his hairline at the sight of Damian's wet face.

"Have Cook prepare a breakfast tray to take up to Miss Beringer's room."

"Right away, sir."

"I want you to deliver it personally, but before you do, there's something I wish to send up with it."

"Yes, sir."

The butler hurried off in the direction of the kitchen, while Damian rose and strode to the library. The *Kama Sutra* was on the side table, exactly where he'd been sure Claire would return it. He grabbed a pen and piece of paper from his desk, scribbled a quick note, attached it to the front of the pages, and brought the bundle back to the dining room.

A moment later, Andrews appeared with the tray. Hot tea, a selection of scones, and pots of jam and clotted cream. Damian nodded his approval, slipped the *Kama Sutra* underneath the checkered napkin, and watched as the butler headed off toward the stairs.

Damian stood staring after him and rubbed his damp chin thoughtfully.

He wished there was another way to win this bet. Hell, he wished he could get out of this wager altogether. Claire was turning out to be a downright fascinating woman. A seductive combination of brains and beauty.

What about her prudish behavior, judgmental opinions and waspish tongue?

True, those were unattractive traits, but he had the distinct feeling that if he could just get beneath her tightly controlled exterior, there was a hot-blooded woman waiting to get out. Waiting for the right man to stoke her fire and set her passions free.

The things I could teach her! Christ, the things I did to her last night in my dreams!

Damian's body shuddered as he vividly remembered some of the delightfully wicked things he'd done to her while he'd been asleep. In particular, how he'd pleasurably punished that pert mouth of hers by teaching her exactly how a man preferred a woman to use her mouth.

He gasped out loud. What was he thinking? Allowing himself to fantasize about Claire was sheer lunacy. She was a respectable virgin. Hell, what he was doing to her with this oral seduction was bad enough. He didn't intend to feel even guiltier than he already did.

He set his mouth into a determined line.

I only have the weekend to win this bet, my little virgin. Let's see how much more of this erotic teasing you can take before you break. Before you finally beg me to put an end to your sexual frustration.

I can make a woman come using just my words....

He was looking forward to that moment more than he'd care to admit. Unfortunately, he was afraid it was no longer solely for the purpose of keeping his horse.

Chapter 7

Claire paced her bedroom furiously. How dare Damian Hunt speak to her like that? Asking which was her favorite *Kama Sutra* drawing, as if he were casually inquiring about the weather?

She was beyond shocked, but obviously she was no better than he was now. After all, the salacious images had affected her the same way they did him.

They give me pleasant dreams.

Damian had expressed a preference for the drawing of the man with six women. And the way he had so wantonly described it!

One impaling herself on his stiff cock....

Claire tilted her head curiously. So the English word for *lingam* was *cock,* was it? Interesting.

She slapped a hand abruptly across her mouth. "Oh, lord, what has that man done to me?"

The restless edginess she'd felt first thing that morning returned. She'd never felt this way before, never experienced this gnawing tension that seemed to be yearning for something, some way to ease it. This was all Damian's fault. He had set off something inside her that she didn't understand.

A knock at her door caused her to spin around in fright. Surely he hadn't followed her up to her bedroom?

Well, there was no way Damian Hunt was going to upset her more than he already had. She crossed the room and locked the door, then leaned her full weight against it for good measure.

Let's see how he reacts to that!

A muffled voice floated through the wood. "Miss? It's Andrews, miss, come with a breakfast tray."

She opened her mouth to send him away, but her stomach loudly rumbled a protest. She was still famished.

Grudgingly, she unlocked the door and opened it a crack. Sure enough, it was the butler carrying a tray with what looked like tea and scones. She stared hard beyond his shoulder, but there was no sign of Damian lurking anywhere in the hallway.

Sighing deeply, she pulled open the door.

"Andrews, I want you to take a message to my brother. Tell him I need to see him as soon as he wakes."

"Yes, miss." The butler put the tray down on her dressing table.

"And do you know your master's schedule for today?"

"I believe he and Master George will be shooting today."

"Thank you, Andrews."

The butler gave her a nod, and left. Claire quickly re-locked the door.

She crossed the room slowly, her mind racing. If Damian planned to shoot today, it meant he'd be out of the house for most of the day, unable to torment her further with his wicked comments about that book. And once she told George how improperly Damian had acted, surely he'd send for their carriage to take her home immediately.

With any luck, she'd be gone from here within hours.

Yes. She'd seen the last of the *Kama Sutra*, and she was determined that she'd *heard* the last about it from Damian as well.

With a sigh of relief, she approached the tray, fixed herself a welcome cup of tea, and slathered a scone with jam. The fresh pastry was flaky perfection, and she savored every delicious bite. If Sarah was indeed the cook, Claire would happily forgive her ineptness as a lady's maid.

She spread jam over a second scone and was reaching to pour herself another cup of tea when she noticed an odd bump underneath the napkin. She'd been so hungry she hadn't even laid the linen in her lap, but now she put down the teapot and reached for the checkered material. Lifting it up, she took a moment to register what her eyes were seeing.

The *Kama Sutra* lay on the tray.

My favorite picture is the man with six women.

Claire shivered. Damn him! Why couldn't she get Damian's shocking words out of her head?

Imagine! One lovely lady spreading herself for his eager mouth.

That couldn't really be true, could it? A woman offering herself to a man like that?

Good lord. Oral. Mouth. *Oral congress* didn't actually mean kissing, it meant *this!*

And, based on the smile she remembered seeing on the woman's face, she'd been enjoying it.

Claire bit her lip. Did every woman get pleasure from that act? What would Damian's mouth feel like between her own legs?

Good lord, Damian's never personally had six women at the same time, has he?

Claire jumped up from her chair, grabbed the *Kama Sutra*, and was a hairsbreadth from throwing the scandalous bundle of pages into the fire when she realized there was a note pinned to the front of it.

Don't read it, you fool, you're only asking for trouble.

What could Damian have to say to her after their little imbroglio in the dining room? An apology, perhaps?

Not if he'd sent up the *Kama Sutra* with the breakfast tray.

With shaking fingers, she pulled open the note.

Pick your favorite position, Claire, and we'll discuss it later. It will make for interesting intellectual stimulation.

She let out a strangled cry, and crumpled the note in her fist. She had to get out of here. Away from this house, away from its host, and away from this book. But with George still abed, she couldn't go very far.

She anxiously crossed the room and looked out the window. Yes. A walk in the garden would soothe her nerves. And give her some solitude, away from Damian's seemingly ever-present reach.

Striding to the wardrobe, she grabbed a light shawl, unlocked the bedroom door, and marched down the stairs and out the front door without so much as a word to anyone.

⁂꙰(☙�*)꙰⁂

Damian felt better after a punishing ride across his fields in the crisp morning air. He'd needed to get out of the house after that little episode at breakfast with Claire, had even ordered his groomsman to saddle up Thunder to remind himself why he'd agreed to this appalling bet. Never mind that he was a fool to take any chances with his prized horse before its first race.

It had been an exhilarating ride, but now that it was over, Damian realized grimly that he hadn't been able to accomplish his real goal—to outrun his thoughts of Claire and the untenable position he'd put her in.

Put them *both* in.

It was getting increasingly more difficult to justify what he was doing. Yes, he had a reputation as a shameless ladies' man, but all those ladies in question had been willing partners. He'd never forced a woman in his life. Not that he was forcing Claire, exactly. Just pressuring her a little.

As she was pressuring him.

Putting pressure on the base of your spine, you mean.

Well, yes, he was feeling a little sexually frustrated. All right, extremely frustrated. Claire was a beautiful woman. He'd be the first to admit that he wouldn't mind having her in his bed. Christ, she'd been the star of his erotic dreams last night, doing some things he'd never even tried with a flesh-and-blood lover.

She's a virgin, you bastard!

True, but she'd still technically be a virgin when he was done with her, as George was so quick to point out. She just wouldn't be as innocent as she'd been.

He grimaced. George's rationale had never sat well with him, but Damian had agreed to this bet, so there was no one to blame but himself for the dilemma he now faced. Thank goodness he and George would be out shooting for most of the afternoon. At least that would give him a few hours respite from this quandary.

With a sigh, he turned his horse's head in the direction of the stables, only to pull up short a moment later. Was that Claire in the rose garden? What could she possibly be doing out here in the cold? She wasn't even wearing a proper coat!

He paused. Maybe her blood was so fevered with lust that she'd needed a spot to cool down. Maybe she was so close to the edge that just another little push from him would be enough to win this bet, and get her on her way back to her precious, virginal, straight-laced life.

He gave Thunder a sharp kick, urging him in the direction of the garden. Claire's head snapped up at the sound of the pounding hooves, and he clearly saw the panic in her eyes when she recognized him. But Damian couldn't give her a chance to bolt and run as she had in the dining room. He was dismounted and striding toward her before his horse had come to a complete stop. She stared as he neared, eyes wide as saucers, and backed away from him slowly until she found herself hard up against one of the brick garden walls.

She was adorable when she was ruffled like this. Caught off-balance, she seemed vulnerable. So unlike the haughty woman of last night, or even this morning. As he watched, a wayward curl loosed itself from her bun, and he imagined running his fingers through her hair, shaking it completely loose of that prim and proper hairstyle.

What would she look like with her blond hair set free to curl wildly around her pretty face? What would it feel like against his hands, his skin?

He could almost imagine its cool silk sliding through his fingers.

Stay in control! Don't let her affect you like this.

"Claire." He heard the cool smoothness in his own voice, and congratulated himself on his restraint.

"My—my lord." She pulled her shawl tighter around her shoulders.

"Damian," he insisted, giving her his best smile. "I thought we were on a first-name basis after this morning."

She blinked rapidly but didn't rise to that bait, so he made a show of looking slowly around at the garden.

"Tell me, Claire, did you happen to notice how many of the *Kama Sutra* drawings take place outside?"

She groaned at that reference, burying her face in her hands, but there was nowhere for her to run to escape the conversation. The wall was behind her, and he was solidly in front.

He pressed his advantage. "I think there's nothing more thrilling than making love in—"

Her head came up, her eyes shooting daggers at him. "Having sexual congress, you mean! A man like you doesn't make love, he only makes conquests."

Damian raised an eyebrow in surprise, but he ignored the insult, concentrating for the moment on the fact that she was actually talking about this.

"All right. There is nothing more thrilling than sexual congress in the open air. I think my favorite way is to brace the woman against a wall, just like this one behind you, then wrap her legs around my waist, and—"

"Why are you doing this to me? Why?"

He ignored the niggling of his conscience and concentrated instead on ending this sordid charade right here and now. She already hated him for being a wastrel and a womanizer, and she'd only hate him more if she knew he was doing this just to win a bet and keep his horse.

He needed this over and done with. He set his jaw in resolve.

"I can see you're excited, Claire. Your breathing is quick and shallow. Your breasts are rising and falling, tempting me, making me wonder what it would be like to hold them in my hands, to wrap my lips around your luscious pink nipples and suck on them until you're squirming with pleasure."

He reached out and ran his index finger quickly down the column of her throat. "I can see the blood pounding right here in your enticing white neck at the thought of it. I'd love to kiss that perfect hollow there at the base of your throat, and slowly move my mouth down your alabaster skin, exploring every inch of your soft flesh."

He was trying to weave a sensual spell around her, to catch her so deeply with his words that she would be helpless with need and powerless to resist. Then he could finally throw her over the edge.

Placing both his hands on either side of her head, he leaned dangerously close, wanting her to feel the pure male heat of his body. She put her palms up to fend him off, but, unexpectedly, she didn't push him away. No. Instead, she ran her fingers almost greedily over the hard plane of his chest. He inhaled sharply in surprise, and when she raised her head, the look in her eyes stole the next words from his throat.

Bloody hell. She wanted this.

Prim and proper Claire Beringer wanted him.

It took all his willpower to hold himself still, when every cell in his body urged him to lean in closer and kiss her, to take her up on the longing reflected in her blue eyes.

But that was not part of the bet.

I can make a woman come using just my words.

His moment of enforced paralysis was all she needed to regain her virgin sensibilities. She blushed scarlet, dropped her hands from his chest as if he were the Devil himself, and slipped underneath his arms in a mad dash for the house.

Chapter 8

She wanted him.

Claire folded her arms stiffly across her chest and paced her room with her mind racing.

She wanted Damian Hunt. Despite the fact that he was a wastrel and a womanizer, a gambler and a lush, she wanted him. She wanted his hands on her body, his mouth on her skin, and, God help her, she even wanted his cock inside her.

The innocent crush of a twelve-year-old girl had turned into the not-so-innocent yearning of a fully grown woman, made all the more potent now that she knew just exactly how a woman wanted a man.

And all those things Damian had said to her in the garden? Yes, she wanted all that, as well.

...to hold your breasts in my hands, wrap my lips around your luscious pink nipples, explore every inch of your soft flesh....

Her body tingled at the thought of it. Ached with the need of it. Good lord, how much of this could a person take before she simply went up in flames?

"But what if it's a game he plays with every woman he meets? Woos her just to see how far she'll let him go?"

She couldn't bear to think that he was just after what he could get.

She bit her lip. It was true that Damian's words had been blatant and bald since she'd arrived, but when she'd looked up into his eyes in the garden, she could have sworn that she'd seen the set of his face change perceptibly. Shock, then realization, then a deep heat had chased themselves in his blue eyes as he'd recognized her feelings.

He wanted her, too.

But why such a surprised reaction, if seduction had been his plan all along?

Was there something else going on here? Perhaps. But for the moment, all she could seem to concentrate on was the idea of being seduced by Damian Hunt.

Would he want her on her hands and knees, like in one of the *Kama Sutra* drawings? Bent over backwards so he could have access to her breasts while impaling her with his cock? Legs draped over his shoulders so that she was powerless when he took her?

She fanned herself with her hand. "Dear lord, what *am* I thinking?"

There was no denying that Damian was pure temptation, sin packaged in a perfect male body, an expert seducer of women. He was acting as his nature—and his reputation—dictated. But why was she, Claire Beringer, a woman who'd rigidly held herself to such proper, virginal standards all her life, in danger of so easily disregarding her own nature now?

"Because he's opened a door inside me that refuses to be closed."

What was behind that door? The secrets of pleasure. She was as sure of that as she was sure of the knowing smiles on the faces of the women in the *Kama Sutra* drawings. But what did that pleasure feel like? She'd touched herself last night, but somehow she was sure it would feel completely different if it were Damian's hands that were doing the touching. With all his experience, he undoubtedly knew just where to kiss and caress to give a woman maximum pleasure.

And what was wrong with feeling pleasure? Nothing. As long as one was safely married to said pleasure-giver.

At least in respectable society.

The thought was like a bucket of cold water. A woman's virginity was the most valuable possession she could bring her husband. And even though Claire fully expected to end up an old maid, a woman's virginity was still a precious thing, especially to a proper, respectable lady. To even think of doing what she'd been thinking of doing was wickedness, sheer madness. She had to get away from this house, and away from the danger that Damian represented.

"Why hasn't George come to me yet?" She glanced at the clock on the mantle. It was almost noon. Surely her brother was awake by now!

Despite the rumbling of her stomach, she refused to go downstairs for luncheon, lest Damian tempt her again. An hour later, a low knock on her door brought her instantly across the room, but it wasn't George, it was only the butler Andrews with a lunch tray.

Nerves frayed almost to the breaking point, Claire ordered him to go find her brother and send him to her immediately.

The butler hesitated.

"Now, Andrews. This instant. I must see him."

The whinny of horses drew her attention to the bedroom window. With a sinking feeling, she quickly crossed the room and looked out. Damian and George, followed by a small retinue of grooms carrying shotguns, were heading off in the direction of a nearby wood with three hounds hot on their heels.

Damn her brother! All her life she'd had to cope with him thinking of her as a mere nuisance, but the one time she really, truly needed him, he chose sport over family duty.

She sighed resignedly. "Send Sarah to me, Andrews. I think I should like a bath."

Damian sat his horse, not paying much attention to the shouts of his men as they rousted birds or to the shotgun cradled loosely in his arm. He was still reeling from Claire's reaction this morning in the rose garden.

She wanted him.

The discovery somehow took a huge weight off his shoulders. He could urge her now to her sexual peak without such awful guilt.

"She sent me a frantic message through your butler," George was saying, eyeing the sky, waiting to take his shot. "Demanded that I come to her as soon as I woke. Imagine!"

Damian pulled himself out of his thoughts. "What?"

George took aim and fired, smirking even though he missed his target. "Accept it, old chap. You've lost the bet. Claire will no doubt insist we leave this house immediately. You've failed to thaw the block of ice that is my sister, as I knew you would."

Damian frowned. Claire wanted to leave? Immediately? No. He couldn't possibly have misread the signal in her eyes this morning. She wanted him. So why— wait a minute. Of course. She wanted him, but she was obviously afraid of wanting him.

As any proper virgin would be.

"I'd like to stop by your stables when we're through here," George added with a sly grin as he handed his shotgun down to a groom to be reloaded. "I want to look at my new horse."

Thunder. Damian cursed under his breath. This whole complicated mess had evolved because he didn't want to lose his precious horse. But somehow the animal was rapidly losing its value in his eyes. Especially when stacked up next to Claire.

"One more night, George."

"Pardon?"

"The weekend is not yet over. You owe me one more night."

"I know my sister, Damian. Another night isn't going to make any difference."

"I'll need you to keep to your room. Don't come down for supper. Let me have some time alone with her."

George raised an eyebrow. "What do you intend—"

"I intend to use nothing but my words. Exactly as we agreed. If she doesn't look like a woman by tomorrow morning, then I will gladly hand over my horse."

George considered for a moment, and then shrugged. "Very well. After all, I have no doubt you'll get nowhere with."

Damian set his jaw and signaled to his grooms. The men beat the bushes until they flushed out a covey of partridge. Ignoring the excited barking of the dogs, Damian raised his shotgun, took careful aim and fired.

There'd be fowl for supper tonight.

The afternoon bath helped take Claire's mind off her wait for George, but unfortunately it did nothing to take her mind off Damian. No. Once Claire was in the tub, all she could think about was Damian's hands on her bare flesh.

Alone in the room—and protected by the privacy screen the maid, Sarah, had set up—Claire laid her head back on the edge of the copper container and let her hand glide slowly down her body, imagining it was Damian's hand, his long, graceful fingers on her.

She remembered Damian's words from earlier in the garden. *Your breasts are tempting me, making me wonder what it would be like to hold them in my hands.*

She slipped a second hand into the water, and cupped one around each round globe of flesh, imagining Damian squeezing them gently. Mmm. That was nice, but she wanted more. What else had he said? *Wrap my lips around your luscious pink nipples and suck on them until you're writhing with pleasure.*

Yes. She wanted his mouth to tease her sensitive tips—right there—until she was squirming helplessly beneath his attention. Her nipples were hard just at the thought of what his mouth would feel like on them. How could he do that—excite her with just his words?

Slowly move my mouth down your alabaster skin, exploring every inch of your soft flesh.

She trailed her fingers farther down her body. The slickness of the water let her hands slide over her skin, easing the friction, but increasing the lubrication so that she could concentrate on the sensual feel of her fingertips on her bare flesh. She paused wherever the contact was particularly pleasurable—the sensitive area around her navel, the gentle curve of her waist—until she came to the juncture of her thighs.

Without hesitation this time, she pushed a finger through her tight curls and explored beneath. Would Damian touch her here before plunging his cock inside her? Just thinking of his hands—or, dear lord, his mouth—on her there made her body suddenly jerk beneath the water, almost as if it was attempting to get away from her own fingers.

The movement abruptly broke the sensuous spell she'd woven around herself. Her eyes flew open and she sat up straight in the tub, spilling water over the edges onto the wooden floor with the sudden change of position. Dear lord, what had possessed her since she'd come to this house? She'd turned into a shameless wanton. What was it about Damian Hunt that tempted her to throw her precious reputation right out the window? Damn the man. She had to see George. She had to leave here immediately.

She picked up the soap and gave herself a cursory scrubbing, rinsed briskly, and quickly toweled dry.

Sarah arrived a short time later to help her dress, and Claire purposely chose a high-collared, long-sleeved gown, hoping to gird herself physically as well as mentally. The neighing of horses signaled the men's return around four o'clock, and Claire resolved that if George didn't come to her before supper, she would go downstairs to find him.

After all, Damian wouldn't dare to speak to her like that with her brother present.

Damian could smell the mouth-watering aroma of partridge *en Chartreuse* even as he stood in the drawing room, pouring himself a drink. He hoped Claire would like it. Hell, he found himself hoping she liked everything connected to him lately. His library. His food. Him.

He made a disgusted sound and upended his scotch. Bah. She would never like him. Especially if he was successful in what he'd set out to do this weekend.

How pathetic was he?

Why didn't he just throw in the towel and give George his bloody horse? Wouldn't that be less painful than what he was doing—prolonging this awful bet, even when he knew how wrong, how outrageous his actions were?

He might actually have conceded, folded up his cards, if Claire had just looked at him in the rose garden this morning with a miserable, haunted or persecuted look in her eye. That might have been the final straw that caused him to break. But she hadn't. She'd looked at him as if she'd wanted him. And, God help him, he certainly wanted her. So he'd resolved to put her out of her sexual misery in a way that would give her pleasure. Actually, he had always intended to give her pleasure, but now it would give him pleasure to give her pleasure, knowing how much she wanted that pleasure.

Bloody hell, was he really trying to rationalize this?

He dragged an unsteady hand through his hair and poured himself another scotch.

It was probably too much to hope that Claire would come down in time for a drink before dinner. He wanted to get his final plan started as soon as possible, but she would likely delay as long as possible before realizing that George had no intention of visiting her room. Only then would she come downstairs to seek him.

Which gave Damian plenty of time to drink.

To buck up his courage. Or drown his doubts.

However this little drama turned out, it would all be over with by tomorrow. After this weekend, he could go back to his aimless, carefree existence, unfettered by any moral qualms. Back to his familiar routine, where he knew the rules of the game, and any woman he met knew the rules of a relationship with him.

It was what he wanted. Much easier that way. So why did he feel as if he'd always have a black mark on his soul after today?

He sighed, reaching for the crystal decanter again. There were times, and this was definitely one of them, when he wished he didn't hold his liquor as well as he did. He would dearly love to be able to feel the potent alcohol relax his tense body.

He wondered if it might help to forgo a glass altogether.

Chapter 9

"Where is my brother?"

Damian looked up from his meal to see Claire standing in the dining room doorway. As he'd expected, he was nearly done with his partridge before she'd finally broken down and come in search of George. The delicious meal he'd hoped to share with her had tasted more like lumps of coal, his tension growing the longer he had to wait to start this end game. In fact, he'd only been able to wash the meal down with his best port.

Yes, forget about mere wine, he'd gone straight for the hard stuff, as he had in the drawing room.

He'd been playing nervously with the stem of his glass, his mind going back and forth between possibilities. She was going to come. She wasn't going to come. She had to come or else she'd starve to death.

Bloody hell, he wanted this damn bet over with once and for all.

"I said, where is George?"

He stared at her now, standing rigid there in the doorway. Despite her ramrod posture and that repressively awful dress she was wearing, she looked beautiful.

Dear lord, did that mean the alcohol was finally working on him? No, his observation wasn't liquor-induced, she really *was* beautiful. He couldn't tear his eyes away from her.

She, on the other hand, wasn't looking at him at all. Her gaze, curiously enough, seemed locked on his left hand, on the fingers running up and down the stem of his glass. He saw her swallow hard. What could that mean?

He cleared his throat.

"Claire, please sit down." He gestured to the empty chair on his right. "I hope you like partridge. Cook makes a wonderful pastry pie of it with carrots, onions, sausages and cloves. Delicious for a cold winter's day."

Good God, he was blathering, and not for the first time with her. This same thing had happened last night when he'd seen her in his drawing room. Usually he was a smooth-tongued devil with the ladies, even beautiful ones. Why then did Claire so frequently make him tongue-tied?

Stop thinking about your tongue *in connection with her!*

"Where is George, my lord?"

He winced at her use of his formal title. She had obviously retreated behind her prim and proper façade. First her dress, and now this. It must mean she'd truly been frightened by her feelings this morning in the garden.

His job tonight would be all the harder because of it.

"I'll tell you about George if you'll join me at the table."

If possible, her posture became even more rigid. "If he isn't here, he must be in his room. I'll just go upstairs and—"

"Claire. Sit. I promise I won't bite." A slow smile pulled at his lips, and he lowered his voice. "Unless, of course, you want me to. Did you happen to read the *Kama Sutra* section on love bites?"

She blushed scarlet, a color which Damian thought was very becoming on her. He'd stake his left ear that she hadn't read that particular part of the book, but before she could gather her wits and come up with some outraged virginal retort, he shouted for his butler.

"Andrews!"

He appeared behind Claire's right shoulder. "Yes, sir?"

"A plate for Miss Beringer."

"Certainly, sir."

As soon as he'd gone, Damian motioned to Claire. "George gave me a message for you. Sit down and I'll tell you."

"I can't."

Damian cocked an eyebrow. "Why not?"

"I can't be alone with you."

"Don't trust yourself?"

She turned that deep red color again, and Damian silently rejoiced. She did still want him, but was struggling valiantly to resist. He hoped the wall she was trying to build between them was not yet set in stone.

"Don't be absurd," she insisted, her voice a little breathless. "It simply isn't proper."

"Cook tells me you barely touched your ham at lunch, and I could hazard a fairly accurate guess that you didn't get down much of your breakfast either. You must be starving. This is one of her best recipes. Sit. Please."

Claire refused to budge from the doorway. "What message did George have for me?"

Damian sighed loudly and pushed away his plate. "He's feeling unwell. Might have caught a chill while we were out shooting this afternoon. He's decided to keep to his room tonight, but wanted you to know that the two of you will be leaving after breakfast tomorrow morning."

The relief was evident in her eyes. "We'll be leaving? Tomorrow?"

Damian nodded. "Yes. Now come. Sit with me."

Andrews returned with a steaming plate, and laid it at the empty place next to Damian at the table. Damian rose and held out Claire's chair.

"You don't want to insult my cook now, do you? Especially since you've been making her do double duty as your personal lady's maid."

He saw her blink slowly, as if digesting his words, but her eyes were now focused for some reason on his mouth. She inhaled deeply, and Damian decided it must be the delicious aroma of the partridge calling to her. A moment later she sighed and pushed herself off the doorframe, took two steps into the room, and sat.

"That's better." He reseated himself. This scene was an eerie replay of breakfast, but he had high hopes that this meal would turn out differently than that one. He poured her a small glass of port. "Now, I know you don't drink, but you might feel a bit more relaxed if you tried some of this."

He prepared himself for a stern lecture on the evils of alcohol, but she silently lifted the glass and swallowed the liquid in its entirety.

Damian's eyebrows shot to his hairline. He expected her to cough and sputter, and then to roundly curse him. Instead, her eyes watered and her mouth fell open as she struggled to catch her breath, but not one word of reprimand passed her luscious lips.

What the hell was going on here?

Wait. She stared at my fingers, then at my mouth. She drank my port, despite all her lofty principles.

Bloody hell, she was his! Suddenly he knew it as certainly as if he'd witnessed Thunder cross the finish line at Ascot. Despite that high-necked, long-sleeved gown, despite her formal use of his title, she was signaling her consent. He had her within his grasp.

Something shifted in his chest.

"Claire," he breathed. "Beautiful Claire."

She blinked rapidly to clear the water from her eyes. "Don't call me that." Her voice came out low, raspy, not yet recovered from the shock of the wine.

Damian thought it the sexiest sound he'd ever heard.

"Why not?" he murmured, reaching out to run his index finger gently down the side of her face. "You are beautiful. I told you so last night."

"You say that to every woman."

He chuckled. "You may think so, but I assure you I do not. And anyway, didn't we agree yesterday to be perfectly honest with each other?"

She looked away, but nodded.

"Come. Eat something. Or else the wine will go straight to your head."

She picked up her fork and toyed with the partridge pie, while he refilled his glass, and then refilled hers as well. What the hell? If she deigned to have another glass, it would only help his case. Make her relax a bit.

As small talk might.

He put down the decanter and cleared his throat. "I was remiss this morning in not asking how you liked your room. I hope you found everything to your satisfaction?"

She pushed a potato around her plate. "The room is lovely."

"You weren't uncomfortable then?"

She took a breath. "Of *course* I was uncomfortable. It's a very improper arrangement. Why did you put me there, Damian?"

Ah. Her honest reply. But at least she was back to using his Christian name. That was progress.

"Why?" He shrugged. "Because it's the best room in the house. A lady's room."

"Is that an honest answer?"

A small smile tugged at the corners of his mouth. "Partly. I also hoped being so close might make you think of me while you slept. It certainly made me dream about *you*. Very pleasant dreams."

She squirmed on her seat and kept her eyes on her food. "Did you dream about me in one of the *Kama Sutra* positions?"

He threw back his head and laughed. This honesty business was bringing out a remarkable side of Claire. Was she truly asking him if he'd made love to her in his dreams?

"I dreamt about you in *several* of the *Kama Sutra* positions, if you must know the truth. Plus a few more that I made up myself."

She inhaled sharply, but still refused to look at him. "Have you—have you ever had six women at once?"

Damian's mouth fell open. "What? Heavens, no! I admit I have a certain reputation, but even *you* can't think me as wicked as that." He reached over and put his index finger underneath her chin, bringing her head up so he could meet her eyes. "One woman at a time is my limit, Claire. And my preference."

She frowned. "Then why did you say that was your favorite drawing? Why do you envy Captain Burton, if it's not for his sexual exploits?"

A small tic worked in Damian's jaw. Claire could have no idea what she'd just asked him, how her question went to the very heart of who he was as a man. Bloody hell, it turned out he'd opened up a can of worms with this honesty thing.

He reached for his port and drained the glass. The alcohol burned his throat but offered him no reprieve. She was looking at him expectantly, waiting for his answer.

He shifted uncomfortably on his chair. "Claire...."

She obviously realized she'd hit a nerve. "The truth, Damian."

He stared into her eyes. He'd wronged her this weekend—deliberately set out to corrupt an innocent, and he still wasn't done with her yet—so perhaps it was only fair that he strip himself naked, emotionally at least, for her. An odd sort of quid pro quo. But strangely enough, he found he wanted to answer her question. Wanted to make this confession, and wanted to make it to her.

He didn't let himself dwell on why he wanted her to think better of him than she obviously did.

"I'll tell you," he agreed, "if you promise to answer an equally personal question for me."

She hesitated, and then nodded.

Damian ran a hand through his hair. "Very well. First of all, rest assured I believe that picture is mere fantasy. Wishful thinking. I've never personally met a man who's had six women at once.

"Second, Captain Burton was translating an ancient text. He did not personally experience all those positions. Well, at least I don't think he did.

"But to answer your question about why I envy him...." He shifted in his chair. "That's a bit more difficult. I know that the world sees me as a ne'er-do-well, and, in truth, I suppose I am. But that's not the real me, or at least that's not the man I'd hoped to be. I pass my time with women and cards and alcohol because—well, frankly it's because there's nothing else to occupy my time."

"What?"

"It's the truth. All my life I've felt trapped by my title, my station in life. I'm not allowed to work. I'm not allowed to join the army. I'm the sole male Atherton heir, and my father very early on made it clear that I represent the only legitimate continuation of the Hunt bloodline. You have no idea how that responsibility weighs on me, Claire."

He blew out a frustrated breath. "I admire Captain Burton because I'd much rather be off exploring some exotic part of the world than constantly having to think about my own safety and my duty to the future of my family title. Instead of living,

I have to read about life through my books, experiencing the world second-hand, as it were. I've never even been outside England's borders. You can't know how frustrating that is, how maddening to be idle, when I'd much rather be active, out there meeting life head-on."

He shook his head. "It sounds rather pathetic, doesn't it? *I* sound pathetic. You probably think I should be counting my blessings instead of cursing my fate."

He waited for her reaction, but rather than the look of disgust he expected to see on her face, he saw one of profound relief. Her brow uncreased, her frown eased, and a certain peace seemed to settle over her features. Now what on earth accounted for that?

Well, at least she wasn't castigating him. Relieved, he leaned back in his chair. "You're the only person I've ever admitted that to. Not even George knows as much about me."

"Then I thank you for your trust," Claire said quietly. "But why haven't you married? If you were to wed and produce an heir or two, you could then devote your life to all those things you long for."

"Bloody hell, you do go right to the heart of the matter, don't you?" Damian grimaced. "The honest answer is that I haven't found the right woman yet. And I'm not about to let my father, or anyone else, tell me who to wed."

Now that his confession was made, Damian felt suddenly awkward. Emotionally exposed. Vulnerable. He cleared his throat and sat up straight in his chair.

"Now," he said briskly. "It's my turn to ask a question. And remember, you promised me an honest answer."

Claire folded her hands carefully on the table, and seemed to hold her breath.

Damian looked deeply into her eyes, and gave her his most seductive smile. "Do you want me, Claire?"

She couldn't possibly mistake his meaning, especially since she'd had almost twenty-four hours with the *Kama Sutra*.

Damian watched as she froze in place like a scared rabbit, trembling slightly, fear in her eyes. But then her face underwent a remarkable transformation. Her initial fear was replaced by a fierce look of longing, followed quickly by a frantic look of shame. Her gaze dropped from his eyes to his mouth, then to his hands, and back up to his eyes again.

"Yes," she whispered, then gasped. "I mean, no! I can't possibly. No. Oh, God, Damian. Yes. The honest answer is yes." She buried her head in her hands.

Despite the fact he'd already known how she felt, hearing the words out loud sent a hot rush of blood to his head—and his groin. His cock tightened instantly.

Your cock is not part of the bet!

He set his jaw. He had to stick to his plan, even if this ache in his body wished otherwise.

"Sweet Claire," he murmured, reaching out to pull her hands gently away from her face. "I know exactly what you're feeling. This longing, this restlessness inside you is sexual tension. I can help you. I can ease this tautness."

A look of profound despair came over her face. "You can't help me. You'll only ruin me!"

"No, no." He squeezed her hands reassuringly. "I won't ruin you. There's a way to give you release that will leave your virginity intact. I won't touch you. I swear it. I'll do it with words."

"I—I don't understand."

"I'll teach you. Please, Claire, let me help you."

She stared at him for an endless minute before she opened her mouth to answer.

Damian held his breath. The entire bet hung on her next words. Bloody hell, he could care less about the damn bet—he felt like his entire existence hung on her next words. He wanted her more desperately than he could ever remember wanting a woman in his life. Even if his role was to be no more than verbal.

"All right," she breathed.

The sharp jolt of relief and heady excitement that shot through his body was almost akin to a sexual climax, so strong it threatened to knock him right off his chair. He had to get a grip on himself.

"Good." He swallowed hard and fought to steady his voice. "Now, I want you to go upstairs and undress slowly. I want you to imagine that it's *me* removing each piece of clothing, teasing it from your body, until you're completely naked and ready for me. Then I want you to put on your robe, lie on your bed, and wait for me. I'll give you fifteen minutes before I come upstairs."

"Damian—"

"Hush, Claire. Don't be afraid. I'll come to you through our connecting door. No one will see us. No one will ever know about this. I promise."

Chapter 10

Claire barely made it up the stairs to her room.

Good lord, what had she just agreed to? To let Damian teach her the secrets of pleasure. If she stopped to think about the consequences of that decision, she'd lose her nerve entirely.

No. She wouldn't back out. She wanted this, and she wanted Damian.

What a revelation it had been downstairs to discover that Damian Hunt wasn't a wastrel after all. He was just a man trapped in a position of responsibility who was passing time in perhaps not the best or most constructive way. She might pity him for that, but at heart he was not the scoundrel she'd originally thought him to be.

All her defenses had dissolved at his surprising disclosure, and now the only thing left was her desire for him.

I want you to undress slowly.

Her unsteady fingers flew to the top of her high-necked gown before she forced herself to calm down, to take her time with the buttons there. Slowly. He'd said to undress slowly.

She took another deep breath, then another, until her racing heart slowed. She purposely unbuttoned each fastening, focusing on revealing her body inch by deliberate inch, opening her gown to the waist. Opening herself. Yes. She was literally and figuratively opening herself to this experience.

Imagine that it's me removing each piece of your clothing...

She closed her eyes and slowly slipped the dress off her shoulders, then slid her arms out of the sleeves, all the while imagining Damian's fingers urging the material down.

...teasing it from your body...

She slid the dress past her waist, and then her hips, until it fell in a puddle onto the floor.

...until you're completely naked.

Damian wanted her naked. But of course he would. Most of those women in the *Kama Sutra* drawings were naked. It was obviously the way these things were done.

Still, she was surprised at how much *she* wanted to be naked.

For him.

Her fingers went to work on her undergarments.

Good lord, it had been sheer torture in the dining room to watch his fingers running up and down the stem of his wine glass and imaging them running over her body, to watch his mouth while she longed for those lips on her bare skin.

She trembled as her hands glided over every bit of skin she revealed. Would

Damian's fingers feel this soft, or would his masculine hands be rough against the smooth skin of her body? Oh, how she longed to find out!

She desperately wanted to put an end to this restlessness, this frustrating tension she felt deep inside. And she knew instinctively that Damian was the only one who could do it. She wanted him. She wanted him despite the fact that wanting him would ruin her.

There's a way to give you release that will leave your virginity intact. I'll do it with words.

Yes, she could well believe it. After desiring him for nine years, she could easily imagine all she'd need was the sound of his deep, rich, honeyed voice speaking illicit words of passion to send her into a glorious swoon. Just look what he'd already done to her! This breathlessness, the racing pulse, the pounding heart.

Before she realized it, the rest of her clothes lay in a pile around her ankles. She stood perfectly naked, every inch of her skin tingling with anticipation, every nerve ending awake and alive, her body singing with an acute awareness she'd never felt before.

And with it came a moment of panic. What was she thinking? If she and Damian took this step, she'd be changed forever, no longer the pure maiden, no longer a woman above reproach.

This might be her only chance to experience the ways of a man and woman. And to experience it with the very man she would choose.

Resolutely, she stepped out of the discarded heap of clothes and crossed the room to the wardrobe to fetch her robe. She slipped it on and tightened the sash, glancing at the clock on the mantle. How much time had passed since she'd left Damian?

I'll give you fifteen minutes before I come upstairs.

In a rush, she scooped her clothes from the floor and shoved them into the bottom of the wardrobe, closing the door. She listened intently for any sound of Damian next door in his bedroom, but all was quiet.

Lie on your bed and wait for me.

Despite her resolve, her breath caught in her throat. Dear lord, this was really going to happen.

He had to stop drinking.

Damian forced his hand away from the decanter of port, and pushed his chair back from the table. He'd lost count of how many glasses he'd had since Claire had rushed upstairs.

Bloody hell, he'd been trying to drown out one particular part of his conversation with her. *I'm not the man I'd hoped to be....*

The discussion over supper had been a painful reminder of exactly how much Damian disliked himself. Disliked his life, his reputation, even his character. It was a subject he tried assiduously to avoid, but tonight Claire had forced him to brutally face it.

How had he sunk so low, become a man like this? As soon as this weekend was over, he was going to change his ways and start taking some responsibility for his aimless, hollow life. It was well past time he did.

In fact, if he was any kind of man at all, he'd forget this awful bet and let Claire

Beringer leave here exactly as she'd arrived—an innocent virgin.

No, no, you don't really want that.

No. Unfortunately, he wasn't that strong.

His groin tightened painfully. She was upstairs right now, removing her clothes, imagining his hands teasing them off her body. He inhaled sharply at the erotic images that flooded his mind. Claire slowly exposing her lush breasts, Claire shyly revealing her feminine quim. Dear lord, she thought she was feeling frustrated this weekend? She had no idea what it was like for him! And worse—if he went through with this bet, he would make absolutely certain she was satisfied, while having no satisfaction himself.

Served him right for agreeing to this outrageous wager.

He groaned.

There was no way out of this except to finish what he'd started. It's what he wanted. It's what she wanted. Besides, she wasn't nearly as innocent as she'd been when she'd arrived. He'd seen to that with his campaign of the *Kama Sutra.*

Do you want me, Claire?

Oh, God, Damian. Yes.

Her words had ricocheted through his body to light up every nerve ending in his skin. Insuring her sexual release would be his pleasure as well as his punishment.

Bloody hell, how much time had passed since she'd gone upstairs? Was it fifteen minutes already? He pulled the watch from his waistcoat pocket. It didn't matter what the time read, he couldn't wait any longer.

"Andrews!"

The butler immediately appeared in the doorway. "Yes, sir?"

"I'm retiring early. Make sure none of the staff bothers me—or Miss Beringer— tonight."

"Yes, sir."

He had to force himself not to take the stairs two at a time, but it was hard when he knew what a prize was waiting for him upstairs. He forced his feet to walk past Claire's bedroom door, resisting the temptation to barge right in and get started.

"Bloody hell." He pulled at his cravat to give himself some breathing room, and reluctantly took the final few steps to his own door.

His valet was waiting to undress him.

"Just my jacket and waistcoat, Jenkins," he said, handing the valet his cravat, and thinking up a quick lie. "I'm going to stay up and read for a—"

Wait a minute. He had intended to visit Claire in his shirt and trousers, but why not meet her on her own terms, naked except for his dressing gown? If he was destined to remain celibate tonight, at least he could have the vicarious thrill of being naked with her.

Even if they would be yards apart.

How ironic that the notorious womanizer Damian Hunt was determined to take no pleasure in his womanizing tonight.

He shook his head in amazement. Claire Beringer had affected him more in two days than any woman had in the last two decades.

He didn't know quite what to make of that.

Claire lay still as a statue on top of her bedspread. The low voices and movement next door clearly told her that Damian had come upstairs.

A shiver of anticipation raced through her body.

Tonight, this gnawing restlessness inside her would be quelled. Tonight the secrets of man and woman would be revealed.

Well, she supposed she already knew what those secrets were by her perusal of the *Kama Sutra*, but tonight she would know how the experience felt.

She squeezed her legs tightly together in anticipation.

She was still at a loss as to how Damian was planning to ease this ache inside her using words. The drawings in the *Kama Sutra* clearly showed that during sexual congress the man and woman had to be together in some fashion. His cock inside her. His mouth on her quim. His fingers playing with her.

Damian's room was quiet now. In fact, all she could hear was the crackling of the fire in her grate. How long would it be before that connecting door opened, and her life would change forever?

Good lord, her skin felt as if it were on fire. Her hands fisted at her sides with restless anticipation, and her head ground back into her pillow.

The soft *click* of a latch suddenly commanded all her attention. Her gaze flew to the door as it opened, and Damian, clad in a silky blue dressing gown, stepped through it.

She gasped. Dear lord, was he naked beneath his robe, as she was? The thought of Damian's bare body so close by—her fantasies made flesh, literally—wrenched a small moan of longing from her lips.

"Claire."

He crossed the room slowly and came to stand by the side of her bed. He was even more gorgeous in the firelight, with the warm glow of the flames highlighting the outline of his impressive body and his perfect face.

"Beautiful Claire."

She shivered beneath his intense stare, but there was nowhere else she'd rather be than right here with him at the receiving end of his rapt attention.

He smiled at her, that heart-stopping smile she remembered from when she was twelve. The one she'd fallen in love with.

"Are you ready?"

She swallowed hard, then nodded.

His gaze swung away from her suddenly, searching the room. He took three steps toward the copper tub that was still nearby from this afternoon's bath. He walked past it, but stopped next to the privacy screen. Gathering it up in his arms, he brought it back and set it up about six feet from the side of her bed, then turned back to her.

She looked at him curiously. "What—?"

"Hush, Claire, let me explain. Now, did you do as I asked earlier? Did you think of me as you were undressing, imagine it was me removing your clothing?"

She could feel herself blush, but hoped he couldn't see it in the shadowy light of the room. "Yes."

"And did it excite you?"

She inhaled sharply. "Yes."

"Good. This time, I want you to listen to my words, concentrate on the sound of my voice, and do exactly as I say. I want you to imagine that my voice is my mouth, my fingers. My voice will caress you exactly as I desperately long to do, and your own hands will be my instrument."

She frowned, not understanding.

"I'm going to stand behind that screen and make love to you with my words, while you make love to yourself with your hands. You will have complete privacy. And total control over your body. I will tell you what to do, and you will do it."

She gasped as his meaning suddenly became clear. Damian was going to tell her how to touch herself? And stand behind that screen while she was doing it?

He held up a hand to stop any protest.

"Do this, my sweet, and I promise you an end to this burning restlessness you feel, an amazing climax that you can't even begin to imagine. Do you trust me, Claire?"

She stared into Damian's glittering blue eyes, clear now with something akin to stark honesty. She did trust him. Whatever his original reason had been for giving her the *Kama Sutra* and bringing her to this agitated physical state, she trusted him now to take gentle good care of her.

A feeling of rightness descended on her, and she nodded.

He let out his breath in a rush, as if he'd been holding it. How remarkable. Had he honestly thought she'd deny him what she herself most desired?

"Claire." His voice was rough with an emotion she couldn't interpret. "You are the most extraordinary woman I have ever met. I swear I will make this good for you."

He moved behind the privacy screen.

Claire took a steadying breath, preparing herself, waiting for his next words.

"Close your eyes, sweetheart. Then take your right hand and bring it to your face."

Dear lord, this was it. There'd be no turning back now, not that she wanted to turn back. She wanted Damian. She wanted *this*. Her heart started to race with anticipation as her eyes drifted closed and her hand moved to her face.

"Now slide your fingertips lightly from your forehead down your nose... across to your cheek... and over to your mouth. Think about how that feathery sensation feels on your smooth skin. Imagine those are my fingers running over you, exploring your perfect face, imprinting your skin with my touch."

Claire did as he said, visualizing Damian's long, graceful fingers gliding over her features, claiming her—at least for tonight—as his own. It was a lovely fantasy. A small sigh escaped her lips.

"That's right, beautiful Claire. Enjoy it. Tonight is all about feeling, sensation, and your pleasure. Now open your luscious lips and put two fingers into your mouth. Imagine they're my fingers. Suck on them gently. Make me wet with your tongue."

Such decadent, scandalous words. Claire's hand shook slightly as she slipped her index and middle fingers into her mouth. She sucked on them shyly at first, and then rolled her tongue around them, surprisingly fascinated by the soft yet scratchy sensation of her rough tongue on her smooth skin. Would Damian's fingers be this smooth in her mouth? What would they taste like?

"Mmm."

"Good," he approved from behind the screen. "Now move those fingers slowly down the graceful column of your neck. Imagine it's my mouth there, trailing a path of kisses along your enticing throat, pausing at the sensitive hollow near your collarbone to tease you with my tongue. Leave a trace of wetness to show where I've been, Claire. To mark my territory."

"Yes." Her body was his territory. He was claiming her. Claire shivered in delight as she slid her wet fingers down the path Damian described, lingering for a moment at the indentation at the base of her throat. Ooh, that was nice. She never realized how sensitive that spot was. In her mind's eye, she could almost picture Damian's mouth here.

"Now I want you to continue to slide your hand down farther, across your chest. Slip it beneath your robe to your breast, and rest just the tip of your index finger on your nipple."

Claire's eyes flew open at that bald suggestion, her startled gaze going to the privacy screen. There was no sign of Damian—he was well hidden behind it. She swallowed hard. She'd enjoyed this game so far, but now they were getting into dangerous territory. First her breasts, and then it would surely be her—

"Damian—"

As if he knew she needed reassurance, his voice floated over the screen, low and encouraging. "Don't think, Claire. Only *feel*. Feel how wonderful these sensations are."

She forced her head back down onto the pillow. Of course she'd known that her entire body would be involved in this lesson. It was only logical, given what she'd seen in the *Kama Sutra*. But emotionally it was another matter entirely. Especially with Damian so close by.

Do you trust me, Claire?

Yes.

"Wet your fingers again," he commanded quietly. "Then bring one fingertip to your nipple."

"All right." Taking a deep breath, she closed her eyes and followed his instructions.

"Good," he said after a moment, as if he could see she'd done it. "I want you to lightly rub your fingertip back and forth across the tip until that precious peak rises up and shows you exactly how much it likes what we're doing to it."

Claire slowly drew her finger back and forth, sliding easily because of the wetness of her fingertip. She felt her nipple growing tauter with each stroke, becoming incredibly sensitive to her touch. She moaned, low.

She heard Damian's answering groan from behind the screen. "Beautiful Claire. You're so honest in your response, so expressive. I want to hear exactly how you're feeling. Talk to me. Don't hold back. It makes me want to please you even more."

Claire's finger paused on her nipple. Damian liked to hear what she was feeling? A thrilling little shiver raced through her body. This experience was turning out to be verbal as well as physical.

She heard Damian take a breath. "Try capturing your nipple between your two fingers, like a scissor, and squeezing gently."

She did. That sensation was even nicer than her fingertip. "Ooh..."

"Now take your fingernail and flick it across your taut tip."

Without hesitation, Claire raked both her fingernails across her tight nipple, inhaling sharply at the strong jolt of pleasure. Good lord, that was so much better than what she'd done to herself last night, or even this afternoon in her bath.

"A woman's breast is one of the most sensitive parts of her body, Claire,"

Damian murmured. "I could worship at your breasts for hours, showing you all the ways I could pleasure you. With my tongue. With my lips. With my teeth. I'm fantasizing about your breasts right now, sweetheart. Would they be a perfect fit for my hands, I wonder? Or would that luscious flesh spill over my fingers, giving me even more of you to enjoy?"

Claire dreamily moved her hand to cup her breast, imagining Damian's hand there. "Would my size please you?"

"You're perfect," he assured her. "I'd tease your breasts until you begged me for more. And then I'd gladly give you more. I'd slowly move my fingers lower, down your stomach, around to the curve of your waist, following the feminine flare of your hip, and finally to your very woman's center at the junction of your thighs. Go on, Claire. Your hand is my hand. Let me feel you."

Damian's voice was like a drug. The more he spoke, the more she wanted him to speak. He was weaving a sensual spell around the two of them so that nothing existed for her beyond the sound of his words. Hypnotic, intoxicating, his deep, rich voice urged her on. She let her fingers trace a path that followed his verbal fantasy, finally coming to rest on her tight curls.

Where the reality of her nakedness once again made her eyes snap open and her gaze fly to the privacy screen.

She heard a quick rustle of movement there, but Damian was obviously still hidden safely behind it.

"Claire," he said quickly. "I want you to sit up slightly on your bed, propping your back against the headboard."

She frowned.

"Do it," he urged. "Just recline slightly against the headboard. You'll understand why in a moment."

"All right." Puzzled by the command, she inched slightly up the bed and propped herself into a reclining position against the headboard.

"Good." Damian paused for a moment. "Now bring your hand back to your luscious quim."

Claire felt herself blush, but she closed her eyes and dutifully brought her right hand back to rest on her tight curls.

"With your left hand, I want you to spread your feminine lips apart."

She swallowed hard, but did as he asked, realizing now why he'd asked her to move. She had easier access to herself in this position.

"Now, a man knows a woman is ready for him when she becomes wet. Stroke yourself, Claire. Are you wet for me?"

Claire's head arched back against the headboard in embarrassment, even as her finger explored her soft feminine flesh. Good lord, she *was* wet. Wetter even than she'd been in the bath water. But this was a different kind of wetness. More slick and slippery than damp.

"Claire. Are you wet for me?"

Damian's heated demand made her squeeze her eyes even more tightly closed, but she couldn't deny her body's response to him. "Yes."

Damian inhaled sharply. "Beautiful Claire. A man uses a woman's wetness to help slide his cock inside her. Let your fingers be my cock, sweetheart. Slide those two fingers deep inside you and tell me how it feels. Tell me how I feel inside you."

Damian inside her. His cock impaling her. The vivid image stole Claire's breath, and she spread her legs wide, plunging two fingers inside herself. She knew she ought to be mortified at her wanton action, but it was impossible. This felt too good. And she knew in her heart that Damian's cock would feel even better, especially if it sank deep inside her like this.

She moaned loudly at the self invasion, and added a third finger, sliding in and out. But it wasn't enough, not nearly enough, when what she really wanted was Damian filling her.

She let out a frustrated sound.

"Easy, Claire, easy," Damian soothed. "Listen to me. I'm going to make you come. I'm going to give your body the release it craves. Just listen to my words and feel what I say. Your body will do the rest. Now with your thumb, find the little button above the entrance to your body where your fingers are."

Claire rooted around her soft folds with her thumb, and inhaled sharply when she brushed across the nub of flesh that Damian must have been referring to. He obviously heard her cry of discovery.

"Good girl. Now with your fingers still inside you, curl them until you can rub up against the inside of your body."

Claire frowned, but curled her fingers in a come here gesture until she could touch herself from the inside. Ooh, what was this spot? It felt so incredibly sensitive!

"Now I want you to concentrate. I want you to move your fingers and your thumb and your body until those three sensations are all you can feel, all you can focus on. Until there's nothing else in the world but what's happening between your legs. Keep moving until it feels so good that you think you can't stand it anymore. And then keep going. Keep going until your body breaks from the sheer pleasure of it. I want you to come, Claire. Your pleasure will be my pleasure. Let me make you come."

Ah, his words again. Such suggestive, sensual words. Claire could feel herself fall under the spell of them, and she began to move her hand and her body, rocking on the bed, setting a pace that was all pleasure.

"You have total control over your body."

She heard Damian's low commentary now in the background, urging her to imagine he was inside her, his cock driving into her, his body sending her toward some peak she needed to reach. Yes, that's what she wanted. Damian's cock impaling her body, spearing her soul, piercing her core. She wanted them together, naked, in every position of the *Kama Sutra*. Her hand continued to move as she felt her pleasure build. It was him. He was inside her. He was doing this to her. They were making love. Lord, it felt so good she could barely breathe.

"Come for me, Claire."

"Oh, oh, oh—Damian!"

She screamed as something shattered deep inside her, her body contracting violently around her fingers, the pleasure almost doubling her over on the bed. Spasms of sensation jerked her body again and again, wave after wave of pleasure, until she was drained, exhausted, and utterly breathless. And through her haze of wondrous awe, she heard Damian's low whisper.

"Well done, sweetheart."

Chapter 11

Damian clenched his hands into fists so tightly that his fingers threatened to gouge holes in his palms.

The pain was the only thing keeping him from climaxing right here and now behind Claire's privacy screen.

Private, my ass.

Damian had purposely set up the screen so that the fold in the two panels had let him enjoy a wickedly licentious view of everything Claire had done to herself. But he'd been suitably punished for his sin, because the sight of her in the throes of ecstasy while he'd been forced to stay behind this screen had nearly driven him insane.

Bloody hell, his cock was straining so hard right now that one touch from his own hand would have sent him right over the edge.

No, no, this is about her pleasure. Mine must wait until I'm alone in my bedroom.

He took a deep breath, then another. Christ almighty, had he ever met a woman as innately passionate as Claire Beringer? As tactile, as physical, as sensually adventurous? He couldn't name one jaded woman of his acquaintance who could hold a candle to Claire's innocent ardor. And the most amazing thing of all was that she didn't even realize it.

He could still hear her moaning now with the remnants of her pleasure, her breathing rough and ragged. Those satisfied sounds made his cock jerk, demanding release, but he purposely ignored it. Gritting his teeth and gathering his control, he stepped from behind the screen and slowly made his way to her bedside.

She was tangled in her robe, her hair askew, limp as a rag doll. She looked a mess, but a very satisfied mess.

"Claire." He reached out a hand to gently brush a stray lock of hair off her face. "You were magnificent. Tell me, did that please you? Are you feeling a bit more relaxed now?"

She blushed scarlet, but a shy smile tugged at her lips.

Damian's heart did a strange flip in his chest. Bloody hell, he hadn't seen that smile on Claire's face since—when? He searched his memory. Since she was twelve years old. Since he'd teased her as a child or complimented her in order to put that smile there. Christ, he hadn't realized until just this instant that she hadn't smiled—not once—this entire weekend. Did her prim and proper lifestyle so rarely give her reason to?

What a tragedy that would be.

"You have a beautiful smile." He dragged his index finger lightly across her lips.

Before he realized it, she'd opened those full lips and sucked his finger inside her mouth to run her tongue over it.

His cock responded with a corresponding jolt of pleasure, as if her mouth were wrapped around him there. He gasped out loud and pulled his finger away. "Claire."

"I want you, Damian."

He sucked in a breath. "No, no. You don't know what you're saying. You wanted a release from your frustration, that's all. I gave you that."

"I know exactly what I'm saying," she insisted quietly. "I want us to be like those people in the *Kama Sutra*. I want to know what that feels like."

Bloody hell. Visions of making sweet love with Claire swam before his eyes, but he forced himself to shake his head.

"No. I promised that you'd still be a virgin after this. Let me do at least one noble thing in my life, sweetheart."

In response, her right hand moved deliberately to the tie of her robe. She loosened the sash, and her hands spread the material wide, exposing all of her luscious flesh to his view.

"Claire!" Despite his resolve—and certainly against his better judgment—Damian's gaze devoured her body. Christ, she was even more alluring up close. Her pert breasts were topped with tempting pink nipples, her narrow waist perfectly complemented her curvaceous hips, and the tops of her creamy white thighs framed her lush woman's center. He drank in every inch of her, from tip to toes. Short of plucking out his eyes, there was no way he was going to deny himself this incredible sight.

"Touch me, Damian."

He swallowed hard and clenched his hands into fists by his sides.

"Please," she begged. "If we're not going to have sexual congress -"

"—make love," he insisted, his gaze flying to her face. "If we ever did this, it would be making love, Claire. Believe me, no one could ever do anything less with you, sweetheart."

"Yes. I want that. I want to make love with you, Damian."

He gritted his teeth, and sent her a pleading look. "I can't. No. Don't tempt me like this, Claire. I'm only a man. As God is my witness, I want you more than my next breath, but I'm trying to protect you here!"

She stared at him for a long moment, an indecipherable look in her eye. "Then just touch me. I want to know what being a woman feels like."

He let out a strangled groan. If he touched her there'd be no way he could ever *stop* touching her. He'd be lost.

"Please," she insisted, low. "Because of the *Kama Sutra*, I've seen what being with a man looks like. But I want to know what it feels like."

"Your future husband will have that pleasure."

She made a small sound. "I think we both know there will be no husband for me, Damian. Grant me this favor."

Christ almighty, this was all his fault. He'd done this to her, changed her from an innocent into a sexually aware woman. How had he ever thought he could verbally seduce her and then simply walk away?

Just touch me.

He took a deep breath. It was going to take all his strength of will, but—

"All right."

She relaxed with a sigh, gifting him with another one of those shy, heartbreaking, I-trust-you smiles.

Bloody hell.

"Take off your robe and move over on the bed," he rasped, his mouth dry.

His mention of the word robe suddenly reminded him of the thin material covering his thick cock. How on earth would he be able to hide his erection from her if they were lying side by side? He supposed he'd just have to pleasure her so thoroughly that all she could think about was her own body.

And Damian Hunt certainly knew how to pleasure a woman.

In fact, he was going to retrace the path of her fingers, showing her how much better his mouth could make her feel.

She'd inched across the bed, and now he climbed in next to her, being careful to keep his robe pulled tightly closed. He propped himself up on one elbow, and stared down into her expectant face.

"You're so beautiful, Claire." He traced two of his fingers lightly down her slim nose and across to caress her cheek. "Open your mouth."

Her smile widened as she obviously recognized what he was doing. She parted her lips and he slid his fingers inside her moist darkness.

"Mmm." She purred low in her throat and eagerly began to suck on his fingers and swirl her tongue around him. Damian's cock started to throb, and he struggled not to come right there next to her. Bloody hell, she was a vixen in virgin's clothing. Or, rather, in no clothing. When was the last time he'd had a woman this enthusiastic in his bed? He pulled his fingers out of her mouth, grabbed her chin with his hand and kissed her.

Her small gasp of surprise allowed him to slip his tongue past her lips to explore inside her mouth. He felt her tense, but his teasing tongue soon coaxed her to play with him like she had with his fingers, and soon they were tangling together and she was exploring his mouth as avidly as he was hers.

He pulled away, breathless. "Sweet Claire. You taste so good."

He moved his mouth to her long white neck, licking and nibbling his way down, while she made appreciative little cooing noises and arched her head back to give him greater access. Loving her reaction, he laughed low in his throat and paused at the hollow near her collarbone to swirl his tongue there, teasing her.

"Oh, Damian, that's so much better than my fingers."

"Yes? And how about this, sweetheart?" His lips deliberately traced the path that her own fingers had taken across her chest, and slowly mounted the soft rise of her breast to suck her nipple into his mouth.

"Damian!"

Her fingers tangled in his hair as he laved her hard tip with his tongue, rolled it between his lips, and scraped it gently with his teeth. She was moaning loudly now, and her hands were actually holding his head tight up against her breast. A surge of pure male pride shot through him.

He gently wrapped his fingers around her soft flesh, not the least bit surprised to discover that Claire's breast was the perfect size for his hand. It seemed designed just for him.

He could have stayed there for hours, molding her shape to his hands, imprinting her flesh with his possessive touch. But after several long minutes of attention, he pulled his mouth away and gave her tight nipple one last stroke with his beard-shadowed chin, which elicited another gasp of pleasure from her.

"Did all that feel better than your fingers, sweetheart?"

"Oh, God, Damian, yes."

"Good. Then tell me what you think of this." He kissed his way slowly down her stomach. Her skin was like the finest silk, smooth, soft, cool to his heated touch. Lush and luxurious. A feast to be savored and explored. He was falling in deep here, deep into her feminine allure. Was there any part of Claire that wasn't perfect?

He moved his lips across to the soft feminine indentation of her waist, and around to the luscious curve of her hip. Exactly the path she'd taken earlier. But when he paused there, he could feel her body tense.

She knew where he was headed.

"Damian."

"Open your legs for me, sweetheart."

"Damian."

"You've seen this position in the *Kama Sutra* drawings, Claire."

"Yes, but—"

"I promise it will feel better than your fingers."

"Oh, God, Damian…"

"You said you wanted us to be like those people in the book."

"But I thought it would be—I mean—"

"You thought it would be with my cock inside you."

She sucked in a breath. "Yes."

"I want to make you come with my fingers, Claire. My fingers and my mouth."

"Damian."

"I love the way you say my name like that. Breathless. Pleading. Desire mixed with a touch of dread. Don't be afraid, Claire. I want you, sweetheart. Don't deny me this."

She sighed deeply, and he felt her legs relax, parting slightly. A shudder of joy and anticipation—and yes, pure male victory—zinged through his body as he moved to position himself between her pillowy white thighs. He laid a gentle kiss on the soft flesh there.

He spread her feminine lips apart with his thumbs and stared for a wondrous moment at the treasure before him.

"You are so beautiful, Claire."

She groaned with something that could have been embarrassment or trepidation, but he'd have none of that. This was Claire, his beautiful, perfect Claire. He was determined to show her exactly what a jewel she was.

With one long sweep of his tongue, he caressed the full length of her sex. She was wet and more than ready for him and tasted like cinnamon and sugar on his lips. Her body jerked and arched up off the bed, but he wasn't about to let her inhibitions prevent her from enjoying this intimate contact. His tongue found her sensitive little button, and he flicked back and forth against it quickly. Urgently. Insistently. Her hips jerked rhythmically with the contact, and soon she was moaning in time with his tongue.

That's it, sweet Claire, just enjoy this.

When he felt she was ready for more, he sucked that luscious little button into his hot mouth and sank two fingers deep inside her.

"Oh, oh—"

He stroked her from the inside, curling his fingers, knowing just the spot that would make her wild with pleasure. He matched the rhythm of his fingers with the rapid tempo of his mouth and simply let nature take its course. Within moments he felt her body start to gather and tighten with the beginnings of its climax, and he silently rejoiced that he was the first man who would bring Claire to this monumental peak.

"Damian—oh, God—Damian!"

She broke apart around his fingers even as she screamed his name, her body shuddering and spasming, jerking and clutching desperately at him. He did his best to prolong her pleasure with his hands and his mouth, as she buried her fingers deeply into his hair in order to keep him close to her as long as possible.

Several moments later, when her hands finally released their death grip on his head, he gently withdrew his fingers and replaced them with his mouth, eager to taste the evidence of her pleasure.

"Damian."

This time his name on her lips sounded somehow different. Reverent, like a prayer. He'd never heard a woman speak his name in quite that way before. It sent the oddest thrill through him.

"You taste like heaven, Claire. Did you enjoy that?"

"I never knew. I mean, those pictures didn't—"

"Just say yes, sweetheart. Tell me I satisfied you. My male pride demands it."

"Oh, yes. Yes, yes, yes!"

He laughed low in his throat. Bloody hell, he loved her spirit, her enthusiasm, her absolute honesty. He pushed himself up on his hands and knees and inched back up the bed, kissing her quickly on the lips before lying alongside her.

"Anything else that my lady might want, to make sure that her needs are completely met?" he teased, smiling into her love-flushed face.

A look of earnest thoughtfulness came over her features. "Well…."

Damian's eyebrows shot up in surprise. There couldn't possibly be anything more he could do to please her. Christ, she'd come twice in the last ten minutes!

"What is it?" he said with a frown.

"I…."

"Yes?"

"I would, um, like…."

He ran the back of his finger lightly down the side of her face. "Don't be afraid to ask me if there's something you really want, Claire."

Even as he said it, his mind made a mental scan of the *Kama Sutra* drawings. She obviously had something particular in mind. What was it she wanted to try?

"I really, really want…."

"Yes? What do you really want, Claire? "

"To touch you, Damian. I want to know what a man feels like."

Bloody hell, why hadn't he seen that coming? Possibly because he was so focused on her needs. Her wants. But obviously, this was one of her wants.

Good lord. Claire's sweet hands on him.

"Please, Damian, I'll never have this chance again."

He blew out a breath. "You keep saying that, sweetheart, but all it takes is one man to see what a prize you are—"

"Please."

Christ, he was so hard, so close to the brink, that he was afraid one touch from her fingers would be all it would take to send him right over the edge. Still, how could he deny her, when—if he was honest with himself—he desperately longed for this himself?

You long for more than that, you sod. You long to bury yourself deep inside her.

Yes. He longed to hear her scream his name again, and he wanted it this time to be his cock that drove her to it, his body above hers, forcing her to that wondrous sexual peak. He shuddered at the thought of how much he wanted it.

"All right," he breathed. "But just touch. And when I say stop, you must promise me to stop. Those are my rules."

Claire looked up at him with such an expression of gratitude on her face that he was reminded of the hero-worship he used to see in her eyes when she was twelve. Bloody, bloody hell. How could any man resist her?

He swallowed hard.

"Will you take off your robe so that I can see all of your body?"

Christ, she was going to strip him of all his defenses—had done so already, truth be told. Half an hour ago he thought he'd be vicariously naked with her, now it was going to happen in actual fact. His fantasy come true.

Just don't let me embarrass myself by coming immediately in her hands.

Not trusting himself to speak, he yanked at the tie of his robe, and slithered out of the silk garment. Claire's heated gaze swept slowly over his chest, down his stomach, and stopped at his groin, which tightened even more under her intense scrutiny.

"Your body is beautiful, Damian."

He groaned low in his throat, his cock jerking in reaction to her praise, eager to be in her hands. As if she knew the extreme state of his frustration, she gently reached out her fingers and wrapped them around him.

Damian gritted his teeth so hard he thought his jaw would break. How was he supposed to resist her? It was patently impossible! His cock thrust into her fingers, luxuriating in the friction.

"Bloody hell, Claire, your hands feel so good. They make me want to be inside you so badly."

"I want that, too, Damian."

Yes, he'd known that. She'd made that perfectly clear at the beginning. Could he risk it? Risk one delicious plunge inside her luscious body just to give them both a taste of what making love would feel like? One quick dip, one luxurious feel, before he pulled out of her and surely spilled his seed like some untrained youth?

His head swam with the temptation, and his fingers found their way between her legs. Bloody hell, she was so wet, so ready for him.

So perfect for him.

She inhaled sharply. "Damian…."

He needed to get her to the same frenzied state he was in. If he could push her as close to coming as he was, maybe just one plunge of his cock would send her over the edge and satisfy her wish to know what sexual congress felt like.

But then she won't be a virgin, you bastard.

True, but she wanted this, she said so, even knowing she wouldn't be a virgin afterwards. She was going into this with her eyes open.

"Damian, please."

She wanted this. He wanted this. Unable to deny himself any longer, he moved to position himself over her body, spreading her legs apart.

"Are you certain, Claire? If I do this, you'll feel pain at my first thrust, as every virgin does." Sweat broke out on his forehead with one last effort to restrain himself. "If you're not absolutely certain, tell me to stop right now."

She looked up at him, her eyes clear. "I'd never tell you to stop."

That was all the permission he needed. With a groan, he sank his cock inside her.

He heard her sharp intake of breath, but there was no way he was going to feel guilty. Her body was incredible, soft and lush, and her feminine sheath fit his cock like a tailor-made glove. A cry of pleasure ripped from his throat, and his well-intentioned decision to withdraw from her after one quick dip flew right out the window. This felt too good to stop. He slid his hands underneath her rear cheeks and he held her up to better take his next thrust.

She gasped again, but it was a different sound this time. Still one of surprise, yes, but this time more of an interested surprise.

That sound penetrated his thick haze of lust. What the hell was he doing?

He wanted—no, needed—to make this as good for Claire as it was for him.

It took every ounce of his willpower, but he withdrew almost clear of her body, then slid himself back in, slowly and deliberately, letting her feel every potent inch of his cock.

This time it was her cry of pleasure that rang in his ears.

He smiled and stroked deep inside her again. Christ, her body was so wet and welcoming that making love with her felt right. Natural. Like the easiest thing in the world. Her hands locked tightly onto his hips, and she held on to him as he built a rhythm that had them both panting within seconds.

Bloody hell, he wasn't going to last. But he'd known that from the start.

"Sweetheart, come for me. Come with me!" He was determined to take her with him when he tumbled into that abyss of pleasure.

"Oh, Damian!"

Her cry of release mingled with his hoarse shout as they climaxed together, bodies rocking, flesh to flesh. He held onto her tightly, desperately sucking in air, as jolt after sharp jolt of pleasure spiked through his cock.

Incredible.

Christ almighty, had sex ever felt like this before? This long, drawn-out, agonizing march to satisfaction that climaxed in such pure shock waves of total bliss? He was spent, exhausted, absolutely sated, and he'd been brought to this state by a virgin.

No, not just a virgin. Claire.

His Claire.

I'm never going to let you go, sweetheart.

He collapsed in a satisfied heap on top of her, enjoying the feel of his blood singing through his veins when the bedroom door opened with a crash.

"What in the bloody hell is going on in here?" George stopped abruptly, his mouth falling open, obviously taking in the scene in front of him.

Damian's head jerked up from where it was nestled on Claire's shoulder. Damn. He'd explicitly told the servants not to bother him or Claire tonight, but he'd forgotten completely about George.

George, who was supposed to stay in his room while Damian verbally seduced his sister.

Verbally seduced.

Damian scrambled to his feet, grabbing for his robe, noting that George's face had turned the most unnatural shade of purple.

"George, I can explain—"

"Explain?" George looked from his sister back to Damian. "Is this how you use words?"

He took three determined strides across the room, hauled back his fist and smashed Damian in the face. Damian went down in an undignified heap, holding onto his nose. Christ, he was bleeding!

"The only thing you need to explain, you bastard," George observed coldly, "is how quickly you will marry my sister."

Marry Claire?

"Yes," Damian agreed, "I'll marry your sister, George. Gladly."

Chapter 12

Claire was shaking like a leaf, clutching her robe tightly to her body, trying desperately to hide herself from George's accusing eyes. He looked absolutely furious standing there by the side of her bed, looming over Damian.

All she'd wanted tonight was to know what being with a man felt like—just once in her life—so that she could live out the rest of her spinster days with at least that precious knowledge. No, that wasn't quite true. She'd wanted to know what making love with Damian Hunt felt like. It had to be him. The man she'd adored since she was twelve.

But instead of the precious memory she'd hoped for, here she was, publicly exposed, caught naked in bed with her brother's best friend. Her reputation was beyond repair, ruined forever.

Which was undoubtedly the reason Damian had agreed to George's heated demand that he marry her. How ironic that one of society's biggest reprobates should have a streak of chivalry in him after all. No, that wasn't fair. She'd seen the true Damian Hunt tonight, the man inside the miscreant. He was honorable and admirable. But she couldn't possibly accept his offer, even though—if she was honest with herself—she had to admit she was madly in love with him.

Being forced to wed because of circumstance was no basis for a happy marriage. And what had Damian said earlier tonight? *I'm not about to let my father or anyone else tell me who to wed.*

No. She couldn't let Damian suffer that fate. This awful situation was all her fault. She had selfishly forced him to make love to her, but she would never let George force him into marrying her.

Dear lord, her heart felt like it was breaking.

If she couldn't have Damian, she would hie off to a nunnery as soon as she left here, since no man would ever compare to him. Best to remove herself from the world of men altogether. Yes, she'd go to the nearby Abbey of St. Jude. He was the saint of hopeless cases, wasn't he? And who could be more hopeless than she was? To be in love with a man who only agreed to marry her because he'd ruined her as she'd requested.

What a dreadful mess her carefully ordered life had become!

A serene calm descended on Damian after George's demand that he wed Claire. Never in a million years had Damian considered he would tie himself to a woman at this point in his life, but Claire truly seemed like the right woman. Christ, she was so sensual and tactile he could spend a lifetime educating her in the ways of passion, and he would enjoy every minute of it.

Maybe instead of the sexually jaded females he'd been pursuing all these years, he should have been seducing virgins. How ironic was that?

No. It had to be Claire. It was only Claire he wanted. Claire with her sharp intelligence and her incredible passion. The fact that he was honor-bound as a gentleman to marry her after ruining her—as George was rightly insisting—paled in comparison to the simple fact that she was perfect for him in every way.

He held a hand to his bleeding nose and stood, shoulders squared, his robe slightly askew.

"Yes, George, I'll marry your sister."

Claire made a strangled sound from the bed. "No, George, he won't."

Surprised, Damian turned to look at her. "Claire—"

"Hold your tongue, Claire," George ordered.

Damian watched as Claire frantically elbowed herself into a sitting position, careful to hold her robe to her chest in an effort to cover her nakedness. His mouth watered at the sight. He wanted to be back in bed with her, embarking on an erotic exploration of all the positions in the *Kama Sutra* with her. Claire on top of him. Claire straddling his lap. Somehow he knew that his adventurous Claire would enjoy that as much as he would.

"I will *not* hold my tongue," she vowed, her right hand fisting nervously in the bedspread. "And I will not marry Damian."

"What?" Damian gasped.

"You will do as I say," George thundered.

"No, George." She straightened her back in defiance, but Damian could see that she was shaking. "Tomorrow we will go home, and next week I will go to St. Jude's."

"What?" George roared. "No well-bred woman from a family of our caliber is going to join a nunnery!"

Damian stared at Claire, flabbergasted. She was refusing to marry him? After the incredible sex they'd just shared? She'd rather become a nun than make love with him ever again?

Bloody hell, had he so totally misjudged her? Had she told him the plain truth, then, when she'd said she simply wanted to *use* him as a man in order to know what sexual congress felt like?

He'd never been used for sex before. The idea left a bitter taste in his mouth.

Especially because he'd fallen in love with her. Christ almighty, he was a bloody fool. But why was she so determined to turn him down? George had mentioned just last week that no one had ever even made an offer for her, so why would Claire spurn the attentions of a man who wanted to marry her, a man who held such a high place in society? Was it his infamous reputation she resented, perhaps? Did she think it beneath her pristine reputation to marry a notorious rake? He bristled at the thought. Well, the fact remained that he would someday be an earl. Society forgave rich and titled men many faults. It was inconceivable that she'd turn him down.

Anger burned his face, but Claire was no longer looking at him. In fact, she was staring fixedly at the fingers she was now twisting into her bedspread. Well, he'd have none of it. If she was going to refuse to wed him, she'd have to look him in the eye to do it.

He set his jaw, put a hand under her chin, and forced her gaze up to meet his. He was stunned by what he saw there. The look of pain and longing on her face told him the truth. Claire Beringer didn't hate him, she loved him! But if that were the case, why was she refusing him? His anger immediately evaporated and he sat down on the edge of the bed.

"I can't let you do it, Damian," she whispered, her eyes watery. "I can't let you marry against your will. This is all my fault."

Bloody hell. She thought he didn't want her.

"Oh, he'll do it," George promised ominously. "And if he refuses, it will be pistols at dawn."

Claire gasped, but Damian wiped away a stray tear from her cheek with his thumb and smiled at her.

"It's all right, Claire. Truly." There was so much more he wanted to say to her—*I want this, I want you, I love you*—but not with George standing there.

He gave Claire another smile, one that he hoped conveyed everything he was feeling, and he was reassured when she tentatively smiled back at him.

Thank God. Everything was going to be all right. He took her hand in his and gave it a gentle squeeze.

"I pity you to be leg-shackled to my sister," George observed acidly from the foot of Claire's bed. "But you wouldn't be in this situation now if you'd just stuck to the rules of the bet."

Claire frowned, and she switched her gaze to her brother. "Bet?"

Damian's stomach fell to his feet. "George!"

"Damian wasn't supposed to touch you. He wagered that he could make you come using just his words." George deliberately eyed Claire's nearly naked state. "Obviously the arrogant bastard was wrong."

Claire's head whipped around to face Damian, a look of uncertainty on her face. "This weekend was all about a *bet*? Everything you did? You bet that you could—could—"

Damian felt sweat break out on his brow. "Claire, listen to me—"

She jerked her hand out of his. Her furious eyes snapped back to her bother. "And you agreed to this bet? My own brother?"

George shrugged. "I thought it was a safe bet. Given your rigid—and frigid— attitude, I never dreamed you'd give a known scoundrel like Damian Hunt more than the time of day. And even if you did, as long as he used only his words to seduce you, you'd *still* be a virgin. Either way it turned out, you'd be untouched." He looked her over once more. "I certainly never expected this. Christ, the first time I heard you scream I convinced myself it must have been the wind whistling through the trees. Claire Beringer, seduced by Damian Hunt? Impossible! The second time I heard you, I actually got out of bed, but by the time I made it down the hall, the two of you were, well…. Now there's only the wedding to plan."

"I will never marry Damian Hunt."

"You'll do as I say!" George thundered.

Damian swallowed hard. "Please, sweetheart, let me explain."

"Get out. Both of you, get out of this room this instant!"

George shrugged again. "As you wish. We'll continue this tomorrow. Damian, I'd like to inspect my new horse, Thunder, in the morning."

Claire's face drained of all color, only to flush beet red the next moment as she glared at Damian. "You bet your horse you could do this?"

If looks could kill, Damian knew he'd be a dead man.

"It was my prized new racing stallion." Bloody hell, that defensive explanation sounded pathetic even to his own ears.

"Get out!"

"That's more like it, Claire. Back to your shrewish, termagant ways." George glanced at Damian. "You've made your bed, my unfortunate friend. Your marriage bed, that is. And now you're going to have to lie in it. For the rest of your accursed life."

Claire pounded her fist into the mattress. "I will never marry Damian Hunt!"

"We'll see about that," George replied, but by the furious look on Claire's face as the two men left the room, Damian feared that nothing he or George could do would change her mind.

Chapter 13

I will never marry Damian Hunt.

Claire's furious pronouncement rang in Damian's ears. She slammed her bedroom door and threw home the lock, leaving him and George in the hallway.

But there was no bolt on the connecting door between the two master suites.

He dashed to his room, listening to her scream, cry and throw things next door. Obviously she was also thinking of the connecting door, because he heard her pile furniture there, undoubtedly to keep him out.

The force of her fury gave him pause.

What should he do? Try and explain that the bet was simply an attempt to liven up a boring winter's night, a wager that had somehow gotten horribly out of hand? Reason with her to accept his proposal? Or should he simply respect her decision because he'd wronged her so greatly?

No, no, no, the thought of Claire in a nunnery, her fiery passion hidden forever beneath a staid sister's habit, was more than he could bear.

This awful situation was all his fault, not hers.

Since that day years ago when he'd realized his father intended to protect him from all harm—from life—for the sake of the family title, Damian had been aimless, wandering through his days with no purpose other than pleasure. Drinking. Gambling. Women.

Now, for the first time, there was something he truly wanted, something he desperately needed. Claire. And he'd be damned if he'd let her go without trying everything humanly possible to keep her.

Her room was quiet now, and maybe that was a good thing. If she'd finally spent her anger, worn herself out, perhaps now she'd listen to reason. Or hopefully to her own heart. She loved him. Yes, Damian was sure of that. He'd seen it in her eyes. He just prayed the feeling was still there inside Claire somewhere, not snuffed out completely by the ignominious revelation of the bet.

Damian was a man on a mission. A pile of furniture, no matter how high, was not going to bar the door against his heart's desire.

He tightened the sash on his robe, and momentarily considered changing into proper clothes. Should he gird himself for the confrontation ahead? No, he'd use every weapon in his possession to win Claire, even his naked body, if he had to. Especially if he had to. Sex between them had been incredible. Letting his body convince her they belonged together could be potent persuasion.

Taking a deep breath, he padded to the connecting door, pausing there to press his ear against it. Had Claire fallen asleep after her terrible tirade? That would help his cause immensely. There was no way he was going to gain entrance to her room in silence, so if she was asleep, perhaps he could make some headway before she realized what he was doing.

He put a hand on the doorknob, put his shoulder to the wood, and pushed.

Claire rubbed the heels of her hands into her eyes, and shifted her head on the pillow. She was exhausted, drained, shattered. She'd vented her rage over her unbearable situation, and now she longed for the oblivion of sleep to escape her troubles, if only for a while.

But sleep would not come.

In frustration, she twisted onto her side. God, her head hurt. No, it was more than just her head. Her heart hurt as well.

The events of the last hour had simply been too painful.

It's all right, Claire. Truly...

Just when she'd begun to believe Damian's reassuring words, that he might actually care for her, that her life would have the happy-ever-after she'd never dared hope for, she'd found that it had all been a cruel joke. A lie. The result of a callous, heartless, vile bet.

Damian wagered he could make you come using just his words.

What a fool she'd been! That had been his motive for pursuing her all weekend. Not that he'd liked her or cared for her. Even now, her ears rang with the hateful words. No, wait. Her ears weren't ringing. It was more of a scraping sound she was hearing.

Prying her eyes open, she sat up unsteadily on the bed, searching out the origin of the sound. In disbelief, she watched as the mound of furniture she'd piled in front of her door moved. Slowly, deliberately, and only so far as to allow a figure to slip into her room.

"Damian!"

His gaze flew to her on the bed. "Claire..."

Good lord, he was still wearing his robe. She could see the skin of his chest where the silk material gaped open, and it took all her strength of will not to let her gaze drop below his waist. The things his body had done to her! Intimate things that meant nothing more to him than a means to win a bet.

"Get out of my room this instant," she hissed, "or I will scream the house down."

He quickly crossed to her bedside. "I need to speak with you. Please."

"You are despicable—"

"Yes."

"—contemptible—"

"Absolutely."

"—abominable, loathsome, and horrid."

"All that and more."

"And I hate you!" She buried her head in her hands, no longer able to look at him, at the face that had become so precious to her. The face of a liar.

He dropped to his knees by the side of her bed, and reached for one of her hands.

"You don't hate me, Claire. You *love* me. I know it. I saw it in your eyes earlier. You love me, and I love you."

Her head jerked up with a snap. What was this? Just as she was giving vent to her anger and starting to feel a bit better, his outrageous declaration stole the litany of accusatory words from her throat.

"You can't actually expect me to believe anything you say, you—you *bastard*."

He winced. "Nonetheless, it's true. I love you. I'll love you for the rest of my life, if you'll just give me the chance. Say that you'll marry me."

Her mouth fell open. Dear lord, he actually looked as if he meant it. His face wore such an expression of guilt and regret. She shook her head in disbelief. "This is just because of the bet."

He made a disgusted sound. "The bet was an asinine thing. I was drunk and bored when I suggested it, and George insisted he name the woman. When he picked you, I told him I'm no seducer of innocents."

"And yet you did it."

He blew out a breath. "It was unconscionable, I know, but I made myself believe him when he said you'd remain a virgin either way it turned out. It's just that none of us expected things to go this far."

She raised an eyebrow. "And how did your horse become part of this?"

He reddened under her gaze. "George wagered his townhouse in London that I couldn't do it, and when I initially refused, he demanded my new racehorse in forfeit."

"I see."

"Damn it all, he can have the bloody horse, Claire. I only want you."

She stared at him, trying to figure out the truth. He was so vehement, so insistent. Her bruised and battered heart longed to believe him, but her head swam.

He ran a finger down the side of her face. "Don't you see, Claire? I've fallen in love with you. With your brains and your beauty, and your incredible passion. I never meant to ruin you."

She inhaled sharply. Damian was right. He'd tried hard to resist her, even begged her to tell him to stop.

"I suppose that *was* my fault. Yes. I insisted on it, didn't I?"

"It was no one's fault," he vowed. "It's what we both wanted. I could no more have resisted you than I could my next breath. I had to have you. I want you still. Right now and for as long as we have on this earth. Marry me, Claire."

Claire's breath caught. He really did mean what he was saying. She could see it in his eyes, in the pleading set of his features. Good lord, he was even on his knees! He truly wanted to marry her. This wasn't just because of George's threat.

She thought for one wild moment of turning him down, to hurt him as deeply as he'd hurt her. But that would be like cutting off her nose to spite her face.

She'd be Damian Hunt's wife. This went beyond even her childhood dreams, but she was no longer that child, and she knew Damian's scandalous reputation well. She had to go into this with her eyes wide open.

"We need to talk about some things, Damian."

"Anything."

She took a deep breath. "First… all your women."

"Trying out those positions in the *Kama Sutra* should keep us busy for at least a few years, sweetheart. And then there are those other positions I mentioned, the ones I've fantasized about in my head. No, I don't think you need to worry about me ever having time for another woman, Claire. Your passion is something I look forward to spending a lifetime exploring."

"Damian, I'm serious."

"So am I." He took her hand and laid her palm over his heart. "I love you, Claire. There will be no other women. Now. What else?"

Claire bit her lip. "I'm afraid you'll resent me. If we wed, I'd be tying you down and preventing you from fulfilling your dream of going off to see the world."

He gave her a smoldering gaze. "I must say I like the thought of you, er, tying me down, although I'd much rather tie *you* down. Preferably with silk scarves."

She looked at him, not understanding.

"It's one of those other positions I mentioned," he murmured, his blue eyes turning hot.

Claire felt herself blush. Did he mean he would tie her down and make love to her? She would be helpless to stop him from doing whatever he wished with her? *Oh, my.* She shivered violently and wondered what other ideas he had in his deliciously wicked mind.

"Seriously, my love," he said, giving her a smile, "sharing life with you will be adventure enough for me. And if we feel the need for some extra excitement, we'll go to meetings of the Royal Geographical Society together. I'd love to share our mutual passion for knowledge with you as well. Anything else?"

"Your father wants heirs."

Damian laid a gentle hand on her stomach. "You may already be carrying my child, Claire. Have you considered that?"

She gasped.

"What we did is how children are made. Surely you know that."

Good lord, how could she possibly refuse to marry him if there was a chance she was carrying his child?

"Oh, Damian."

He let out a deep sigh. "I love the way you say my name like that. Like I'm the only man in the world. Well, I intend to be the only man in your world from now on, Claire. So I'll ask you one more time. Will you marry me?"

She stared into his eyes, at the love she could clearly see there. Was there any woman in the world luckier than her?

"Yes, Damian, I'll marry you."

He let out a victorious shout and leaned in to kiss her. She welcomed his mouth, opening her lips when he demanded entrance, tangling her tongue with his.

They savored the kiss until Damian put a hand on her arm. "Let's seal this agreement with more than just a kiss, Claire."

"What precisely did you have in mind, my lord?" she asked, trying to sound innocent. "I don't have any silk scarves here in my room."

He gave her a smoldering glance. "I was thinking of letting you choose a position from the *Kama Sutra*. Earlier today in my note, I asked you to pick a favorite. Have you?"

Claire thought for a moment, and then smiled. "Yes. But you'll have to come up here on the bed for me to show you."

Damian made the leap from floor to mattress almost quicker than Claire's eye could follow. She laughed at his eagerness.

He lay on his back, stretching out his long body, one hand under his head. "And now?"

"Now take off your robe."

"As my lady wishes." With one swift move, he shrugged out of the blue silk.

Claire took a moment to look him over. The fire in the hearth threw light and shadows over the planes and valleys of his body, dramatically highlighting his hard muscles and taut skin. And his thick cock. He was perfect from head to toe, and he was all hers. Now and forever. And on top of that, he loved her.

"Don't make me wait," he groaned. "I'm desperate to see you, as well."

She smiled at him then, and she knew it wasn't her usual shy smile. No, this was a smile meant only for Damian. A knowing smile. A secret smile. She rose to her knees next to him on the mattress, pulled at the tie at her waist, and slid her own robe from her body.

Damian let out a deep sigh. "I'll never tire of looking at you."

And by the heat in his eyes, she actually found the confidence to believe him.

"Now, about that position...."

"Hmm." She slowly moved to straddle his hips. His cock rose up to meet her as she settled herself on top of him, slowly taking every inch he could give her, deep inside her body. He groaned his approval even as she gasped at the possessiveness of his penetration.

She could feel him all the way to her heart.

"Damian?"

"Yes, sweetheart?"

"I saw this position in the book, and I liked the sense of control it seemed to give the woman. But...."

"But?"

"Well, what am I supposed to do now?"

He had the grace not to embarrass her by laughing at her ignorance.

"Move. Just move your hips whichever way makes you feel good. Whatever you do, I won't last long. This is just too good, sweetheart."

She began to roll her hips, feeling his cock stroking deep inside her. Ooh, she liked this. She moved faster and Damian gasped, grabbing onto her hips with his hands, guiding her movements.

She closed her eyes and let him take charge, quickening their pace, until her breathing became as ragged as his. She splayed the fingers of both hands across his chest and held onto him as she felt her body begin its fierce contractions, tightening around him, claiming him for her own. In response Damian's body shuddered beneath her hands, his cock jerking inside her, his sharp cries of pleasure echoing in her ears.

When her body finally eased its violent trembling, she collapsed onto his chest with her right hand over his heart. She could feel that precious organ beating crazily beneath her fingers, and she smiled. Damian loved her. He really and truly did.

"Amazing," he breathed. "That may very well become my favorite position as well. But I think we owe it to ourselves to try out the other sixty-three."

She lifted her head to look at him. "Sixty-three?"

"Mmm. There are sixty-four positions described in the *Kama Sutra*. I've counted them. Then again, one of the positions I have in my head might turn out to be our favorite. At any rate, I highly recommend we try them all before we make any final decisions."

She laughed and hugged him close, and then raised an eyebrow. "You know, Damian, I just realized something. Technically, you did win that bet with George."

He paused. "That's debatable. I may have made you come with words, but did I forfeit that victory when I made love with you? Truthfully, I think I won the bigger prize when you agreed to marry me, sweetheart."

"Still, by rights, you should at least be able to keep your horse."

"Hmm. We'll speak with George in the morning, shall we? Right now, I have something more pleasant in mind. It's called position twelve."

Claire blew out a breath. "You're incorrigible. How soon can we wed?"

"We'll post the banns next Sunday." He looked at her and chuckled. "I can hardly wait to hear what society will say. Imagine. Damian Hunt, confirmed provocateur, doing something as utterly conventional as getting married. They'll think you've reformed me."

"They'll think you've corrupted me, more like."

Damian laughed outright. "Let them think what they will, sweetheart. Come to think of it, let George think what he will. You and I know the truth. I love you with all of my heart, and I'm looking forward to having the adventure of my life with you."

About the Author:

The Bet *is Leigh Court's second* **Secrets** *novella. Her first,* The Disciplinarian, *is in* Volume 15.

Leigh's been writing since age eleven, starting with wild adventure stories for her elementary school newsletter, then growing up to be a television news journalist whose work took her on real life adventures.

She now writes sexy romantic fiction because she wants her readers to be able to escape into a story guaranteed to have a happy ending.

Leigh loves to hear from her readers! You can contact her at leigh@leighcourt. com or at www.leighcourt.com.

Men you've been dreaming about!

Secrets

Satisfy your desire for more.

*F*eel the wild adventure, fierce passion and the power of love in every *Secrets* Collection story. Red Sage Publishing's romance authors create richly crafted, sexy, sensual, novella-length stories. Each one is just the right length for reading after a long and hectic day.

Each volume in the *Secrets* Collection has four diverse, ultra-sexy, romantic novellas brimming with adventure, passion and love. More adventurous tales for the adventurous reader. The *Secrets* Collection are a glorious mix of romance genre; numerous historical settings, contemporary, paranormal, science fiction and suspense. We are always looking for new adventures.

Reader response to the *Secrets* volumes has been great! Here's just a small sample:

> *"I loved the variety of settings. Four completely wonderful time periods, give you four completely wonderful reads."*

> *"Each story was a page-turning tale I hated to put down."*

> *"I love **Secrets**! When is the next volume coming out? This one was Hot! Loved the heroes!"*

Secrets have won raves and awards. We could go on, but why don't you find out for yourself—order your set of **Secrets** today! See the back for details.

Secrets, Volume 1

A Lady's Quest by Bonnie Hamre
Widowed Lady Antonia Blair-Sutworth searches for a
lover to save her from the handsome Duke of Suther-
land. The "auditions" may be shocking but utterly
tantalizing.

The Spinner's Dream by Alice Gaines
A seductive fantasy that leaves every woman wishing
for her own private love slave, desperate and running
for his life.

The Proposal by Ivy Landon
This tale is a walk on the wild side of love. *The
Proposal* will taunt you, tease you, and shock you. A
contemporary erotica for the adventurous woman.

The Gift by Jeanie LeGendre
Immerse yourself in this historic tale of exotic seduction, bondage and a concubine's
surrender to the Sultan's desire. Can Alessandra live the life and give the gift the
Sultan demands of her?

Secrets, Volume 2

Surrogate Lover by Doreen DeSalvo
Adrian Ross is a surrogate sex therapist who has all
the answers and control. He thought he'd seen and
done it all, but he'd never met Sarah.

Snowbound by Bonnie Hamre
A delicious, sensuous regency tale. The marriage-shy
Earl of Howden is teased and tortured by his own
desires and finds there is a woman who can equal his
overpowering sensuality.

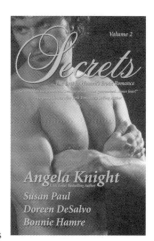

Roarke's Prisoner by Angela Knight
Elise, a starship captain, remembers the eager animal
submission she'd known before at her captor's hands
and refuses to become his toy again. However, she has
no idea of the delights he's planned for her this time.

Savage Garden by Susan Paul
Raine's been captured by a mysterious and dangerous revolutionary leader in
Mexico. At first her only concern is survival, but she quickly finds lush erotic nights
in her captor's arms.

Winner of the Fallot Literary Award for Fiction!

Secrets, Volume 3

The Spy Who Loved Me by Jeanie Cesarini
Undercover FBI agent Paige Ellison's sexual appetites
rise to new levels when she works with leading man
Christopher Sharp, the cunning agent who uses all his
training to capture her body and heart.

The Barbarian by Ann Jacobs
Lady Brianna vows not to surrender to the barbaric
Giles, Earl of Harrow. He must use sexual arts
learned in the infidels' harem to conquer his bride. A
word of caution—this is not for the faint of heart.

Blood and Kisses by Angela Knight
A vampire assassin is after Beryl St. Cloud. Her only
hope lies with Decker, another vampire and ex-merce-
nary. Broke, she offers herself as payment for his services. Will his seductive powers
take her very soul?

Love Undercover by B.J. McCall
Amanda Forbes is the bait in a strip joint sting operation. While she performs, fellow
detective "Cowboy" Cooper gets to watch. Though he excites her, she must fight the
temptation to surrender to the passion.

Winner of the 1997 Under the Covers Readers Favorite Award

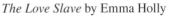

Secrets, Volume 4

An Act of Love by Jeanie Cesarini
Shelby Moran's past left her terrified of sex. International film star Jason Gage must gently coach the young
starlet in the ways of love. He wants more than an act—
he wants Shelby to feel true passion in his arms.

Enslaved by Desirée Lindsey
Lord Nicholas Summer's air of danger, dark passions,
and irresistible charm have brought Lady Crystal's
long-hidden desires to the surface. Will he be able to
give her the one thing she desires before it's too late?

The Bodyguard by Betsy Morgan & Susan Paul
Kaki York is a bodyguard, but watching the wild,
erotic romps of her client's sexual conquests on the
security cameras is getting to her—and her partner, the ruggedly handsome James
Kulick. Can she resist his insistent desire to have her?

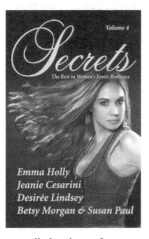

The Love Slave by Emma Holly
A woman's ultimate fantasy. For one year, Princess Lily will be attended to by three
delicious men of her choice. While she delights in playing with the first two, it's the
reluctant Grae, with his powerful chest, black eyes and hair, that stirs her desires.

Secrets, Volume 5

Beneath Two Moons by Sandy Fraser
Step into the future and find Conor, rough and masculine like frontiermen of old, on the prowl for a new conquest. In his sights, Dr. Eva Kelsey. She got away before, but this time Conor makes sure she begs for more.

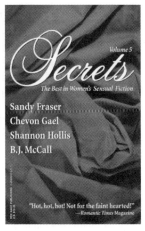

Insatiable by Chevon Gael
Marcus Remington photographs beautiful models for a living, but it's Ashlyn Fraser, a young exec having some glamour shots done, who has stolen his heart. It's up to Marcus to help her discover her inner sexual self.

Strictly Business by Shannon Hollis
Elizabeth Forrester knows it's tough enough for a woman to make it to the top in the corporate world. Garrett Hill, the most beautiful man in Silicon Valley, has to come along to stir up her wildest fantasies. Dare she give in to both their desires?

Alias Smith and Jones by B.J. McCall
Meredith Collins finds herself stranded at the airport. A handsome stranger by the name of Smith offers her sanctuary for the evening and she finds those mesmerizing, green-flecked eyes hard to resist. Are they to be just two ships passing in the night?

Secrets, Volume 6

Flint's Fuse by Sandy Fraser
Dana Madison's father has her "kidnapped" for her own safety. Flint, the tall, dark and dangerous mercenary, is hired for the job. But just which one is the prisoner—Dana will try *anything* to get away.

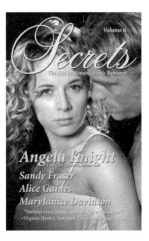

Love's Prisoner by MaryJanice Davidson
Trapped in an elevator, Jeannie Lawrence experienced unwilling rapture at Michael Windham's hands. She never expected the devilishly handsome man to show back up in her life—or turn out to be a werewolf!

The Education of Miss Felicity Wells by Alice Gaines
Felicity Wells wants to be sure she'll satisfy her soon-to-be husband but she needs a teacher. Dr. Marcus Slade, an experienced lover, agrees to take her on as a student, but can he stop short of taking her completely?

A Candidate for the Kiss by Angela Knight
Working on a story, reporter Dana Ivory stumbles onto a more amazing one—a sexy, secret agent who happens to be a vampire. She wants her story but Gabriel Archer wants more from her than just sex and blood.

Secrets, Volume 7

Amelia's Innocence by Julia Welles
Amelia didn't know her father bet her in a card game with Captain Quentin Hawke, so honor demands a compromise—three days of erotic foreplay, leaving her virginity and future intact.

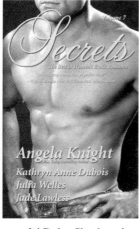

The Woman of His Dreams by Jade Lawless
From the day artist Gray Avonaco moves in next door, Joanna Morgan is plagued by provocative dreams. But what she believes is unrequited lust, Gray sees as another chance to be with the woman he loves. He must persuade her that even death can't stop true love.

Surrender by Kathryn Anne Dubois
Free-spirited Lady Johanna wants no part of the binding strictures society imposes with her marriage to the powerful Duke. She doesn't know the dark Duke wants sensual adventure, and sexual satisfaction.

Kissing the Hunter by Angela Knight
Navy Seal Logan McLean hunts the vampires who murdered his wife. Virginia Hart is a sexy vampire searching for her lost soul-mate only to find him in a man determined to kill her. She must convince him all vampires aren't created equally.

Winner of the Venus Book Club Best Book of the Year

Secrets, Volume 8

Taming Kate by Jeanie Cesarini
Kathryn Roman inherits a legal brothel. Little does this city girl know the town wants her to be their new madam so they've charged Trey Holliday, one very dominant cowboy, with taming her.

Jared's Wolf by MaryJanice Davidson
Jared Rocke will do anything to avenge his sister's death, but ends up attracted to Moira Wolfbauer, the she-wolf sworn to protect her pack. Joining forces to stop a killer, they learn love defies all boundaries.

My Champion, My Lover by Alice Gaines
Celeste Broder is a woman committed for having a sexy appetite. Mayor Robert Albright may be her champion— if she can convince him her freedom will mean they can indulge their appetites together.

Kiss or Kill by Liz Maverick
In this post-apocalyptic world, Camille Kazinsky's military career rides on her ability to make a choice—whether the robo called Meat should live or die. Can he prove he's human enough to live, man enough… to make her feel like a woman.

Winner of the Venus Book Club Best Book of the Year

Secrets, Volume 9

Wild For You by Kathryn Anne Dubois
When college intern, Georgie, gets captured by a
Congo wildman, she discovers this specimen of male
virility has never seen a woman. The research possibilities are endless!

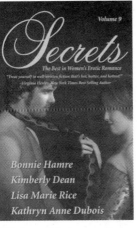

Wanted by Kimberly Dean
FBI Special Agent Jeff Reno wants Danielle Carver.
There's her body, brains—and that charge of treason
on her head. Dani goes on the run, but the sexy Fed is
hot on her trail.

Bonnie Hamre
Kimberly Dean
Lisa Marie Rice
Kathryn Anne Dubois

Secluded by Lisa Marie Rice
Nicholas Lee's wealth and power came with a price—
his enemies will kill anyone he loves. When Isabelle
steals his heart, Nicholas secludes her in his palace for a lifetime of desire in only a
few days.

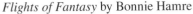

Flights of Fantasy by Bonnie Hamre
Chloe taught others to see the realities of life but she's never shared the intimate
world of her sensual yearnings. Given the chance, will she be woman enough to
fulfill her most secret erotic fantasy?

Secrets, Volume 10

Private Eyes by Dominique Sinclair
When a mystery man captivates P.I. Nicolla Black
during a stakeout, she discovers her no-seduction rule
bending under the pressure of long denied passion.
She agrees to the seduction, but he demands her total
surrender.

The Ruination of Lady Jane by Bonnie Hamre
To avoid her upcoming marriage, Lady Jane Ponson-
by-Maitland flees into the arms of Havyn Attercliffe.
She begs him to ruin her rather than turn her over to
her odious fiancé.

Jeanie Cesarini
Bonnie Hamre
Dominique Sinclair
Kathryn Anne Dubois

Code Name: Kiss by Jeanie Cesarini
Agent Lily Justiss is on a mission to defend her country
against terrorists that requires giving up her virginity as a sex slave. As her master
takes her body, desire for her commanding officer Seth Blackthorn fuels her mind.

The Sacrifice by Kathryn Anne Dubois
Lady Anastasia Bedovier is days from taking her vows as a Nun. Before she denies
her sensuality forever, she wants to experience pleasure. Count Maxwell is the perfect man to initiate her into erotic delight.

Secrets, Volume 11

Masquerade by Jennifer Probst
Hailey Ashton is determined to free herself from her
sexual restrictions. Four nights of erotic pleasures
without revealing her identity. A chance to explore her
secret desires without the fear of unmasking.

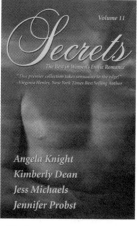

Ancient Pleasures by Jess Michaels
Isabella Winslow is obsessed with finding out what
caused her husband's death, but trapped in an Egyp-
tian concubine's tomb with a sexy American raider,
succumbing to the mummy's sensual curse takes over.

Manhunt by Kimberly Dean
Framed for murder, Michael Tucker takes Taryn
Swanson hostage—the one woman who can clear him.
Despite the evidence against him, the attraction is strong. Tucker resorts to uncon-
ventional, yet effective methods of persuasion to change the sexy ADA's mind.

Wake Me by Angela Knight
Chloe Hart received a sexy painting of a sleeping knight. Radolf of Varik has been
trapped there for centuries, cursed by a witch. His only hope is to visit the dreams of
women and make one of them fall in love with him so she can free him with a kiss.

Secrets, Volume 12

Good Girl Gone Bad by Dominique Sinclair
Setting out to do research for an article, nothing could
have prepared Reagan for Luke, or his offer to teach
her everything she needs to know about sex. Licentious pleasures, forbidden desires… inspiring the best
writing she's ever done.

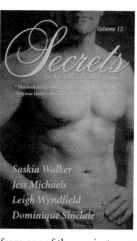

Aphrodite's Passion by Jess Michaels
When Selena flees Victorian London before her evil
stepchildren can institutionalize her for hysteria,
Gavin is asked to bring her back home. But when he
finds her living on the island of Cyprus, his need to
have her begins to block out every other impulse.

White Heat by Leigh Wyndfield
Raine is hiding in an icehouse in the middle of nowhere from one of the scariest men
in the universes. Walker escaped from a burning prison. Imagine their surprise when
they find out they have the same man to blame for their miseries. Passion, revenge
and love are in their future.

Summer Lightning by Saskia Walker
Sculptress Sally is enjoying an idyllic getaway on a secluded cove when she spots a
gorgeous man walking naked on the beach. When Julian finds an attractive woman
shacked up in his cove, he has to check her out. But what will he do when he finds
she's secretly been using him as a model?

Secrets, Volume 13

Out of Control by Rachelle Chase
Astrid's world revolves around her business and she's
hoping to pick up wealthy Erik Santos as a client. He's
hoping to pick up something entirely different. Will
she give in to the seductive pull of his proposition?

Hawkmoor by Amber Green
Shape-shifters answer to Darien as he acts in the name
of long-missing Lady Hawkmoor, their ruler. When
she unexpectedly surfaces, Darien must deal with a
scrappy individual whose wary eyes hold the other half
of his soul, but who has the power to destroy his world.

Lessons in Pleasure by Charlotte Featherstone
A wicked bargain has Lily vowing never to yield to the

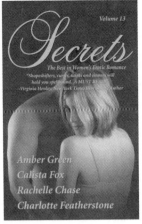

demands of the rake she once loved and lost. Unfortunately, Damian, the Earl of St.
Croix, or Saint as he is infamously known, will not take 'no' for an answer.

In the Heat of the Night by Calista Fox
Haunted by a curse, Molina fears she won't live to see her 30th birthday. Nick, her for-
mer bodyguard, is re-hired to protect her from the fatal accidents that plague her family.
Will his passion and love be enough to convince Molina they have a future together?

Secrets, Volume 14

Soul Kisses by Angela Knight
Beth's been kidnapped by Joaquin Ramirez, a sadistic
vampire. Handsome vampire cousins, Morgan and
Garret Axton, come to her rescue. Can she find happiness with two vampires?

Temptation in Time by Alexa Aames
Ariana escaped the Middle Ages after stealing a kiss
of magic from sexy sorcerer, Marcus de Grey. When
he brings her back, they begin a battle of wills and a
sexual odyssey that could spell disaster for them both.

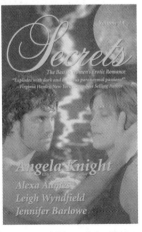

Ailis and the Beast by Jennifer Barlowe
When Ailis agreed to be her village's sacrifice to the
mysterious Beast she was prepared to sacrifice her vir-
tue, and possibly her life. But some things aren't what they seem. Ailis and the Beast
are about to discover the greatest sacrifice may be the human heart.

Night Heat by Leigh Wynfield
When Rip Bowhite leads a revolt on the prison planet, he ends up struggling to
survive against monsters that rule the night. Jemma, the prison's Healer, won't allow
herself to be distracted by the instant attraction she feels for Rip. As the stakes are
raised and death draws near, love seems doomed in the heat of the night.

Secrets, Volume 15

Simon Says by Jane Thompson
Simon Campbell is a newspaper columnist who panders to male fantasies. Georgina Kennedy is a respectable librarian. On the surface, these two have nothing in common... but don't judge a book by its cover.

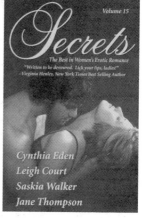

Bite of the Wolf by Cynthia Eden
Gareth Morlet, alpha werewolf, has finally found his mate. All he has to do is convince Trinity to join with him, to give in to the pleasure of a werewolf's mating, and then she will be his... forever.

Falling for Trouble by Saskia Walker
With 48 hours to clear her brother's name, Sonia Harmond finds help from irresistible bad boy, Oliver Eaglestone. When the erotic tension between them hits fever pitch, securing evidence to thwart an international arms dealer isn't the only danger they face.

The Disciplinarian by Leigh Court
Headstrong Clarissa Babcock is sent for instruction in proper wifely obedience. Disciplinarian Jared Ashworth uses the tools of seduction to show her how to control a demanding husband, but her beauty, spirit, and uninhibited passion make Jared hunger to keep her—and their darkly erotic nights—all for himself!

Secrets, Volume 16

Never Enough by Cynthia Eden
Abby McGill has been playing with fire. Bad-boy Jake taught her the true meaning of desire, but she knows she has to end her relationship with him. But Jake isn't about to let the woman he wants walk away from him.

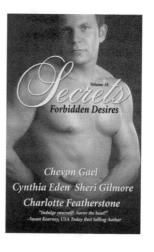

Bunko by Sheri Gilmoore
Tu Tran must decide between Jack, who promises to share every aspect of his life with her, or Dev, who hides behind a mask and only offers nights of erotic sex. Will she gamble on the man who can see behind her own mask and expose her true desires?

Hide and Seek by Chevon Gael
Kyle DeLaurier ditches his trophy-fiance in favor of a tropical paradise full of tall, tanned, topless females. Private eye, Darcy McLeod, is on the trail of this runaway groom. Together they sizzle while playing Hide and Seek with their true identities.

Seduction of the Muse by Charlotte Featherstone
He's the Dark Lord, the mysterious author who pens the erotic tales of an innocent woman's seduction. She is his muse, the woman he watches from the dark shadows, the woman whose dreams he invades at night.

Secrets, Volume 17

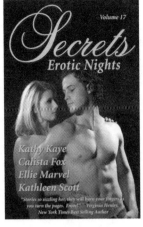

Rock Hard Candy by Kathy Kaye
Jessica Hennessy, descendent of a Voodoo priestess, decides it's time for the man of her dreams. A dose of her ancestor's aphrodisiac slipped into the gooey center of her homemade bon bons ought to do the trick.

Fatal Error by Kathleen Scott
Jesse Storm must make amends to humanity by destroying the software he helped design that's taken the government hostage. But he must also protect the woman he's loved in secret for nearly a decade.

Birthday by Ellie Marvel
Jasmine Templeton's been celibate long enough. Will a wild night at a hot new club with her two best friends ease the ache or just make it worse? Considering one is Charlie and she's been having strange notions about their relationship of late… It's definitely a birthday neither she nor Charlie will ever forget.

Intimate Rendezvous by Calista Fox
A thief causes trouble at Cassandra Kensington's nightclub and sexy P.I. Dean Hewitt arrives to help. One look at her sends his blood boiling, despite the fact that his keen instincts have him questioning the legitimacy of her business.

Secrets, Volume 18

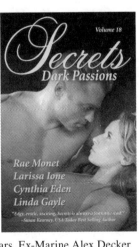

Lone Wolf Three by Rae Monet
Planetary politics and squabbling drain former rebel leader Taban Zias. But his anger quickly turns to desire when he meets, Lakota Blackson. She's Taban's perfect mate—now if he can just convince her.

Flesh to Fantasy by Larissa Ione
Kelsa Bradshaw is a loner happily immersed in a world of virtual reality. Trent Jordan is a paramedic who experiences the harsh realities of life. When their worlds collide in an erotic eruption can Trent convince Kelsa to turn the fantasy into something real?

Heart Full of Stars by Linda Gayle
Singer Fanta Rae finds herself stranded on a lonely Mars outpost with the first human male she's seen in years. Ex-Marine Alex Decker lost his family and guilt drove him into isolation, but when alien assassins come to enslave Fanta, she and Decker come together to fight for their lives.

The Wolf's Mate by Cynthia Eden
When Michael Morlet finds "Kat" Hardy fighting for her life, he instantly recognizes her as the mate he's been seeking all of his life, but someone's trying to kill her. With danger stalking them, will Kat trust him enough to become his mate?

Secrets, Volume 19

Affliction by Elisa Adams
Holly Aronson finally believes she's safe with sweet Andrew. But when his life long friend, Shane, arrives, events begin to spiral out of control. She's inexplicably drawn to Shane. As she runs for her life, which one will protect her?

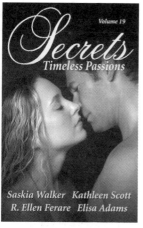

Falling Stars by Kathleen Scott
Daria is both a Primon fighter pilot and a Primon princess. As a deadly new enemy faces appears, she must choose between her duty to the fleet and the desperate need to forge an alliance through her marriage to the enemy's General Raven.

Toy in the Attic by R. Ellen Ferare
Gabrielle discovers a life-sized statue of a nude man. Her unexpected roommate reveals himself to be a talented lover caught by a witch's curse. Can she help him break free of the spell that holds him, without losing her heart along the way?

What You Wish For by Saskia Walker
Lucy Chambers is renovating her historic house. As her dreams about a stranger become more intense, she wishes he were with her. Two hundred years in the past, the man wishes for companionship. Suddenly they find themselves together—in his time.

Secrets, Volume 20

The Subject by Amber Green
One week Tyler is a game designer, signing the deal of her life. The next, she's running for her life. Who can she trust? Certainly not sexy, mysterious Esau, who keeps showing up after the hoo-hah hits the fan!

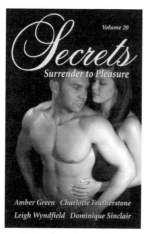

Surrender by Dominique Sinclair
Agent Madeline Carter is in too deep. She's slipped into Sebastian Maiocco's life to investigate his Sicilian mafia family. He unearths desires Madeline's unable to deny, conflicting the duty that honors her. Madeline must surrender to Sebastian or risk being exposed, leaving her target for a ruthless clan.

Stasis by Leigh Wyndfield
Morgann Right's Commanding Officer's been drugged with Stasis, turning him into a living statue she's forced to take care of for ten long days. As her hands tend to him, she sees her CO in a totally different light. She wants him and, while she can tell he wants her, touching him intimately might come back to haunt them both.

A Woman's Pleasure by Charlotte Featherstone
Widowed Isabella, Lady Langdon is yearning to discover all the pleasures denied her in her marriage, she finds herself falling hard for the magnetic charms of the mysterious and exotic Julian Gresham—a man skilled in pleasures of the flesh.

Secrets, Volume 21

Caged Wolf by Cynthia Eden
Alerac La Morte has been drugged and kidnapped. He
realizes his captor, Madison Langley, is actually his
destined mate, but she hates his kind. Will Alerac
convince her he's not the monster she thinks?

Wet Dreams by Larissa Ione
Injured and on the run, agent Brent Logan needs a
miracle. What he gets is a boat owned by Marina
Summers. Pursued by killers, ravaged by a storm,
and plagued by engine troubles, they can do little but
spend their final hours immersed in sensual pleasure.

Good Vibrations by Kate St. James
Lexi O'Brien vows to swear off sex while she attends

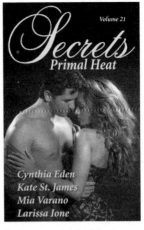

grad school, so when her favorite out-of-town customer asks her out, she decides to
indulge in an erotic fling. Little does she realize Gage Templeton is moving home, to
her city, and has no intention of settling for a short-term affair..

Virgin of the Amazon by Mia Varano
Librarian Anna Winter gets lost on the Amazon and stumbles upon a tribe whose
shaman wants a pale-skinned virgin to deflower. British adventurer Coop Daventry,
the tribe's self-styled chief, wants to save her, but which man poses a greater threat?

Secrets, Volume 22

Heat by Ellie Marvel
Mild-mannered alien Tarkin is in heat and the only
compatible female is a Terran. He courts her the old
fashioned Terran way. Because if he can't seduce her
before his cycle ends, he won't get a second chance.

Breathless by Rachel Carrington
Lark Hogan is a martial arts expert seeking vengeance for the death of her sister. She seeks help
from Zac, a mercenary wizard. Confronting a common enemy, they battle their own demons as well as
their powerful attraction, and will fight to the death
to protect what they've found.

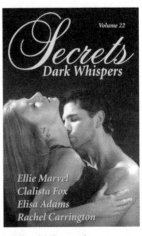

Midnight Rendezvous by Calista Fox
From New York to Cabo to Paris to Tokyo, Cat Hewitt and David Essex share
decadent midnight rendezvous. But when the real world presses in on their erotic
fantasies, and Cat's life is in danger, will their whirlwind romance stand a chance?

Birthday Wish by Elisa Adams
Anna Kelly had many goals before turning 30 and only one is left—to spend one
night with sexy Dean Harrison. When Dean asks her what she wants for her birthday, she grabs at the opportunity to ask him for an experience she'll never forget.

Secrets, Volume 23

The Sex Slave by Roxi Romano
Jaci Coe needs a hero and the hard bodied man in
black meets all the criteria. Opportunistic Jaci takes
advantage of Lazarus Stone's commandingly protective nature, but together, they learn how to live free...
and love freely.

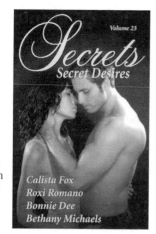

Forever My Love by Calista Fox
Professor Aja Woods is a 16ᵗʰ century witch... only
she doesn't know it. Christian St. James, her vampire
lover, has watched over her spirit for 500 years. When
her powers are recovered, so too are her memories of
Christian—and the love they once shared.

Reflection of Beauty by Bonnie Dee
Artist Christine Dawson is commissioned to paint a portrait of wealthy recluse, Eric
Leroux. It's up to her to reach the heart of this physically and emotionally scarred
man. Can love rescue Eric from isolation and restore his life?

Educating Eva by Bethany Lynn
Eva Blakely attends the infamous Ivy Hill houseparty to gather research for her book
Mating Rituals of the Human Male. But when she enlists the help of research "speci-
men" and notorious rake, Aidan Worthington, she gets some unexpected results.

Secrets, Volume 24

Hot on Her Heels by Mia Varano
Private investigator Jack Slater dons a g-string to
investigate the Lollipop Lounge, a male strip club.
He's not sure if the club's sexy owner, Vivica Steele,
is involved in the scam, but Jack figures he's just the
Lollipop to sweeten her life.

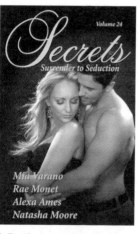

Shadow Wolf by Rae Monet
A half-breed Lupine challenges a high-ranking
Solarian Wolf Warrior. When Dia Nahiutras tries to
steal Roark D'Reincolt's wolf, does she get an enemy
forever or a mate for life?

Bad to the Bone by Natasha Moore
At her class reunion, Annie Shane sheds her good girl
reputation through one wild weekend with Luke Kendall. But Luke is done playing
the field and wants to settle down. What would a bad girl do?

War God by Alexa Ames
Estella Eaton, a lovely graduate student, is the unwitting carrier of the essence of
Aphrodite. But Ares, god of war, the ultimate alpha male, knows the truth and becomes obsessed with Estelle, pursuing her relentlessly. Can her modern sensibilities
and his ancient power coexist, or will their battle of wills destroy what matters most?

Secrets, Volume 25

Blood Hunt by Cynthia Eden
Vampiress Nema Alexander has a taste for bad boys.
Slade Brion has just been charged with tracking her
down. He won't stop until he catches her, and Nema
won't stop until she claims him, forever.

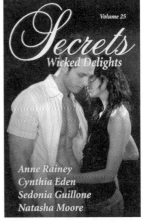

Scandalous Behavior by Anne Rainey
Tess Marley wants to take a walk on the wild side.
Who better to teach her about carnal pleasures than
her intriguing boss, Kevin Haines? But Tess makes
a major miscalculation when she crosses the line
between lust and love.

Enter the Hero by Sedonia Guillone
Kass and Lian are sentenced to sex slavery in the Con-

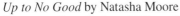

federation's pleasure district. Forced to make love for an audience, their hearts are
with each other while their bodies are on display. Now, in the midst of sexual slavery,
they have one more chance to escape to Paradise.

Up to No Good by Natasha Moore
Former syndicated columnist Simon "Mac" MacKenzie hides a tragic secret. When
freelance writer Alison Chandler tracks him down, he knows she's up to no good. Is
their attraction merely a distraction or the key to surviving their war of wills?

Secrets, Volume 26

Secret Rendezvous by Calista Fox
McCarthy Portman has seen enough happily-
ever-afters to long for one of her own, but when her
renowned matchmaking software pairs her with the
wild and wicked Josh Kensington, everything she's
always believed about love is turned upside down.

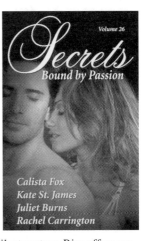

Enchanted Spell by Rachel Carrington
Witches and wizards don't mix. Every magical being
knows that. Yet, when a little mischievous magic
thrusts Ella and Kevlin together, they do so much
more than mix—they combust.

Exes and Ahhhs by Kate St. James
Former lovers Risa Haber and Eric Lange are partners
in a catering business, but Eric can't seem to remain a silent partner. Risa offers one
night of carnal delights if he'll sell her his share then disappear forever.

The Spy's Surrender by Juliet Burns
The famous courtesan Eva Werner is England's secret weapon against Napoleon. Her
orders are to attend a sadistic marquis' depraved house party and rescue a British spy
being held prisoner. As the weekend orgy begins, she's forced to make the spy her
love slave for the marquis' pleasure. But who is slave and who is master?

Secrets, Volume 27

Heart Storm by Liane Gentry Skye
Sirenia must mate with the only merman who can save
her kind, but when she rescues Navy SEAL Byron
Burke, she seals herself into his life debt. Will her
heart stand in the way of the last hope for her kind?

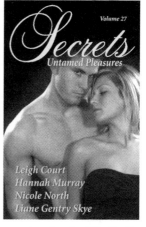

The Boy Next Door by Hannah Murray
Isabella Carelli isn't just looking for Mr. Right, she's
looking for Mr. Tie Me Up And Do Me Right. In all
the wrong places. Fortunately, the boy next door is just
about ready to make his move...

Devil in a Kilt by Nicole North
A trip to the Highland Games turns into a trip to the
past when modern day Shauna MacRae touches Gavin
MacTavish's 400-year-old claymore. Can she break the curse imprisoning this *Devil
in a Kilt* before an evil witch sends her back and takes Gavin as her sex slave?

The Bet by Leigh Court
A very drunk Damian Hunt claims he can make a woman come with just words. He
bets his prized racehorse that he can do it while George Beringer gambles his London townhouse that he can't. George chooses his virginal sister, Claire, for the bet.
Once Damian lays eyes on her, the stakes escalate in the most unpredictable way...

Secrets, Volume 28

Kiss Me at Midnight by Kate St. James
Callie Hutchins and Marc Shaw fake an on-air
romance to top the sweeps. Callie thinks Marc is a
womanizer, but as the month progresses, she realizes
he's funny, kind, and too sexy for words, damn it.

Mind Games by Kathleen Scott
Damien Storm is a Varti—a psychic who can communicate telepathically to one special person. Fear
has kept his Vartek partner, Jade, from acknowledging their link. He must save her from the forces who
wish to see all Varti destroyed.

*Release
Date:*

*December
2009*

Seducing Serena by Jennifer Lynne
Serena Hewitt has given up on love, but when she
interviews for a potential partner she's not prepared for her overpowering sexual
attraction to Nicholas Wade, a fun-loving bachelor with bad-boy good looks and a
determination to prove her wrong.

Pirate's Possession by Juliet Burns
When Lady Gertrude Fitzpatrick bargains with a fierce pirate for escape, but unwittingly becomes the possession of a fierce privateer. Ewan MacGowan has been
betrayed and mistakenly exacts revenge on this proud noblewoman. He may have
stolen the lady's innocence, but he also finds the true woman of his heart.

The Forever Kiss
by Angela Knight

Listen to what reviewers say:

"*The Forever Kiss* flows well with good characters and an interesting plot. ... If you enjoy vampires and a lot of hot sex, you are sure to enjoy *The Forever Kiss*."

—*The Best Reviews*

"Battling vampires, a protective ghost and the ever present battle of good and evil keep excellent pace with the erotic delights in Angela Knight's *The Forever Kiss*—a book that absolutely bites with refreshing paranormal humor." **4½ Stars, Top Pick**

—*Romantic Times BOOKclub*

"I found *The Forever Kiss* to be an exceptionally written, refreshing book. ... I really enjoyed this book by Angela Knight. ... 5 angels!"

—*Fallen Angel Reviews*

"*The Forever Kiss* is the first single title released from Red Sage and if this is any indication of what we can expect, it won't be the last. ... The love scenes are hot enough to give a vampire a sunburn and the fight scenes will have you cheering for the good guys."

—*Really Bad Barb Reviews*

In *The Forever Kiss*:

For years, Valerie Chase has been haunted by dreams of a Texas Ranger she knows only as "Cowboy." As a child, he rescued her from the nightmare vampires who murdered her parents. As an adult, she still dreams of him—but now he's her seductive lover in nights of erotic pleasure.

Yet "Cowboy" is more than a dream—he's the real Cade McKinnon—and a vampire! For years, he's protected Valerie from Edward Ridgemont, the sadistic vampire who turned him. Now, Ridgmont wants Valerie for his own and Cade is the only one who can protect her.

When Val finds herself abducted by her handsome dream man, she's appalled to discover he's one of the vampires she fears. Now, caught in a web of fear and passion, she and Cade must learn to trust each other, even as an immortal monster stalks their every move.

Their only hope of survival is... *The Forever Kiss*.

Romantic Times Best Erotic Novel of the Year

Object of Desire
by Calista Fox

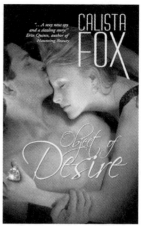

Listen to what reviewers say:

"Bombings, kidnappings and hot, hot sex fill the pages of this engaging story. Not only are the alpha hero and heroine strong, they have intriguing flaws too."
—*Romantic Times Magazine*

"...a sexy new spy and a sizzling hot story."
—*Erin Quinn, author of Haunting Beauty*

"*Object of Desire* delivers sizzling sensuality, emotional complexity, and an intriguing story—everything I've come to expect from Calista Fox!"
—*Rachelle Chase, author of The Sin Club and The Sex Lounge*

"*Object of Desire* was a very good book! The plot was fast paced, the adventure was thrilling, and the espionage angle added a whole new edge to the book. The developing relationship between Devon and Laurel was fun to watch, and the romance between them was intense! ... I loved it!"
—*Romance Junkies*

In *Object of Desire*:

When treasure hunter and spy Laurel Blackwood raids Victoria Peak in Belize to recover a rare Mexican fire opal rumored to evoke dark desires and passions, she unwittingly sets off a sequence of dangerous events—and finds herself in the midst of a battle between good and evil... and lust and love. Being chased through the Yucatan jungle is perilous enough, but Laurel must also keep the opal from falling into the hands of a deadly terrorist cell, a greedy Belizean dignitary, and one particularly hot and scandalous treasure hunter named Devon Mallory.

For ten years, Devon has had his eye on the thirty-million-dollar prized opal and his heart set on winning Laurel for keeps. But her web of secrecy and now her betrayal over recovering the legendary stone without him has Devon hell-bent on stealing the opal from her and collecting on the massive pay-out. Unfortunately for Devon, there is much more to Laurel Blackwood than she lets on. And soon, he's caught in the eye of the storm—falling under her sensuous spell, willing to put his own life on the line to help her protect the mystical jewel.

But Devon will eventually have to decide which gem is his true object of desire...

Check out our hot eBook titles available online at eRedSage.com!

Visit the site regularly as we're always adding new eBook titles.

Here's just some of what you'll find:

A Christmas Cara by Bethany Michaels

A Damsel in Distress by Brenda Williamson

Blood Game by Rae Monet

Fires Within by Roxana Blaze

Forbidden Fruit by Anne Rainey

High Voltage by Calista Fox

Master of the Elements by Alice Gaines

One Wish by Calista Fox

Quinn's Curse by Natasha Moore

Rock My World by Caitlyn Willows

The Doctor Next Door by Catherine Berlin

Unclaimed by Nathalie Gray

Finally, the men you've been dreaming about!

Give the gift of spicy romantic fiction.

Don't want to wait? You can place a retail price ($12.99) order for any of the *Secrets* volumes from the following:

① online at **eRedSage.com**

② **Waldenbooks, Borders, and Books-a-Million Stores**

③ **Amazon.com** or **BarnesandNoble.com**

④ or buy them at your local bookstore or online book source.

Bookstores: Please contact Baker & Taylor Distributors, Ingram Book Distributor, or Red Sage Publishing, Inc. for bookstore sales.

Order by Title or ISBN #:

Vol. 1: 0-9648942-0-3 ISBN #13 978-0-9648942-0-4	**Vol. 13:** 0-9754516-3-4 ISBN #13 978-0-9754516-3-2	**Vol. 25:** 1-60310-005-9 ISBN #13 978-1-60310-005-2
Vol. 2: 0-9648942-1-1 ISBN #13 978-0-9648942-1-1	**Vol. 14:** 0-9754516-4-2 ISBN #13 978-0-9754516-4-9	**Vol. 26:** 1-60310-006-7 ISBN #13 978-1-60310-006-9
Vol. 3: 0-9648942-2-X ISBN #13 978-0-9648942-2-8	**Vol. 15:** 0-9754516-5-0 ISBN #13 978-0-9754516-5-6	**Vol. 27:** 1-60310-007-5 ISBN #13 978-1-60310-007-6
Vol. 4: 0-9648942-4-6 ISBN #13 978-0-9648942-4-2	**Vol. 16:** 0-9754516-6-9 ISBN #13 978-0-9754516-6-3	**Vol. 28*:** 1-60310-008-3 ISBN #13 978-1-60310-008-3
Vol. 5: 0-9648942-5-4 ISBN #13 978-0-9648942-5-9	**Vol. 17:** 0-9754516-7-7 ISBN #13 978-0-9754516-7-0	*Vol. 28 Release Date Dec. 2009*
Vol. 6: 0-9648942-6-2 ISBN #13 978-0-9648942-6-6	**Vol. 18:** 0-9754516-8-5 ISBN #13 978-0-9754516-8-7	**The Forever Kiss:** 0-9648942-3-8 ISBN #13
Vol. 7: 0-9648942-7-0 ISBN #13 978-0-9648942-7-3	**Vol. 19:** 0-9754516-9-3 ISBN #13 978-0-9754516-9-4	978-0-9648942-3-5 ($14.00)
Vol. 8: 0-9648942-8-9 ISBN #13 978-0-9648942-9-7	**Vol. 20:** 1-60310-000-8 ISBN #13 978-1-60310-000-7	**Object of Desire:** 1-60310-003-2 ISBN #13
Vol. 9: 0-9648942-9-7 ISBN #13 978-0-9648942-9-7	**Vol. 21:** 1-60310-001-6 ISBN #13 978-1-60310-001-4	978-1-60310-003-8 ($14.00)
Vol. 10: 0-9754516-0-X ISBN #13 978-0-9754516-0-1	**Vol. 22:** 1-60310-002-4 ISBN #13 978-1-60310-002-1	
Vol. 11: 0-9754516-1-8 ISBN #13 978-0-9754516-1-8	**Vol. 23:** 1-60310-164-0 ISBN #13 978-1-60310-164-6	
Vol. 12: 0-9754516-2-6 ISBN #13 978-0-9754516-2-5	**Vol. 24:** 1-60310-165-9 ISBN #13 978-1-60310-165-3	

Red Sage Publishing Order Form:

(Orders shipped in two to three days of receipt.)

Each volume of *Secrets* retails for $12.99, but you can get it direct via mail order for only $10.99 each. Novels retail for $14.00, but by direct mail order, you only pay $12.00. Use the order form below to place your direct mail order. Fill in the quantity you want for each book on the blanks beside the title.

_____ *Secrets* Volume 1	_____ *Secrets* Volume 12	_____ *Secrets* Volume 23
_____ *Secrets* Volume 2	_____ *Secrets* Volume 13	_____ *Secrets* Volume 24
_____ *Secrets* Volume 3	_____ *Secrets* Volume 14	_____ *Secrets* Volume 25
_____ *Secrets* Volume 4	_____ *Secrets* Volume 15	_____ *Secrets* Volume 26
_____ *Secrets* Volume 5	_____ *Secrets* Volume 16	_____ *Secrets* Volume 27
_____ *Secrets* Volume 6	_____ *Secrets* Volume 17	_____ *Secrets* Volume 28*
_____ *Secrets* Volume 7	_____ *Secrets* Volume 18	*Vol. 28 Release Date Dec. 2009
_____ *Secrets* Volume 8	_____ *Secrets* Volume 19	
_____ *Secrets* Volume 9	_____ *Secrets* Volume 20	Novels:
_____ *Secrets* Volume 10	_____ *Secrets* Volume 21	_____ *The Forever Kiss*
_____ *Secrets* Volume 11	_____ *Secrets* Volume 22	_____ *Object of Desire*

Total _____ *Secrets* Volumes @ $10.99 each = $_____

Total _____ Novels @ $12.00 each = $_____

Shipping & handling (in the U.S.) $_____

US Priority Mail:

1–2 books .... $ 5.50	
3–5 books $11.50	
6–10 books $14.50	
11–28 books................ $25.00	

UPS insured:

1–4 books $16.00	
5–10 books $25.00	
11–28 books...................$29.00	

SUBTOTAL $_____

Florida 6% sales tax (if delivered in FL) $_____

TOTAL AMOUNT ENCLOSED $_____

Your personal information is kept private and not shared with anyone.

Name: (please print) _____

Address: (no P.O. Boxes) _____

City/State/Zip: _____

Phone or email: (only regarding order if necessary) _____

You can order direct from **eRedSage.com** and use a credit card or you can use this form to send in your mail order with a check. Please make check payable to **Red Sage Publishing**. Check must be drawn on a U.S. bank in U.S. dollars. Mail your check and order form to:

Red Sage Publishing, Inc. Department S27 P.O. Box 4844 Seminole, FL 33775

It's not just reviewers raving about *Secrets*. See what readers have to say:

"When are you coming out with a new Volume? I want a new one next month!" via email from a reader.

"I loved the hot, wet sex without vulgar words being used to make it exciting." after *Volume 1*

"I loved the blend of sensuality and sexual intensity—HOT!" after *Volume 2*

"The best thing about *Secrets* is they're hot and brief! The least thing is you do not have enough of them!" after *Volume 3*

"I have been extremely satisfied with *Secrets*, keep up the good writing." after *Volume 4*

"Stories have plot and characters to support the erotica. They would be good strong stories without the heat." after *Volume 5*

"*Secrets* really knows how to push the envelop better than anyone else." after *Volume 6*

"These are the best sensual stories I have ever read!" after *Volume 7*

"I love, love, love the *Secrets* stories. I now have all of them, please have more books come out each year." after *Volume 8*

"These are the perfect sensual romance stories!" after *Volume 9*

"What I love about *Secrets Volume 10* is how I couldn't put it down!" after *Volume 10*

"All of the *Secrets* volumes are terrific! I have read all of them up to *Secrets Volume 11*. Please keep them coming! I will read every one you make!" after *Volume 11*